SHE HAD TO ESCAPE—
OR BETRAY HER LOVE

"I want to go ashore, Brian," Sydne insisted. "I've been on this ship for five consecutive weeks and I'm overdue for my leave!"

"You'll just have to survive a while longer, won't you?" Brian's voice was a husky caress.

Sydne's heart began its familiar clamoring. His merest touch could turn her bones to water, and his kisses wiped all thought of resistance from her mind....

But this time he didn't touch her. His worried eyes scanned the horizon. "Brian, what's wrong?" she asked in concern.

"It's the weather," he admitted grimly. "Hurricane warnings."

Sydne's throat tightened. Now she couldn't walk out—not when danger and financial ruin threatened the man she loved.

AND NOW...

SUPERROMANCES

Worldwide Library is proud to present a
sensational new series of modern love stories —
SUPERROMANCES

Written by masters of the genre, these longer,
sensuous and dramatic novels are truly in keeping
with today's changing life-styles. Full of intriguing
conflicts, the heartaches and delights of true love,
SUPERROMANCES are absorbing stories —
satisfying and sophisticated reading that lovers
of romance fiction have long been waiting for.

SUPERROMANCES
Contemporary love stories for the woman of today!

EMILY MESTA

FUGITIVE HEART

A SUPERROMANCE FROM
WORLDWIDE

TORONTO · NEW YORK · LOS ANGELES · LONDON

Published October 1982

First printing August 1982

ISBN 0-373-70034-2

Printed in Canada

CHAPTER ONE

As HE HUNG UP the phone, the man in the wheelchair turned toward the young woman sitting across the desk from him. His dark piercing eyes, set beneath bushy brows that matched his shock of gray hair, examined her closely. "Well, I guess that does it for Bob. His leg is broken." Andrew McCallum shook his head. "That means you're going to have to go to the Dominican Republic in his place, Syd. How's your Spanish?"

"I can read better than I speak, but you could say it's fair." Sydne Matheson shrugged her shoulders and added wryly, "Poor Bob. He was really looking forward to this trip."

"That'll teach him to be a physical-fitness nut," Andrew quipped. "Sometimes you can exercise yourself right into the hospital. At any rate, his loss is your gain, Syd—and mine," and at the quizzical look she gave him he smiled wickedly. "You're so pretty to look at."

Although in jest, Andrew had spoken the truth. Sydne Matheson was beautiful in an aristocratic understated sort of way. Her creamy complexion required little makeup. A touch of fawn eye shadow was enough to accent almond-shaped eyes the color of clear amber, which were fringed with long thick lashes. A thin layer of coral gloss moistened her full, rather pouting lips. High cheekbones enhanced the delicate bone structure of an oval face, saved from total perfection by the impudent little nose that added a touch of piquancy to her features.

Perhaps if the handicapped millionaire had said something like that to her six months ago, when she had accepted the position of assistant curator at his private museum, she would not have been able to laugh as freely as she did now. "Shame on you, Andrew. I thought Bob was supposed to be your friend."

"Well, he is." Andrew grinned impudently, looking in obvious admiration at her hair. The rich mahogany tresses with red highlights, worn in a semi-long feathered style, caught the light when she threw back her head, and then fell neatly back into place. "But if we're to spend a few weeks in the Caribbean, I'd much rather look at you in a bikini than at him."

"But I thought—"

"That I would stay behind?" Andrew interrupted. "Not a chance! I want to be as close to that Spanish galleon as I can possibly get when they start bringing up the relics." Seeing her concern, he went on, "Ever since I started my collection I've been wanting to take part in a discovery like this. Being an archaeologist, you don't have to be told what a rare find a galleon that has been lost for more than three hundred years is." He shook his head. "No, Syd, this may be my last chance at such adventure. I'm not a young man anymore."

As if realizing that he had become too serious, Andrew smiled and added in a lighter tone, "Besides,

I've got money invested in this salvage—and I haven't seen Brian Stevens in years. I've told you about him, haven't I?" he asked casually.

"A little," Sydne said, nodding. She was well aware that even though her employer was into his sixties, he was youthful at heart. And perhaps because of the fact that he was confined to a wheelchair, he seemed fascinated with the physically demanding occupation of his friend. "He's the fellow who owns the marine-salvage outfit that found the galleon, isn't he?" She paused briefly. Then, knowing how Andrew liked to talk about his friends, she went on conversationally, "You said it's been a long time since you saw him, Andrew. How many years is that?"

"Four—no, three," he corrected. "I remember because it was shortly after he and Helene got married. He's going to need lots of help with the artifacts from the galleon, Syd. The *Conde de Santander* was supposedly carrying a fortune when it went down."

"And where is the *Conde*?" she inquired.

"Somewhere off Samaná Bay," Andrew replied offhandedly. "I hear the fishing is terrific in that area, so who knows? I might even catch me a big blue marlin."

With an understanding smile, Sydne shook her head and said, "How much time do I have to prepare for this trip, Andrew? I'm afraid I'll have to do some shopping. Everything I own is ideally suited for the climate here in Minneapolis."

"Will a couple of days be enough?"

"If I start right now," she laughed, rising to her feet and heading for the door.

THE SIGN ALERTING THE PASSENGERS to fasten their
seat belts started flashing as Sydne returned to her
seat. Looking out the window, she could see the city
below, spreading out on the banks of the meandering
Ozama River. Buckling her own seat belt, she turned
to Andrew and inquired, "Will your friend be meeting us at the airport?"

"I hope so," he replied. "Brian said he might be
driving into Santo Domingo today."

In the ensuing silence they were conscious of the
landing gear being lowered. Even though Sydne was
a seasoned traveler, she never failed to experience a
certain breathless anticipation the moment the aircraft approached the runway. And she wasn't alone,
if the sheepish smiles of relief exchanged among the
other passengers were anything to go by as the jumbo
jet completed its run on the tarmac. It taxied to a
stop a short distance away from the terminal building
of the Airport of the Americas, where a sign in large
bold letters read: Welcome to the Dominican Republic.

Andrew McCallum and his party remained in their
seats until the rest of the passengers had deplaned.
Then Tim Robbins, a powerfully built man in his
mid-thirties, who had served as an army medic and
had later become Andrew's nurse, carried the invalid
out of the plane.

Sydne, following the two men, paused for a moment as she emerged from the door. Immediately she
was struck by the vibrant colors of an incredibly blue
sky without a hint of cloud, by the purple and yellow
flowers that contrasted so vividly with the lush green
shrubbery bordering the terminal building. Infused

with a sudden sense of joy, she descended the steps, deeply inhaling the fragrant Caribbean breeze that carried the salty tang of the sea.

By the time she joined her companions, Tim had already installed his employer in the folding aluminum wheelchair he always used in his travels.

"I hope you remembered to bring your suntan lotion," Andrew said, grinning at her. With a wink at Tim he added, "And the bikini."

"They're both in my suitcase," she replied, quite used to their teasing.

By the time they entered the terminal, most of the other passengers had already been processed, so immigration and customs formalities took less than half an hour to complete. Once they had been legally admitted into the country, they moved out into the airport lounge.

"There's Brian!" Andrew exclaimed almost immediately.

Sydne looked up at the tall man advancing through the crowd in long lithe strides. For some reason she was surprised to discover that Brian Stevens was much younger than she had expected, somewhere in his early thirties. The fit of the tan slacks he wore suggested well-muscled legs, and his lemon yellow shirt stretched across broad shoulders before tapering to the slim waist of an athlete. Short sleeves exposed sinewy arms covered by a veil of fine dark hair. His light brown hair, streaked no doubt by constant exposure to the sun, offered a contrast to his dark, well-defined brows. The angular features of his face seemed to have been chiseled in bronze, while his skin, tanned to a nut brown, emphasized his deep blue eyes—eyes that now crinkled at the corners as he flashed a broad smile.

"Brian, my boy," Andrew exclaimed with alacrity, offering his hand, "it's good to see you!"

"Hello, Andrew," the man replied in a deep husky voice as he shook the proffered hand. "I don't have to ask how you are. You're certainly looking fit."

"I'm not complaining." The older man grinned. "You know Tim," he said, and while the two men shook hands he added casually, "Brian Stevens, Miss Matheson."

Sydne was too distracted by the newcomer to notice the introduction. There was a certain intimacy in the way Brian's hand closed firmly around her smaller one. Yet his smile faded and his blue eyes took on a cold glint as they moved over her face. When they examined her figure the same way, in the process almost seeming to strip her of her clothes, Sydne suddenly felt terribly vulnerable and self-conscious. The man exuded a raw animal magnetism that she found disturbing. And he certainly wasn't being very polite!

She had met this type before, Sydne admitted to herself, fighting down a surge of annoyance—men who see women primarily as sexual objects. The mocking superior smile curving his full sensual lips told her that Brian Stevens must have drawn his own conclusions about her relationship with Andrew. Incensed by the man's arrogance, Sydne acknowledged him with a disdainful nod of her head.

So this was the Brian Stevens of whom her employer had spoken so fondly! Sydne experienced a feeling of apprehension. This was the man in whose company she was expected to spend a good portion of the coming weeks.

She was glad that in the excitement of the reunion Andrew hadn't noticed her reaction to his friend, hadn't realized she had become very quiet as they followed Brian to the parking lot. He led them to a large blue Dodge van, taking charge of the wheelchair once Tim had installed Andrew in the front seat. And it was the male nurse who helped Sydne board, while Brian loaded their luggage in the back and then slid behind the wheel.

The exhilaration Sydne had felt moments before was totally gone. As the vehicle joined the traffic on Las Americas Superhighway, she looked out of the window. The modern road, spectacularly landscaped and bordered with palm trees, followed the coast. She knew that Santo Domingo, their destination, had been the first city founded by the Spanish conquistadores in the New World.

The island was so beautiful, she mused. From the air it had appeared as a jewel set in the midst of a shimmering cobalt sea. She had caught glimpses of white sand beaches, of small villages surrounded by patterned fields, of towering mountains kissed by mist.

Yes, perhaps her work in this exotic paradise would help her completely regain her emotional stability, she reflected. In accepting the position of assistant curator for Andrew McCallum's collection, she had taken the first step in the right direction....

It still amazed her how fond she had become of the crafty old fox in the six months she had worked for him. Sydne smiled to herself. Perhaps friendship could not be measured in time, for she was sure Andrew returned those feelings. His zest and vitality in spite of his disability had influenced her tremendously during what had been perhaps the most difficult period of her life. And he had been the only man in a long time who had been kind to her without ulterior motives.... But why think of Paul again now, Sydne admonished herself. Shoving aside the feeling of desolation that threatened to surface at his memory, she turned her attention to the general conversation.

"So," Andrew was saying to Brian, "where did you find the *Conde*?"

"We're not sure it really is the *Conde de Santander*," Brian replied, keeping his attention on the heavy traffic. "But the galleon is some miles off Samaná Bay, on the northeastern side of the island. By the way, I've arranged for accommodations for you in Samaná, and for a helicopter to fly you there. Unfortunately there's only room for two passengers."

He paused as if expecting a comment from Andrew, but the older man merely said, "Thank you, my boy."

"I'm driving back to Samaná tomorrow with some equipment," Brian went on. "When is this Syd fellow you mentioned supposed to arrive? I had expected him to come down with you."

Sydne opened her mouth, intending to tell him that she was the archaeologist he had been expecting, but Andrew didn't give her a chance. "Syd is not a *fellow*," he chuckled.

A note of apprehension had crept into Brian's voice when he asked, "What do you mean?"

"*He*'s a *she*," Andrew replied, grinning, "and you just met her."

Sydne could see Brian's frown reflected in the rearview mirror. "You can't be serious!" he burst out.

"But I am, my boy," the old man chortled, as if amused by his own joke. "And don't worry. She'll do just fine."

"Not on my ship, she won't!"

For the second time in a row Andrew beat Sydne to the punch when she started to protest. "Now, now, my boy," he said conciliatorily. "She's been helping Bob with my collection for almost six months, and I don't mind telling you what a splendid job she's made of it."

"I'm sure she's qualified, but that's not the point," Brian countered testily. "Do you realize the situation her presence will create? She'll be the only woman aboard!"

"You make it sound as if your crew would pounce on the first unsuspecting female they came across, Mr. Stevens," Sydne interposed dryly. "I assume we're talking about civilized men, aren't we?"

Ignoring her remark as if she hadn't spoken, Brian asked, "When will Bob be available?"

"Don't count on him." Andrew shook his head. "A broken leg at our age doesn't mend very quickly."

Brian fell silent. At that moment he had pulled onto a curving driveway, and further discussion was prevented by their arrival at the hotel.

Had she not been so upset, Sydne would have been enchanted by the rambling three-story structure painted a light cream color, with red clay tiles on the

slanting roof. It was set in an expanse of carefully
manicured lawns, where trees, shrubbery and colorful flowers added the exotic touch of a lush tropical
garden. An abundance of potted plants carried the
outdoors right into a spacious lobby. The floor was
inlaid with polished Spanish tile, and comfortable-
looking rattan couches and chairs strewn with cushions in gay prints added color to the large area.

Sydne stood a little apart from the others while
Tim and Brian took care of checking them in, and as
they turned away from the gleaming mahogany reception counter she heard Andrew tell Brian that they
would see him at dinner.

Brian Stevens's scowl was a clear indication that he
had not voiced his last objection to Sydne's presence
aboard his ship. But realizing that Andrew must be
weary after the long flight from Minneapolis and the
hours they had spent between planes in Miami, he accepted the delay.

TIM AND BRIAN BOTH GOT UP from their chairs when
Sydne approached their patio table later that evening. Brian had an appraising way of looking at a
woman, she thought with mounting irritation as if he
were evaluating her as a potential bed partner.

"Hello, my dear," Andrew greeted her warmly.
"Were you able to get a nice rest?"

"Yes, thank you," she replied, mentally crossing
her fingers. Actually she had been too disturbed by
Brian's rudeness, by his objections to her presence
aboard his ship, to be able to relax at all. Instead she
had burned up her excess nervous energy by swimming laps in the pool, which had been almost desert-

ed in the late afternoon. But Sydne was reluctant to let Brian know how much he had upset her. After all, she had managed to achieve some amount of relaxation, and she did feel rested—or had, before coming face to face with him again.

He had changed into dark blue slacks and a white silk shirt that she was sure he wore purposely to accent his deep tan. The shirt was unbuttoned sufficiently to allow Sydne a glimpse of dark hair curling on his chest. She caught a whiff of musky after-shave as he courteously seated her between Andrew and himself.

"How about a cocktail before dinner?" Andrew offered solicitously when a waitress came to take their order. "I recommend the *piña colada* as outstanding."

Sydne wasn't much of a drinker. An aperitif was her usual choice on such occasions, but she accepted Andrew's suggestion, and wasn't sorry when her drink came. A chunk of fresh pineapple speared to a colorful maraschino cherry garnished the wide bowl-like glass, which was filled with a creamy concoction. The combination of pineapple, coconut and rum, a perfectly balanced blend, was pure ambrosia; not too tart, not too sweet, it went down smoothly and deliciously.

"Brian was just telling us about the galleon," Andrew told her. Then he addressed his friend. "How long do you think it will take to establish its identity?"

Leaning lazily back in his chair, Brian seemed to carefully consider his reply. "At the rate coral grows in this area, we'll probably have to dig through ten to fifteen feet of limestone." He took a long swallow of his drink before adding, "I don't have to tell you what a monumental task that will be."

"How deep is it?" Tim inquired.

"Luckily only forty feet. The pressure isn't too great at that depth, but it's hard backbreaking work, so we're limiting the shifts to ninety minutes."

"How many divers are you using?" Andrew asked.

"Eight at the moment, for a total of twelve hours a day. We'll be adding two more men as soon as they finish working an oil rig in the gulf—probably within the next two to three weeks."

Andrew looked a little disappointed at the news. "Sounds like it will be a long job," he said.

"You bet," Brian asserted. Looking at Sydne, he added pointedly, "And also hard and dirty. No place for a woman, especially a bored rich girl looking for a thrill—one who will quit as soon as the going gets rough."

At Brian's remark an amused glance passed between Andrew and Tim. It was an easy mistake to make; Sydne Matheson did look expensive. There was poise and innate grace in every gesture, and her excellent taste was reflected by her wardrobe which, although limited by her financial resources, stressed quality rather than quantity.

"For your information, Mr. Stevens," Sydne said with justified indignation, "I happen to earn my living at just this sort of job!"

"Now, now, my boy," Andrew broke in, "you're going to need someone to handle the artifacts you recover from the galleon, and with Bob out of the picture I can't think of anyone more qualified than Sydne here. And don't think she's a bit of fluff because she's beautiful. Why, she's one of the most serious competent people I know!"

"It's all right, Andrew," Sydne interposed dryly, trying not to show the effort she was making to keep her temper in check. "Mr. Stevens has made it perfectly clear that he doesn't require or want my services. Perhaps it's best that I take the next flight back to the States."

When she started to rise, Andrew stopped her. "Wait, Sydne," he said, and took advantage of her hesitation to go on. "Please listen to me for a moment. If after I've finished you still want to go, I won't stand in your way. You know my collection is important to me, but I don't think I've ever told you, or Brian, how important."

Seeing that he had their attention, he paused pensively, as if he were about to bare his soul. Both Sydne and Brian looked at him expectantly as he went on, "When I was crippled in that accident five years ago, I asked myself what would be the point of living. Spending the rest of my days strapped in a wheelchair held very little attraction for me. I was a fighter who had clawed his way up, and I found it a terrible irony that something like this should happen when I had reached the top.

"But I was wrong." He chuckled wryly. "That close brush with death made me pause and think—take inventory of my life."

He took a sip of his drink, shaking his head as he continued. "I don't mind telling you what a frightening yet interesting experience that was. I discovered that, in striving for success, I had neglected perhaps the most important aspects of life. It's funny the things that go through your mind when you think your time is up. Suddenly it didn't matter how much money or how much power I had acquired, how many deals I had made. And little things I had never really thought about before became terribly important—a conversation I had on a fishing trip with my ten-year-old son, for example. You know, that was the only time we ever really talked, and I can't tell you how sorry I was that I'd never taken the time to do it more often. But it was too late. My wife was gone. My children had grown up and were as much strangers to me as I was to them. It was a paradox. I had succeeded, yet failed.

"But you can't turn back the clock. Right then and there I made up my mind to do something about it, something that would enrich whatever time I had left. The trouble was, I had no idea what to do."

Again he paused, and his craggy face broke into a smile as he looked at Brian. "Ah, but I was lucky," he went on after a moment. "I stumbled onto the solution when a certain young man came to me, asking that I back his search for one of those lost galleons." This time he glanced at Sydne. "Mind you, I knew nothing at all about hunting for treasure. Magnetometers and the like were a mystery to me. But I do know human nature, and I was impressed by that young fellow, who presented me with some very convincing arguments. I had him investigated, of course. He had formed a commercial marine-salvage outfit after his release from the navy. He had some capital at his disposal, but an operation like the one he wanted to undertake required much more. Treasure hunting is a very expensive proposition, Sydne, and a long shot at best. But I took the gamble, and by God it turned out to be the best investment I've ever made—for myself and for Western culture. Not only did I make money, but some of the artifacts Brian brought back from his adventures were the beginning of my collection. Other pieces have found their way into museums all over the world. After that I was hooked. Now it's one of the few things that keeps me going.''

Sydne regarded her employer somewhat ruefully when he had finished speaking. Once again he had cleverly turned the tables so that he got what he wanted. And Brian Stevens's eloquent silence was indication enough that Andrew had won the battle. She would *not* be going back to Minneapolis.

BEFORE RETIRING THAT EVENING, Sydne lingered in Andrew's suite.

"You seem a little worried, my dear," he said gently after a moment. "Anything wrong?"

She gave a deep sigh. "I don't know, Andrew. I think we're making a mistake," she admitted. "Or at least I am."

Andrew looked at her quizzically, aware that there was more than met the eye in her antagonism toward Brian Stevens. From the very beginning this uncommon young woman had seemed totally unaware of the devastating effect she could have on a man. She was an enigma, and it had taken time as well as Andrew's extraordinary gift for dealing with people to pierce through the shield of aloofness behind which she hid a wealth of softness and warmth.

"When you came to work for me six months ago I asked myself why—" immediately she stiffened uncomfortably "—why a pretty woman like you would suddenly abandon what seemed to be a very promising career to accept the job I had to offer."

"I already told you," she replied with a slight frown.

"'Personal reasons,'" he quoted. "They must have been pretty important reasons, Sydne. You earned your education at great sacrifice to yourself." He let a few seconds of silence go by before inquiring, "What really happened?"

She took a deep breath. "Andrew, I—"

"Would rather not discuss it. I know," he finished for her. Again he was silent for a moment. "I didn't press the point at that time, because I was happy to get someone with your excellent qualifications to assist Bob with my collection." His face softened as he added, "But that was then, and things are different now. I've grown very fond of you, young lady."

He was a manipulator and Sydne knew it, but that didn't detract from the affection she felt for him. Her long lashes curtained the expression in her amber eyes, which focused on her lap.

"Who was he, Sydne?" he coaxed gently, and waited.

"It doesn't matter," she sighed at last. Only the tremor of her lower lip betrayed the effort it took to keep her voice from breaking when she added, "He was married."

"And you didn't know?"

She shook her head.

"I suspected as much." There was compassion in his eyes when he added thoughtfully, "So you decided to put distance between the two of you. Good for you, my dear. You're a strong courageous young woman, Sydne."

No, I'm not, Sydne wanted to say. *Too many things frighten me!*

"Time is the best healer there is, Syd," Andrew said. "Let it do its work. Put it all behind you, where it belongs."

There was a sheen of tears in the amber eyes when she met his affectionate gaze. "You've been very good for me, Andrew," she said in a small voice.

"It's been mutual," he said, gruffly dismissing her gratitude. "Now get to bed. Brian wants to make an early start."

Once in her own room, Sydne prepared for bed, slipping into a cool nightgown she had packed. But she knew she wouldn't be able to sleep yet. Instead she went out onto the balcony and leaned against the stone railing.

The serenity of the tropical night, the whisper of the sea seemed to deny the turbulent history of this beautiful island, which had seen so much pillage and invasion, war and revolution; tyranny and civil strife. The street below the hotel was almost deserted at this late hour on a week night, although Brian had told them that weekends were another matter entirely.

Brian Stevens.... Sydne shook her head to dislodge her somber thoughts. They seemed so out of place in the pervasive quiet. She closed her eyes to evoke a more romantic scene: of dark-eyed ladies carrying parasols and parading in their open carriages along the narrow cobbled streets of the colonial city of La Hispaniola; of elegant Hidalgos in courtly costumes astride sleek and fiery Andalusian horses, their saddles decorated in silver and gold.

She smiled to herself. She had always had a vivid imagination, and that had been a source of amusement to her friends. But Paul had never laughed. Instead he had encouraged her dreams, until almost without knowing it she had fallen under his spell. The stars twinkling in the velvet sky above reminded her of the silver strands threading the midnight black of his hair. The murmur of the sea was as compelling as his voice uttering those words of love she had so treasured.

The situation had not been unique, Sydne realized now—a handsome mature professor dazzling a lonely young student with his brilliance, his sophistication, his special attentions. He had become her mentor, had obtained for her a post as his assistant that allowed her to continue her advanced studies in archaeology. And then one day she had been overwhelmed by the discovery that the god she worshipped had feet of clay—and a wife besides. Paul had proposed that they set up an "arrangement"....

She had been filled with disgust and had fled, the only solution to gather up the shattered pieces of her heart. But even after all these months, the dull pain, that sharp sense of betrayal, was still there.

But Sydne had more immediate problems—like spending the next few weeks with Brian Stevens, she thought with a sense of foreboding. Only for Andrew would she put up with the arrogance of the man. But it would not be easy; he had a way of getting on her nerves like no other man in all her twenty-four years had ever done.

Heaving a wistful sigh, Sydne glanced at her slim gold wristwatch, a piece of jewelry she treasured because it had been the last gift she had received from her parents. It was almost midnight, and taking into consideration the time difference between Minneapolis and Santo Domingo, she knew a good night's sleep was in order.

If only she *could* sleep!

THE FRONDS OF TALL ARECA PALMS were casting their swaying shadows on the red tiles of the Spanish patio and a couple of youngsters were already cavorting in the sparkling pool when Sydne joined Andrew McCallum for breakfast under the brightly colored umbrellas the next morning. She felt cool and casual in a simple cotton wraparound skirt that tied at the front and a short-sleeved green knit top that hugged the swell of her bosom. Due to the heat of the morning, she wore her wedge-heel, open-toed sandals without stockings.

Always solicitous of her comfort, Andrew asked, "Did you sleep well?" as she took her place at the table.

"Reasonably so," she answered, accepting a menu from the smiling waitress, who appeared immediately.

"I recommend the papaya," he suggested, indicating his own plate.

Sydne examined the menu, and after she had ordered papaya, coffee and toast Andrew commented,

"You should do better than that, my girl. Didn't your mother ever tell you that breakfast is the most important meal of the day?"

"Got to watch my figure," she said with a wink.

"Go ahead and eat," he encouraged with a wolfish grin and a wiggle of his bushy brows. "*I'll* do the watching."

"You old fox, you!" she laughed. Then, looking around for the male nurse, who was never far from his employer's side, she inquired, "Where's Tim this morning?"

"Loading my stuff in the van." Attacking his ham and eggs with relish, Andrew added, "Brian should be joining us any minute now."

At the mention of the man who had caused her to toss and turn for a good portion of the night, Sydne stiffened. But at that moment the waitress returned with her order, and brushing her apprehension aside, Sydne decided she was not going to allow Brian to spoil her breakfast as he had managed to spoil her sleep. She sprinkled lime juice over the golden slices of papaya and then forked a piece into her mouth. "Mmm...delicious," she said, savoring the fresh tangy flavor of the fruit.

An insulated jug of coffee and a plate of toast were also left on the table, and conversation ebbed while they ate.

The prickle of irritation Sydne felt when Brian joined them minutes later told her that this was not going to be an easy day.

"Sit down, my boy," Andrew invited cordially, apparently oblivious to the undercurrent of hostility that existed between his two companions. "Have you eaten?"

Brian nodded. "Yes, thank you, but I think I'll join you for a cup of coffee."

"Help yourself." Andrew indicated the jug on the table.

"No, thanks. Dominican coffee is the best I've ever tasted." To the waitress, who appeared suddenly at his side, he said, *"Un café, por favor."*

"Sí, señor," the girl replied, rewarding him with a dazzling smile that carried much more approval than his choice warranted.

When the waitress returned minutes later with a demitasse of the native brew, Sydne's nostrils flared at the delicious aroma that wafted toward her. Immediately she resented the fact that it smelled so good, as she resented the smile of appreciation Brian bestowed on the girl.

"The helicopter will be here at noon," Brian told Andrew, adding sugar to the tiny cup and stirring it. With reluctant fascination Sydne watched him raise the cup to his lips. He sipped the coffee slowly, obviously savoring it, and when he had emptied the cup he said to Andrew, "That *is* good, my friend. You ought to try it."

Andrew, who had also watched the performance, didn't need more encouragement. "I think I will." He looked at Sydne inquiringly, but she shook her head. She was dying to try it, but even though she was conscious of her childish reaction, she refused to give Brian the satisfaction of knowing she wanted to.

No, this certainly wasn't going to be an easy day,

she told herself once again. At least eight hours of road travel were before her, but that wasn't the worst part. For that whole time her only companion would be Brian Stevens, a man who annoyed her in a way she found most disturbing.

CHAPTER TWO

ABOARD THE BLUE DODGE VAN there were air tanks and hoses that even Sydne, a stranger to diving, recognized as standard equipment. She did not ask about the purpose of a large cylindrical apparatus painted a dull gray. That, along with a hospital bed and other paraphernalia designed to make life easier for Andrew McCallum, occupied the cargo space of the vehicle.

Traffic on Avenida Simón Bolívar was heavy.

Suddenly Sydne jumped, frightened almost out of her wits, when Brian stomped on the brakes as they prepared to make a right turn onto Avenida Máximo Gómez. The driver of a vintage, banged-up Chevy had changed his mind at the last minute and had darted in front of the van without a warning signal.

After skillfully averting what had appeared to be an inevitable collision, Brian cast an amused glance in her direction. "Relax," he said. "Things will get better once we're out of the city."

Slowly Sydne released the deep shuddering breath she had been holding. Her hands were shaking, and she knew her face must be drained of color. But as she began to regain her composure, her irritation mounted at Brian's casual attitude toward the near miss. The man must have ice in his veins, she thought

crossly, darting a fierce look at him. Apparently he
missed it.

As he had very accurately forecast, the traffic remained heavy as they traveled through the city
streets. After circling the rotunda, in the middle of
which stood an equestrian statue of one of the country's patriots, they headed down the Avenida Presi-
dente John F. Kennedy. The broad lanes of the
thoroughfare should have eased her mounting tension, but Sydne was unable to let down her guard.
She was greatly relieved when they finally reached the
Autopista Duarte and left the congested city traffic
behind.

Brian had proved to be a skillful driver who knew
his way around the city, and she resented the fact, as
she did everything else about him.

What was happening to her, Sydne wondered in
confusion. All her life she had considered herself to
be a reasonable person, certainly not one given to
edginess and impulsive judgment. But her disposition
ever since she had come in contact with Brian Stevens
left a lot to be desired. Never in her life had she been
so wary and self-consciously uncomfortable in the
presence of a man. What was there about him that
rattled her so? After all, he was not the first attractive macho type she had ever encountered.

Sydne had been a college freshman when her parents were killed in a head-on collision with a drunken
driver. Tom Matheson, just turned forty, had been
an executive on the rise. Confident of his bright
future, he and his wife, Linda, had lived far beyond
his excellent income. Sydne had grown up in beautiful homes, surrounded by the love of doting parents

and all the comforts and advantages money could buy. She had had ballet and riding lessons, a horse of her own, even a little red sports car for her sixteenth birthday. Expensive clothes filled her closets. Membership at select country clubs, first-class travel and the best of private schools had been the only way of life she'd ever known, until an inebriated stranger brought her world tumbling down. After the tragic loss of her parents she had discovered that their house had been heavily mortgaged. But that was the least of her worries. The proceeds of a hefty insurance policy and the sale of all the remaining property had barely covered the mountain of debts her parents had left behind.

Sydne had been forced to hold a variety of jobs to see her through her remaining college years. This had left little time for dates and all those other pleasures of carefree youth that had been hers before the fatal accident. With a tight class schedule to keep, waitressing had provided her with a reasonable income, and she had supplemented that by tutoring other students. Helping the captain of the football team prepare for final exams had definitely cured her of males, long in brawn and short in brains, who thought of themselves as irresistible. It certainly had not been easy to hammer the intricacies of algebra into the thick skull of a 225-pound octopus, she remembered wryly.

Clouds veiled the beauty of the rugged heartland as the van cruised through small picturesque villages. In each of them Sydne spotted colorful roadside eateries that offered a variety of native foods. There were crisp and salty *chicharrones*, the very popular fried

pork rinds, as well as fried *plátanos*, or large cooking
bananas, which restaurants served as accompaniment
to every meal. Temptingly displayed at fruit stands
were golden bunches of bananas, sweet ripe man-
goes, juicy pineapples, creamy avocados. In the
valleys tender young blades were just poking through
the marshy rice fields, and neat rows of tobacco
plants surrounded thatch-roofed *vegas*, the curing
barns where the harvested leaves were hung up to
dry.

When they had passed several towns, Sydne commented on the fact that even the smallest ones had
baseball stadiums, some of them apparently very
modern and well equipped.

"Baseball is the national pastime," Brian replied.
With a smile he added, "And people take it very seriously here. Actually it's probably the only subject
over which you can get into an argument with a
Dominican. Maybe that's why so many of their
players get to the major leagues. Do you follow the
game?"

"Not really," Sydne replied. "My father took me
to the World Series once, but I didn't care much for
it—perhaps because I didn't understand what was
going on most of the time."

She hoped the exchange had managed to break the
ice, but Brian let the subject drop. Sydne realized
that he probably still resented her presence. He certainly had no inclination for idle conversation.

With a slight shrug, she tried to disregard her
traveling companion. But Brian Stevens was not a
man women found it easy to ignore. Even though
Sydne's own taste ran more toward intellectual

sophisticated men, she was uncomfortably conscious of Brian's masculinity. Her eyes kept wandering to his sinewy arms covered with fine dark hair, to his strong sunburned hands resting casually on the steering wheel. Were those large powerful hands capable of gentle caresses, she wondered.... When she became aware of the thoughts she was entertaining, she felt her face grow hot. To hide her embarrassment, she quickly pretended an absorbing interest in the view once again. She was relieved that Brian didn't seem to notice her discomfiture; for all she knew, the man beside her was totally oblivious to her presence.

"I hope you brought more sensible shoes than those sandals," he said a moment later.

When Sydne turned back to him in surprise, she saw that he was eyeing her ankles—and a good deal of one leg that had been inadvertently exposed by her wraparound skirt. She heaved a sigh, yanking the folds of her skirt together. "I'm sure even you would approve of canvas deck shoes, Mr. Stevens," she replied dryly. She waited for another caustic remark from him, but he only frowned.

Moments later her attention was diverted by a woman with burnished brown skin walking along the side of the road. She was carrying a large basket perfectly balanced on her head, while she swung her arms freely at her sides. Momentarily forgetting the lack of harmony between her and her companion, Sydne started to comment, but then caught herself in time and sat back in frustrated silence. She wasn't going to warm up to this chauvinistic impolite brute, no matter how much Andrew McCallum respected him!

By the time the van had turned off the main highway onto the road leading to San Francisco de Macoris, the uneasy silence was grating on Sydne's nerves. *This is ridiculous,* she told herself. They had a long way ahead. Someone had to make an effort to reach some sort of truce, and it was obvious that Brian Stevens had no intention of making the first move. It would be up to her.

Thinking back on the very brief conversation they had had about baseball, Sydne realized that the probable reason it had failed so miserably was her lack of knowledge on the subject. For the next few minutes she racked her brain for a topic they could discuss, and she could have kicked herself for a fool when she realized that all the time the solution had been staring her in the face.

Before embarking on this adventure, Sydne had brushed up on her knowledge of the ships lost during the early seventeenth century. At that time Philip IV, the king of Spain had been in dire need of enormous sums to maintain his armies in the far-flung empire he had inherited. And with the sea being the only link between Spain and its New World colonies, the ships that carried the royal revenues of gold and silver, precious jewels and merchant's goods were vitally important. Assembled into fleets, they were escorted by mighty war galleons to protect them from their enemies—not only the English, but also the Dutch who, with the end of a twelve-year truce, had threatened to descend upon Castile's Indies.

From Vera Cruz, Portobello and Cartagena de Indias the fabulous treasures of the New World sailed: gold from the mines of New Granada, which is now

Colombia; silver from Peru, in the form of coins or bars, consigned to the silversmiths of Seville; indigo from Honduras; and from Cuba tobacco and copper, the latter bound for Málaga to be cast into bronze cannons to fight the imperial wars.

Man alone was not their enemy, and many of those fabulous treasure ships had been lost to the fury of nature, against which even the mightiest of galleons was powerless. During the ensuing centuries, adventurers like Brian Stevens had searched the seas for those sunken vessels. Within the past decade, the recovery of two such *almirantas*, *Nuestra Señora de la Concepción* and *Nuestra Señora de Atocha*, had made the fortune of men of daring. Brian himself had succeeded once before. What other subject could better bridge the communication gap between them?

"How did you find the *Conde*?" Sydne inquired at last.

Casting an ironic glance in her direction, Brian replied laconically, "Some detective work, a lot of expensive equipment and an incredible amount of luck."

Sydne knew that the Spanish government, eager to protect the king's portion of all the treasures brought from the New World, had kept very accurate accounts of each shipment. What Brian so succinctly described as "detective work" entailed the painstaking screening of thousands of pages of original cargo manifestos, letters, salvage accounts and other such documents meticulously kept for hundreds of years at the colonial archives in Seville. She waited for Brian to continue, and when he did not, decided to give him another chance.

"You make it sound so simple," she said doggedly. "Yet the *Conde* has been lost for over three hundred years. How is it that no one ever found it before?"

"There could be a number of reasons," Brian said with a shrug.

This was like pulling teeth, Sydne thought impatiently, but determined not to give up, she insisted, "Such as?"

"No one looked in the right place."

At first, refusing to believe her ears, Sydne gave him a startled look. Then she exploded, "Oh, I give up!" She had to take a deep breath to steady herself before she spoke again. "Look, Mr. Stevens, all I'm trying to do is behave in a civilized adult manner. Like it or not, we have a long road ahead of us, and on top of that we'll be seeing a lot of each other during the coming weeks—unless your precious ship is the size of the *Queen Mary*, that is."

"The *Adventurer* is by no means the *Queen Mary*," Brian replied, a quirk of amusement twitching the corners of his sensual mouth. "She's just a 130-foot buoy tender that's been refitted for salvage work."

Even in her angry state, Sydne stared in fascination as the chips of ice vanished from the blue eyes that briefly studied her flushed features. Moreover, she could find only a hint of irony in the lazy smile tilting the corners of his mouth. She was startled to discover how tremendously attractive Brian Stevens could be when he wasn't being rude to her. "How long did it take you to find the *Conde*?" she hastened to ask.

"As I told Andrew, we found a galleon. Whether

or not it's the *Conde* still remains to be seen," Brian qualified. "But the hunt took us almost a year from the time we started searching the colonial archives."

"Did anyone survive the shipwreck?" she wanted to know.

Brian shook his head. "Not of the *Conde*. All we learned from the accounts was that the fleet that sailed from Havana in late August of 1622 was scattered by a severe hurricane. Two ships, the *Santa Margarita* one of them, sank within sight of each other. But although much of the fleet was reassembled afterward, no one ever saw the *Conde* again."

"But how did you ever select this area to look for the *Conde*?" Sydne inquired with interest. "Isn't it way off the course the Spaniards usually took on their return voyages to Spain?"

There was a new glimmer of appreciation in Brian's eyes when he looked at her. "You're right, it was. And maybe that's precisely why no one has ever taken into account one small item—the fact that a galleon was sighted somewhere off the northern coast of Hispaniola not too long after the storm."

"But it seems more logical that such a ship would have been on its way from Spain to the New World," Sydne observed thoughtfully, "not the other way around. If memory serves me right, those outbound ships stopped in Puerto Rico for provisions before continuing on to Havana. Samaná Bay is closer to that course, isn't it?"

When Brian smiled at her Sydne could not find any traces of his previous antagonism toward her, and she mentally congratulated herself for her success.

"You're right again, and that's one of the reasons

we can't be sure that the shipwreck we found is that of the *Conde*. It could well be one of the king's galleons carrying mercury to the silver mines of the New World, in which case we could still make a profit from this venture. But it could just as easily be a later wreck, and totally worthless." He paused before adding wryly, "We know the *Conde* was thrown off course by the storm, which may have badly damaged her. She might have been headed for La Hispaniola for repairs, or she might even have run into an enemy. The possibilities are endless, and that's what makes hunting for treasure such a gamble. At any rate, we took the information we had to Hildegarde."

Sydne's delicate brows arched quizzically. "Hildegarde?"

"Hildegarde is a computer," Brian chuckled, and at her surprised exclamation he went on, "With such a large area to cover, we figured we needed to narrow the odds a bit. Hildegarde came up with several possibilities that we thought had some merit, so we decided to approach the Dominican government for permission to conduct our search. We started with Puerto Plata because it was the nearest port, but there was nothing there. After weeks of searching, our largest discovery turned out to be the fuselage of a World War II airplane. So we moved on to Samaná." He paused, then asked suddenly, "Are you hungry?"

"As a matter of fact, I am," Sydne admitted. She had not eaten anything since the light breakfast at the hotel. "How far is it to the next town?"

"A few more miles, but I had the hotel pack us

some sandwiches. There's a brown bag behind your seat. Can you reach it?''

While Sydne searched for the sack, which had slipped under the seat, Brian continued, ''Small towns like the one coming up have very little to offer in the way of dining facilities. The best you can expect is a café or a cantina frequented mainly by the local people.''

Sydne had located the bag, and opening it, she reached inside for the sandwiches wrapped in clear plastic. Holding them up, she asked, ''Ham and cheese or roast beef?''

''Take your pick, '' he replied. ''We'll be stopping up ahead for something to drink.''

Sydne unwrapped the roast-beef sandwich and passed it to Brian. ''So what happened after you got permission from the government?''

She had to wait until he swallowed a mouthful before he replied, ''The next step was to comb the area in a small boat with a sensitive magnetometer until we got some readings. Since those galleons were heavily armed, the best way to find them is to search for unusual masses of metal on the sea bottom. There were a few disappointments, but we finally came across some remnants of a cannon.''

''And the ship?''

''It wasn't there.''

Sydne couldn't contain her curiosity. ''What about the markings on the cannon? Couldn't you identify them?''

''They had been worn smooth by exposure,'' Brian replied. Consumed with impatience, Sydne had to wait until he had finished his sandwich to hear the rest. "At any rate," he finally continued, "after we found the cannon we sent teams of divers to search the area. There's a lot of coral out there, which makes the search even more difficult, since it can easily hide pieces of rigging and even a mast. But we finally found the shipwreck, less than half a mile away from the cannon."

So enthralled had Sydne been with his narrative that she was surprised when he stopped the van. It was not until she looked out the window that she realized they had finally arrived at the town he had told her about. They were parked in front of a dusty cantina, one that at first sight certainly didn't hold much promise. The corrugated roof was stained with rust, and the rickety walls, which had once been painted pink, were now faded and coated with dust.

"This is all there is," Brian announced.

By the time he came around the van to help her, Sydne had already alighted. When he took her by the elbow to guide her inside she was rather alarmed by her response to his touch. She felt something akin to a mild electric shock, and it made her feel curiously warm.

A rough counter, two rustic tables and four chairs were the only furniture in the cantina. The loud hum of an ancient refrigerator tucked away in a corner competed with the lively rhythm of the merengue blaring out of a modern portable radio.

"Beer?" Brian offered. "The local brew is quite good."

"I've never acquired a taste for beer," Sydne replied, wrinkling her nose. She didn't realize her blunder until she saw that the ice chips had returned to his eyes. He had already accused her of being a bored rich girl in search of a thrill; now he probably thought her a snob, she supposed. *But I don't owe him any explanations,* she thought stubbornly, and simply said, "I'd rather have a soda."

He ordered and paid for the drinks, which they sipped standing at the counter, from the bottles. And during that time they had to submit to the curious stares of three men, who apparently didn't see many strangers. Sydne wasn't surprised to find that Brian's reticence had returned by the time they returned to the van.

To break the silence she queried, "Where do tourists go for meals around here?"

"There are few good restaurants outside the capital and the larger cities," her companion replied, and for a moment she believed that the tenuous rapport they had established earlier had survived the episode at the cantina. "Until very recently, Samaná was totally isolated from the rest of the island and was accessible only by sea. You must remember that this country existed under a very repressive tyranny for over thirty years," he went on to explain. "Only recently the new government started restoring colonial buildings that had been left to deteriorate, and developing natural attractions for tourists. There are some beautiful beaches on the windward side that are still practically untouched by man."

Sydne's hopes had floundered as she listened. Even though he had taken the trouble to maintain the flow of conversation, the friendly casual Brian Stevens of the past hour had been replaced by a polite detached stranger whose strong-boned face was set in stern lines. What made this man blow hot and cold so unexpectedly, Sydne wondered in frustration.

They had turned off the main highway two hours earlier, and she didn't think Samaná could be far away. Too tired to try to keep forcing a conversation, Sydne concentrated on the scenery.

It was truly magnificent. The sun had gone down behind the mountains, leaving the mist to settle across the brow of the forest. There was such primitive beauty to this land, she mused, and Brian's words of moments before came unbidden to her mind. Except for the gray ribbon of the road, large stretches of the countryside had probably not changed much since the first Spanish conquistadores had set foot on the island. Suddenly Sydne was filled with a yearning to see those beaches untouched by man.

But how long would the wild beauty last? In a few years there would probably be gas stations, motels and restaurants along the highways, catering to herds of camera-toting tourists who would bring prosperity to the land, but destroy its natural perfection. The thought of billboards cluttering the landscape was unsettling, especially at this quiet hour when even the smokestacks of a sugar mill, looming in the distance like the masts of a ship in a fluttering sea of green, appeared to intrude.

Soon it grew dark, and with even the scenery denied her, Sydne tilted her seat back and closed her eyes.

THE DOOR OF THE VAN CLICKING shut brought her out of her sleep. She straightened up in time to see Brian walking away, toward the lights of a house she could just glimpse through the thick foliage of a garden. She was about to call after him when a figure, unequivocally feminine, stepped out of the shadows to meet him. Sydne strained to get a better look, but all she could distinguish in the gloom was the light color of the woman's dress. Even that was hidden when Brian's tall frame blocked the view, and it seemed from Sydne's vantage point as if they were embracing.

Her irritation growing with every minute that slowly ticked away, Sydne waited impatiently in the van while Brian took part in what had all the earmarks of a clandestine rendezvous. She deliberately turned away from the couple, but finally, catching a movement in the shadows out of the corner of her eye, she couldn't resist the temptation. Brian was returning to the van when, apparently responding to a call from the woman, he paused again. This time when she came up to him, she definitely threw her arms around his neck.

Sydne was staring straight ahead when Brian climbed into the van. "Have we arrived at Samaná yet?" she asked stiffly.

"Just about," Brian replied as he slid behind the steering wheel and turned the key in the ignition. "We should be at the cottage in a few minutes."

They drove in silence for a while, but Sydne couldn't erase the scene in the garden from her mind. "Have you bothered to tell your local conquest about your wife?" she finally asked, unable to keep the caustic tone out of her voice.

Brian's face was set in hard lines as he said harshly, "Stay out of my personal life, okay?"

Despite her self-righteous position, Sydne was taken aback. In the faint light of the dashboard she could see the bitter twist of his mouth. He had accelerated abruptly and was now driving at such a speed that Sydne half expected to crash into one of the trees bordering the road. She clung to her seat.

"Would you please slow down?" she pleaded in a quavering voice.

To her surprise and immense relief he complied immediately. Sydne slumped back in her seat, straining to get a grip on her terror and calm her pounding heart.

Minutes later she saw lights twinkling at the bottom of the hill, and through the dense darkness caught a glimpse of frothy waves breaking on the shore of a small cove. There was a gravel walkway leading to the small cottage. Brian parked the van in front.

Without wasting a second, Sydne jumped out and ran toward the house. After the long hours of tension, the fright of the reckless downhill race had rekindled her anger, and she was seething when Andrew answered her knock, a tall glass in his hand.

"Judging from your entrance," he said dryly, "I don't think I'll bother to ask how your trip was."

"Of all the stupid, rude and contemptible men I've ever met, your Brian Stevens wins first prize!" she flared. "I could wring his neck!"

"Now, now, my dear, it can't be that bad," Andrew said soothingly. "Why don't you have one of these *piña coladas*? They're guaranteed to settle your nerves and improve your disposition." Turning away he called, "Beulah!"

"Oh, stop maneuvering me, Andrew!" Sydne snapped. "The only thing that would make me feel better is to know that I'll never have to suffer that big ape again. Ever!" Only then did her mind register the rest of what Andrew had said, and she paused long enough to ask, "Who's Beulah?"

"A very nice lady that Brian engaged to look after Tim and me for the length of our stay," Andrew explained patiently. "You'll like her."

A tall slender black woman had appeared at Andrew's call.

"Beulah, would you please bring one of these delicious concoctions for Miss Matheson?" he asked after introducing Sydne.

Beulah smiled warmly. "Jes, Mistah Andrew," and before Sydne could react, she had disappeared into the kitchenette.

"Mistah Andrew?" Sydne repeated, startled.

"A colloquial term of respect," Andrew said.

Beulah returned with the cocktail for Sydne just as Brian and Tim entered the room. The two men were carrying Andrew's bed, which they had unloaded from the van.

Sydne took the drink gratefully, and lowering herself into a rattan chair with soft green cushions, she forced herself to ignore the commotion as they tried to get the bed through the narrow front door.

Several minutes later the work was done. Brian declined Andrew's offer of a drink when he came back to the living room. "We'll be leaving first thing in the morning," he told Sydne tersely. "I'll pick you up at seven."

She acknowledged the statement with a nod, and

Brian went out, letting the screen door slam shut behind him.

"Andrew, if I wasn't sure before that this was a mistake, I am now," she said after he had gone. "I don't know how you can expect me to spend five minutes, let alone several weeks, with that man. He's so rude, so—" she groped for the word "—so infuriating! One minute he's acting like a civilized person, and then wham, he's reverted to the Stone Age! And he drives like a maniac! It's a miracle we made it here in one piece!"

Andrew's bushy eyebrows knit in a frown. "Brian isn't normally unreasonable. He's one of the most trustworthy men I know. What happened?"

By this time the *piña colada* had begun to work its magic, and Sydne took a deep breath. "He stopped on the way to meet with a woman," she answered reluctantly. "When he got back to the van I asked him if he had bothered to tell her that he had a wife somewhere. I know I shouldn't have said anything," she admitted ruefully. "I don't know what got into me. At any rate, he was very upset. He was driving so fast that I thought we were going to crash going around those curves on the hill."

Andrew regarded her thoughtfully. "But why did it bother you, Sydne? What's wrong with his meeting a woman?"

"What's wrong!" she repeated, aghast. "The man is married!"

Andrew gave her a probing glance. "Brian was divorced almost two years ago, Sydne. The man is free."

Sydne was so taken aback by this piece of news

that it took her a moment to focus again on his words. "Helene was a pampered society girl who decided she wanted to be a countess or something like that."

"Is that what he told you?" she scoffed, arching a brow.

"Brian has never spoken about his wife to me," Andrew said, shaking his head. "But if I read him right, he's a man who feels things deeply, Sydne. He must have loved the girl, and I think the failure of his marriage affected him much more than he lets on."

Sydne remained unconvinced. Somehow she couldn't reconcile her impression of Brian Stevens with the picture Andrew was painting. She saw him as the big macho type, capable of hurting, not of being hurt.

"Please try to keep an open mind, Syd," Andrew said as if reading her mind. "He's a good man."

"I'll do my best, Andrew," she said after a pause. At the same time she told herself inwardly that men and women must hold different views as to what a good man is. Paul was considered a good respectable man by his peers, and yet.... "Oh, I don't know what's wrong with me," she admitted wearily.

"You're tired, Sydne." Andrew regarded her affectionately. "You'll feel better after a good night's sleep."

"Perhaps you're right," she admitted. "I *am* tired."

"Your things are in the cottage next door, to the right," Andrew said, handing her the key. "I had Beulah unpack what you'll need for the night."

Sydne took the key as she stood up. "Thank you, Andrew."

"If I don't see you in the morning, take care, Syd. Don't work too hard. Remember it takes time to get used to this climate." Watching her go out the door, he smiled whimsically.

CHAPTER THREE

WITHOUT OPENING HER EYES, Sydne reached out and turned off the alarm that had so rudely interrupted her heavy slumber. Six o'clock already. She groaned, feeling as if she had gone to bed only minutes earlier.

She was barely awake as she pushed aside the fine cotton sheet and stumbled out of bed. Determined not to give Brian Stevens another excuse to be nasty, however, she made her way to the bathroom. The cold spray of the shower jolted her back to reality before she could adjust it to a more comfortable temperature.

Minutes later she stepped out of the shower, relaxed and refreshed, and wrapping a towel around her body, stood in front of the mirror to blow dry her hair. She congratulated herself for having taken the time to have her hair cut before her hasty departure from Minneapolis. A visit to Oskar, her expensive hairstylist, took a good chunk out of her limited budget, but it was one of the few luxuries Sydne allowed herself and she felt it was well worth it. Unlike other coiffeurs, who usually despaired of ever taming her unruly tresses, Oskar had taken advantage of the natural curl, achieving a feathered wind-blown style that was not only highly flattering, but also easy for her to keep up.

After she had applied a minimum amount of
makeup, she dressed in a short one-piece jump suit of
yellow terry cloth that attractively molded the curves
of her slender figure. While moving her bags into the
living room she detected a delicious aroma of coffee
and bacon, making her mouth water and the void in
her stomach acutely noticeable. Small wonder, she
mused, remembering that she had hardly eaten anything the previous day. She found Beulah fixing
breakfast in the small kitchenette, and mentally she
thanked Andrew for thinking of her.

"Good morning, Beulah," she greeted the other
woman.

"Good mawnin', missy." Beulah smiled back.
"Breakfast is almost ready. How you like the eggs?"

"Over easy," Sydne answered. Taking a seat at the
table, she inquired, "Are you from the States,
Beulah?"

"No, missy. Ah is fum heah, born and raised."

But her accent sounded straight out of the United
States' Old South, Sydne realized with surprise. Then
she remembered something she'd read during her
quick research on the Dominican Republic. In the
1820s, during one of the periods when the entire
island of Hispaniola had been under the domination
of Haiti, a shipload of slaves had escaped to the
black republic, thinking they would find refuge
there—especially since the Haitian government had
recently freed all slaves in Santo Domingo. The ship
had foundered in Samaná Bay, and the refugees had
settled in the area. But finding it difficult to adapt to
the local way of life, most of them had left. The de-
scendants of those who stayed were still in the area,

and they still kept some of the traditions of their ancestors.

"And do you speak Spanish, too?" Sydne asked.

"Oh, jes, missy. I learnt in school. But at home we kyep in English, like my mama and her mama."

The small cup that Beulah set before Sydne gave her the opportunity to sample Dominican coffee. It was aromatic, strong and sweet, and tasted much better than she had anticipated. Sydne dismissed as petty her gnawing feeling of annoyance that for once Brian Stevens had been right about something. And thinking of him, she found she was still curious about the identity of the woman he had met the night before.

Beulah, having lived in Samaná all of her life, proved a good source of information. She answered all Sydne's questions about the town, inquiries that discreetly led to the occupants of the house at the top of the hill.

By the end of their conversation, Sydne had learned that Francisco Lozano, the owner, was the wealthiest man in the area. He and his wife, Matilde, shared their rambling hilltop mansion with two of his unmarried sisters—both well into their fifties—three sons, and their only daughter, Julia. The nineteen-year-old was probably Brian's *novia*, or girl friend, Sydne deduced. And when Beulah mentioned that the girl was engaged to a rich landowner from Santiago, the second largest city in the Dominican Republic, she understood the reason for the secrecy of their meeting.

So that was why he had been so upset when she had seen them together, she mused. There was no question in her mind that the girl's family would strongly object to any involvement their daughter might have with a foreign adventurer such as Brian Stevens.

That Julia Lozano was attracted to him was understandable. Judging by the hotel waitress's reaction, women responded easily to his charm and good looks. Sydne had to reluctantly admit that even she had felt the power of his masculinity. At the same time, she assured herself that the gnawing feeling in the pit of her stomach could be nothing more than concern for the young Julia. Brian Stevens had the capacity to hurt a girl as badly as Sydne herself had been hurt . . . unless he loved her . . . .

But she immediately discarded the idea. Regardless of what Andrew had said, macho men like Brian Stevens loved themselves far too much to have any real feelings left for anyone else. Their hearts were in their glands.

Sydne sighed, sipping the last of her coffee. She had promised Andrew that she would do her best to get along with Brian, and she was determined to keep her word.

She had finished her breakfast when she heard him at the door. Getting up from the table, she said goodbye to Beulah, thanking her sincerely for the meal.

The minute Brian looked at her, his blue eyes as hard as tempered steel, she knew he was displeased about something. And he didn't leave her guessing.

"Where do you think you're going, dressed like that?" he demanded, gesturing at her long bare legs. "I won't have you parading around the ship half-naked."

Sydne's mouth dropped open. Surely even he could not be so rude. But all she had to do was look at his face again to know she was not mistaken, and her good intentions immediately went up in smoke. "How dare you!" she gasped. "I'm dressed perfectly respecta—"

"Look, lady, you're not going on a cruise," Brian interrupted her bluntly. "You'll be the only female aboard the *Adventurer*, and I don't want you distracting the men. Every hour we spend out there costs me money." Handing her one of her bags, he jerked his head toward the bedroom. "Now get back in there and change into something decent—and hurry up. We're late."

Sydne's cheeks were burning with fury, and she felt an overwhelming urge to inflict physical damage. Instead she snatched the bag from his hand and stomped into the bedroom, where with trembling hands she fumbled with the zipper of her jump suit.

"Oh, that egotistical domineering man!" she muttered. Never in her life had she met anyone who could make her lose her temper like Brian Stevens did.

The stab of pain from a fingernail that split to the quick evoked images of Brian Stevens being drawn and quartered that gave Sydne a measure of malevolent satisfaction. The vision helped her regain some control of her temper while she finished changing.

Brian examined her critically when she reappeared. Her checkered red-and-white shirt, tapered at the waist, did nothing to disguise the fullness of her heaving bosom, and her denim jeans fit just snugly enough to mold the curves of her hips and buttocks without hugging them too tightly.

"We could always stop by the local convent and

borrow a habit from the nuns,'' she suggested sweetly.

A muscle twitched in Brian's cheek, but he made
no reply to her sarcasm as he picked up her bags.
Smiling inwardly at her successful dig, Sydne followed him down the gravel path to the van.

BRIAN MUST HAVE BEEN to the wharf earlier, Sydne realized as soon as they got there. The equipment they
had brought from Santo Domingo had already been
transferred to the outboard-motor launch, which she
boarded, reluctantly accepting Brian's help. She was
a little puzzled by the curious sensations that rippled
through her when he grasped her by the waist to
lower her onto the deck.

When he had followed her aboard he handed her a
wide-brimmed hat woven out of a green palm leaf.
''You'd better put this on,'' he ordered.

Sydne took the hat, and ignoring him, laid it on the
bench beside her.

A helpful Dominican came over to cast off the
lines, and Brian started the motor. With all the
equipment they carried, the craft sat low in the water.
But Brian steered it skillfully through the motley fishing vessels toward the mouth of the enormous U-
shaped bay.

It was a beautiful morning. The sun shone brightly
on the clear blue waters and reflected off the windows of the large hotel perched on a promontory. Up
in the surrounding hills, set amid lush foliage, were
the houses of the prosperous and the prominent,
Sydne knew. She thought of Julia Lozano, who perhaps at this very moment was watching their progress

from her window. Resisting the temptation to look back, she wondered if Brian would wave at his secret *novia*.

About half an hour later they passed near a beautiful little island, where a large building gleamed white amid the luxuriant vegetation. It appeared deserted, as was the small stretch of white sandy beach.

"That's Cayo Levantado," Brian volunteered. "The hotel is closed now for some reason. I'm not sure why."

It was nine o'clock by the time the laden motor launch gained the open sea, and Sydne was beginning to feel the effects of the sun on her sensitive skin. She was about to reach for the hat Brian had given her when he said, "You'd better put on that hat before you get sunstroke."

His suggestion was enough to make her change her mind. Still smarting from his earlier treatment, she tossed dryly over her shoulder, "Your concern for my health is very touching, Mr. Stevens."

"Let's get one thing straight, Miss Matheson." The tone of his voice made Sydne turn and face him, and his expression promised that she wouldn't like what she was about to hear. "I own this outfit," he said, "and when I tell you to do something, you do it. No arguments; you just do it. Is that clear?" At the sight of her pursed lips he added, "Now put that hat on."

For a moment Sydne defiantly held his glance. Then she turned away and grudgingly clapped the hat on her head.

Suddenly she realized how childishly she was behaving. She had never reacted so unreasonably

toward a man before. Brian Stevens seemed to bring
out the worst in her nature, she admitted guiltily.
Why couldn't she simply be herself when she was
with him? The man must have some redeeming qualities for Andrew to hold him in such high esteem—
only she had yet to discover them. . . .

Perhaps it was the chemistry between them, she
mused wryly. There were those who believed in love
at first sight, so why couldn't the opposite be true?
And for two people who had detested each other at
sight, she and Brian were being forced to spend too
much time alone together. Hopefully their colleagues
aboard the *Adventurer* would act as a buffer.

How Brian was able to find his way to the ship, she
had no idea. They were out in the middle of a road-
less ocean with no land or any other point of reference in sight. But suddenly there it was, a white dot in
the distance—the *Adventurer*.

The name suited the man who owned it, Sydne
mused. Who else but an adventurer would take on
the challenge of wrenching from the sea a prize it had
claimed so long ago?

AS THE MOTOR LAUNCH APPROACHED the ship, it
entered a channel marked by brightly colored buoys.
Sydne imagined this was probably the path the
Adventurer had followed through the reef to its present position, where it was now moored with heavy
steel lines.

Their arrival had been observed from the ship, and
apparently the crew had been alerted to the presence
of a woman on the launch, for all the men had gathered topside. A chorus of whistles and good-natured

if somewhat rowdy remarks reached Sydne's ears as they pulled alongside.

Two men wearing brief swimming trunks that displayed their lean bronzed bodies to perfection jumped aboard the launch.

"Chuck Bates, my second-in-command," Brian said, indicating the sandy-haired man in the lead.

In his early thirties, he was almost as tall as Brian, Sydne noted, and his brown eyes were as warm as his welcoming smile. She liked him immediately.

"Kenny Felton, one of our divers. Miss Matheson, our archaeologist."

"Wow!" Kenny grinned, pumping her hand enthusiastically. "I can't believe it! I never had an archaeology professor who looked like you!"

The second man was very young, Sydne judged— in his early twenties. He was wiry and smaller than the other two, but he had a winning grin and a mischievous twinkle in his clear blue eyes. If she had ever wished for a younger brother, she would have wanted one like Kenny, she decided.

"Welcome aboard the *Adventurer*, Miss Matheson," Chuck was saying. "I hope we can make you comfortable."

He didn't seem to resent her presence aboard as Brian did, Sydne observed in surprise. His welcome appeared genuine.

"Thank you, Chuck," she answered sincerely. "And my name is Sydne—Syd to my friends. I hope you'll be one."

"Nothing would please me more," the tall man answered gallantly.

"Me, too," Kenny put in, and Sydne laughed.

Once aboard, she was immediately surrounded by a group of men, many of different nationalities. Some were wearing swimsuits, while others wore portions of their black wet suits. Every one of them was anxious to be introduced and to shake her hand. Most of them were young, Sydne noticed, although Rod McKenzie, an Australian, was well into his forties and Bernardo Rivero, a charming Spaniard, was in his mid to late thirties. Claude Dumas, from Marseilles, was slightly built, as was Enrico "Ricco" Martelli, an Italian who surprised Sydne and drew guffaws from the others when he kissed her hand.

"Don't you pay no mind to that skinny Eyetalian," someone scoffed. "He thinks he's Marcello Mastroianni."

"*Beh!* But it was I who taught the great Mastroianni all he knows!" protested Ricco, rolling his eyes to the sky.

"Yeah, and you have five *bambini* to prove it!"

Sydne joined the chorus of laughter until Brian, who had been conferring with Chuck, broke through the crowd. "All right, boys, break it up," he said good-naturedly. "The show is over. Back to work."

Protesting mildly, the men dispersed, leaving Sydne free to follow their boss.

"This way," Brian said, leading her below deck to a small cabin. They both went inside.

Only when Brian began collecting his belongings from the locker did she realize he had relinquished his quarters to her.

"Please don't trouble yourself on my account," she rushed to protest. "I don't want any special treatment because of my sex. I can use the accommodations assigned to the man you were expecting."

Brian paused in his packing and gave her a smile charged with irony. "Nothing would please the men more." When she didn't react, he added, "I told you before that this is not a luxury liner, Miss Matheson. There *are* no other cabins. The man was expected to bunk in with the crew."

He paused, as if enjoying her embarrassment. "Like it or not, you *will* receive special treatment, and here are some rules to follow. Number one—" he counted with his fingers "—stay away from the men. You are here to work, not flirt."

Sydne opened her mouth to protest indignantly, but Brian didn't give her a chance. "Number two," he went on, "the men are used to running around in their birthday suits, so unless you're looking for a thrill, stay away from the areas that will be off limits to you—the berthing area, for one." Sydne looked at him mutely. She had no argument there.

"Number three, this cabin has a private shower," he said, opening the door to show her, "but if you want to use the head—the toilet—get one of the fellows to make sure no one is using it, and then to make sure you're not interrupted." The order brought a flush to her face, but he appeared not to notice.

"Number four, you are to be fully clothed while on board—and before you open your mouth to object," he hurried to say, "I'll tell you why, only to avoid further arguments. First, because you must use extreme care in exposing yourself to the sun. It's much more intense here in the tropics than at other latitudes, and that fair skin of yours could easily be broiled to a crisp. I can't afford the time it would take to rush you to the nearest hospital with third-degree burns.

"Secondly, of course, you're the only woman aboard, as you know, and the less temptation you put in the way of the men, the better it will be for all concerned. We're working twenty-day shifts, with ten days off in between. There are eight divers on duty at all times in addition to the crew, and believe me, at the end of twenty days the men are really looking forward to some female companionship. Do I make myself clear?"

"Is that all?" she asked testily.

"For now. If I've overlooked anything, you'll be the first to know."

He zipped up his duffel bag and went to the door. With his hand on the knob, he turned and faced her. "Make yourself at home," he said with an edge of mockery in his voice. "I'll be back in an hour to introduce you to your colleague, Dr. Marín, who seems to be the only male aboard you haven't met yet."

And with that, he left.

Dr. José Marín, or the Professor, as he was called by the crew, was the archaeologist assigned by the Dominican government to act as liaison with the salvagers. His duties included the recording of artifacts recovered from the shipwreck. If indeed the galleon proved to be the *Conde de Santander*, it would be perhaps the richest find ever made in Dominican waters.

Dr. Marín turned out to be a small, sparse, middle-aged man with crackling black eyes and a luxurious mustache. He had a rich café au lait complexion and he protected his balding pate with a black baseball cap. His dedication to his profession had made him one of the topmost authorities in his field, Sydne knew, and she felt privileged to work with such a man. She soon discovered that he had a delightful personality, and his easy rapport with Brian and the crew made her own first hours on board more pleasurable.

"I never expected to be working with such a lovely young lady," he had exclaimed gallantly when Brian introduced them. "Come, my dear, I will show you what I've done so far."

A large canvas awning had been set up aft to provide shelter from the relentless tropical sun, since the burning rays made the steel deck and the assorted metal equipment hot to the touch.

"Here are the first items we recovered," Dr. Marín said, pointing out a row of clay jars encrusted with sand and coral. The jars, in various stages of being cleaned, had been used on the galleon to carry water, wine, olives and pine pitch. "These were found strewn around the shipwreck and are only the beginning," he explained. "We expect a much larger number of artifacts, which will have to be recorded, cleaned and carefully packed for transportation. But these will keep us busy for the time being."

"Yes, of course," Sydne agreed. Items such as these might not have as much dollar value as the treasures of gold and silver Brian expected to recover from the *Conde*, but from an historical point of view they were just as precious.

Some of the jars were broken, and gesturing toward them, Dr. Marín said, "Perhaps we'll be able to put some of these back together again. Isn't it remarkable? They have been underwater for more than three centuries!" This was a man who obviously enjoyed his work, Sydne mused, observing his delight. As she knew herself, a passion for the past was one of the main attributes of a good archaeologist.

Although history had always been one of her own favorite subjects, she had really stumbled into archaeology when Paul had come into her life. It was he who had shown her how fascinating reconstructing the past, discovering old civilizations, could be. Three centuries, ten—it didn't matter. Artifacts invented and used by peoples long lost in history were their legacy to evolving humanity. They had sown the seeds of progress, had laid the foundations for modern survival. After all, the first tribe to use a plow had taken the initial step in creating the technology that put a human being on the moon....

Sydne was going to enjoy her new colleague's stimulating company, she knew. Already she felt much more relaxed, much less defensive as she learned the routine their work would follow.

SYDNE HAD A SPLITTING HEADACHE when she woke up early the next morning. If she had any doubts as to its origin, they were dispelled when she looked at her face in the small mirror on the cabin wall. She had a painful sunburn. It had been the curse of her life never to be able to achieve that beautiful golden tan she so admired in other women. But any length of time she spent in the sun turned her skin to a boiled-lobster red before it peeled off. The previous day she had used liberal amounts of screening lotion before exposing herself to the sun, yet here she was with a sunburn on her very first day. It was a good thing she had changed out of that jump suit, she conceded with chagrin. At least her shirt and jeans had provided some protection against the burning rays. "Damn Brian Stevens," she muttered to herself. "Does he always have to be right?"

The cool shower she took was a blessing, and an application of moisturizer assuaged the sting on her face and arms before she dressed. The cabin was small and cramped, and skinning her shin on the narrow bunk did little to improve Sydne's outlook this morning. How did a man as big as Brian Stevens manage to move about in such little space, she wondered. He was over six feet tall, perhaps two or three inches over. And with those broad powerful shoulders—Sydne caught herself up. What was she doing even thinking such thoughts, she asked herself crossly.

After gulping down a couple of aspirins to soothe her throbbing head, Sydne finished dressing and made her way to the galley. Dr. Marín was already there.

"You look a little under the weather this morning, my dear," he said, sympathetically eyeing her. "And your face! You must use some protection from the sun!"

"I did, but as you can see it wasn't much help," she admitted ruefully. "It never is."

"There must be something we can do," he replied, shaking his head in commiseration. And to Gus, the

Dominican cook, he asked, "Why don't you fix some coconut oil for Miss Matheson?"

"Coconut oil?" Sydne repeated.

"With a few drops of iodine," the Professor explained, "it will not only protect you from the sun, but will also give you a beautiful golden tan. Guaranteed," he said, grinning.

That was too good to be true, Sydne thought skeptically. Her attempt to smile came out as a wince.

"Headache, too?" Dr. Marín inquired solicitously.

"I already took some aspirin," Sydne said with a weary sigh, pressing her fingers to her temples. "I'll be all right after I've had some coffee."

"What you need is a hearty breakfast," Dr. Marín said. As if by magic, a hearty breakfast appeared before her. Gus had already expressed his opinion that a few extra pounds would turn the skinny American girl into a stunning woman, and apparently he had made it his responsibility to put some meat on her bones. To her horror and his delight, Sydne had consumed every delicious morsel he had served her the day before. Now, facing the mountain of creamy scrambled eggs, crisp bacon slices and golden hashbrowns on her plate, Sydne gave an inward groan, knowing that her appetite was big enough to polish them off.

"No, Gus, please!" she protested. "Just coffee and toast."

"You'd better eat it, my dear," Dr. Marín interposed. "It will make you feel better. And besides, sea air does wonders for the appetite. With only a skimpy breakfast you'll be ravenous in less than an hour."

Everyone seemed determined to feed her, Sydne mused wryly. And she *was* hungry. . . .

KEEPING HER DISTANCE from the men was easier said than done. Apparently Brian had neglected to lecture his men as he had her, for it was *her* work that was interrupted that morning. First Kenny lingered for a while after turning in a pistol decorated with brass plates. Then Ricco, who had recovered a wine decanter, seemed reluctant to leave.

"The grandees knew how to live well, no?" he said, admiring his find.

"Oh, yes," Sydne replied, pointedly continuing with her work. "Life in the New World was not as primitive as most people think. Although by royal decree Spanish vessels could only transport articles of Spanish origin, there was a great deal of smuggling going on, and luxury items were much in demand. This decanter, for instance, may very well have come from Germany or Bohemia."

"How did a *bellisima donna* like you get involved in archaeology?" Ricco inquired with a provocative smile. "I thought all historians were like the Professor over there."

It was a subject Sydne didn't care to discuss. "And what is the father of five *bambini* doing so far from his brood?" she inquired in return. "By the way, where is your family, Ricco?"

"In Sorrento, where we live," he replied, and something in his voice betrayed his longing.

"You miss them terribly, don't you?"

"Yes, I do," he admitted with a sheepish smile. "*Mia moglie,* Constanza, and all the girls."

"Are all five of them girls?"

"We're still trying for the boy," he said with a philosophical shrug. "Maybe next time."

"Will you go home to see them on your next leave?"

"The air fare is too expensive—" he shook his head "—and I have to save my money. Perhaps after this job is over I'll have enough to open my own diving school and stay with my family. Diving jobs take you away from home too often. It's not good for a man to be alone."

"Will you have enough after this job?"

"If we get half as much as we expect, I'll be... *come si dice*... sitting pretty. Brian has promised us a good cut of the profits, and according to the cargo manifesto the *Conde* was carrying close to ten million at today's rates."

"Ten million?" Sydne repeated. And that wasn't taking the contraband into consideration.

"More or less," Ricco said, nodding emphatically. "Even after the Dominican government takes its share we stand to make a fortune. It's a big project. Brian took a chance going after the *Conde*," he added, "but he knows his business. He's *intelligente*— you know... sharp."

If it is *the Conde,* Sydne thought to herself. Aloud she said, "You like him, don't you?"

"He's fair in business—" Ricco shrugged his shoulders "—and a man you can count on when you're down there," he added, pointing toward the sea.

"Is he also a diver?"

"But of course!"

"Oh!" Sydne gasped. The metal spatula she had been using to scrape a clay jar had slipped and cut her finger.

"Let me see," Ricco said, taking her hand to examine the injury. "It's bleeding."

But Sydne quickly pulled away. Her gaze had met with a pair of cold blue eyes as Brian advanced in their direction. "It's nothing," she blurted out. "I'll be all right."

Her sunburn did not account for the heat she felt on her cheeks as she covertly watched Brian talk for a while with Ricco, who was showing off the wine decanter he had found. What did it matter if he had seen the diver holding her hand, Sydne silently fumed. The situation had been perfectly innocent. She knew it and Ricco knew it, but did Brian? To him it might have looked. . . .

Why did she care what Brian thought of her anyway, she argued. And why did she find herself thinking of him in a sexual way, the way she hadn't thought about any man for a long time? Over and over she had told herself that she disliked him, so what was this strange excitement she felt whenever he was near? Was it a natural physical attraction, seeing him, as he was now, standing tall and bronzed in his brief swimming trunks? Seeing the rippling muscles of his back, his broad shoulders, his powerful arms, the cloud of dark hair covering the expanse of his chest and his long strong legs planted firmly apart? There was a jagged scar on his right thigh, she noted, and it looked as if it had been caused by sharp teeth.

To date almost everything that had transpired between them—every word, every gesture—had carried hostility and resentment. Each time he had looked at her his eyes had been cold or charged with irony or anger. Yet Sydne couldn't forget the strange sensations she had felt when he had taken her arm to guide her into that dusty cantina, or when he had grasped her waist to help her onto the motor launch. She was confused by her conflicting emotions.

This was only her second day aboard the *Adventurer*. For the next eighteen they would meet at every turn. There was no way to avoid it—not on this ship. Brian Stevens was as hard as granite, as cold as ice. There was no gentleness in him, no glimmer of friendliness. He had already shed one wife, he was having a secret affair with a woman engaged to another man, and still Sydne had not known a moment's peace since he had walked into her life.

CHAPTER FOUR

SYDNE TRIED TO AVOID BRIAN as much as she could, but even though he did not seek her company it was inevitable that they would run into each other frequently. She was settling into the routine of the ship more easily than she had expected to, and the men were becoming used to her presence, which she tried to make as inconspicuous as possible. The two men who had been on leave at her arrival—Nikko, a Greek, and Randy, a Texan—were back. Claude and Rod were gone; Ricco and Chuck would be next. Already she knew she would miss these last two. She enjoyed talking to Ricco about his faraway family, admiring the pictures of them he proudly showed her. And Chuck was becoming a friend.

"Hi," Chuck said, interrupting her thoughts. "Are we keeping you busy?"

"No complaints so far." Sydne returned his smile, taking from him a coral-encrusted split bar that had served as ammunition for the cannon.

"Dr. Marín was telling Brian what an excellent job you've been doing," he volunteered. "He's very impressed."

"Dr. Marín or Brian?"

"Dr. Marín," he clarified, but quickly added,

"I've known Brian for a long time, Syd, and he knows a good thing when he sees it."

Sydne wondered what he meant by that remark. "How long have you known him, anyway?" she asked casually.

"About ten years. We served together in the navy."

"You must have been very young," she commented, resisting the temptation to ask about Brian. Here was a man who probably knew him better than anyone else aboard.

"Just twenty," Chuck answered with a grin. "Brian's almost two years older. We had good times together."

"Are you married, Chuck?" Sydne asked curiously.

"Nope," he answered wryly.

"Is there anyone special?"

"Er, not really."

"You don't sound too sure!" she teased. Sydne had already learned that he was a quiet man who usually didn't talk about himself. When he blushed, she hastened to add, "I'm sorry, I didn't mean to pry."

"It's all right, Syd," he reassured her. "Friends shouldn't be afraid to ask questions of each other, and we are friends, aren't we?"

"I hope so, Chuck," she said, deeply touched. "I do need a friend."

"Well, you may count on me, madam," he sallied, and in a rare mood of confidence he began talking about himself. "There isn't really much to tell. After two years of college I realized that more book learning wasn't for me, so I joined the navy. As I said, that's where I met Brian. He was released before me, and right away started his marine-salvage outfit. I went to work for him when I finished my hitch. It's been a good association," he added, "both personally and professionally."

"Do you have any family?"

"One sister. She's married to a doctor in upstate New York. Her kids, aged three and five, are a couple of little devils. Remind me to show you their pictures some time."

The affection with which he spoke of his nieces suggested to Sydne that Chuck would make not only a good dependable husband for some lucky girl, but also a fond father. She wondered if Brian was fond of children, and again was tempted to ask. No, she decided firmly, it wouldn't be fair to pump Chuck for all she wanted to know about the enigmatic Mr. Stevens—things like his background, his family, his marriage. At any rate, she told herself sternly, Brian's life story was none of her business. It was enough that they had been able to keep the peace.

He had kept his distance, yet there were times when Sydne had the uneasy feeling that someone was watching her. She would look up to find those icy blue eyes on her, making her shiver...with apprehension?

The number of relics the divers had recovered was mounting. In addition to the clay jars, the sea had yielded navigator's dividers, tarnished silver spoons, matchlock muskets, as well as an assortment of swords and daggers, cannonballs and cast-iron shot. A pair of ivory handles, one of them inlaid with pre-

cious stones, must have once graced the walking
sticks of a grandee. Sydne suspected they were just
forerunners of the treasures to come.

Material vacuumed from the sea bottom was emptied into metal baskets, which were hoisted aboard.
This mass of mud, sand and blocks of coral had to be
broken up and examined for possible valuables. The
roar of the compressor that operated the airlift was
deafening, so much so that the crew often had to
shout in order to be heard.

"Hey, Sydne, look what I found!" someone
yelled. Kenny was coming toward her at a run. He
had peeled off his helmet, and the water dripping
from his wet suit was leaving a trail on deck. "Can
you believe it? It's a book!"

"A book!" Both Sydne and Dr. Marín put down
their tools.

"Careful how you handle it," warned the Professor, taking the book away from Kenny. "It's a
miracle!" he exclaimed. "It's intact!"

"It was wrapped in this," Kenny said, holding up
layers of what once had been oilcloth.

"How is it possible?" Sydne breathed in awe.

"I wouldn't even attempt to explain how it was
preserved in that corrosive brine for all this time,"
Dr. Marín replied. "It must have fallen off the ship
and been buried immediately after the shipwreck."
Gingerly he opened the book. "It's a diary of some
sort," he said.

"A diary?" a deep voice asked.

Sydne gave a start. It was Brian's voice, and it
came from so near that she felt the warmth of his
breath on the nape of her neck.

"It looks like a woman's diary, written in Spanish, of course," the Professor replied, showing the book to Brian. "A passenger, perhaps. The first entry is dated June 29, but the year is not mentioned."

Taking the book, Brian read the first page, which Sydne could see was written in a small elegant hand. He translated aloud:

"I am seventeen today. Mother gave me this book because she said that now I am a woman grown, I could confide to it all the things I can't bring myself to tell another soul."

He paused and regarded Sydne in a curious way. "It's a young girl's diary." After glancing briefly at the last entries, he added, "Unfortunately there's no mention of the ship." To Sydne's surprise he closed the book gently and held it out to her. "You might like to read it."

Before accepting it, Sydne looked to the Professor for approval. "May I?"

"But of course, my dear. It's only fitting."

"Thank you." Sydne took the book from Brian's hand, and when their fingers brushed the steely flint was back in his eyes. But for an instant, she was sure, it had not been there.

THE EXCITEMENT OVER THE DIARY DIED quickly, but not for Sydne, who kept it in her cabin. That night, propped up in her narrow bunk, she read the same passage Brian had translated. For some reason, even in private she felt like an intruder, just as she had that afternoon listening to his words. Perhaps he had felt

the same way and had been reluctant to continue—or
was he simply not interested in the naive confessions
of a young woman? Was she being unfair? Was there
more depth of feeling to the man than she was prepared to admit? She shook her head impatiently.
Why did everything she thought about these days
seem to revolve around Brian Stevens?

Overcoming her scruples, Sydne returned to the
diary.

The things I feel inside me cannot be put into
words. Perhaps they can be, but I don't know
how. So I will not write in this journal every day,
because there isn't really that much to tell. My life
goes on, one day very much like another. I go to
the chapel and I pray. I think I will save these
pages for only the important things.

Sydne closed her eyes and mulled over the words she
had just translated. More than three hundred years
ago a girl of seventeen had not known how to put her
feelings into words. Some things hadn't changed that
much; she herself often had the same problem.

Who was this mysterious girl whose dilemma mir-
rored her own, she wondered. Already, across the
distance of centuries, their lives had touched. Perhaps that young author, who had obviously gone
down on the very ship Sydne herself was helping to
salvage, would not mind sharing her innermost
secrets with her. Somehow she felt that to be true.

The next entry was dated September 10. It was
brief, yet very moving: "Father told me today that I
am soon to marry. The news frightens me."

Sydne read on.

November 11

I've always known the day would come when I would leave my home, my family and all the things that are dear to me to take my place with the man who will be my husband and my lord. Yet now that the day is near, I find myself wishing with all my heart that time would stand still.

Father is very pleased, for the match will unite two noble lineages and establish an important alliance between our houses. But there is winter in my heart, and I only pray that I will be able to love the man he has chosen for me. His name is Felipe. A beautiful name, but it's all I know of him.

December 10

Today I received presents from Felipe that, as expected, were magnificent. But the jewels and cloth of gold could not chase the coldness that I feel in my soul. Perhaps I was expecting more—a kind word, a simple note in his own hand to let me hope. . . .

December 31

Christ's birthday was sad for me this year, knowing that this is the last one I shall spend in the bosom of my family. Tomorrow, with the New Year, I shall leave this house where I was born, where all my memories were made.

The only thing that gladdens me is that my beloved Doña Ana will stay with me after the marriage. It was her ample bosom that cushioned all my tears as a small child, her gentle hands that soothed all my hurts. But what can she do now to protect me against what is to come? I pray my lord is kind.

The entries that followed were comments on the journey, and Sydne read them with interest. The girl wrote exclusively of the experiences on the road, as if afraid to record her inner feelings. Putting herself in the place of the bride to be, Sydne had a good idea what these feelings must have been, and fear was high on the list. How terrifying it would be for any young woman to find herself bound for life to a man about whom she knew nothing at all. But arranged marriages were a custom as old as time itself. Matches had often been made for the glory of a house, for the gain of property, for an alliance that would establish peace—all sorts of reasons without one thought given to the women themselves. It was their duty to obey, and there was no escape except the cloister.

Finally Sydne found what she had been looking for. It was written in a tremulous hand.

January 7
It's almost dawn, and in a few hours I shall meet my lord. There is no turning back.

Later on the same day she had added:

The party that rode out of the castle today to meet our train was led by a man all dressed in black. His eyes, his hair, his short-trimmed beard were also black, and astride his mighty black stallion he resembled a black angel, beautiful and frightening at the same time. I had been told Felipe was young and handsome, and this man certainly was that. But there's no warmth in his eyes when he looks upon me, no kindness in his voice when he speaks to me. I know I am not beautiful, but do I displease him so much that he holds me in contempt? The wedding is tomorrow, and I've never been so afraid.

January 8

The noises of revelry died down in the hall a long time ago, and the fire that burned so brightly in the hearth when I came into this chamber is now only embers. I am alone, shivering in the cold, but it is much more than this that makes me tremble. I have tried to prepare myself to obey the demands my lord would make upon me this night, as mother and Doña Ana had warned. They were evasive, and I was not sure of their meaning. But when Felipe came in a while ago he looked upon me with those eyes of winter, which seemed to have the power to strip me of my robes.

"So it is a child I must take to wife," he said, but I think mostly to himself.

"I am not a child, my lord, but a woman," I replied.

His smile was mocking when he came to me and put his hands on my shoulders. He is very tall, and I had to tilt my head back to look upon his countenance. I do not know what I was expecting—perhaps a gentle kiss upon my lips— but what happened then took me by surprise. At first his lips were warm on mine, and it was very pleasant. Then his tongue darted inside my mouth, and as I struggled in his embrace I tried to push it away with my own.

Suddenly what I thought to be repulsive changed. But it was too late, for my husband's lips had left mine and his hands no longer held my shoulders. I know my cheeks must have been flushed, for I could feel them burning when Felipe regarded me with scorn.

"I am not a man to take an unwilling woman to his bed," he told me, "let alone a reluctant child. Good night, madam. I shall disturb you no further."

Before I could speak, he was gone. And yet I wished that he had stayed.

A tear fell on the old parchment, very close to another age-old stain. It was stiflingly hot in the cabin, and Sydne felt she had to get out. She threw a robe over her pajamas and went up on deck.

Leaning against the railing, she noticed the underwater lights and remembered that the men had been talking about an evening dive. Was Brian there in the dark depths, trying to break through the shell of coral? The roar of the compressor kept on, and she could see the tiny dark figures of the divers deep down in the sea. One of them was surfacing.

Suddenly Sydne caught her breath, and her mouth went dry. Even in wet suit and diving helmet she could recognize Brian as he climbed up the side of the ship.

"What are you doing here?" he demanded. The

tone of his voice was cold and hostile; why would Sydne expect anything different?

"I couldn't sleep," she replied, nervously licking her lips. "It was too hot in the cabin."

"You shouldn't be here alone."

He turned and began to walk away, but her voice stopped him. "Brian?"

When he faced her again, Sydne swallowed before she asked, "Why did you stop reading the diary today—the one Kenny found?"

The tall man seemed to hesitate. "I'm not interested in the confessions of a young girl," he said at last. "Now get back to your cabin."

Sydne didn't know what she had hoped to hear. She only knew disappointment as she stood there, bathed in moonlight, the soft breeze fluttering her hair and the folds of her flimsy robe.

A few moments elapsed before Brian turned and walked away.

EVEN WITH ALL THE OCEAN around her Sydne had yet to take a dip. Her new bathing suit lay forgotten at the bottom of her suitcase. This was not at all what she had envisioned when she had been told that a Caribbean trip was in the offing, and she often looked with longing at the men, who frequently discarded their wet suits and plunged overboard to cool off.

"You look a little limp today, Syd," Kenny pointed out one day. "The water is great. Why don't you put your tools away and come for a swim with us?"

"Well, I. . . ."

"You can swim, can't you?"

"Believe it or not," she said with a grin, "I was on the swim team during my sophomore year in high school."

"Hey, that's great! How come you've never gone swimming with us?" Without waiting for an answer Kenny added, "Ah, never mind, you qualify. Get your bathing suit and let's go!"

The invitation was too tempting to resist. "Dr. Marín, would you mind if I leave you for a little while?" she asked.

"Go right ahead," the Professor encouraged. "Enjoy yourself. It's about time."

Sydne gave him a grateful smile and ran to her cabin. In a few minutes she had shed her damp shirt and jeans, applied a liberal dose of the coconut oil Gus had mixed for her and slipped into her swimsuit. It was a flesh-colored, one-piece knit that molded the peaks and valleys of her figure to perfection. The deep plunging V neckline did little to hide her firm full breasts.

"Wow!" Kenny exclaimed when she appeared on deck. "You've been holding out on us, Syd. What a terrific body!"

"Oh, Kenny, stop it!" she laughed, feeling young and carefree for the first time in a long, long time. "Let's go! The last one in the water is a rotten egg!"

She stood poised for a moment before slicing through the air in a graceful arc and plunging into the blue, crystal-clear water. Even without a mask she could see a great distance underwater, and the number of figures that dove after her told her that no divers were left on deck.

The water was warm, and Sydne frolicked in it until she grew tired. It had been a long time since she had done any swimming, and she was almost out of breath by the time she returned to the ship. She was closely followed by Kenny, who had tried to kiss her in the water and apparently hadn't given up hope.

Ricco and Randy were just climbing on deck and Sydne was wrapping a towel around her wet hair when Brian appeared. He had been diving until sunrise, and apparently had gone to sleep after that. But he was awake now, and advancing toward her like the wrath of God.

The divers were left standing openmouthed as Brian took Sydne by the arm and propelled her none too gently below deck and into her cabin.

"What the hell do you think you're doing?" he demanded angrily.

Recovered from her initial shock, Sydne found her tongue. "What does it look like I'm doing?" she snapped back. "Swimming! Is that a crime?"

"In that?" Brian pointed at the wet swimsuit that clung to every curve of her body like a second skin.

"Oh, don't be such a prude! You make it sound as if I were naked, and I'm getting sick and tired of being ordered around!" she cried passionately. "I'm a person, not a robot like you! No wonder your wife left you. I don't blame her!"

There was a stunned silence, during which her words seemed to hang in the air between them. Sydne could have bitten her tongue out. "Th-that was a cheap shot," she stammered. "I'm sorry."

The face of the man before her held an unreadable expression. "So you don't think I'm human, do you?" he asked in a low husky voice that was just above a whisper. "I'm going to show you how very wrong you are."

Trembling like a captive bird, Sydne was caught in a grip of steel and pulled against him. If it hadn't been for the heat of his skin and the wild tattoo of his heart, his bare chest could have been a wall of granite.

"Please don't," she breathed in protest. Ignoring her words, Brian grabbed a handful of her hair and pulled her head back. His mouth, wide and full lipped, descended on hers, forcing her lips apart. His tongue invaded the recesses of her mouth in a savage punishing kiss that sent her senses reeling. She was aware of the taste of his ravaging lips, of his scent, of his desire as his hands pressed her back to mold her body to the length of his.

She arched against him, striving to get closer... closer, as if to fuse their bodies together. Suddenly she was no longer the vanquished; she was the aggressor. Her arms encircled his neck, and her fingers dug and tangled in his hair as she met and challenged the violence of his passion with her own. An overwhelming desire made her blood rush in a pulsating torrent through her veins.

She moaned in protest when, as suddenly as he had captured her, he thrust her away. "Damn you, witch!" he whispered hoarsely. Bitterness was written on his rugged face before the impenetrable mask fell into place and he stalked away.

Without his support Sydne's legs gave way, and she fell to the floor on her knees. The fire that had burned so hotly in her blood only moments earlier had vanished, and she was shivering with cold. Her teeth were chattering and she couldn't stop trembling. She wanted to cry.

How could this man play havoc with her senses? What had happened to the sensible Sydne Matheson she had been all her life? And who was this frightening, almost primitive stranger who had lived secretly within her until Brian had unleashed her with one kiss?

IT WAS a shaken and demure Sydne who emerged from her cabin later. Her unruly hair was tied with a ribbon away from her face, which would have been pale except for the golden tan her skin had acquired.

Her appetite gone, she pushed food around her plate listlessly before she gave up and went back to her work. She was unaware of the glances exchanged among the crewmen as she made her way aft without acknowledging their greetings.

Even the Professor was rather quiet, and Sydne was glad to lose herself in her work of recording the latest addition to the mounting collection. But her heart was not truly in it, for even a brass astrolabe, a forerunner of the modern sextant, failed to arouse her interest.

"Hi, Syd." She had not noticed that Kenny was standing beside her until he spoke. "I'm sorry about earlier," he said contritely. "Was the old man very rough on you?"

"He didn't spank me, Kenny," she said dryly. "I'm a big girl now."

"Geez, I've never seen him so mad! He looked like the devil himself was after him when he left your cabin."

"Good. I hope he caught up with him."

Kenny looked puzzled. "Who?"

"The devil, silly," Sydne attempted to quip. "Run along, Kenny. I'm busy now."

"Okay, okay, I get the message!"

Sydne realized that his feelings had been hurt and reminded herself of how very young he was. "Oh, Kenny, I'm sorry. I'm not mad at you really. It was bound to happen sooner or later." After a pause she went on, "Brian—Mr. Stevens and I have been at odds with each other from the start. We just get on each other's nerves, that's all." She gave him a bright smile. "Don't give it another thought."

"Okay, Syd. Hey, listen, my leave starts tomorrow. Will you meet me in Santo Domingo next week when your turn comes? Maybe we could go dancing or something."

In another week she could leave the ship, get away from Brian—perhaps even get a new perspective on her problem. Could she wait a whole week without going out of her mind? "That sounds like a terrific idea, Kenny," she said at last, "but let me think on it."

"All right." Kenny frowned, and to hide his disappointment added petulantly, "But I'll be leaving early."

"I'll let you know tonight." Sydne smiled as she added, "Now run along and let me get some work done."

Perhaps an evening of dancing and fun with Kenny was the remedy for what ailed her, Sydne mused. Being trapped on this ship for so long was making her lose her bearings. She decided to accept the invitation.

What would she have done if it had been Brian who had asked her for a date, was her next unbidden thought. Would she have accepted, knowing that if he tried to make love to her, she was not sure she could deny him?

She laughed derisively. Deny him, or deny herself? She remembered too clearly her response to Brian's kiss. But it certainly wasn't love flaring between them. In love there was passion, of course, but also tenderness and caring—things Brian knew nothing about. Did he love Julia, or was he simply playing with her? Had he made love to her, arousing her to the same pitch of frightening passion he had awakened in Sydne?

And what *did* Brian feel for her? Anger? Yes! Desire? Yes! Both emotions had been blatantly present in that kiss, which she tried to forget and could not. They had been there in those bright blue eyes before the mask had fallen into place, where it still remained each time he looked at her.

"I can't go on like this!" she said, then realized she had spoken aloud.

"What did you say, my dear?" Dr. Marín said after a moment. "It's very hot today. Why don't you get some rest?"

It had been calm all day with hardly a breeze. In the days of sailing ships they would have been adrift with empty canvas.

"Perhaps you're right," Sydne admitted wearily. "I'll finish this tomorrow."

She made her way to the cabin, where she stripped off her clothes and let her body cool down before she lay on the bunk—the same bunk where Brian had

slept before her. Some of his clothes were still there
in the locker, where his male scent faintly lingered.... She had to take her mind off these
thoughts, Sydne decided, reaching almost desperately for the leather-bound volume placed carefully beside her bed.

Her fascination with the diary was growing. More
and more she could identify with the mysterious
woman who had gone down with the galleon. She
opened the book to the page she had marked and began to read.

January 25
This castle is much larger and colder than the
one where I was born—or perhaps it only seems
that way because it is so lacking in company.
Oh, there are many servants, but at home I had
mother and my three sisters to fill it with laughter and warmth. There's none of that here, for
Felipe continues to keep his distance, and at
night I shiver alone in my great bed.

Still I cannot forget or understand the feelings
my lord's kiss stirred within me. They come
back to me sometimes when I see him, so tall
and beautiful, like the black angel of our first
meeting. Although my duties keep me busy, I
still have time to ponder the effect he has upon
me.

Sydne paused in her reading, her heart constricted
with pity for the young girl who had been so frightened and alone. What kind of man had this Felipe
been that he could be so cruel to his bride? Why

couldn't men understand the tender feelings of a woman? With a sigh she returned to the diary.

February 25
My lord still calls me "child." I don't like it at all, but when I told him so this morning he said that Cristina is too grand a name for such a small girl like me.

So Sydne finally knew her name!

To please me, he will call me Tina, which he says is more appropriate. Perhaps I should not like it, but I do. It's his special name for me, and I hope it brings us closer together. I'm so lonely!

For many pages Tina wrote of her new life as a chatelaine, inserting notes here and there about her relationship with her husband. Felipe was not a cruel man, as Sydne had suspected after reading the narration of their first encounter. From Doña Cristina's notes she began to draw a mental image of him: a handsome, arrogant, virile young man who tolerated his child bride with amusement and even found occasion to be kind. Sydne read about Cristina's gratitude for any crumbs of affection from Felipe. One incident, which had taken place almost two months after their marriage, was particularly heart wrenching.

March 5
I am deliriously happy, because today my lord has shown me kindness. He had seen that I was

not content, and as a gift to lift my spirits, bought me a beautiful exotic bird that comes from the New World and has feathers as bright as jewels—green, red and blue. I laughed when it hung upside down from its perch, and Felipe was pleased that I enjoyed his gift. I hope my lord is becoming fond of me.

Reading each entry, Sydne learned how, little by little, the two strangers who had been united for reasons other than love began to know each other. That Doña Cristina was falling in love with her handsome husband became apparent when she wrote:

April 3
To think that only a few months ago I was afraid to face my lord, and now it's only he who brings light into my world. One look, one word from him is all I need to make a day seem brighter. It's only now that I understand what mother meant when she said that there would be feelings I could never tell another soul. I tried to tell Father Tomas, and he gave me penance for being wicked.

And perhaps I am. Each time I see Felipe, or even when he's in my thoughts, I long to touch him, to cover his face with kisses, to be held in his arms against his heart. But there is more, much more—things I have never felt except on our wedding night when my lord kissed me. But those feelings are much stronger now. At times I smile when he speaks, as if I knew what he was saying, yet I haven't heard a word because all my efforts have gone to control the urge to throw myself at his feet and beg him to love me. But this I know is wrong, and so I must control myself.

Doña Cristina may have been young and naive, Sydne mused, but there was nothing wrong with her womanly instincts. As if in confirmation, one of the very next entries told of the consummation of their love.

I am drowsy with joy, for it is joy I feel from deep within me to the very surface of my skin. I may still be small and frail, but my lord thinks me a child no longer. How can I express what a night of bliss this has been? My mother's warnings were for naught, for there was nothing unpleasant to endure. To touch my lord at last, to be touched by him—could anything be more wonderful? The gift of love is in our hearts!

In the space of a few months the timid young girl had grown into a woman and conquered the man who had believed her a child. "The gift of love is in our hearts," Sydne repeated aloud, unable to repress a wry smile. Doña Cristina's dreams of love had finally come true.

And what of her own, Sydne wondered. Would she ever find love? Her thoughts moved unbidden to Brian Stevens once again. But she could not possibly fall in love with him! He seemed to possess none of the warm qualities she had always admired in a man. What she felt for him was obviously nothing more than a very strong physical attraction.

Six bells alerted her that it was time for dinner, and she slipped off the bunk, tenderly replacing Doña Cristina's journal on its shelf.

"YOU SEEM very pensive this morning, Syd. Are you all right?"

Sydne gave a start. "Yes, of course I am," she exclaimed. Then, realizing how defensive she sounded, she smiled at Chuck, who was regarding her quizzically. "What are you doing here anyway?" she said more amicably. "I thought you were going on leave."

"Change of plans." He shrugged noncommittally. "I'll go after Brian gets back."

Sydne tensed at the mention of his name. "When will that be?"

"Three, four days at the most. He's never gone much longer than that."

He doesn't have to go far to get what he wants, she thought crossly. Aloud she asked, "Why so soon? I thought leaves were ten days long."

"For the crew," Chuck elaborated. "Brian and I make other arrangements. One of us has to be here at all times."

"Why? Doesn't he trust the men?"

"It's not that," Chuck replied, shaking his head. "Diving is not without risks, Sydne, and even though we use the safest methods and equipment possible, one of us should be here in case of emergency."

Sydne frowned. "I suppose you're right," she conceded.

"You'll be taking your own leave soon," Chuck commented, changing the subject. "Got any plans?"

"I'll probably spend most of the time in Samaná with Andrew McCallum," she replied noncommittally. "And I have a date with Kenny in Santo Domingo. We plan to go dancing, see the sights, I suppose. I never had the chance when we arrived because Brian was in a hurry to get back."

"Ah, yes, that's when he collected the decompressor."

Sydne was surprised. "I didn't think a decompressor was necessary when working at forty feet."

"It's just a precaution," Chuck answered. "At thirty-three feet we're already working under heavier pressure," he went on to explain. "Our divers are experienced, but there's always the possibility of air embolism."

"How dangerous is it down there, Chuck?" she asked, an edge of apprehension in her voice. "Tell me frankly."

"Not very. We keep a close watch on the men to make sure that they don't stay underwater longer than is safe. They have spare tanks in case of equipment failure, but right now the major risk is from the excavation itself. A diver can dig himself into a cave and become trapped. Aside from that," he went on, "there are the regular mishaps of working reefs. Some coral is as sharp as a razor and can slice your hands without your even noticing. Then, too, we have our share of earaches, sore backs from lifting rocks that are too heavy and the like, but Moose can take care of them."

Moose, Sydne knew, was the closest thing to a doctor they had aboard. He was an ex-marine medic whose lanky frame and large head had earned him the nickname.

"After Brian gets back," Chuck continued, "we're going to set some TNT charges."

"Isn't that dangerous?"

"Not really, but it was something he had been trying to avoid."

"Why?"

"Because he didn't want to disturb the ecology of the reef," Chuck replied. "But the explosions will be controlled, to prevent unnecessary destruction."

"Why is he doing it now?" Sydne asked curiously.

"To gain time. So far we've been lucky that the weather has held, but we're running into the hurricane season. I, for one, don't relish the thought of being caught by one of those monstrous storms in the middle of this reef. We might end up keeping company with the galleon down there."

"Could we get away quickly in case of a hurricane?" Her tone was apprehensive.

"Sure. The first thing we did out here was to mark a channel through the reef—" the one she had noticed on arrival, Sydne realized "—and we keep a close watch on the weather reports."

She thought for a moment before asking, "How long do you think it will take to dig through the coral, Chuck? Brian mentioned you'd probably have to go through ten or fifteen feet of the stuff before reaching the shipwreck."

"That's a good estimate. A sunken ship is an ideal place for coral to grow, Syd. You see, it needs oxygen and something to attach itself to. The crevices, angles and planes of a shipwreck make it an ideal perch," he explained. "As for how long it will take, who knows? Probably a few more weeks, if we're lucky and the weather holds. The TNT charges should save us some time."

"Who's going to set them?"

"Brian, of course." At her frown, he added, "Don't you worry about him, Syd. He knows what he's doing."

Sydne was taken aback. Was her reaction so obvious? "And why would I worry about him?" she protested indignantly. "We're not exactly bosom buddies, or haven't you noticed? We can't even exchange two words without getting into an argument."

Chuck's smile was whimsical when he remarked, "He hasn't been in the best of moods lately, I admit."

"Is he ever?" she asked rather tartly.

"Oh, you'd be surprised." He grinned. "Perhaps a couple of days ashore will improve his disposition."

"I'll bet they will," Sydne scoffed. She didn't bother to make any remark about the female companionship he was obviously enjoying.

"He has a lot riding on this operation, Sydne." Chuck's voice was serious now.

She looked away for a moment before asking, "What will happen if the galleon down there is not the *Conde*?"

"As the chief investor, he'll take a bath."

Hesitantly she asked, "What made him take such a risk, Chuck?"

He started to reply, but a cry from one of the crewmen interrupted him. "Hey, Chuck, we've got company!"

Sydne saw him tense and then relax at the sight of the familiar Dominican coast guard cutter. A light aboard the cutter flashed several times, and she realized it must be a signal. "What are they saying?" she inquired.

"Just checking that we're all right," Chuck replied. To the crewmen he said, "Flash back three times that all is well."

"Aye, aye, sir," the man acknowledged.

"Why three times?" Sydne asked.

"By previous arrangement, if our message is not repeated three times it's a sign of trouble. That's why we don't use the radio."

"What kind of trouble?" she persisted, apprehension creeping into her voice.

"The possibility of pirates aboard," Chuck answered reluctantly.

"In this day and age?" Sydne exclaimed, aghast. "You've got to be kidding!"

"I wish I were," Chuck replied soberly. "But it's happened before and it could happen again."

"When?"

"When we found the first galleon, off the Florida Keys. The situation was pretty hairy, believe me. We were unarmed except for one rifle."

Sydne had turned deathly pale, and when Chuck noticed the fact he was immediately contrite. "I'm sorry, I didn't mean to frighten you," he said, taking her cold hand in his.

"Was. . .anyone hurt?"

"Nothing serious," he said dismissingly.

Sydne had to bite her lip to hold back the question

that was struggling to come out. "Were you hurt?" she said at last.

"No, I wasn't," Chuck replied, finally. "One of the crew was, but it was just a scratch. We were lucky." He paused before adding, "So far, out here we have recovered artifacts that, although of historical value in themselves, would not attract pirates, Sydne. But once we break into the galleon, and if there is a treasure to be found, we'll have to tighten security drastically."

"But how would anyone know there is a treasure?"

"People talk." He shrugged. "Word gets around. But don't you start worrying about it, Syd. It may never come to pass."

"Oh, I hope not," she said fervently.

LIFE ABOARD THE *Adventurer* BEGAN at sunrise when, after an early breakfast, the first team of divers began to prepare their gear for their descent. Usually their conversation and the clatter of their equipment woke Sydne up. Never an early riser, she would turn over on her narrow bunk and go back to sleep for another hour or so.

She had not seen Brian after their last clash, and it was with conflicting emotions that she thought of their next meeting. With luck she would already be gone when he returned. She didn't know how she could face him again after what had happened between them, yet too often she found herself scanning the horizon for his arrival.

The next two days were overcast with slightly

choppy seas. Since the whole crew was on the alert for hurricane warnings, Sydne tried to blame the weather for her depression. But she knew that really had nothing to do with her mood. She had been convinced that not seeing Brian Stevens for a few days would help her regain her balance, but he was never far from her thoughts.

Even the journal added to her troubles. Doña Cristina's passion for her husband only served to make Sydne more painfully aware of her own torturous feelings for Brian. Finally she put the book aside, unable to read more about their obvious happiness. *Don't think about him,* she told herself over and over, fighting the primitive stranger within her who wanted to give herself completely to the man who had brought her to life. His voice, his scent, his touch, his kiss were embedded in her nervous system, working on her sensitivities until she wanted to cry out. The fact frightened her, for there was no doubt in her mind about what Brian would do if he knew of her inner struggle. He was ruthless and he would not hesitate to use her. To save herself, she could never let him see how very vulnerable she had become.

CHAPTER FIVE

FINALLY THERE WERE only four more days before her leave. Sydne had spent almost three weeks aboard the *Adventurer*. Her work was progressing, and her inner turmoil was, as well.

Many of the artifacts recovered had been packed in crates for transportation to Santo Domingo, where, by arrangement with the authorities, they would be displayed for a time at the Museum of the Royal Houses before they were divided between the government and the salvagers. The coast guard cutter would take the relics and Sydne directly to the capital. She would miss seeing Andrew right away, but she was planning to visit him on her way back, after she had seen something of the city.

If she did come back, that was. Right now all her instincts were telling her to run as fast as she possibly could. Yet she had given her word to Andrew that she would stay.... No, she could not disappoint him. She'd probably be all right again after a few days away. At least the weather had improved, with clear blue skies and gentle breezes that provided relief from the unrelenting heat.

Crating the findings had kept Sydne and Dr. Marín busy, and it was with relief that she finally turned in for the night. Yet she was strangely restless, and sleep

proved elusive. Brian had been gone for three days.
Sydne couldn't chase from her mind the thought that
perhaps at that very moment he was making love to
Julia under the light of the same moon she could see
shining through her porthole.

But in four days she herself would be leaving the
ship. She would go dancing with Kenny, would see
the sights, and for ten marvelous days would forget
that Brian Stevens even existed. . . .

After tossing and turning for hours, Sydne gave up
trying to get to sleep and switched on the light. She
picked up the diary, hoping that reading would relax
her.

The king has summoned my lord to Madrid,
where he is to be appointed to a post in the New
World. It is with mixed feelings that I look upon
such an honor, for Felipe does not wish to ex-
pose me to the perilous journey. But to the ends
of the earth I shall follow my love. I'm not
afraid of the fury of man or of nature—perhaps
I am just a little—but the thought of life without
Felipe terrifies me. In this my heart is set. I shall
not be left behind.

Apparently Doña Cristina got her wish, for soon
thereafter she was recording her impressions of the
sea voyage. Her entries about it were few and far between, however. Sydne had already discovered that
Cristina had not been a woman to bother writing
about petty complaints. She only recorded her great
joys and sorrows, and Sydne suspected that, with little to do during the long trip, the lovers had found

ways to while away the time. She found proof that her suspicions had been well-founded in a later notation.

I have unveiled the secrets of bliss, of the joy that commands my burning soul. I'm no longer child or woman scorned. Our passion grows, my lord, my own, forever and ever more.

Doña Cristina did not fail to record her impressions of her arrival in the New World, and as an historian of kind, Sydne found the information interesting. But for many months the entries had reflected the woman's preoccupation with the fact that she was still childless. The pages were filled, as well, with her inner struggle between her staunch religious beliefs and the consuming passion she felt for her husband.

My lord, my love, how I yearn to bring you the most precious gift of our love! But yet I fear that I am barren. So many nights of love have failed to bring forth the blessed fruit.

Perhaps it is God's justice. The union of our bodies is meant only for His glory in procreation, and I am so terribly wicked that when my lord touches my flesh, the pleasure I feel is so intense that it sets my blood on fire. I have done penance and prayed for forgiveness, but how can He grant it when I feel no repentance for my sin?

To add to her dilemma, just months after arriving in the New World the woman discovered that her beloved Felipe had developed a roving eye. She faithfully recorded her misery.

Had I not seen it with my own eyes, I would
have denied it to my dying breath. But there they
were, in tight embrace, my lord and the Indian
maiden with the face of a madonna. How could
he have betrayed my love, after I have imperiled
my immortal soul to satisfy his every whim? Is
my body so unsatisfying that he seeks the em-
braces of another?

Oh, my lord, had thou thrust thy sword into
my breast, the pain could not have been greater!

The final blow came when she learned that the Indian woman had conceived her husband's child.
Doña Cristina must have been prostrated with grief,
for her notes during this time were rambling and in-
coherent. The next dated entry was months later,
confirming Sydne's suspicions.

It's been a long time since I have written on these
pages. I have been very ill, both in body and in
soul. I never knew that I could hate Felipe, but
hate him I did for betraying my love.

And yet he's been so kind and loving, showing
his repentance in a hundred ways. He's begged
my forgiveness, and how can I deny it when my
life without him would have no meaning?

Still, there is that child, whose very existence
is a dagger twisting in my heart, reminding me
that another woman has given him what I could
not. But there's no hate within me now, only
deep sorrow—for myself, for Felipe, for the
child, because the gift of love that we had was

frail and has been shattered. Can we ever put the pieces back together again?

For many weeks Doña Cristina's entries were random and dispirited, but finally one day her tone changed.

At last the Lord has heard my prayers! I am with child, and life is good again. I have not yet told Felipe. Only Doña Ana knows, and I have sworn her to secrecy. Why haven't I told Felipe that his seed has taken root within my womb? It is not revenge, I tell myself, but because I wish to savor this knowledge alone for just a little while longer.

But I wonder. He loves me, I know, and I love him still. Yet even though I have forgiven, I cannot forget. Perhaps the child will help me. I pray to God that He will, as well.

Doña Cristina had recorded her own inner feelings while she carried the child in secret, and then her husband's joy when she gave him the news. Finally everything seemed to be going their way. Then Felipe was summoned back to Spain by the king. Doña Cristina argued that she should go with him, but Felipe would not hear of endangering her or the child. At last she had relented.

Felipe had already gone when the child arrived... stillborn. Doña Cristina's entries were charged with bitterness and remorse, blaming herself for being incapable of producing a live child. It was in this frame of mind that she received the news that her husband

was in the hands of the Spanish Inquisition. Her
reaction was recorded in heart-wrenching words.

How can the Lord God allow such horrors? To
accuse Felipe of heresy, when it is I who should
suffer the fires of Hell! I, who profess to be
pious in my hypocrisy. Because even though I
said I had forgiven my husband, I truly had not.
It is I, Lord God, who should be put on the rack
of torment to expiate my sins.

But even as I write those words, my heart
rebels. I can no longer believe in a God who
allows such cruel injustice, nor can I pray. I have
booked passage to Spain on the ship that leaves
tomorrow, and am carrying with me all the gold
and jewels I have been able to collect to buy my
lord's freedom. May God forgive me, because I
love Felipe much more than I love Him.

The remaining pages were blank, and Sydne
guessed that the end of the story lay at the bottom of
the sea.

She was crying when the door of her cabin opened
suddenly. "Are you all right?"

Startled, Sydne opened her tear-filled eyes in surprise. It was Brian. He was back!

"I'm sorry if I startled you," he went on. "I
knocked, but I guess you didn't hear."

Averting her face, Sydne wiped her hand across
her eyes, but it was too late. He came in, uninvited.

"What's wrong?" he asked, frowning.

"Nothing—nothing at all."

"Then why are you crying?" Before she could tell

him to mind his own business, Brian noticed the diary lying open on her lap. "Oh, I see," was all he said.

Sydne sniffed, lifting her chin in defiance. "I suppose you think me a fool."

"For crying over the diary of a woman dead for more than three hundred years?" he asked wryly, sitting on the bunk beside her. Gently his hand cupped the nape of her neck and his thumb rubbed her chin. "I bet you cry at the movies, too."

She thought he was laughing at her, yet when she looked into his eyes, the intimate caress she saw in their blue depths made her feel all warm, all quivery inside. A dry sob invited his smile before his lips brushed hers with unexpected tenderness, and it never occurred to Sydne to object when he gathered her into his arms. Heaving a weary sigh, she rested her head on his broad chest, feeling his hand stroking her hair.

"It's so sad," she murmured, giving one last sniffle. And soothed by the comforting warmth of his body, which she could feel through the thin silky fabric of his shirt, she went on to tell Brian the story of Doña Cristina and her Felipe.

"That was a long time ago," he whispered into her hair when she finished.

Held so close to his heart, Sydne felt incapable of moving. "Do you think she could have saved him?"

"I doubt it. He may have been already dead by the time she heard he was in the hands of the Inquisition," he said gently. "News took a long time to reach the New World in those days."

Sydne hesitated before saying, "She loved him terribly, you know, even though she had been forced to marry him. She said their love was a gift.''

"Love always is," Brian said huskily. Then he drew back, and holding her at arm's length, he regarded her quizzically. "You should get some sleep," he said at last. "It's late."

STILL BASKING IN THE GLOW of Brian's tenderness, Sydne slept peacefully for the first time in a week. But she didn't know how to react when she ran into him in the passageway the next morning on her way to the galley. Without a word, but with a searching look, he stood aside to let her pass. She did so as quickly as possible, trembling inside.

After a quick breakfast with Dr. Marín, Sydne resumed her duties. Her attention was often diverted from her work, however, and she stole frequent glances at her watch. The teams worked for ninety minutes, she knew. Each diver went down two or three times a day, with two hours between shifts to allow their bodies to eliminate the nitrogen that accumulates in the bloodstream when working at a depth of forty feet. The first team would be coming up soon, and Sydne was sure Brian would dive with the second team.

She spotted him immediately when he appeared on deck. He would stand out in a crowd, she thought, let alone a small group of men. He must have felt her gaze, because he looked up suddenly and met her eyes. She turned quickly away, feeling her cheeks flush with color. When she dared to look again he was gone.

Dipping silver coins in acid solution to remove

coral incrustations and tagging and recording new artifacts didn't take Sydne's mind off the time that was ticking by so slowly. But she pretended to be busy when the divers returned aboard, all the while conscious of the tall figure in the black wet suit— where he was and what he was doing.

The day went by at an agonizingly slow pace, and although she found Brian looking in her direction several times he never came near her. A siesta after lunch helped her bear the worst heat of the day. Stripped down to her panties and bra, Sydne tossed and turned on the bed in a kind of stupor that allowed no rest. Finally she got up and dressed, and was about to leave the cabin when the ship lurched suddenly in spite of its mooring.

Sydne rushed to the deck, where the crew and divers had assembled. Immediately she noticed that Brian was not among them.

"What happened?" she inquired anxiously.

"Dunno," Randy replied, "but it was weird."

"Where is Brian?"

"Down there—" Kenny pointed toward the sea "—working the airlift."

Sydne felt the blood drain from her face. "Alone?" Her voice was almost inaudible.

"Yep," Kenny answered. "He should be coming up any minute now."

But when minutes ticked by and Brian did not appear, Sydne started going quietly out of her mind. Visions of Brian trapped under a pile of coral and waiting for help persisted.

"Shouldn't someone go down to make sure he's all

right?" she finally said tremulously. "He may be trapped down there."

"Hey," Nikko called from the bridge, "the radio just announced that the Dominican Republic has had an earthquake."

Sydne held on to the nearest object to keep herself from falling. The image of Brian suffocating underwater was sharper than ever in her mind. As if in a dream she heard someone say, "He's coming up." She stood aside while the men gathered around Brian when he was safely aboard.

"We were about to send someone after you," Randy told him.

But Brian was looking at Sydne, and her eyes refused to look away from his. She was still frozen with fear, and realized she had probably turned deathly pale. She couldn't speak. She stood there, staring at him with eyes that could not get enough of seeing him alive and unharmed.

"I felt the vibration, but I wasn't sure what was going on," Brian said when Randy finished telling him about the earthquake. "I should have known something was wrong when all the fish disappeared so suddenly." While his attention was occupied, Sydne slipped away to the shelter of her cabin.

THE EARTHQUAKE FORCED SYDNE TO ALTER her plans, because Dr. Marín had left on the coast guard cutter for Santo Domingo to make sure his family was unharmed. His absence made her own presence on the *Adventurer* imperative. She accepted the situation with trepidation and avoided Brian, terrified that she had given her feelings away.

But on the ship the size of the *Adventurer* it was not easy to hide, especially when Brian seemed determined to find her. When someone knocked on her door that evening, Sydne knew it was him. She opened the door and faced him, trying to appear nonchalant.

"Yes?"

His brows arched quizzically before he said, "It's a warm night. I thought perhaps you'd like to go up on deck for a breath of fresh air."

"Thank you, Mr. Stevens," she answered coolly, ignoring the twinkle in his blue eyes, "but I'm tired. I plan to go to bed early."

"Mr. Stevens?" he repeated, catching her by the waist and drawing her to him. "I thought we were past that stage."

She wedged one arm between them, desperately trying to resist the temptation to remain in his arms and conscious of the wild beating of her heart. "Nothing has changed between us," she objected feebly.

He chuckled, holding her closely. "Don't be a fool," he said into her hair, pressing his lips to her temple. He lifted her chin and bent to kiss her, but Sydne turned her face away.

"No!" she breathed, struggling awkwardly to free herself.

Brian released her. "Don't run away from me, Sydne," he said gently.

"I'm not, but I do want to be alone," she said firmly, summoning all her strength.

"Are you sure?"

"Yes."

Brian gave a sigh. "Okay. Good night, Syd."

"Good night, Mr. Stevens."

He gave her a wry smile before going out. All Sydne's control deserted her as soon as the door closed behind him. She covered her mouth with her hand to stifle the sob that, for some bewildering reason, was struggling to surface. "No!" she told herself sternly, "I won't cry!"

But she did anyway—tears that were hot and bitter because she had really wanted to be held in his arms, to receive his kisses, to glory in his touch. And it was all wrong! There was no love between them, only desire, she told herself over and over. It was a desire so strong it clouded her reasoning. No, she couldn't let him use her just to satisfy his vanity. And she had to get away—especially now that she had betrayed herself during those agonizing moments when he had been in danger.

THE HURRICANE SEASON WAS UPON THEM, and two new divers had arrived from the States to speed up the salvage operation. Ernesto "Ernie" Beltran and Ray Padilla, two young Cubans raised in Miami, had been on Brian's payroll for some time. They were the men Brian had mentioned who were working on an oil rig in the gulf.

Excavation of the shipwreck was going well, and everyone hoped that imminent access to the galleon would help establish its identity. There was anticipation in the air as more and more valuables were brought aboard each day, the most important discovery so far being lengths of gold chain found by Ernie during his first day on the job.

Since that night when he had come to her cabin, Sydne had discouraged any conversation on the two occasions when Brian had approached her. With all the new finds to record and tag, her excuses had appeared valid. But struggling with her ambivalent feelings kept her awake once again that night. The walls of her cabin seemed to be closing in on her. At last, certain that Brian was taking part in the evening dive, she went out on deck.

She didn't notice his quiet approach until he was standing beside her.

"Have you ever been underwater, Syd?" he asked softly. When she shivered and shook her head, he went on, "It's another world, babe, a world of silence. It's like nothing you've experienced before." He paused briefly. "Imagine you're floating in clear blue air. Then you come across a forest of sea fans swaying with the current, as graceful as ballerinas dancing to music no one can hear. Imagine coral formations in colors you've never seen, teeming with such life and beauty that they take your breath away."

Sydne's first inclination had been to run away, but now it was too late. In that brief moment of hesitation she had been reluctantly caught up in the spell cast by Brian's low husky voice. She was dreamily aware of his arms slipping around her, of being drawn against him.

"I'd like to share all that beauty with you, Syd," he murmured as he pressed his lips to her temple. "Will you let me?"

The magic of his voice, his physical nearness were robbing her of the strength or will to resist. A shiver of delight went through her when he turned her to face him, and as if mesmerized, she watched as he bent his head. His lips were warm and soft, yet firm, and they covered hers gently, moving oh, so seductively, so lingeringly, before the tip of his tongue traced the contours of her lips and coaxed them apart. The pitiful remains of Sydne's defenses crumbled completely, and she melted in the strong arms that held her. His tongue was probing and exploring the recesses of her mouth, tasting the sweetness within, stirring sensations never felt before. She had known other kisses, but not like this. No, never like this.

"Oh, babe, this is what I've been wanting since I first saw you," Brian murmured huskily, holding her even tighter against him. Sydne trembled as the warmth of his lips traced the slender column of her neck, lingering at the pulse in her throat. The caress swept her into a whirl of emotions that set her heart thumping wildly, erratically. She moaned as his hand slipped inside her dressing gown to cup her breast and his fingers rubbed her nipple gently, causing it to harden. Honey was flowing through her, and she pressed herself against his length. Their proximity betrayed his desire, his need for her.

Through the fog of sensations that enveloped them came the sound of voices approaching, and Brian released her with a choked groan. Sydne's legs were so shaky when he let go that she had to hold on to the railing for support, had to struggle to regain a measure of composure. Moments later the voices faded away again, and she let go of the breath she had been holding. Reason began to return, and with it the realization of what she had been doing. What if no one had interrupted them? She had given in completely to her own traitorous desires.

"Don't go," Brian whispered, reaching for her hand, as she pulled herself erect.

"Let me go!" she hissed. "Let me go and don't come near me again."

His face was lost in shadow as she gazed up at him, but he released her when she drew away. With as much dignity as she could muster, she made her way back to her cabin, all the time resisting the temptation to break into a run.

A CHORUS OF WHOOPING and hollering made Sydne pause in her work the next afternoon. Unable to contain her curiosity, she went to the forward section to investigate the commotion. The divers had all gathered around Nikko and, obviously excited, were inspecting the contents of a rubber bucket.

"What's going on?" Sydne inquired, and the group parted to let her through.

"Look, Syd—" Nikko grinned proudly "—and tell me if these are what I think they are."

Sydne gave him a quizzical look before her eyes fell to the contents of the bucket. It was almost half-full of metal disks, some of which had been worn smooth by exposure. Others were tarnished or heavily incrusted with sulfide and bits of shell.

"Watch out," Nikko warned her when she reached for one of them. "The edges on some of these babies are as sharp as razors. Look." And to stress his words he showed her a long cut on one of his fingers.

"Thanks for the warning," Sydne replied. "And you'd better see Moose about that cut."

"Sure, as soon as I hear what you have to say about these." Nikko grinned again. "Well, are they really silver coins?"

Sydne picked one up at random and examined it closely. It was heavily tarnished, but she had no doubt in her mind that it certainly was a silver coin. In vain she searched for one that had retained its markings.

"I'm sorry," she said at last. "I can only guess that these are Spanish *reales*, but someone with more knowledge of coins than I have could probably tell you for sure."

Unable to hide his disappointment, Nikko echoed, "*Reales*, eh?"

He was let down, Sydne suspected, mostly because he had never heard of them. She tried another approach. "I'm sure you've heard about the pieces of eight of pirate lore. Each one was a peso worth eight *reales*—hence the name."

Nikko seemed more pleased with that explanation, and when she bent to pick up the bucket he said, "Here, let me, Sydne. That's too heavy for you." She let him carry it aft.

Counting and recording the coins was going to be a long job, especially since Dr. Marín hadn't returned yet from Santo Domingo. Sydne was immersed in the task when Brian appeared. She went on with her work, pretending he wasn't there while he examined the coins.

"You'll need help with these," he said briskly. "I'll send someone over."

"Thank you. I could use another pair of hands," she answered, her tone businesslike.

When Brian went away without saying more, Sydne tried to shake off her disappointment. But she had made it perfectly clear that she didn't want anything to do with him—and he seemed to have got the message!

So what *did* she want from him, Sydne asked herself in frustration. In her confused state of mind she lost count and had to start all over again.

To her relief, Kenny arrived a few minutes later and took over the count. She couldn't seem to concentrate on the simple task. "They certainly don't look like much, do they?" the young man commented, the disappointment in his voice as obvious as Nikko's had been.

"Oh, but they will, once they've been cleaned and classified, Kenny. I'm sure these are very valuable coins," she told him. Mostly to take her mind off Brian, she elaborated on the subject. "You know, in the old days the coin was accepted as international currency. You could even say that it was, in a way, the ancestor of our dollar, since the *real* was patterned after the German *taler*."

"How so?" Kenny inquired, now visibly interested.

"Well, the trading houses of the time marked pieces of eight in their books by a symbol that intertwined the letter *p* and the number *8*," Sydne went on. She began to illustrate her explanation on a piece of paper. "But that took too much time, so they started using a form of shorthand to speed up their bookkeeping. By reducing the *8* to an *s*, and the *p* to a vertical line, they ended up with the dollar sign.''

"Hey, that's great!''

"Now take these particular coins," Sydne continued. "We can't see their markings now, but we can use our imaginations, right?" After he nodded enthusiastically she continued, "The Spaniards had a mint in New Granada—now Colombia—so let's suppose these coins came from there. In that case, they would have New Granada printed on one side, like this—" she illustrated on her piece of paper "—and these would be the Columns of Hercules, representing Gibraltar. The waves at the bottom symbolized the Atlantic. The other side would have the name and coat of arms of the king of Spain, or his likeness.''

"You really know your stuff, don't you, Syd?" Kenny said in admiration. He handled the coins with greater respect as he went back to counting them.

In the ensuing silence Sydne's mind wandered from the task at hand and along lines she had tried to avoid. Again she could hear Brian's voice telling her of the wonders of the sea. He had offered to share that beauty with her, and she had refused him. She felt a pang of regret—only because she was longing to see that world, Sydne assured herself. But all the time she knew she was deluding herself.

"Kenny, would you take me diving sometime?" she asked on impulse.

"Sure," Kenny agreed immediately. "I'll take you any time you want. Just say the word. Have you ever used diving gear?"

"No, I've never tried diving," she had to admit. "But I can swim like a fish, as you know.''

"Well, if we were back in the States you'd have to

be a certified diver," Kenny pointed out. When her face reflected her disappointment, he quickly added, "But I don't think that will be necessary here. At any rate, it's easy to learn the basics. I can teach you if you want me to."

"Will you?"

"Sure." He grinned. "How about tomorrow morning? I'm not going on duty until eleven."

"It's a deal." She smiled back.

Kenny left after finishing the count, and Sydne went about her work, thinking of the promised adventure. It took her mind off Brian.

But it was Brian who was waiting for her the next morning when she appeared in her bathing suit, ready for her lesson.

"Where's Kenny?" she asked with apprehension.

"On duty," Brian replied without batting an eye. "Are you ready for your lesson?"

Sydne hesitated, uncomfortably aware that they had caught the attention of several crew members. "I suppose I am," she reluctantly conceded.

"Then you'd better fetch a beach robe—and a hat."

Taken aback, Sydne asked, "Where are we going?"

"You don't expect to learn the use of diving gear here on deck, do you?" Brian said, crossing his arms over his chest and watching the play of conflicting emotions across her face. When she hesitated, he challenged, "Do you want a lesson or don't you?"

Sydne pursed her lips with annoyance. "Yes, I do," she answered shortly.

"Then go get your things," Brian said, grinning, "and don't take too long. We haven't got all day."

None too pleased by the turn of events, Sydne went back to the cabin, where she collected her beach robe and the hat Brian had given her the day he had brought her aboard the *Adventurer*. When she returned to the deck, he helped her board the motor launch. As she had done previously, she sat facing forward.

Brian began to whistle softly as he steered the craft through the buoy-marked channel. His good humor only served to increase her apprehension.

"Where are we going?" she inquired at last, turning to eye him warily.

"There are only two places that are safe for a first diving lesson," Brian replied pleasantly. "A pool or a beach."

"Which one are we using?" As if she had to ask.

"Remember the beaches I mentioned on our way from Santo Domingo?"

"The ones you said were practically untouched?"

Brian bobbed his head and smiled. "That's where we're going."

No matter how much she wanted to see the area, Sydne didn't relish the idea of being alone with Brian on a deserted beach. "I thought you said we didn't have all day," she reminded him.

"It's not too far," he replied, undaunted by her lack of enthusiasm. "Besides, I'm taking the day off, and so are you. Rank has its privileges." He winked at her.

"How very considerate of you!" she exclaimed.

"I knew you'd appreciate it." He grinned, disregarding her sarcasm. "Better put on your hat."

Sydne turned and faced him defiantly. "You really enjoy ordering me around, don't you?"

"I enjoy everything to do with you, babe," he said with laughter in his voice. "Even that nasty temper of yours."

"Oh!" she fumed, turning away from him. Hearing his chuckle of enjoyment only increased her fury.

About an hour later they had reached the coastline.

"Is it much farther?" she asked impatiently.

"We're almost there."

Soon afterward the launch approached the most beautiful beach Sydne had ever seen. Against a lush background of coconut palms and other tropical vegetation was a strip of white waves. It seemed deserted and quiet, except for the cries of gulls, and the crystalline waters changed color from deep blue to green and turquoise as they neared the shore.

Brian turned off the motor and jumped into the water to push the launch ashore. Then he scooped Sydne up in his arms to carry her to dry land.

"Put me down!" she demanded, feeling foolish and decidedly vulnerable.

He obliged, lowering her feet to the sand. But he held her against his bare chest much too long before finally letting her go, and Sydne felt her face grow hot.

Totally unruffled, he began to unload the diving gear, which he placed neatly on the sand.

"This is the weight belt," he said when he was

ready to start the lesson. Eyeing her figure appre-
ciatively, he added, "I'd say you weigh about one
hundred and fifteen pounds, right?"

His guess was accurate, and after Sydne nodded he
inserted lead weights on the belt, which he then put
aside.

"I hope the flippers fit you," he said next, kneel-
ing before her and letting his hand slide down her
calves before lifting each foot to put on the rubber
fins. Sydne was reluctant to touch him, but had no
choice but to place her hands on his shoulders to
maintain her balance, biting back a protest at the way
he was touching her leg. "How's that?" he inquired.

She wasn't quite sure what he meant. "They fit,"
she admitted crossly.

"This is the buoyancy compensator," Brian went
on. He showed her an inflatable vest that, to Sydne,
looked very much like the Mae Wests whose use was
religiously demonstrated at the beginning of trans-
oceanic flights. "We call it BC for short. It helps you
stay afloat and save air by swimming on the surface
until you reach the point where you wish to dive. See
this?" He held up what looked like a short hose with
a mouthpiece at the end. "You inflate the BC by
blowing on this and deflate it by pushing the valve
here at the end."

Next came the air tank, and he showed her the
regulator, attached to the tank with a black hose.
"Now, hold the mouthpiece between your teeth,
close your lips around it and breathe only through
your mouth, understand?" At her nod, he added,
"Try it."

Sydne did as she was told.

"Good girl." He grinned. "One of the most important things to remember during an ascent from the deep is not to hold your breath. It's a good idea to hum, in fact. Okay, let's put this on."

She slipped her arms through the shoulder straps he held out. Brian had to steady her when he let go of the tank.

"Yes, it's heavy," he chuckled, "but buoyancy will compensate for that in the water."

He adjusted the straps, and Sydne knew she was turning several shades of red as he casually turned her hips this way and that. The quirk of amusement curling the corners of his mouth told her he was enjoying her embarrassment as he secured the straps and finished adjusting the weight belt.

Brian put on his own equipment in a fraction of the time he had taken with her. "Ready?"

Again Sydne nodded, too flustered to speak.

"Shall we?" he said, taking her by the hand.

She was glad of his support as they made their way awkwardly to the water. Ducks might be used to webbed feet, she decided, but she wasn't!

They waded into the water until it reached a little above Sydne's waist. There Brian showed her how to clear her mask, spitting on the glass and washing it off until it squeaked. He laughed at the face she made when she spat, and Sydne gladly could have clobbered him.

"If water gets inside your mask, all you have to do is press down the top, look skyward, and blow through your nose," he instructed. "Let's sit on the bottom and try it. Remember, breathe only through your mouth and try to relax."

Biting into the mouthpiece, Sydne experienced a surge of panic when the water closed over her head. No matter how hard she sucked, not enough air was reaching her lungs. She scrambled to the surface again, gasping for air.

Brian followed her. "What's the matter?"

"I—I couldn't breathe!" she gasped, her chest heaving.

"Let me check the regulator." After he did, he stated, "It works fine."

"But I couldn't breathe!" she argued.

"All right, put the mouthpiece back in your mouth and try again before going under. You're too tense," he said calmly, kneading the back of her neck with his strong fingers. "Just relax and breathe normally."

Sydne readjusted her mask and breathed through the mouthpiece. Brian let her practice for a few minutes before he took her hands and lowered her to the bottom again, where they sat crosslegged facing each other.

Sydne could breathe normally now, and followed his signal to shake out the water that had entered her mask and was getting inside her nose. After this operation was completed Brian stood up.

"Very good," he encouraged. "Now we're going to take off our masks underwater and put them back on again. After that we'll do buddy breathing. That means that you're going to take off your mouthpiece and breathe through mine. Take two good breaths and hold them. Then repeat exactly what I did and let me breathe through yours. Okay?"

They sank down to the bottom again, and after removing and readjusting the masks, Sydne emptied the water accumulated inside, this time without any sense of panic. Then Brian grabbed her shoulder strap with his left hand and with his right offered her his mouthpiece. After she had taken two deep breaths as he had instructed, he put it back in his own mouth. She repeated the operation as he had performed it, and after the practice was completed they swam side by side close to the sandy bottom, holding hands. Sydne paddled along, marveling at the speed the flippers gave her, even without the use of her arms. She was elated when they swam toward a school of tiny silver fish, which darted in all directions at their approach.

The water was so clear that it seemed more like green air. It was a marvelous weightless sensation, almost like flying, to be suspended in this wonderful world, where small patches of grass poked through the white sand and swayed with the current. Then Brian made her go through the same drill once more. Sydne was disappointed when he ended the lesson.

"You did very well," he said, removing her tank on the shore. "I'll make a diver out of you yet."

She flushed at his compliment, her reserve forgotten. "I wish we could go back underwater," she said wistfully.

"We will after lunch," he assured her. "Let's take a break now. Would you like to explore the beach?"

"I'd love to."

Brian finished putting the gear away and then extended his hand to her. She accepted without reluctance, and hand in hand they began to follow the crescent-shaped shoreline.

"It is as you said," she breathed. "Untouched."

The white sand beneath their feet was as fine as powder. It was dotted here and there with fallen coconuts, and with shells in soft pastel hues. She picked up several and examined them with the delight of a child. They walked for a long time before Brian suggested they turn back.

"Hungry?" he asked when they had returned to the launch.

"Ravenous!"

"Good." He grinned at her fondly. "Let's see what Gus packed for us."

He spread a blanket on the sand under the shade of the trees before collecting a picnic basket and a cooler from the launch. There was cold fried chicken, hard-boiled eggs, potato salad and pickles, all of which Brian served on paper plates. He also produced a bottle of chilled white wine that he poured into plastic cups, and between the two of them neither a crumb nor a drop was left.

After clearing away the plates, Brian stretched out on his back, folded his hands behind his head and closed his eyes. Sydne glanced at him with indecision before she stretched out next to him. They lay like that in companionable silence for a while, enjoying the cool breeze playing over their bodies. Then Sydne said, "Brian?"

"Mmm?"

"Thank you."

"For what?"

"For such a marvelous day."

"It's not over yet."

"I know." Sydne turned her head to look at him and found him propped up on an elbow, watching her in a way that made her feel quivery inside. Suddenly she felt awkward and tongue-tied, and not knowing what to do with herself, she started to get up. But Brian held her back by the hand. "Don't go in the sun without protection," he said, handing her a bottle of coconut oil.

She took it and applied the oil to her arms and legs, but when she was finished, he tugged at her hand. "Lie down and let me do your back."

At first Sydne was tense under his touch. The movement of his long fingers felt like a caress. But as his hands stroked her back, a delicious warmth began spreading through her body, and she relaxed. She was almost purring in contentment by the time Brian rubbed the oil on her legs, lingering on the sensitive area behind her knees and stroking her thighs in a way that made her entire body tingle with curious excitement. She didn't object when he turned her onto her back and began to spread the oil on her throat and shoulders, gently pushing aside the straps of her swimsuit.

And she was lost in the sensation of his touch when he bared her breasts. His knowing hands stroked circling caresses on the soft mounds and then rolled the top of her suit down to her hips. All the time he stroked and caressed her, igniting the fires of her flesh until she was aching with longing.

His lips traced the line of her jaw and glided down the column of her neck, lingering at the pulse of her throat before they continued down to her breasts.

There he nibbled and teased the crests with his tongue until her nipples hardened, and he took them in his mouth one by one.

With a moan, Sydne threaded her fingers into his hair, holding his head to her breasts. She didn't want him to stop the agonizing pleasure. Never had she felt so alive. Every inch of her skin was brought to awareness, responding to his caressing hands and lips, carrying her on a crest of desire so intense it made her tremble.

He paused only to seek her lips, which he claimed in a kiss that seemed to devour her. But when he began to ease her bathing suit lower, Sydne returned to reality with a jolt. If she didn't act immediately they wouldn't be able to stop....

"No!" she moaned, rolling away from him. Her cheeks were stained crimson as she readjusted her bathing suit with shaking fingers. "Stay away from me!"

Brian's eyes were startled. "What in blazes gets into you?" he asked, rubbing his bare chest with his palm.

"Enough sense to realize what you're trying to do!" she choked indignantly. "Did you expect me to swoon just because you flexed your muscles? Well, I'm not going to, you hear me? I'm not going to!"

Brian sat back on his heels and laughed.

"What's so funny?" she demanded with indignation.

"It won't work, Sydne." After his laughter had subsided there was still a quirk of amusement at the corners of his mouth.

"I haven't the faintest idea what you're talking

about," she said, edging away as he moved toward her.

"Yes, you do," he said gently, continuing to advance. "You're hiding behind all that anger just to keep me away."

"That's a lie!"

"Is it?" he said, reaching for her hand. "It won't work, Syd. I ought to know. I tried it, remember? One look at you and I knew that if I didn't keep you away, this would happen. I want you, babe, and you want me. All the anger in the world won't change that."

"Is that the same line you feed Julia?" she scoffed, slapping his hand away.

"Julia?" he repeated, his brow creasing into a puzzled frown.

"Yes, or have you conveniently forgotten?" she taunted. "You know, Julia Lozano. Remember her? The girl you met in the garden the night we arrived in Samaná?"

Brian grinned. "Ah, so you know her name."

"Of course I do!"

His eyes shone mischievously. "You sound jealous, Syd."

"Jealous!" she cried indignantly. "You must be out of your mind—and don't sound so smug!"

"I'm not!"

"Well, then, I'm sorry, but you're barking up the wrong tree. If you thought that bringing me to a romantic setting like this would make me fall into your arms, I've got news for you. I'm just not going to!"

Her outburst only seemed to increase his amuse-

ment. "You've obviously formed a very poor opinion of me, babe. I just wanted to show you what a
nice fellow I can be."

"Ha!"

"For a moment there I thought I was making a
pretty good case."

"Ha!"

"You're being very childish, you know."

Sydne opened her mouth to protest and then closed
it again before exploding, "Oh, you're insuffer-
able!"

Brian chuckled. "So what do you expect me to do?
I'm not going to apologize for making love to you,
and I might as well tell you that I'll probably do it
again next chance I get. I said I wanted you. I still
do."

"I'll bet!" Sydne scoffed.

With a wicked grin he answered, "No contest."

"Oh, this is ridiculous!" she flared at him.
"Please take me back to the ship!"

"Now?" He frowned. "I thought you wanted another diving lesson."

"Forget the lesson. Take me back now!"

Brian heaved a weary sigh. "All right, Sydne, if
that's what you want."

Reluctant to get near him, Sydne kept her distance
while she warily watched him collect the diving
equipment, abandoned on the beach after her lesson.
The anger that had made her blood boil only
moments earlier was slowly decreasing in intensity,
leaving an empty feeling of desolation in its place.
Concentrating her attention on clearing away the remains of their lunch, she tried not to look at Brian.

But she found it impossible to keep her eyes away from the muscles rippling under his tanned skin while he rinsed the sand off their masks and flippers. Those broad shoulders that she had caressed during the moments of blissful intimacy they had shared, those sinewy arms that had held her. She could almost feel them beneath her fingers again....

She closed her eyes, trying to erase the memory of how vibrantly alive she had felt in his arms, of how sweet his kisses had tasted. To remember would only serve to make her yearn for those experiences again, she knew. But still lurking in her mind was her suspicion about his involvement with Julia Lozano—an involvement Brian had not even bothered to deny. Instead, he had laughed at her.

Once again Sydne berated herself for having let her feelings become so transparent. She meant nothing to Brian Stevens. All he saw in her was another conquest, another source to feed that incredibly enormous macho ego of his. For what other kind of man would expect her to give in so easily to his desires?

Brian's voice broke through her thoughts. "Are we all set to go now?"

Sydne didn't answer, but simply crossed the strip of sand with as much dignity as she could muster under the circumstances. As she approached the launch she went around to the other side, across from where he stood, making it clear that she didn't want his help. She was no longer angry; she just couldn't bear for him to touch her again. In the past hour she had become painfully aware of how frail her resistance really was.

Brian made no comment about her maneuver to

avoid him, but when she glanced at him covertly she saw undisguised amusement in his expression. How expressive were those beautiful blue eyes of his, she mused against her will. But let him laugh if he wanted; she didn't care. It was no longer a question of pride. It was a question of survival.

Seeing that Sydne had boarded the boat by herself, Brian collected the picnic basket and the blanket. He placed them on the floor of the launch, and then, taking advantage of an incoming wave, pushed the vessel out to sea until it was deep enough for the motor's propeller to clear the sandy bottom. When the water reached his chest, he hoisted himself up and clambered aboard. His weight and bulk made the small boat rock perilously, and Sydne had to hold on to the sides with both hands to keep her balance until it had righted itself. Brian didn't comment on her silence, instead applying himself to starting the motor, which coughed a couple of times before finally sparking into life.

This time they didn't follow the coast as they had on their way in. While Brian steered the launch directly out to sea, Sydne looked back toward the beach receding in the distance, until all she could distinguish was a thin line of greenery. It, too, was lost from sight in what seemed a matter of minutes. A lovely sight that had vanished as quickly as the happiness she had known, she mused.

The crystalline waters still shimmered under the burning sun, and she looked up at a pair of gulls gliding by on a draft of wind. The birds came so close to the launch that she could clearly see each feather on their extended wings, their short pink legs tucked under their tails. In spite of all the beauty that surrounded her, however, the joy had gone out of the day, and Sydne found herself wishing she had never come to the Dominican Republic.

"Don't forget your hat," Brian said after a while.

Absently she reached for the wide-brimmed shade and put it on without argument. His reminder failed to get a rise out of her, as it had in the past.

"Why so gloomy, Syd?" Brian asked gently. "I thought you had enjoyed the day."

Oh, why can't he leave me alone, Sydne silently wailed. It was obvious that she couldn't stop her depression from showing, but she was damned if she was going to give Brian the satisfaction of talking about it. "I did—most of it," she replied dryly.

"Look, babe, about what happened—" he began.

"I don't care to discuss it," she cut him off stiffly. "We all have our weak moments, Brian. That's all it was. Don't read any more into what happened between us."

Then she sat in isolated silence, until a tiny white dot on the horizon announced that they would soon be back aboard the *Adventurer*.

Several minutes passed before Sydne realized there was another vessel near the ship. She hoped it was the Dominican coast guard bringing Dr. Marín back—and making it possible for her to get away from Brian! But it couldn't be the coast guard, she soon realized. Smaller than the *Adventurer*, the vessel had remained hidden by the bulk of the salvage ship until this moment.

Sydne couldn't help remembering what Chuck had told her earlier about the pirate attack on the galleon

Brian and his crew had found off the Florida Keys. Her sense of foreboding only increased as she turned and looked inquiringly at Brian.

"Brian, what are we going to do?" she asked tensely as he turned off the motor.

For a few seconds there was silence as the launch rose and fell with the sea. Then Brian said, "There's a kit stowed away in that little compartment at the prow, Sydne. Get out a flashlight and hand it to me, will you, babe?"

The lack of urgency in his voice made Sydne realize that he was trying not to alarm her. But his actions were more than sufficient indication that he was worried. Following his lead, Sydne tried not to show her fear as she scrambled to the prow. She got out the small waterproof duffel bag Brian had mentioned, which contained, among other things, a first-aid kit and the flashlight he had requested.

Sydne made her way back to the stern of the launch, and after handing Brian the flashlight, she sat as close to him as she possibly could without impeding his movements. All of a sudden the prospect of danger seemed to have dissolved their differences and joined them in a common cause.

While Brian signaled the ship with the flashlight, Sydne found herself praying that the people in the other boat were not hostile. The launch would never be able to outrun the pirate vessel, if indeed that's what it was. And she was very worried about the fate of her friends on the *Adventurer*.

It wasn't until this moment that she realized how important those men had become to her. The discovery didn't take her by surprise, however. She had a tendency, she knew, to become too attached to people she liked, and even though this characteristic had caused her many disappointments throughout her life, the closeness she had shared with the crew of the *Adventurer* had encouraged this pattern.

"Will they see the signal?" she inquired after Brian had flashed the light several times without getting a response from the *Adventurer*.

"It may not be visible in this weather," he replied. "All we can do is keep trying."

Aware that Brian had a lot on his mind at the moment, she didn't bother to ask what they would do if the *Adventurer* was under attack. What could they do? Unconsciously she moved closer to him, seeking reassurance from physical contact. As if he understood, Brian put an arm around her shoulders. There was no sexual innuendo in the gesture, only one of protection, and Sydne offered no resistance when he drew her closer to him. When he looked at her she gave him a feeble smile that didn't hide her apprehension.

"It's going to be all right, babe," Brian told her gently, accompanying his words of reassurance with a swift kiss on her temple.

For some reason, his gentleness brought tears to her eyes and a lump to her throat. She was so tired of the loneliness of her existence! How wonderful it would be to let herself love this man as she wanted to love him—without doubting his affection, without fears of betrayal.

She let her arm slip around his waist as he continued to signal the ship. . .twice, three times more. And at long last there was a flashing response from the deck of the *Adventurer*.

"They've seen us!" Sydne exclaimed, but Brian's attention was concentrated on the message being transmitted. Remembering Chuck's explanation, she tried to see if the message was being repeated three times. If it was, she couldn't tell, but being so close to Brian she could feel the tension ebbing from his body as he deciphered it. Unable to contain herself, she queried at last, "What are they saying?"

Brian's expression was enigmatic as he regarded her worried features. "The other ship is friendly," he told her.

"Do you think they're telling the truth?" Her voice was filled with doubt.

"It's hard to say," Brian replied cryptically. "But there's only one way to find out, isn't there?"

In spite of the tension of the moment, Sydne became aware of a delicious feeling of warmth rippling through her. His eyes, she saw, had fastened on her mouth. The feeling increased when he raised his sun-bronzed hand to trace the soft curve of her cheek with his fingers, then continued down the length of her slender throat. By the time she realized his intention, Sydne wanted his kiss too much to refuse it.

His mouth was warm and sweet on hers as he savored the responses she could not hold back. His lips, his teeth, his tongue combined to tease, to caress, to nibble and then caress again. Each seductive movement made her want more. There had never been a kiss like this—so sweet and yet so full of passion that it made her go weak with desire. How she wished that it would never end!

But it had to, and it was Brian who ended it, looking deep into her amber eyes, which reflected her longing. Sydne didn't care that her feelings were so obvious. To be held in his arms like this, to feel the wild beating of his heart so close to hers made any danger bearable. She was only grateful that if the end was near, she had had the chance to live this moment in Brian's embrace.

There was no hesitation in her hand as it smoothed away the lines that came to his brow. With a feather-light touch she caressed his tanned cheek in a gesture meant to erase the troubled clouds that came to his eyes. She wanted to say, "I love you, Brian," but she never got the chance, because her words were silenced by a kiss that held a note of burning need, of desperation. Her body, trembling like a captive bird's, was crushed in an embrace so fierce it was almost painful in its intensity.

Brian released her suddenly and, without a word, turned to start the motor. *So this is it,* she thought, watching his somber face as the old outboard went through its routine of coughing and sputtering and then roaring into life. Once he had the launch under control, he reached for her hand and held it in his own large warm one, as if trying to communicate some of his own courage to her. But although Sydne was no longer frightened, she couldn't help being nervous as the launch dipped and climbed through the trough of waves raised by the early-evening wind.

And in her mind rang the question, *are we riding into a trap?*

DISTANCES AT SEA are highly deceptive, Sydne had learned. In most cases it took longer than she expected to reach objectives that, to the naked eye, seemed close. The launch was not a speedy craft—it had only seemed that way to Sydne during their mad race back to the salvage ship—but it took almost three quarters of an hour for them to come within shouting distance of the seventy-five-foot, gleaming white yacht that was prudently anchored a good distance away from the reef where the *Adventurer* was moored. They were still too far away to see the expressions on the faces of the men aboard, and Sydne's wariness did not lessen even when she saw a hand waving.

"Andrew!" Sydne finally exclaimed, realizing who it was. "It's Andrew!" Enormously relieved, she waved back delightedly, turning to look at Brian as she did so. He seemed pleased to see his old friend, but not overly surprised by Andrew's unexpected appearance.

A shadow of doubt instantly began to take form in Sydne's mind. Was this visit really unexpected, she wondered. Had Brian been aware of the identity of the strange vessel and purposely withheld the information from her?

Thinking back over the past hour of suspense, Sydne realized that all along he must have known there had been no danger. Otherwise he would have been more cautious during their approach. It all made sense now. As macho as he was, Brian was no fool.

He might not be a fool, but she certainly was, Sydne admitted, feeling her temperature rise. With every second the suspicion was becoming a full-fledged certainty in her mind. She had played right into his hands, acting the way she had in the face of danger. How stupid could she be? She had almost told him that she loved him! Oh, Lord, how Brian must be laughing at her now!

The launch was just nosing alongside the elegant yacht. Then and there Sydne vowed that when Andrew sailed back to Samaná, she would be going with him. Blindly, without looking back at Brian, she accepted the hand one man aboard the yacht offered her.

"How good to see you again!" Andrew was saying, but his welcoming grin began to fade when he saw her face. "What's wrong, Sydne? You look like you're about to burst into tears."

She forced a smile as she bent down to hug the dear old man. "You old fox, you scared me half to death!" she countered. "When we saw this yacht we thought pirates were attacking the *Adventurer*."

"Good heavens, I've been called many things in my life," Andrew admitted wryly, "but 'pirate' wasn't one of them."

"I never dreamed it could be you," Sydne continued, making her voice sound normal. "What are you doing here?"

"Tim and I went fishing this morning," Andrew replied enthusiastically, "and since we weren't too far away, we decided to pay you a visit." Sydne was well aware that fishing was only an excuse, but she refrained from commenting. She was a little bewildered when Andrew looked past her and asked, "And tell me, my boy, how are things coming along? Any luck in determining if it's the *Conde*?"

Waiting for Brian's response, Sydne involuntarily

stiffened her back—in spite of her resolution to act normally and not to let him see how terribly ashamed she was of her earlier conduct.

"Not yet, but we're making progress," Brian replied, shaking his friend's hand. "When did you get here?"

"Earlier this afternoon," Andrew replied. "I wanted to board the *Adventurer* for a closer look at what's going on, but the captain of this tub—" he encompassed the luxurious yacht with a wave of his hand "—wouldn't hear of getting any closer to the reef. He wouldn't budge an inch, even when I told him I'd buy the damned thing. So here we were, in the middle of a perfect Mexican standoff until you got back from wherever it was you and Sydne went today." With a mischievous twinkle in his dark eyes he added, "I certainly would consider it a consolation to know that at least you were enjoying yourselves."

Brian had chuckled at Andrew's account of his troubles, and now he replied ruefully, "Well, you know what they say about all work and no play, old friend. Yes, I had a great time. I think Sydne did, too—didn't you, Syd?" He winked at her.

Sydne was so furious with him at that moment that she could have slapped his face. She controlled herself with difficulty. "Yes, Andrew, of course I did," she said instead, adding, "Brian was kind enough to teach me a little scuba diving, so that I can go down to see the shipwreck."

Sydne wasn't sure she had sounded very convincing, for Andrew looked from one to the other as if doubting the truth of her statement. But he said

cheerfully, "You'll have to tell me all about it sometime, Syd. I'm glad to see that the two of you have
finally hit it off. I always knew you would."

Sydne didn't have to look at Brian to know that he
must have been thoroughly amused by Andrew's
comment. She would have been amused, too, if the
circumstances had been different.

But she was distracted from such speculation by
Andrew's next question. "What are the chances of
my getting aboard the *Adventurer*, Brian? I know it's
not going to be easy with my wheelchair and all, but I
wish we could give it a try."

A young boy in a starched white uniform appeared
at this point, carrying a tray of tall frosty glasses. At
the sight, Sydne realized how thirsty she was, and she
gratefully accepted one of the drinks. It turned out to
be a refreshing mixture of rum and lime juice flavored with sprigs of fresh peppermint leaves, delicious
and icy cold.

Brian, in turn, took a glass from the tray and
scratched his head thoughtfully. "Well, the transfer
would take some time and it'll be dark soon—" he
began.

"You don't have to worry about that, my boy,"
Andrew interrupted confidently. "I already thought
of it. We came prepared to spend the night right here
on this spot, so we can try it in the morning. How's
that for planning?"

It was clear that the old man would not be easily
dissuaded from his purpose. He was like a little boy
intent on a new toy, and a denial would disappoint
him bitterly.

Sydne knew how much visiting the salvage ship

would mean to Andrew. After all, he had a financial stake in the operation, and he had come so many miles, had sat ashore in his wheelchair for so many weeks, just to be near the salvaged galleon if and when it turned out to be the *Conde*. She prayed that Brian would find a way to grant his wish.

But if there was one thing she knew about Brian Stevens, it was that he seemed to have the same weakness for the engaging old fox as she did herself. No wonder her employer thought so highly of him, Sydne mused. She imagined Brian would do anything in his power for his friend—whether out of gratitude for his continuing financial help or out of love, it didn't matter.

She felt a surge of relief when she heard Brian say, "Okay, Andrew, we'll give it a try in the morning."

Andrew was beside himself with joy. "I knew it! I knew you would find a way to get me aboard the *Adventurer*! Thank you, my boy! And now, to celebrate the occasion, will you and Sydne be my guests for dinner this evening?"

Sydne was a little shaken by this unexpected invitation. She didn't relish the idea of traveling back and forth between ships alone with Brian. As a matter of fact, she had no intention of spending any time at all alone with the man again. But she couldn't refuse Andrew's invitation, and she racked her brains for a graceful way to get out of it.

After Brian had accepted for both of them, Sydne smiled. "Thank you, Andrew, but I wonder if it would be too much trouble to include Chuck Bates in the dinner party. He's Brian's second-in-command, you know. Of course, I really wouldn't mind letting

Chuck take my place if you've already planned on having only two of us."

She refused to look at Brian, but she wondered what his reaction might be.

"But that won't be necessary, Syd!" Andrew was protesting emphatically. "There's enough room for all of you, and more. And you're right, I should have thought of Chuck." He turned to Brian and said, "You will ask him for me, won't you, my boy?"

"Of course," Brian assented.

Sydne was beginning to feel a little better about the whole thing now that she could count on Chuck being there. And Andrew was right about the yacht; it was capable of accommodating a much larger party. Perhaps she could even manage to spend the night. With only Andrew and Tim aboard besides the crew, there were probably a few cabins vacant. She would see about it later, Sydne promised herself, returning her attention to the conversation.

Tim had joined them by this time, and he and Brian were discussing the best way of moving the invalid from one ship to the other. Brian agreed with the yacht's captain that it wasn't advisable to move the vessel any closer to the reef. Andrew would have to be lowered onto the launch, which would take him out to the *Adventurer*. There they would use some of the hoisting equipment they had aboard to lift him up without jolting him too much. Brian promised he would have some type of harness ready by morning.

There shouldn't be any problem with the older man using his wheelchair on deck, Brian decided, as long as he didn't expect to go below. But this restriction presented no problem for Andrew, who had no desire to tour the salvage ship. His interest lay solely in the relics that had been recovered from the shipwreck.

After a long discussion on the subject and another round of drinks, Brian looked at Sydne and said, "I think we'd better get going."

Sydne saw her plans to speak in private with Andrew evaporate. She had really wanted to tell him that she had had enough of the salvage and that she wanted to go home.

Well, she consoled herself with the thought that she might get her opportunity this evening. She had definitely made up her mind that she was not going to go back to the *Adventurer* after the dinner party.

She got up gracefully from her chair, and after saying goodbye to Andrew and Tim, followed Brian toward the launch.

He climbed down to the smaller boat before she did and caught her in his arms as she was being assisted by one of the yacht's crewmen.

"You can put me down now, Brian," she said a little testily when he held her much too long, as if reluctant to let her go.

The smile he gave her seemed a little wistful, but after releasing her without a word he took his place at the stern.

Settling herself on her usual bench, Sydne looked up to find Andrew and Tim watching them. She felt color rising to her cheeks at the thought that they had witnessed that brief telltale moment between Brian and her, but she decided that they couldn't have made much out of it. Feigning a cheerfulness she was far from feeling, she smiled and waved at her employer and his male nurse, who both waved back.

As the launch covered the distance to the *Adventurer*, Sydne pretended Brian wasn't even there. He knew she was aware that he had taken advantage of her, she was sure, and her pride wouldn't let her reopen the subject, even to accuse him. What was the point? She would gain nothing by it except to shame herself.

She was relieved that Brian didn't even try to start a conversation. As soon as they arrived Sydne went to her cabin to shower and change for dinner. Locking her door, she removed her swimsuit and then reached inside the locker for her robe. Catching sight of her reflection in the mirror made her grimace in dismay. What a sight she was! Salt water had dried in her hair, leaving it stiff and sticky, and the wind had blown it in all directions. Her sunburned face would probably be smarting by morning. Not even Dr. Marín's coconut oil remedy would save her this time.

Sydne was glad she had decided not to confront Brian, after all. When she accused him of trying to seduce her, he would probably have handed her a mirror.... "The ultimate put-down," she said to her reflection, smiling gruesomely.

Well, she didn't have much time to make herself presentable for the dinner party—much less beautiful. According to the mirror, she had a great deal of work to do.

While in the shower she shampooed her hair, trying to adhere to the water rationing that had been imposed on the crew. Brian had once warned her that salvage work would be tough and dirty, and he had been right. As Sydne had soon discovered, the *Adventurer* was no place to wear anything remotely resembling a dress. On several occasions she had wondered what had possessed her to pack the long white satin lounging pajamas that had been hanging in the locker since her arrival. But that was in the past. Tonight, especially after what she had seen in the mirror, Sydne was determined to dress up. She needed the frills of femininity to boost her sagging ego, and thanked her lucky stars for Andrew McCallum, who had provided her with the occasion and the opportunity to do so.

She was pleased with the glossy silken texture of her hair as, later, she ran a brush through it. Shampooing it had done wonders, and even though she knew she was probably going to pay dearly for it, the touch of sun on her skin, once the sting had been assuaged with a little moisturizer, was highly becoming against the whiteness of her outfit. The pajamas tied around her neck in a halter, leaving her back completely bare to her waist, and there was a sensuous quality in the feel of the soft satiny fabric against her skin.

As she was dabbing perfume along the curve of her throat, there was a knock on the door. Rather than rushing to answer it, she took her time, touching the fragrance to her pulse points, taking one last-minute check in the mirror and collecting a small clutch purse before opening the door.

Brian, too, had changed, into brown slacks and a casual but elegant, long-sleeved shirt in a cream color that went well with his hair, still slightly damp from a recent shower. He had recently shaved, she also noted, as the scent of musky after-shave wafted to her nostrils.

Sydne had the satisfaction of seeing Brian's eyes widen as he took in her appearance. To be able to produce such an effect on him gave her a heady sense of power. Knowing how he made her feel, she was ready to give a little of the same back. She was playing with fire, she knew, but at the moment her pride demanded some tribute from Brian, one that would allow her to salvage a shred of her self-esteem.

What wouldn't she give to have him trembling with passion for her, she mused, acutely aware of a stirring within her. As she looked into his blue eyes, she saw the desire she had inspired and felt a pang of regret that he had admitted only to wanting her, not to loving her..... Afraid to dwell too much on this point, she smiled and said, "I'm ready, Brian. Shall we go?"

The way his eyes fastened on her mouth made her aware of what was on his mind. Stepping quickly out of the cabin, she closed the door behind her, leaving him little chance to satisfy his wish. Together they went up on deck.

After taking so much care with her appearance, Sydne's ego was gratified to have Brian as a witness to the commotion created by her emergence there. Crewmen and divers flocked from every corner of the ship to look at her, and the air was rent with wolf whistles. The noisy demonstrations subsided a bit as soon as the boss appeared at Sydne's heels, but not much. Brian didn't seem greatly disturbed by the calls and teasing remarks that followed them as they walked toward the launch.

Chuck, who was already waiting for them, wore casual slacks and a dressy long-sleeved shirt, just as Brian did. Both men looked handsome in the extreme, and Sydne began to feel giddy with the unreality of it all. So far the evening could be considered every woman's dream—receiving the admiration of so many men while going out with two of the most attractive ones. Determined to enjoy herself, she accepted Chuck's hand to board the launch, where Brian was already waiting for her.

Her feeling of euphoria didn't protect her from the sensations that coursed through her as Brian caught her and held her to him. Sydne shivered a little and her breath quickened slightly when his broad hand, splayed out on the bare skin of her back, lightly traced the line of her spine in a sinuous caress. Her gaze rose to meet his, and, realizing he was aware of her slightest reaction to his touch, she pulled abruptly away. She was grateful that her action coincided with Chuck's coming aboard.

But a moment later Sydne was grating her teeth in frustration. By some unspoken agreement, Chuck had taken over the steering of the launch, while Brian sat next to her on the bench. No matter what she did, Brian Stevens always came up the winner! She had held all the aces tonight until the moment he touched her, and then she had lost the game again. If she had any sense at all, she would lay down her cards and run as fast as her legs could take her!

At that moment Brian's arm went casually around her shoulders, interrupting her thoughts. Not wanting to create a scene in front of Chuck, Sydne merely stiffened her back and pursed her lips to show her displeasure. Brian seemed to take no notice of the signals she was sending out, however, and a few minutes later his hand began absently stroking her upper arm.

"Stop that!" Sydne muttered, hoping Chuck couldn't hear her over the roar of the outboard motor.

The wind had caught her hair as she turned her head, and even after she pushed it away from her face, a wayward strand hung temptingly across her mouth. Undaunted by the anger he could see sparking in her amber eyes, Brian brushed the lock aside, letting his fingers touch her lips as he did so. Then he slipped his arm around her shoulders once again.

Sydne fumed in silence for the rest of the way.

Andrew wasn't quite ready for them when they arrived at the yacht, so at Sydne's request a steward took her below, where she could repair the damage the wind had done to her hairstyle. The moment's privacy gave her a chance to examine the luxuriously appointed cabin the crewman had told her was vacant.

Even though it wasn't huge, it was still larger than the one she had taken over from Brian on the *Adventurer*. Instead of a narrow bunk to sleep on, there was a bed, securely fixed to the floor, with a nice firm mattress. The walls were paneled in glowing wood.

It would be nice to spend a night away from the salvage ship for a change, Sydne mused—nice to enjoy some of this marvelous comfort, and most of all, to get away from Brian. Inner peace was what she needed—now more than ever after the day she had spent in his company. She had to admit, though, that there had been certain moments she had wished would never end. . . .

After refreshing her lip gloss, Sydne felt ready for the rest of the evening. With the idea of remaining aboard the yacht firmly in mind, she left the cabin to join the party in the saloon.

"My goodness, you look fantastic!" Andrew exclaimed as she came in.

"Thank you, kind sir." She smiled flirtatiously, accepting another of the cool drinks she had enjoyed that afternoon.

"Chuck was just telling me about the artifacts they brought up today," Andrew informed her. "I can't wait to see them."

"Anything interesting?" Sydne asked.

"More cannonballs, and some pottery fragments with parts of a Latin inscription," Chuck replied. "Perhaps you can make something out of it."

"Maybe even the name of the ship," Andrew put in hopefully.

"I'll take a look at them tomorrow," she replied. "But don't get your hopes up too high, Andrew. In the seventeenth century Latin was commonly used throughout Europe."

At that point dinner was announced, and they all filed into a beautiful wood-paneled dining room with all the comforts of home, Tim pushing Andrew in his wheelchair. The meal itself was a little disappointing, however. The fresh snapper, served with a coconut sauce, would have been very good had it not been overcooked, as were the vegetables that came with it. Sydne ate little of both, satisfying her hunger mostly with the tossed green salad, fried plantains and seafood soup. Absently she noted that, for all the luxury aboard the yacht, not much attention had been given to the kitchen help. Gus was a much better cook.

As it turned out, after all her worrying about it Sydne didn't have to ask to spend the night on the yacht. Andrew himself suggested the idea during the meal, except his invitation also included the two men. Much to Sydne's dismay, Chuck declined the offer so that Brian could remain aboard and oversee Andrew's transferral to the *Adventurer* in the morning. And since the working day started early for the salvagers, the second-in-command returned to the ship shortly after dinner.

Sydne still wanted to discuss with Andrew the possibility of her going back to Samaná with him, so she patiently waited to broach the subject. She would have preferred to discuss the matter in private with her old employer, but since Brian's interests were also involved, she realized she probably shouldn't leave him out. It was already late in the evening when she finally opened the discussion, starting by asking when Dr. Marín was expected back.

"We still don't know," Brian replied. "His house didn't suffer any damage, but his wife is terrified of earthquakes. She still refuses to be left alone, and he's very worried about her."

"But if he's unable to come back, won't the government send someone else in his place?" Sydne inquired.

Brian's face wore a quizzical expression. "Dr. Marín insisted that he wants to return to the ship himself. It shouldn't be much more than a few days."

"I realize that you've been carrying a load big enough for two people, Syd," Andrew interjected, "but couldn't you hold on for a few more days, my dear? Dr. Marín will be back soon, and things will get back to normal."

Normal, she thought wryly. Nothing had been normal for her since she'd come to the Dominican Republic! And Dr. Marín's return wouldn't solve her problems, of which the work load was the least of her worries.

But at this point neither Andrew nor Brian would take very kindly to her walking out on the job. Dr. Marín's duty was to the Dominican government. He was a knowledgeable man, highly respected in his field and scrupulously honest. The salvagers' relationship with the government had been so harmonious chiefly because of his willingness to make things easier for both parties involved. If he were unable to return to the project, and if Sydne walked out, the salvage team would have no one to look after their interests.

Sydne hesitated. Brian had staked his future on this project, but he was not alone. The other men on the *Adventurer* had many dreams invested in it, too. She thought of Ricco, who had to leave his family in faraway Italy for months on end so that he could earn enough to eventually return home for good. And there were others—Claude, Bernardo, Rod, Nikko—who had also come from distant places, leaving loved ones behind. Each one of them had his dreams, dreams that, after all their effort and sacrifice, could be so easily jeopardized by someone selfish and uncaring.

Until this moment, Sydne had been so involved in her own emotional upheaval that she hadn't realized how much the team depended on her, and she was too much of a professional to let her personal feelings make her forget her duties. She had to keep trying. Loving Brian was her own misfortune, for which other people shouldn't have to pay. She would have to learn to live with her feelings, and avoid falling into the trap of believing that he might someday love her in return.

Sydne had been silent while all these thoughts chased through her mind. Becoming aware that both Andrew and Brian were waiting for a response from her, she finally smiled and said, "I'm sure I can hold the fort for a few more days, Andrew."

The decision made, she felt weary, physically and emotionally weary, and bidding the men good-night, she went to her cabin to seek refuge in sleep. Yet she was still wide awake when, much later, she heard the footsteps that told her Brian was retiring to the cabin next door. For a long time after that she lay in her bed staring at the ceiling. How close they were, with only a thin plank of wood between them, yet how very far apart in their emotional needs!

An hour later Sydne was still restlessly tossing and turning. She had gone to bed naked, and having nothing else to wear, she dressed again in her lounging pajamas and tiptoed out of her cabin. She didn't really know where she was going or what she was looking for at that hour, then decided that a drink might settle her nerves. Everyone else had gone to bed, but she had noticed a well-stocked bar in the saloon. She found her way there and poured a hefty dash of brandy into a snifter, which she took with her up on deck.

Ignoring the lounge chairs on the afterdeck, she stood by the railing, sipping her drink and pensively watching the lights of the *Adventurer*. The hull of the ship appeared like a white ghost in the moonlight.

"Did I tell you properly how very beautiful you look tonight?" said a very familiar husky voice behind her.

Abruptly she turned. Brian was leaning lazily against the frame of the door that opened onto the afterdeck. The light was behind him so she couldn't see his face. Oh, why did her heart have to beat faster at the sight of him, when she knew he felt only desire for her, not love? It was an effort not to betray her agitation when she said dryly, "I suppose anything would be an improvement over this afternoon."

She heard him chuckle before he said, "Don't you know that beauty is in the eyes of the beholder?" Then he came nearer, so near that she felt his warm breath brush her cheek. "And I always find you beautiful, babe. Very lovely, very desirable....."

Sydne knew he was going to kiss her, but even though she hungered for that kiss in every fiber of her being, she turned away. Her action didn't help. She felt him remove the brandy snifter from her nerveless fingers and place it on a nearby deck table. She felt his warm lips following the soft curve of her bare shoulder, and he pushed her hair aside to reach the nape of her neck. The pattern of kisses he traced across her back wrenched a reluctant sigh of pleasure from her, pleasure that grew in intensity when his hands slipped around her waist and under the satiny fabric of her halter top, cupping the naked flesh of her breasts.

She was tremblingly aware of his desire when, turning her around to face him, he drew her against the hardness of his muscular body. "I need you, babe," he whispered intensely as she turned her face away. "I need you now."

His mouth was seeking hers, but she was afraid that if he kissed her she would be lost, as she had been earlier that day. Time and place had saved her then, and now the memory of his deception caused her anger to flare anew. She pulled away, and her words were deliberate when she said, "But neither of us is in any danger now, Brian," before she turned and ran away.

TRANSPORTING ANDREW TO THE *Adventurer* proved to be quite a production, but the harness Brian had prepared made the operation easier and safer for the older man.

Sydne had her hands full that day, doing her regular work and fielding the myriad of questions Andrew kept throwing at her with childlike curiosity. He examined every artifact already recorded and tagged, as well as all the new items the divers continued to bring in.

Despite her work load, Sydne was able to piece together the pottery fragments with the Latin inscription, found the previous day. As she had feared, the words failed to shed any light on the identity of the sunken vessel. Although this disappointed Andrew, he still felt privileged to have firsthand contact with the relics.

Midafternoon marked the end of his visit, and a repetition of the earlier procedure reinstalled the aging millionaire on board the luxurious yacht. Amid cheerful goodbyes from the salvage crew he headed back toward Samaná.

Sydne was glad that the day's activities had prevented her from dwelling too much on her relationship with Brian—not to mention the events on the beach or aboard the yacht.

But in the privacy of her cabin her worries returned in full force. Judging by the way he had treated her all day, Brian had resumed his easygoing but relentless campaign to win her—a campaign that was proving quite effective in breaking down her resistance. So far Sydne had purposely refused to admit that his assessment had been correct, that she had been hiding behind her anger. But now she had to concede that, yes, she had been as much to blame as he for everything that had happened between them.

All along she had known that she couldn't trust herself where Brian was concerned. Yet she had gone to that deserted beach with him, had almost told him on the boat that she loved him. Even last night, after she had realized how he had tricked her, she had almost succumbed to her own desire for him when he had told her that he needed her. She had been a fool; she had been weak—and all because she loved him.

She loved his strength; she loved the way he could stir her to passion. But most of all she loved that wonderful gentleness he was capable of. She even loved his sense of humor, she admitted crossly to herself—even when she was trying so desperately to maintain the anger that had become her only defense.

CHAPTER SIX

THE FOLLOWING DAY Sydne finally got her chance to dive down to the shipwreck. When the time came, she held the mask to her face so that the fall wouldn't dislodge it, and without hesitation dropped backward into the sea. Somehow she managed to control her fear when the water closed over her head and she was blinded by the masses of bubbles that rose all around her. But when water rushed into her mask and burned the inside of her nose, she quickly shot for the surface, where in panic she yanked off the mask, sputtering and choking.

Brian immediately surfaced beside her and helped her stay afloat. "Are you all right?" he asked. At her nod he instructed, "Inflate your BC."

That was easier said than done, but she finally managed to do it. "I couldn't breathe!" she gasped, gulping for air but afloat at last.

He gave her a chance to catch her breath before inquiring, "Do you want to go back to the ship?"

Sydne was so nervous by this time that she was sorely tempted to say yes, but she knew she would always regret it if she did. "Not on your life!" she answered firmly.

"That's my girl!" Brian smiled encouragingly. "Okay, Sydne, let's take it slow and easy. Just try to

relax. j here's nothing to be nervous about.'' He
waited for a few seconds, and when she had readjusted her mask and stuffed the mouthpiece back
into her mouth he said, "Good. That's right, breathe
evenly and relax. Tell you what, I'll let you swim a
little on the surface until you're ready to go down,
okay? Take your time. There's no hurry. I'll stay
with you."

Brian never ceased to amaze her. He was not only
an excellent instructor, he was a patient one, as well.
Once again he was displaying the kindness so effective in disarming her.

Comforted by his presence, Sydne tried to take a
grip on her fear. She submerged her head, but following Brian's suggestions she swam on the surface
until she could feel confident that air was reaching
her lungs when she breathed through the regulator.
The glass of the mask allowed such a clear view that
even from the surface she could see the divers working below, as well as portions of the shipwreck still
encased in a shell of coral. After a little while her
nerves settled and her breathing became easier. It was
then that Sydne signaled to Brian that she was ready,
and she even had the presence of mind to deflate her
BC before she bent double and dove downward.

The water in this area was so clear that visibility
was almost perfect. As they began their descent what
had appeared to Sydne as nebulous dark patches
began to take form, like a picture slowly coming into
focus. Slowly the blotches turned into intricate colonies of living coral, bursting with color.

The eerie song of the regulator and the rush of
bubbles that it expelled each time she exhaled were

the only sounds in this magic world of stillness. But as Sydne went farther down the water pressure made her ears begin to hurt. Suddenly the instructions Brian had given her came back to mind, and just as he had shown her, she pinched her nose shut through the hollows of her mask and blew out. Her ears popped with a loud squeak that she found uncomfortable, but then she saw that Brian had been watching her and was smiling behind his mask. When he saw that she was looking at him, he made a circle with his thumb and index finger to signal "okay."

Sydne had to pause again to clear her ears when they had reached a depth of thirty feet, but once the discomfort had passed she began experiencing the same exhilarating sense of weightlessness she had discovered only two days earlier. This time, however, it was accompanied by a kind of rapture as she entered a marvelous fantasy world where rainbow-hued coral cities rose around her.

Poised in this blue green transparency, seeming to hang suspended from a ray of sunlight, a silver barracuda fixed its big glassy eyes on Sydne. The fish looked so beautiful that even the sight of its menacing teeth didn't frighten her as she watched it open and close its mouth. She was aware that the rhythmic action, as much as it served to increase the animal's ferocious appearance, was also its normal way of breathing. Or perhaps her lack of fear was due to Brian's reassuring presence.

The smooth ease with which her diving companion moved through that clear, blue green atmosphere, leisurely beating his flippers, was beautiful to watch. In spite of his size he released only a few bubbles of

spent air in comparison to the noisy long trail she left
behind. The fact made Sydne realize that she was
breathing too fast, and she told herself to relax.
Otherwise she would be running out of air soon, and
she certainly didn't want to return to the surface
yet!

Her attention returned to the barracuda, just in
time to see the fish disappear with a flick of its tail.
As if by magic, one moment it was there and the
next, poof! It was gone.

As they dove deeper, Sydne was able to get a closer
look at an outstanding profusion of marine life.
Walls of living coral loomed above the shipwreck,
and a variety of colored fish played their games of
hide and seek, poking their noses into the holes and
gliding around the corners, totally unperturbed by
the presence of the divers.

The wreck site was swarming with a crowd of
hungry groupers and yellowtails, frantically feeding
on the tiny crabs and worms churned up by the airlift. Nikko, operating the lift, paused in his arduous
task to wave at Sydne. A few feet away, Claude, in
the process of loosening the sea floor, was wrestling
with a pitchfork. Rod and Bernardo paused in their
struggles to lift a box of grenades as Sydne stopped to
investigate the contents. The old ammunition was
fused together and encrusted with coral.

Sydne had just waved and was swimming away
when a flash of gold under a loosened piece of coral
caught her eye. She swam quickly toward it. The
edges of the coral were as razor sharp as Chuck had
told her they were, and being very careful to avoid
cutting herself, she picked up the small disc she had

seen. Upon closer inspection, she realized it was a golden *escudo*. She had made her first find!

Filled with excitement, she turned toward Brian and waved. Once she had his attention she held up the coin for his inspection. Again he made the "okay" sign before beckoning her away from the shipwreck.

Sensing intuitively that Brian wanted to show her something special, she slipped the coin inside the bra of her swimsuit and followed him. They swam close to the sandy bottom punctuated by atolls, until they came upon a forest of the sea fans he had described to her as ballerinas. And that was exactly what they looked like, Sydne thought, their long branches reminiscent of ostrich plumes in mauve, rose, pink and yellow, breathtakingly beautiful as they gently swayed with the current.

As she and Brian left the sea-fan forest they ran into a school of fish striped in blue and gold. The fish, not at all disturbed by their presence, simply opened their ranks to let them through. There before them lay a beautiful garden created by hundreds of sea anemones. The innocuous-looking flowers had captured an unsuspecting yellowtail in their poisonous tentacles. The spectacle served as a grim reminder of the constant struggle for survival that existed in this magical world.

A field of large sponges, growing in a variety of shapes, formed a marine vista that reminded Sydne of pictures she had seen of southwestern landscapes. She was admiring what looked like towering rock formations when Brian touched her on the shoulder and called her attention to a giant clam lying on the sea bottom. The creature must have measured at least three feet in diameter, and for Sydne's amusement, Brian tapped its shell as if knocking at a neighbor's door to borrow a cup of sugar. Although impeded by her mouthpiece, she wished she could laugh when, disturbed by such outrageous treatment, the animal began working its valves and expelling jets of water to close its habitat to intruders.

But Brian was saving the best for last. He took Sydne by the hand and led her through a narrow channel in the coral, where at the end they found an immense cavern. Not knowing what to expect and a little fearful of finding the cave occupied by an unfriendly creature, Sydne was hesitant as she followed him inside. But once there she halted, awestruck.

Sunrays, filtering through holes in the ceiling, fell on sculptures of living coral in every shape and color imaginable. It was a palace of marvels, a wonderland of beauty so mesmerizing that when Brian tapped her on the shoulder to let her know it was time to go, Sydne shook her head, refusing to leave. He had to signal to her again and pointed to his watch before she realized she had only a few minutes of air left and had to start back. But when she followed him out of the cavern, she did so with great reluctance, promising herself that she would return.

As they slowly began their ascent, pausing at intervals to adjust to the change in pressure, Sydne caught herself humming a religious hymn. The sight of the sun reflecting on the surface above, playing shadows along the reef, gave her the sense of being in a cathedral or some other sacred place.

"Enjoy yourself?" Brian asked as they took off their diving gear aboard the *Adventurer*.

"It was wonderful!" Sydne replied fervently.

"When we get back to Florida I can have you certified," he said, capturing her waist and drawing her against him.

"Certified as insane?" she taunted, choosing to ignore his meaning.

He threw back his head with a hearty laugh. "Ah, babe," he chuckled, "I see your tongue is as sharp as ever."

Terribly conscious of the strong muscles of his thighs pressing against hers, Sydne tried to resist the shiver of excitement that went up her spine. The inadvertent reaction triggered a combination of longing and fear within her. "With you around," she said, placing the palms of her hands flat on his chest and pushing him away, "there's little chance it will become blunt. Please let me go," she added when he didn't release her.

He did so with a deep sigh of resignation, and Sydne told herself she should be glad she had escaped the danger of his nearness instead of feeling disappointment. She didn't know what she wanted anymore, she admitted, exasperated. Brian's touch was thrilling and exciting, but she was afraid of her own reactions. And yet when he did ignore her, she couldn't wait to be near him, to be touched by him again. At this rate she really was making tremendous strides toward a padded cell, she mused as she headed toward her cabin.

Brian followed at her heels, and standing behind her while she opened the door, he put his arms around her. The unexpected gesture reawakened the gamut of conflicting emotions she was trying so hard to fight.

"You're only wasting precious time, you know," he said, lifting her easily as he moved inside and kicked the door shut behind him. "Instead of sparring with words, we should be doing this." Pushing her hair aside, he pressed his lips to the nape of her neck, nibbling and caressing, fanning the flame of desire that was rapidly growing within her.

Sydne's skin prickled under the teasing caresses his warm lips trailed over the curve of her shoulder. Then his hands left her waist to pull down the top of her bathing suit and cup her breasts. His lean strong fingers kneaded the soft mounds and rubbed their sensitive crests, filling her with a tingling anticipation. She wanted more!

"Please stop," she pleaded without conviction.

"That's not what you want," he said, turning her in his arms to face him. Pressing little tantalizing kisses to the corners of her mouth, he teased her lips apart until they yielded the sweetness within to his demanding thoroughness. Then it was she who was tracing the contours of his mouth with the tip of her tongue, she who was taking little love nips at his lower lip. Her aggression seemed to have the same effect on him as his own love play had had on her, for his hold tightened fiercely before he lowered her onto the bunk. His mouth descended once again, seeming to devour her...absorb her.

As she breathlessly stroked the smoothness of his flanks, Sydne became increasingly aware of the sensual pleasure building within her. The hard muscles of his back and shoulders seemed to ripple under her fingertips, as soft as silk, as undulating as the sea.

She felt a sense of loss when he withdrew his mouth, and opened her eyes to see that his were bluer than they had ever been before. "You have eyes like brandy," he said huskily, "and you're just as inebriating."

With a sigh he eased himself away slightly, and she could see that he was fighting for control. "I want to make love to you," he stated seriously, "but not here, not now."

It was then that Sydne became aware of noises overhead—and the fact that she was lying almost naked in his arms.

Brian must have seen the alarm in her eyes, because he drew her into his embrace again before she could get away. "Don't fight it, my love," he said softly into her hair. "You want this as much as I do."

Sydne wanted to deny it, but could not. Oh, why did she have to be so weak? Her eyes were brimming with tears when he lifted her chin to look into them. "It's going to be all right, babe," he said gently, brushing her lips with his. A few minutes later he let himself out of her cabin.

Sydne had been tremendously attracted to the cold hostile Brian Stevens, but against this passionate tender lover she was totally powerless. Yes, it was true that she wanted him as much or more than he wanted her. He could have had her right then and there!

And yet he had held back, as if she really mattered

to him. Did she? Or was he only trying to prove that he could make love to her anytime he pleased?

"Well, he won't!" Sydne said out loud, rolling over on the narrow bunk. Now that she was alone she could think clearly, an impossibility when Brian was near. There was clearly no hope of escaping his fascination as long as she was trapped on the ship. The only way to recover her faculties was to get away quickly. She was due for her leave, and now that Dr. Marín had finally come back from Santo Domingo, she would demand that Brian let her go. She needed time to think things over, to put them in their proper perspective.

There was no future in having an affair with Brian, she admitted achingly. At any rate, it wasn't an affair that she wanted. Brian could offer physical gratification, that was obvious, but to him women were nothing more than instruments of pleasure. His wife, Julia Lozano, herself—had he loved any of them?

He had called her "my love," yet he hadn't said that he loved her. Any man could *want* a woman, she thought dejectedly. But more tender feelings—wanting to share each other's lives, have children, grow old together—were apparently alien to Brian. But Sydne wanted all those things: she wanted them with him.

And she wasn't alone. As sure as the sun must rise, so must Julia Lozano.

"I'M AFRAID IT'S IMPOSSIBLE," Brian replied when Sydne asked to be taken ashore. "I can't spare anyone at the moment."

"But I'm overdue for my leave!" she protested

hotly. "I've been on this tub for five consecutive weeks!"

"Then you'll survive another four days," he said calmly.

"Four days!"

"That's when the men return from their leave. You may go then."

"I don't want to wait four days! I want to go now!" Sydne insisted. "I *have* to go now. I'm getting off this ship if I have to swim!"

Brian regarded her soberly. "Why the rush, Sydne? Is anyone waiting for you ashore?"

"That's none of your business!"

"Ah, but it is," he said, eyeing her possessively. "Everything about you is my business, babe."

"Don't you 'babe' me!" she protested indignantly.

"You never objected before."

Sydne couldn't stop her flush. Brian had only called her "babe" during intimate moments. "Well, I do now," she put in stubbornly.

Brian cupped the nape of her neck with one hand and rubbed his thumb over her chin. The familiar gesture was so tender, so much a part of why she was attracted to him. "Why, Syd?"

"Brian, I have to get away," she said in a tremulous voice. "I need some time to myself to think things over."

"Why are you so afraid to let your feelings show?" he inquired gently. "Is it so hard to trust me?"

"Why should I trust you?" she said, bitterness in her voice. "I saw you with Julia, Brian. You were

holding her just as you do me. Tell me, is it the same
with her?'' With a sob she spun on her heel. She
didn't want him to see her cry.

WITH ITS ASSORTMENT OF PANELS and floats, the hose
of the airlift had the appearance of a voracious sea
serpent looming over the shipwreck as Brian swam to
the point where the excavation had been called to a
halt.

Turning, he motioned to Chuck to bring the airlift,
and together they began to dig. Failing to find
anything, they moved forward another fourteen feet
until they reached a pile of wooden planks, and then
a mound of debris. Here again they applied the airlift. In a few minutes they had uncovered an object
that might have been portions of a cannon truck. The
men looked at each other and nodded in agreement
before beginning their ascent to the ship.

''How does it look?'' Dr. Marín inquired avidly
when the divers finished removing their gear.

''We're close,'' Brian answered. ''Let me show
you.'' He made his way to the worktable that had
been set up in the shade and spread out a map he had
made of the shipwreck. ''Here,'' he said, sketching in
pencil, ''is the galleon. Because of the conditions
prevailing in the area, we think there may be a list to
starboard. The animal bones we've found seem to in-
dicate that we've been digging near the forward section, where the livestock was kept, so we're going to
transfer our efforts to this area—'' again he pointed
with the pencil ''—where we hope to gain better
access to the treasure room. In order to do that we're
going to dig a transversal trench at this point.'' To

Chuck, who with Rod and Bernardo had joined them, he said, "If we reduce the diving teams to two men at a time, we'll be able to operate the airlift for a few extra hours a day. That should speed things up a bit."

The men nodded in agreement.

Brian glanced at the dark clouds gathering over the horizon and frowned. "Anything new on the weather report?"

"Nothing so far," Chuck answered, "but we're keeping in touch with the Miami weather bureau."

"Good. Let's continue monitoring around the clock. I don't like the look of the sky. Another thing," he added. "We should move the *Adventurer* directly above the work area to make it easier to haul the larger blocks of coral and the metal baskets."

After the men dispersed Brian moved toward Sydne, who was sifting coral fragments through a fine screen, her cheeks streaked with coral dust.

"Hi, babe." Standing behind her, he slipped his arms around her waist. "Any luck?"

Sydne stiffened. "Some rusty nails and a musket ball," she replied, brushing a wayward strand of hair from her face. In vain she struggled against the combination of weakness and excitement that invaded her when he pressed a kiss on her temple.

"You look tired," he said gently. "Why don't you go below for a while? Take a shower and get some rest."

"A shower!" she repeated with longing. "But you said we had to save water."

To stretch their supply, Brian had given orders to cut down on water consumption. Showers had been limited to a group total of forty-five minutes a day, and to Gus's delight even paper plates were being used in the galley.

Now Brian turned her in his arms to face him, and his blue eyes regarded her tenderly. "You take my turn in the shower, babe."

"Oh, Brian, I couldn't!" she protested, touched by his offer. As many swimmers know, a casual diver doesn't require any protection in the warm waters of the Caribbean. But anyone who spends long hours at a stretch underwater has to wear a rubber wet suit in order to retain his body heat. If he doesn't wash off the salt left after the seawater evaporates, a diver's skin becomes irritated, and he is miserable in his wet suit. She couldn't let that happen to Brian. "Could I go swimming instead?" she offered. "It would cool me off just as well as a shower and save water, too."

Brian hesitated briefly. "All right," he agreed, "but I'll go with you."

Rushing to her cabin to change, Sydne pushed away the little scolding voice that was telling her she was a fool to let him get close to her again.

When she reappeared moments later in her bathing suit, Brian had discarded his wet suit and now wore only a pair of white swimming trunks.

"Do you think I could see the shipwreck again?" she asked him.

"Sure, babe." He collected the diving gear and helped her put it on.

This time there was no sense of panic when Sydne went underwater—only that exhilarating weightlessness, that sense of wonder at entering a fairyland where time and space seemed suspended. There were no words to describe the colors that existed beneath the surface. The same barracuda she had seen before watched the intruders with little curiosity. It seemed to have become a permanent fixture in the area, so much so that the divers had named it Albert. A school of striped sergeant majors swam boldly by, and Sydne was elated when a colorful parrot fish came to feed from her hand.

Suddenly she froze. A large dark shadow had appeared out of nowhere. It was a blue shark, perhaps ten feet long, and it was so close that Sydne could clearly see the numerous scars on its dull gray sides. All her instincts screamed for flight, but Brian was instantly beside her. Holding her firmly in place, he forced her to face the animal as it swam majestically in circles around them. Sydne had seen sharks in aquariums, but this one seemed larger than life. Petrified, she had no idea how much time passed before the monster finished its tour of the area, and after it had gone she had no desire to remain underwater any longer. All she wanted was to return to the safety of the ship as quickly as possible.

"Are you okay?" Brian asked when they resurfaced.

Sydne couldn't find her voice. She even forgot to inflate her BC until he reminded her. She couldn't get out of the water soon enough.

"I'm sorry you had such a fright," Brian said in an apologetic voice, noting how pale she was after they had climbed up on deck. "But I couldn't let you swim away from the shark. That's the worst thing you could do," he explained. "Always face them."

Face them, she thought with a shudder. At this

moment she couldn't even bear to face a picture of one.

"There were many sharks in this area when we arrived," Brian was saying conversationally, "but they went away after we started working the airlift. They're more sensitive to sustained noises than humans are, and the vibration of the compressor has kept them away. We've become so accustomed to it, that I didn't even notice it had been turned off," he added wryly.

Neither had she, Sydne realized. The constant roar of the mechanical monster had become a part of life. "I'm—I'm all right," she finally managed to say, hating herself for being such a coward.

"A little fear is a good thing, sweetheart," he said gently, as if reading her mind. "I'd rather go down there with a confessed coward than with a fearless fool who takes unnecessary chances. You'll be all right." And he slipped his arm around her shoulders in a comforting hug.

As THE DAYS PASSED Sydne became aware that she and Brian were being watched by the rest of the crew. In such a close community there was bound to be gossip about their relationship, and the fact that the men would single her out as Brian's property irked her. Kenny and Ricco, who had sought her company before, now kept their distance, and aside from Brian she had contact mainly with Dr. Marín and Chuck. Sydne felt alone in her struggle, and the weather added to her problems.

Since the prevailing winds had dropped, the relentless tropical sun had turned the *Adventurer* into a daily oven. The men dripped with sweat as, using sledgehammers and drills, they chipped away at the huge blocks of coral that were lifted aboard. Some of the blocks were so heavy that, in order to move them from one place to another, they had to be hoisted back into the water, where buoyancy aided in their handling.

Chunks of coral were everywhere. Some of them yielded items they had hoarded for centuries—buttons, belt buckles, nails. But no other objects of value had been recovered for some time, and there was a great deal of tension, as if each member of the crew were holding his breath.

Debris was also a serious problem. The tons of coral fragments inspected and discarded—actually the skeletons of living organisms—began to smell foul as they dried in the sun. They had to be collected regularly and dumped into the sea, away from the work area.

Between shifts, crew and divers alike kept busy breaking coral chunks, and even Gus abandoned his galley from time to time to take part in the arduous task. On occasion a glittering object was swallowed in the avalanche of coral fragments, rotten wood and sand spewed out from the mouth of the airlift. Then the men had to search for the elusive bit of metal with their arms buried up to their elbows in the muddy pile. It was in this way that a gold medal was found, its inscription reading, *Sante Francisce, ora pro nobis*.

"*Sante Francisce, ora pro nobis*—Saint Francis, pray for us." Dr. Marín frowned.

"But which one?" Sydne inquired. "Saint Francis of Assisi or Saint Francis Borgia?"

"That, my dear, I'm afraid I can't say," Dr. Marín admitted ruefully.

The medal didn't cast any conclusive light on the identity of the ship. But if the saint was Saint Francis Borgia, canonized in 1671, then the galleon could not possibly be the *Conde de Santander*, which had been lost in 1622. If only Doña Cristina had seen fit to record the years in her diary, Sydne thought in frustration. But somehow the woman had judged that detail unimportant. And if the galleon was not the *Conde*, if there was no treasure to be found, then what would happen to Brian?

AFTER THEIR ENCOUNTER with the shark, Sydne saw very little of Brian until late the following night. When someone knocked softly on her cabin door, she had no doubt about who it was. Aware that letting him in would lead to a situation she wanted to avoid, Sydne was tempted to pretend she was asleep. Perhaps if she didn't answer he would just go away, she thought wildly. But when the knock came again it seemed to echo the siren song that mariners of old couldn't resist—even when they knew it would lead them to their destruction. She wanted—she needed Brian's kisses. She longed so much to be held in his strong arms, to hear his husky voice murmuring in her ear. . . .

No! Sydne stopped herself sternly. Where was her willpower? Determined to send him away, she opened the door resolutely.

"Hi, babe," he said softly, and the way he looked at her made her resolution weaken. "I was hoping you were still up."

"I—I was about to go to bed," she stammered.

"Great idea!" Before she could even think of stopping him, Brian had stepped inside the cabin and closed the door behind him. "Too bad there's only room for one," he added with a crooked grin, eyeing the bedding she had already turned down. "But where there's a will there's a way."

Sydne looked away from his probing gaze, her cheeks hot. "It's late," she began.

Disregarding her excuses, Brian framed her flushed face with his hands. "Much too late!" he whispered before his lips met hers. He drank deeply of the sweetness of her mouth. Then, taking her by the hand, he led her toward the narrow bed.

"Oh, Brian, no!" she protested feebly. Yet she allowed herself to follow him.

"Lord, how I need you!" he groaned as, sitting down, he encircled her waist with his arms and buried his face in the swell of her breasts.

Sydne had tried to stay away, had tried to deny the truth. But all the things she wanted out of life she wanted with Brian—no one else. He had only to touch her and she was putty in his hands. And she felt more than just desire for him. Tenderness invaded her heart as she cradled his head to her breast, as if in this way she could hold him safe against the world, could soothe his pain, his worries, his need. "Oh, Brian," she sighed, stroking his hair gently and pressing her lips to his temple. She longed to tell him how very much she loved him, but the words died with her sharp intake of breath. He had unbuttoned her pajama top and was kissing her breasts, turning her flesh to jelly. If he hadn't pulled her onto his lap she might even have fallen. Her body ached for more, cried to be a part of his.

"I love you," he murmured, kissing her hungrily. "I love you, Sydne. I love you!"

He had said it—said the words she had longed to hear, the words she wanted so badly to say to him. She loved him, too—loved him desperately....

"No!" she gasped, struggling to free herself from the arms that held her prisoner. "No, I don't want your lies!" Suddenly she was blinded by tears.

"Stop it!" Brian said, capturing her hands, which were pushing him away. "Damn it, Sydne, I'm telling you once and for all that there's nothing between Julia Lozano and me! You've made it all up in your head, and I'm not going to let your suspicions keep us apart, do you hear me?"

In spite of her effort at control, a tear dripped down each of her cheeks. "Oh, babe," he groaned, loosening his insistent hold and kissing her hands, "don't do this to us!"

She could almost believe he meant what he said. She desperately wanted to, in fact. But his was a power she wouldn't easily be able to break away from once she had submitted to it, and she still wasn't sure she could trust him. She turned her face away and gave a shuddering sob.

After a tense moment he let go of her. Sydne backed away against the bulwark, clutching her pajama top to cover herself.

"I'm not going to force you, Sydne." Brian's voice sounded tired as he rose to his feet. "I can wait. It won't be easy, damn it, but I will."

THE NEXT DAY started badly for Sydne. To begin with, she overslept for the first time since she had been aboard the salvage ship. She was usually awakened by the noises of activity shortly after daybreak, but this morning she slept undisturbed through the whole thing. She shouldn't have been surprised, considering that she had cried for what seemed like endless hours after Brian had left her. The few hours of troubled sleep she had managed hadn't done much to relieve her physical and emotional weariness.

Now Sydne practically jumped out of bed when she found out how late it was. She was immobilized, however, by the stab of pain that shot behind her lids when she tried to open her eyes. Lacking the strength to get up, she remained where she was, hoping her misery would soon fade.

As she lay there Sydne tried to keep the scene with Brian out of her mind, but it kept coming back—over and over, just as it had through the long night. Things had reached a critical point between them. She had to make a decision, one she would have to abide by the rest of her life. Brian had told her that he loved her, and even though she wanted to believe him more than anything she had ever wanted in her life, Sydne couldn't erase the memory of his meeting with Julia.

Yet with each passing day she found it more difficult to resist his continuous advances, the growing intimacy that had become a part of their relationship and that she craved with both body and soul. She acknowledged the probability that her need for Brian would continue to grow each minute she remained aboard the *Adventurer*, until his lies no longer mattered. She would end up settling for whatever he wanted to give her, for however long.

For the first time in her life Sydne didn't know what to do. When she had discovered that Paul was married, she had wasted no time in putting distance between them, even though in so doing she had given up a job she loved. Now she had to decide whether to walk out on Brian and the men of the *Adventurer* and save herself, or to remain faithful to her duty and take a chance on being able to survive a tumultuous love affair.

A knock on her door interrupted her self-examination. It had to be Brian; who else ever came to her cabin? Hoping to avoid another confrontation, she refrained from answering and feigned sleep when she saw the door opening. She tried to breathe regularly when he quietly entered her cabin and stood over her, watching her in silence.

"What's the matter, Sydne?" Brian asked gently. "Are you ill?"

Realizing that Brian hadn't been taken in by her performance, she kept her eyes closed, still refusing to look at him when she answered, "I have a headache."

After all the tears she had shed during the night, Sydne didn't think she had any left, but she felt the telltale weakness overcoming her as he sat on the edge of the bunk and tenderly touched her face. "Have you taken anything for it?"

"No, I just need some rest."

"Have you any aspirin?"

"In the locker."

She felt his weight shift from the bed and heard him rummaging through her things. He filled a glass with water.

"Here you are, babe," he said. When she tried to raise her head he added, "Let me help you."

Putting his arm around her, he lifted her up so that she could swallow comfortably. When she had taken the pills he eased her down again. She welcomed the coolness of the damp washcloth that he ran gently over her face and neck.

"Don't try to work today, babe. Stay here and get some rest," he murmured, brushing her hair back from her face and tenderly stroking her cheek. "I'll look in on you later, but promise you'll send for me if there's anything you need, okay?"

Sydne was so choked up with tears that she couldn't answer. Instead she simply bobbed her head, and he dropped a gentle kiss on her brow before he left the cabin, closing the door softly behind him.

It was then that the dam broke, and she turned her face to the wall, weeping raggedly. It didn't matter what she kept telling herself—that the long years of loneliness she had known were what made her so vulnerable to the wonderful tenderness Brian showed her; that that was what made her body respond so quickly, so intensely to his passion. She not only loved Brian, she needed him, and her heart refused to accept what her mind dictated as the only intelligent course of action left to her: to leave the ship, to forget Brian.

For the next hour or so Sydne crossed and recrossed the first line between an exhausted wakefulness and sleep. When she finally opened her eyes again the pain had lessened considerably. The temperature inside the cabin was ovenlike, however, and her body was drenched in sweat.

Dreaming in vain of a cool shower, she sponged herself down, then liberally splashed eau de cologne on her body, relishing the fresh feeling even though she knew the relief would only be temporary. Disregarding Brian's previous warning about her dress code, Sydne pulled on a pair of shorts and a loose cotton top that would allow the maximum ventilation for her overheated body.

Ricco and Dr. Marín were eating their lunch by the time she made it to the galley.

"Hello," she greeted them as she subsided onto a chair at the table.

Both men answered, but it was Dr. Marín who inquired, "How are you, my dear? Brian said you weren't feeling well this morning."

"Nothing serious," she replied. "I'll be back at work this afternoon." It wasn't until she looked at Ricco and noticed how awkwardly the diver was trying to ignore the conversation that Sydne realized how the Professor's words could be misconstrued. Maybe by now the Italian thought that she and Brian had spent the night together, and she tried to mask her embarrassment.

"You looked exhausted, Sydne," Dr. Marín continued, oblivious to the awkwardness of his two companions. "I'm afraid much of the blame is mine for letting you carry the burden alone for so long and missing out on your leave. You must talk to Brian about sending you ashore as soon as possible."

That would be the perfect solution, Sydne silently agreed. "We've already discussed it, Dr. Marín, and I'm just waiting for the launch to return ashore— probably tomorrow or the day after." Trying to change the subject, she turned to Ricco. "How's your family, Ricco? Have you heard from them lately?"

The diver smiled and nodded. "I got three letters in the last mail. Constanza sent me some snapshots of Gina's birthday party."

"Gina is your youngest, isn't she?"

Again Ricco nodded. "She turned six last month."

"I'd love to see the pictures sometime," Sydne said sincerely.

That was all the encouragement he needed, and resuming his former friendliness toward her he pulled an envelope out of his shirt pocket. "Thought you'd never ask," he said, grinning.

He spread the photographs on the table, and for the next few minutes both Sydne and Dr. Marín admired pictures of the large Italian family celebrating the child's birthday—a birthday her father had missed. Then Ricco looked at his watch and jumped to his feet. "*Mamma mia*, I've got to run! I'm diving in ten minutes and still have to suit up."

"I hope you'll be home for the next celebration, Ricco," Sydne said.

"I hope the same— No, keep them for me until I get back," he said when she started to return the photographs to him. "I haven't got time now. Give them back to me later, okay?"

"Sure, Ricco," Sydne called after him, and when he had gone she and Dr. Marín finished looking at the pictures.

"Thank you, Gus," Sydne murmured as the cook set a plate of food in front of her. She wasn't really hungry, but decided that some food in her stomach would help dissipate the effects of the aspirin Brian had given her earlier.

"Well, I'm off to take my nap," Dr. Marín said a few minutes later. It was his custom to rest through the worst heat of the day before resuming his work in the afternoon, a habit Sydne herself found helpful in such a sultry climate.

"I'll see you later, doctor," Sydne replied.

"Don't go back to work unless you feel up to it," he admonished in a fatherly voice. "I can take care of things until you get back from your leave."

She felt grateful for his concern. "I'm all right now, Dr. Marín," she said warmly. "Have a nice nap."

After he had left, Sydne toyed with the food on her plate for a few more minutes before pushing it away and concentrating on her cup of coffee. Two or three crew members came and went with no more than a brief greeting exchanged, affording Sydne the time to plan her coming shore leave. For the time being she decided to postpone her decision about whether or not to return. Dr. Marín was right; she was exhausted and in no condition to make an intelligent choice. Perhaps once she had spent some time away from Brian's influence, things wouldn't seem as bleak as they did at this moment.

Two days earlier Brian had told her she could take the launch when it returned ashore, but now she wasn't sure if he would keep his word and let her go. He'd better, she thought, becoming aware of a gnawing feeling inside her that she knew wouldn't leave her until she was actually under way.

So immersed was she in her own thoughts that she jumped and almost spilled the remains of her coffee when she heard Brian's voice speaking to her.

"W-what?" she stammered looking at him with eyes that were wide and bewildered.

"I asked how you were feeling," Brian replied. "Headache all gone?"

"Yes, thank you. I'm fine."

He gave her a searching look. "You still look a little green around the gills," he quipped. "If I didn't know better I'd say you have quite a hangover, babe."

She wasn't in the mood for joking, and his attempt at levity fell flat. "Brian, you said that I could go on my leave when the launch returns ashore," she reminded him.

Keeping his attention on the coffee he was pouring into a cup, he didn't meet her eyes as he answered, "Yes, I said that, didn't I?"

The gnawing feeling inside her became a knot. Sydne jumped abruptly to her feet. He couldn't go back on his word now; he simply couldn't! "Yes, you did! Oh, Brian, don't do this to me, please!" She was almost in tears and hated herself for not being more assertive. "I need a break, Brian. I must get some rest!"

Seeing her obvious agitation, Brian put his coffee cup on the table and took her in his arms. With all the fight suddenly gone out of her, Sydne let herself be drawn into his embrace.

"Calm down, love," he said gently as he stroked

her hair. "I said you could go and you will. I'll take you myself. I promise. There are so many beautiful places I want to show you in—"

Without letting him finish she pulled away from him. "No!" she exclaimed explosively.

He raised a dark brow as he echoed, "No?"

She shook her head emphatically. "I don't want you with me, Brian! I need to be alone!"

He started to say something, but at that moment Kenny came running into the galley. "Brian!" he cried. "Oh, thank God I've found you!"

"What's wrong?" Brian inquired, and Sydne could see that he was instantly alert.

Kenny was almost out of breath. "It's Ricco," he panted.

"Ricco!" Sydne exclaimed.

Kenny nodded. "There's been a cave-in. He's trapped down there."

Sydne's eyes swung quickly to Brian, but he had already started out of the galley. As soon as she could make her legs move again she followed the men up on deck, where a scene of frantic activity met her eyes.

All the divers were suiting up for the rescue mission—Brian, too. At the same time he was interrogating Bernardo, who had been diving with Ricco when the cave-in had occurred.

Sydne moved toward them.

"How much air do you think he has left?" Brian was asking.

"If his equipment wasn't damaged, he should have enough for half an hour," Bernardo answered, his face pale from having witnessed the harrowing experience. "We couldn't have been down there more than ten minutes when it happened."

"We're ready, Brian," Rod called.

"Hold it a minute," Brian replied, facing the anxious men. "I want three of you to come with me now. The rest will wait here until needed."

Every one of the divers volunteered, but Brian picked Bernardo, Nikko and Rod to accompany him. The others remained on deck, waiting impatiently to be called to the aid of their friend.

Sydne searched their faces for some sign that she could take as encouragement for Ricco's fate. All she saw was deep concern, perhaps even fear, because an accident like this was a grim reminder of what could happen to any one of them—a warning that in spite of their experience and training, none of them was completely safe in this profession.

Some five minutes later Brian surfaced alone and climbed aboard. Sydne was among those who gathered anxiously around him to hear the news about the situation below.

"Okay, here it is," Brian told the group. "A wall of coral caved in, trapping Ricco inside. We think he's still alive. We could hear some faint metallic sounds that might be a signal he's sending. He should have enough air to last him about twenty minutes more. But that's only an assumption, so let's try to get him out in less time than that. Kenny, Ray, you two get down there and help with the rescue operation. Take turns with Rod and Bernardo on the airlift. Ernie, Claude and Randy, you stand by to take over from them in ten minutes' time. We have to work fast. There's no time to lose, and fresh men work faster. Let's go."

"Brian?" Sydne called. When he turned to her she asked anxiously, "Isn't there anything I can do?"

He touched her face gently. "You can pray, babe."

With a feeling of dread Sydne watched him turn away abruptly, to be swallowed up by the treacherous sea. Twenty minutes was such a short time! *Oh, God, don't let Ricco die like this,* she prayed fervently.

Then Chuck came up to her. "Sydne, would you mind helping Gus get some coffee for the men?" he asked.

Grateful to have something—anything—to do, she immediately replied, "Yes, yes, of course," and ran to the galley. She told the cook what was happening and he set about preparing a large pot. As she waited distractedly, Sydne spotted the photographs of Ricco's family she and Dr. Marín had been admiring only minutes earlier. She started collecting them to put back inside the envelope, but as she did so she couldn't stem the disconsolate tears that ran down her cheeks. This mischievous little birthday girl, on the other side of the Atlantic, was totally unaware that her father might never return home. It was with a terrible feeling of impotence that Sydne took the coffeepot Gus had prepared and the stack of Styrofoam cups up to the men waiting on deck.

She was almost there when the drone of the compressor changed to a sort of squealing, high-pitched noise. The mood of the men changed instantly from expectancy to fear. One of the divers was already running toward the compressor, and he switched it off.

"What's wrong?" Sydne asked the first man who accepted a cup of coffee from her. He was a crewman whose name she didn't know, but his face had turned ashen.

"The compressor has gone out," the man replied soberly.

Sydne's hand was shaking so much she almost spilled the coffee. "But that means the airlift can't be used!"

The man looked at her and nodded. "Exactly."

Afraid of the answer, she still forced herself to ask, "How—how long will it take to repair?"

Bleakly the man shook his head. "Too long."

A couple of mechanics summoned by Chuck were already beginning to take the compressor apart when Brian and the first group of rescuers reappeared on the surface. "What happened to the compressor?" Brian asked impatiently as soon as he came aboard. "The airlift is dead."

Chuck shook his head. "I'm afraid it's more serious than we expected, Brian. Russ says it won't be operational for a while. Apparently one of the seals broke, and the compressor has to be taken apart to replace a bearing. It may take three hours."

Brian cursed under his breath. "We only have minutes, Chuck. See what you can do about it." Without wasting time on lamentations, he immediately directed his attention to reorganizing his forces. In a minute three extra men carrying additional air tanks with them were on their way down to manually perform the airlift's work.

As soon as Brian himself had gone under again, Sydne checked her watch. Barely eight more minutes remained of the original twenty. They would have to hurry if they were going to find Ricco alive. She wanted to hold each minute back with her hands. Chuck, she knew, had given her this choice of serving coffee partly to keep her from going out of her mind with worry. But it didn't help much. She felt totally useless as she hurried below to refill the pot.

She willed her mind to become a blank. She couldn't bear to think of the woman in Sorrento who might be about to lose the man she loved, of the children who might never see their father alive again. Gina was so young she would probably even forget what he looked like....

Only three minutes were left when she returned topside—minutes that much too quickly ticked down to one. *God, help them save Ricco,* she prayed anxiously, clinging tightly to the ship's railing while scanning the rolling surface of the sea. But there was no sign of life.

"Sydne, why don't you go back to your cabin," Chuck said quietly.

Until he spoke Sydne hadn't realized she was crying. "He's dead, isn't he, Chuck? Does that mean Ricco is dead?"

"We don't know, Sydne."

"But twenty minutes are over!" she argued between sobs.

"Yes, I know, but that was only an estimate, and a conservative one at that," Chuck told her gently. "You must remember that Ricco is an experienced diver, and he'll be conserving his air as much as he can. Besides, if there's anything to be done to keep him alive, Brian will do it. Just keep the faith a little longer.''

A dark head surfaced beside the *Adventurer*, but Sydne's vision was so blurred by her tears that she couldn't tell it was Claude until the man removed his mask. He was hoisted aboard in nothing flat and immediately surrounded by the divers.

''How is he?'' was the first question thrown at him.

Still trying to catch his breath, Claude nodded his head. ''He's alive.''

A collective sigh of relief followed his statement.

''He's still trapped, but we've managed to dig a hole through the coral to provide him with air. However, we can't get the tank through yet, so one of us has to stay with him at all times to make sure the hose doesn't get blocked or twisted. That's why Brian sent me back. He wants two more men to help with the digging.''

Chuck selected two men, and as soon as they had gone he turned to Sydne. ''You see?'' He grinned, and with a wink added, ''Brian just bought him another hour. If we're lucky we might have the airlift working by then.''

Sydne gave him a feeble but grateful smile as he went off to check on the mechanics, who by this time had disassembled the compressor, scattering the parts in an order known only to them on a piece of cloth.

For the next while the talk consisted of nothing but bearings and seals and shafts. The meaning of most of it went over her head, but the men seemed to make sense out of it. They seemed particularly discouraged when, some time later, the head mechanic announced that the shaft had been scored.

"What about replacing it?" inquired Chuck, who had been left in charge of getting the compressor back to work as soon as possible.

Russ, the mechanic, told him that they didn't carry a spare and that the shaft would have to be machined before the compressor could be put back to work again—a procedure that would probably take an entire day.

"But we haven't got that much time," Chuck replied firmly. He took a moment to think things through and then queried, "What would happen if we simply replaced the bearing without machining the shaft? Will it work?"

"It may work—for a couple of hours at the most before it breaks down again." The man shrugged.

Chuck didn't hesitate. "Then put it back together and get it to work as soon as you can," he ordered.

"It may ruin the shaft in the process," the mechanic pointed out.

"You said it might give us a couple of hours," Chuck replied succinctly. "Two hours may be all Ricco needs."

FIFTEEN MINUTES LATER the men who had been digging below came up to rest while others took their places. Brian wasn't with them. In fact, Sydne hadn't seen him since the compressor had gone out, and she was becoming worried. Already he had stayed below for much too long, apparently changing air tanks without bothering to surface. She had heard him speak often enough about the possible dangerous effects of pressure on the human body, and she hoped that he would have enough sense not to spend more time below than was prudent, even under the current circumstances. She was thinking along these lines when she spotted Chuck, whom she hadn't seen for a while. He was in his wet suit and apparently on his way to relieve Brian. A rush of gladness washed over her as she saw him disappear beneath the surface.

Then she had to wait impatiently for the familiar dark head to appear, as it did moments later. Like the others, Brian was immediately surrounded and bombarded with questions about the latest developments. In spite of how much Sydne wanted to hear about what had been going on, she waited a little apart from the others before she gathered enough courage to approach Brian and offer him a cup of coffee.

"How is it going, Brian?" she asked then. "How much longer can Ricco stay down there? It's been almost an hour and a half."

Until voicing her question, Sydne hadn't remembered that ninety minutes was the duration of a regular diving shift. Under ordinary circumstances that length of time had never seemed too great to her, but this time it had seemed like an eternity. Then again, there was nothing ordinary about a man being trapped underwater, in an element where he couldn't survive without the use of artificial methods. If it had happened to a complete stranger Sydne would have felt desperately worried, but when that man was a friend the tragedy came even closer to home. She had only known Ricco for a few weeks, and already she felt close to him and his family. So she could well imagine how Brian must be feeling, and could understand why he would need her moral support. She wasn't surprised, therefore, when he put his free arm around her waist, after taking the cup she offered, while he answered her questions about the rescue. To Sydne the gesture seemed totally natural, but for a fleeting moment she wondered what the men on deck with them would think. In a way Brian's gesture was an announcement that Sydne was his woman, that she belonged to him.

"It shouldn't be too long now, babe," he answered. "At least we've been able to get air to him, and he's holding up well enough."

"Is he hurt?"

"That we don't know as yet. The main thing right now is getting him out of there. We'll worry about the rest later."

He had spared her all the time he could, and after draining his cup he went over to see how the mechanics were doing. It only took a few more minutes to finish a job that ordinarily would have taken hours, and when the switch was pulled the familiar roar of the compressor sounded like heavenly music to everyone's ears.

For the first time since her arrival Sydne saw the decompression chamber she and Brian had transported from Santo Domingo being put into use as it was readied to receive Ricco. This was only a precautionary measure, Brian had said, but she wasn't sure if he was telling the truth. After all, Ricco had spent nearly two hours under water.

Soon everything that could be made ready had

been; now all the men had to do was free Ricco from his underwater trap.

Once the airlift was operational again, the job of clearing the coral debris became an easier task. It was approximately a quarter of an hour later when the swarm of divers finally surfaced, pulling Ricco with them. There was a moment of suspense. Everyone seemed to be holding his breath, waiting for a sign of life in the body Chuck and Bernardo held afloat between them. Then Ricco waved a hand. The cheering and whistling that followed were almost deafening, and many of the men jumped into the sea to help bring him aboard.

Sydne found herself crying again, this time tears of happiness and immense relief. She wanted to know if Ricco had been injured, but Moose was examining him and she didn't want to interfere.

From the jokes that soon began circulating among the men, Sydne deduced that Ricco had received no more than a few cuts and bruises in an accident that could so easily have been fatal. Once her mind had been set to rest she went back to the galley, where she sat at the table nursing a cup of coffee and waiting for her nerves to settle down. As she sat there she offered a prayer of thanks for the happy ending to a dramatic afternoon. On the table was the envelope containing Ricco's family photographs, and with a lighter heart she picked it up, intending to return it to Ricco when she saw him again.

During those few hours of suspense and fear Sydne hadn't once dwelled on her own dilemma. When compared to a human life, troubles of the heart seemed almost unimportant. But now the crisis was over. Ricco had been saved, and one day soon he would be joining his wife and children, never to leave them again.

And where would Sydne be then? Riding high on Brian's passion, or nursing a broken heart?

In spite of the tension of the past few days, they held a small consolation. The scarcity of new discoveries had permitted her and Dr. Marín to catch up with the backlog that had accumulated during his absence. Sydne spent what was left of the afternoon doing precisely that as she filled in the details of the rescue for Dr. Marín, who had slept through a good part of the afternoon drama.

She didn't see Ricco at dinnertime, so when she saw Brian that evening she asked about his condition.

"Still a little shaken by the experience, but he seems to be all right," he replied. "In fact, he's refused to go to the hospital for a checkup. Moose says he seems fine, so I can't force him to go if he doesn't want to."

Sydne handed Brian the envelope with the photographs. "Will you return these to him?" she asked. "I'm sure he would like to have them back as soon as possible. And please say hello for me."

"Sure, babe." He slipped the envelope in his shirt pocket and continued with his meal.

Only then did Sydne remember what she and Brian had been discussing in this very room when they had been interrupted by the news of Ricco's accident. Suddenly she felt a little awkward, but the presence of others served as an excuse not to bring up the subject. She knew it had to be discussed between them sooner or later. The later the better, however, since there was sure to be an argument if Brian went back on his promise to send her ashore. Realizing it was cowardly, Sydne finished her dinner and retired to her cabin early, leaving Brian in the galley discussing the rescue operation, which continued to be the topic of the day.

An hour went by and then another, and she was beginning to think that he wouldn't stop by at all that evening when she heard him knocking on the door.

"May I come in?" he said as she opened it, and didn't seem surprised to find her still fully dressed.

This was the first time he had asked her permission to enter her quarters, and Sydne wasn't sure whether she should take it as a good sign or a bad one. "Please, do. I wanted to talk to you, Brian."

The cabin was so small that it seemed really cramped when he stepped in and stood next to her. Most of the other times he had been there she'd found herself wrapped in his arms almost as soon as he arrived, and this closeness without touching felt strange to her. Nervously she invited him to sit on the bunk, which he did, waiting for her to speak up.

"When is the launch going ashore, Brian?" she asked before she let herself become intimidated.

"The day after tomorrow," he answered simply.

"Good. At what time?"

"Around six-thirty."

"In the morning?" Sydne gasped. She'd never been much of an early riser.

He chuckled and said, "You know how early we start around here. Any problem with that?"

"No, of course not. I'll be ready."

He reached for her then, and before Sydne knew it

she was sitting on his lap. "Why are you so determined to get away from me, babe?"

He wasn't really expecting an answer from her. Otherwise he wouldn't have covered her mouth with his own. Sydne's response to his kiss was as it had always been—as it always would be. She gave all the love she had for him, all the sweetness she was capable of, all the passion she felt burning within her. He drank it all from her lips, and in return filled her heart with a longing that only he could satisfy, bringing every nerve in her body to such awareness that she seemed to feel through every pore the hands that caressed her so intimately, so lovingly, so tenderly.

"Why, Sydne?" he murmured almost incoherently between kisses. "Why do you continue torturing us both?"

But she didn't want him to stop loving her! She had told him that with her hands, her lips, her body. Her resistance had already reached its weakest point, and she was lying limp with desire in his arms, her clothing definitely awry. The emotional struggle of the past twenty-four hours had drained her completely of any strength to resist, and at this moment she was his for the taking. How she hated the tears that accompanied her surrender, tears that welled up in her eyes and flowed down her cheeks like a river without her being able to stop them.

Brian didn't see them until he tasted them on her skin. He stopped kissing her abruptly to look at her, but Sydne kept her eyes close to hide her shame at appearing so vulnerable.

"All right, Sydne, you win," she heard him say

bleakly. "You can leave the ship the day after tomorrow. I won't touch you and I won't stop you, if that's what you want."

Her eyes opened in disbelief, and all she managed to say was, "Oh, Brian!"

Heaving a weary sigh, he let her go and rose to his feet. "Good night, Syd." He bent down to kiss her forehead one last time before he left the cabin.

Sydne stared at the door closing behind him, refusing to believe that he had really gone. It was then that she made up her mind that she would not be coming back to the *Adventurer*.

She knew she wouldn't be able to sleep right away, not the way she felt. Instead she began packing her belongings, as if in doing so she was taking a final step that would not allow her to change her mind. She was clearing out the drawer where she kept her jewelry when one of her pearl earrings slipped from her fingers and fell to the floor. It rolled under the bunk, so Sydne had to go down on all fours to look for it. When she did she saw that something else had been dropped there, too. She reached for both items, and the pearl earring came out in her hand along with a shining golden disc. It was the *escudo* she had found during her dive to the shipwreck with Brian. She had completely forgotten about it.

Holding the coin in the palm of her hand, Sydne remembered how she had slipped it inside the bra of her bathing suit while they were swimming. It must have fallen out undetected during the lovemaking that had followed their return to the ship. . . .

And for the first time, Sydne took a good long look at the gold coin. Unlike the silver ones Nikko had found earlier, this one had survived the centuries of burial at sea with all its markings intact. It had been minted in Seville, Spain.

Thoughtfully turning the coin over in her hand, Sydne reviewed in her mind all the artifacts that had already been recovered from the ill-fated ship. Except for Doña Cristina's diary, which didn't really shed any light on the identity of the ship, all the items could have been carried aboard a ship heading toward the New World—not the other way around.

"Wait a minute!" Sydne said out loud. What a fool she had been! There *was* a way of finding out whether it was the *Conde* that Doña Cristina had traveled on, and she would have thought of it had she not been so distracted by Brian Stevens. The ship's passenger list—if Brian had been able to get hold of it!

CHAPTER SEVEN

IN SPITE OF THE ABSENCE of any more valuable finds,
morale continued to run high. Laughter and singing
accompanied the backbreaking work that went on
day after day, making Sydne wonder occasionally if
the good humor and cheerfulness weren't partly a
means of hiding uneasiness. With the hurricane
season upon them, the pace accelerated. Even after
darkness fell the work usually continued, the divers
excavating with the help of powerful floodlights. For
those who worked aboard, chipping at the coral
chunks extracted from the sea, wind that rose in the
evening and the frequent cooling rain brought welcome relief from the heat of the day and the sting of
salt and coral dust that clung so tenaciously to their
sweat-drenched bodies.

Under water, the salvage operation had become a
constant trial of perseverance for the divers, who had
to work in the dense forest of coral lying dead and
broken in the muck at the bottom of the sea. More
and more frequently the airlift jammed and the normal procedure of opening and closing the air hose
was not enough to clear the obstruction. Then
precious hours had to be wasted in disassembling the
equipment.

But quiet descended upon the *Adventurer* late in

the evenings. It was then time to relax, to read, to joke and dream of what to do with the riches that everyone expected to get out of this adventure. While others talked, Reynaldo played his guitar, and the haunting love songs that came from his strings made Sydne long more than ever for strong arms to hold her and a husky voice to murmur in her ear. But Brian had kept his word. She had hardly seen him since he'd last come to her cabin. The way he was looking at her tonight, however, her last evening aboard the salvage ship, told Sydne that his thoughts were following the same path as hers. The realization sent a shiver of excitement through her, one that she was unable and unwilling to control.

She had pleaded, demanded and begged to be allowed to go away, and now that the time was near all she wanted was to be close to Brian again. Two days without his kisses had seemed more like a century. And perhaps he had caught the messages her eyes kept sending in his direction, for she saw him advancing toward her. The surge of emotions that came over her combined incredible joy and agonizing pain.

Wordlessly he took her by the hand and led her aft, to the area where she worked during the day and which was now deserted. Sydne wanted to be kissed so badly that she was sharply disappointed when Brian simply put his arm around her shoulders as he looked out across the dark sea.

"I'm leaving tomorrow," she said at last when he didn't speak. Forcing her voice to sound casual, she added, "Have you any messages for Andrew?"

"Andrew?" he repeated absently. "No, there's no need. We keep in touch by radio." At her exclamation of surprise he went on to explain, "He had one installed in his cottage."

"Why didn't you tell me?" She heard the note of annoyance in her voice and bit her lip.

He gave her a wry look. "So you could call in the cavalry?"

Conscious of her burning cheeks, Sydne refrained from pressing the point. It would only lead to an argument, and that was the last thing she wanted at this moment, her last chance to be with him. What she did want was to touch him, to carry away with her the taste of his kisses, because after tonight he would disappear from her life forever. It hadn't been easy for her to stand by that decision, especially after she had examined the *Conde*'s passenger list, which Brian had copied from the files of the Spanish archives. As it turned out, he had already checked out that lead, and she, too, had failed to find anyone by the name of Cristina. She had then tried for Doña Ana, Tina's faithful old servant, but Ana was such a common name even then that there had been three on the list.

"Please, Brian, let's not argue," she said softly, touching his arm. "Not tonight."

She had the uneasy feeling he could read her thoughts when he looked at her and frowned, and before she could stop herself Sydne reached out and touched his face.

"You seem worried." She smoothed the crease from his brow with her fingers. "Won't you tell me what's wrong?"

"It's nothing, babe," he denied unconvincingly.

She had been watching him all day, trying to fill

her eyes with him. There had been a certain tension about him, especially when he had watched the red and golden rays of a beautiful sunset piercing through clouds that were purple and black.

"Is it the weather?" she insisted.

He seemed to debate with himself before finally admitting, "Yes, I think we're in for a bad time."

"How bad?"

He let a few seconds go by before answering, "A hurricane."

"A hurricane! But the weather bureau hasn't issued any warnings," she argued, arching a delicate brow. "Are you sure?"

He shook his head. "No, I'm not," he admitted wryly, "but all the signs are there, and this *is* the hurricane season."

"What are you going to do?"

He shrugged his shoulders. "Until we know for sure, stay and try to get as much work done as we possibly can." He paused and then with a sigh of exasperation exclaimed, "Damn, we're so close! I'd hate to give up now!" Gazing out again at the mysterious sea, he seemed to be seriously considering how to answer her question. "If the weather holds we're going to continue digging that trench for another day or so," he said at last. "My guess is that the hull is almost totally buried in the sand. If we can only get through a few more feet, we're bound to hit the deck."

Sydne thought of the medal with its ambiguous inscription, of the golden *escudo* she had found and of the consequences if the galleon turned out to be other than the *Conde*. But at this moment Brian had enough on his mind; she shouldn't bring up that particular problem.

Suddenly she realized that she would not be taking the launch in the morning. No matter how much she had insisted on leaving the ship, she could not walk out now that Brian might be facing danger, and perhaps even financial ruin. She would never be able to live with herself if she did. There was really nothing she could do except stand by him and offer her support for whatever it was worth. Apart from her love, it was all she had to give.

All the tenderness she felt for him was shining in her eyes when she looked up and said, "I don't think I'll be leaving tomorrow after all, Brian. I've changed my mind."

His eyes searched her face. "We might be in for a rough time, Sydne," he warned. "Are you sure?"

"Yes, I'm sure," she answered without hesitation.

The blue eyes were no longer clouded as he drew her into his arms, and clinging to him, returning his kisses, Sydne needed no words to tell Brian how much she loved him.

THE SALVAGE WORK CONTINUED as usual, and it was late the following day when Brian was called over to examine a piece of plank that had been brought aboard. It was a section of packing attached to the plank, still secured by a few rusty nails, that claimed all this attention.

"What do you think?" Chuck inquired.

Brian examined it carefully, then looked at his friend quizzically. "A stopper for a leak?" The majority of the Spanish galleons had leaked like sieves.

and this looked suspiciously like a patch-up job. "But that would mean we're close to the hull, not the deck as we had believed." He glanced at his wristwatch. "Let's get our gear."

The water was as unpleasant as the weather. Sediment falling from the metal baskets made for poor visibility in the work area, and the diggers had run into a wall of limestone that was proving difficult to demolish.

After inspecting the work site where the stopper had been found, Brian and Chuck circled the area in an attempt to determine the exact position of the shipwreck. When they had finished, the two men returned to the salvage ship to plot a new plan of action. Sydne and Dr. Marín joined them as the map of the shipwreck was being spread out on the table.

"If our estimate is correct, the upper and lower batteries should be here and here," Brian stated, indicating the site on the map.

Chuck studied the drawing and bobbed his head thoughtfully. "You're going for the cannon." It was not a question.

"It's the quickest way to determine once and for all what we have down there," Brian replied.

"*If* the markings are still intact," Dr. Marín interrupted.

"They should be," Brian said, "or at least some of them might be. And we're close enough to go for it."

Sydne listened to the exchange in silence, watching Brian's face with a sense of foreboding. If the foundry markings on the cannon didn't check with those listed on the *Conde*'s arms list, then the ship below them was not the one they were after. The possibility of a treasure would become more uncertain, but lack of evidence would help Brian decide on a quick course of action in an emergency—like the weather. In the event of a hurricane, the site would have to be abandoned regardless of possible treasure, but at least they would know whether or not to continue with the salvaging later. Brian was the chief investor in the venture, but the other men had been promised a share and they had all worked long and hard to find the *Conde*. They were entitled to choose to abandon the project, as was Andrew. But would Brian give up, Sydne asked herself, realizing how very little she knew about the man she loved.

THERE WAS NO CHANGE in the weather the next day. Two teams of divers worked at the designated task without interruption, and it was late in the afternoon when Brian's estimate proved correct. News that the upper battery had been found spread like wildfire through the *Adventurer*, but it was too late in the day to attempt to haul the cannon aboard. There was no doubt in Sydne's mind that there would be very little sleep that night, at least for her.

Brian had been so busy lately that she had had no opportunity to talk to him in private. When she couldn't find him after dinner she went to her cabin, hoping that he would seek her out. But when hours passed and he failed to appear, the cabin walls began to close in on her and she ventured out to find him.

It took her a while, but she was determined, and she finally found him alone on the darkened bridge, monitoring the weather bureau on the radio.

"Hi, babe." He smiled at her. In the faint light

from the console she could see the lines of weariness on his face as he drew her onto his lap. "You should be sleeping," he remonstrated gently. The palm of his hand was warm on her cheek, and his lips met the sweetness of hers in a long but gentle kiss that stirred her deeply.

"Look who's talking," she retorted, holding his hand against her cheek. When he smiled wryly she added, "Any news on the weather?"

"No change." He shrugged, but she could see he was still worried.

"You're still uneasy."

"I suppose I am," he admitted. "It's just a vague feeling I can't seem to shake. I've seen the signs before—in the Indian Ocean, in the China Sea—just before a hurricane."

"You were in the navy then."

"Uh-huh."

And when he didn't elaborate, she prodded, "For how long?"

"Six years."

"How old were you, then?"

"Old enough."

He seemed reluctant to talk about himself, but she wanted to know all about him. Her next question was silenced with a kiss, however. He needed a shave, and the stubble on his cheeks scraped her tender skin as he nuzzled her throat, but she didn't mind.

"Better get some sleep, babe," he sighed a few minutes later. "Tomorrow is a big day."

"And you?"

"I still have another hour to go."

"Let me stay with you."

"You need your beauty sleep," he teased with a tired smile. "Now scoot!"

Reluctantly Sydne got up from his lap. "Good night, Brian."

"Sweet dreams, babe."

She began to walk away, then stopped and turned to face him. "Brian, what will you do if the galleon isn't the *Conde*? Will you abandon the salvage?"

Brian frowned and regarded her soberly. "We'll find out soon enough," he said at last.

Why won't you tell me, Sydne wanted to ask as she stood there hesitantly. But his frown was a sign that he had no inclination to discuss the subject. It was late, he was tired and Sydne thought it prudent not to insist.

"Good night, Brian," she said again.

She had been a fool, Sydne told herself as she went below, fighting tears of disappointment. She was so in love with him that it had been easy for a moment to let herself believe there could be a future for them. But the same man who kissed her, who touched her and caressed her, would share nothing else of himself. All he felt for her was desire, pure and simple, and she had been stupid enough to believe there was more.

But never again, she promised herself.

DRIPPING STREAMS OF SEAWATER, a greenish loglike tube hung suspended from the hoist of the *Adventurer*. The crew maneuvered the heavy object onto the deck and stood back while Dr. Marín and Sydne began to clean up the cannon, looking for the foundry markings indicating its weight. Three other cannons had already been examined, but after three hundred years at the bottom of the sea, had failed to retain their markings. This one was their last chance.

Little by little the green slime gave way to the gleam of bronze. The markings were barely legible, but after some deliberation they were deciphered: 30q 10 lb.—thirty quintals and ten pounds. The *Conde*'s gun list was carefully scrutinized.

"The cannon's not here," Brian said, his face set in an unreadable mask. He turned and made his way to the bridge.

Sydne's mouth went dry. She wanted to run after him, but instead asked Dr. Marín, "Would it be possible that, even though the cannon is not on the list, the galleon might still be the *Conde*?"

"Anything is possible, my dear." Dr. Marín shrugged. "The Spaniards kept very accurate accounts, but there was a great deal of smuggling going on, as you probably know. Actually, there were times when the contraband was more valuable than the legal cargo. Most of the ships weren't in very good condition, and they were difficult to maneuver. They also had to carry a tremendous supply of armament to protect themselves from their enemies."

An idea began to take shape in Sydne's mind. "Would it be possible for them to remove some of the cannons to make room for the cargo—legal or not?"

"Exactly, my dear." Dr. Marín's eyes sparkled. "You've understood my line of thinking. If they were examined in Havana and couldn't present their total armament, they would have to replace the cannons missing. Mind you, this is just a theory," he hastened to add.

"Of course," she said with a grateful smile, "but I think Brian should know about the possibility."

Before Sydne could look for him, Brian appeared on the bridge to address the crew, who had gathered topside to await his decision.

"As you all know, the identity of the shipwreck is still unknown," he began, "but it's reasonable to assume that it's not the *Conde*. However, we have worked long and hard during the past few weeks to gain access to the galleon, and we're too close now to abandon this project. The *Conde* was not the only galleon carrying gold bullion and valuable cargo, so we still stand a reasonable chance to make a profit. Those of you who choose to continue with the salvage will do so under the same terms we established before. Anyone wishing to step out can pick up his pay and be taken ashore in the morning when we resume work. But let me remind you," he added, "that giving up now will only ensure the loss."

Brian, Sydne realized, must have made this decision beforehand. Why had he refused to tell her? She didn't understand.

Minutes later she and Dr. Marín found Brian pouring himself a cup of coffee in the galley. Together they told him their theory, Sydne eagerly filling in where her co-worker left gaps.

"Keep it to yourselves, okay?" Brian said when they had finished.

"But Brian," Sydne protested, "can't you see that the men might walk out on you?"

"Most of these men have worked for me a long time, Sydne," he told her. "They trust me and I trust them. I want them to make their decision based on facts, not on wishful thinking."

His tone left no room for argument, and with a sinking heart Sydne turned away. But when she emerged on deck she was astonished to see that the activity had resumed as if nothing had happened. Not one single man would walk out on the job, she realized, feeling the sting of tears. Brian was right. He knew and trusted his men and, in turn, was trusted by them. If only he would trust her, too.

And perhaps as a reward for their loyalty, fate stepped in. That night, after a long period of finding little of value, a cache of blackened silver bars was retrieved from the depths, leading the crew to hope even greater treasures lay waiting to be discovered.

IN THE MORNING the color of the sea had changed from blue and green to a gray, and the water had lost its transparency. A vague feeling of apprehension replaced the usual good cheer as the men watched great clouds roll across the sky, seeming to touch the sea. The wind had died down completely; the heat was unbearable. Brian's fears seemed to be turning into reality.

At noon the Miami Weather Bureau finally issued a hurricane warning.

Randy rushed into the galley to convey the news. "But they said it will pass to the northeast," he said, softening the blow. "We should be okay."

"Weather forecasting isn't a precise science," Brian reminded him with a worried frown. "I don't have to tell you what will happen if we're caught by a hurricane sitting in the middle of this reef.''

"What are you going to do?'' Sydne couldn't help asking.

But she could read his thoughts, evident from the expression on his face. Brian turned toward the ominous sea, visible through a porthole. Did he have the right to risk the *Adventurer* and the lives aboard for the sake of an uncertain promise of riches? On the other hand, the men had worked hard. Many of them abandoning other projects to take this one on. They had made it clear they wanted to stay.

Maybe the weather forecast was accurate and the hurricane would bypass them, but there were no guarantees it would. He himself was reluctant to give up now that they were so close to their target, but he couldn't let his own desires endanger the ship's crew. He would have to make a decision soon.

"We'll wait a few more hours,'' he said at last. "If the hurricane hasn't changed its course by five o'clock, we'll stay put. Otherwise we get out fast.''

Randy grinned and went to pass on the word. Chuck, who was sitting with Brian and Sydne at a table, said, "It's very probable that we're in no danger here.''

Brian turned and looked soberly at his friend. "I hope you're right,'' he said.

THE ROAR OF THE COMPRESSOR had been silenced. The weather was worsening, and strong gusts of wind blowing from the southeast whipped up the sea. Waves broke over the submerged reefs around the *Adventurer* in a foreboding prelude of what was to

come. By five o'clock, with no change in the course
of the hurricane announced, Brian sent divers out to
light the channel buoys and make sure the anchorage
lines were secure.

Then there was only waiting.

BY SUNSET, gathering clouds had turned the sky to
molten lead. Then, like a balm, came the rain. It fell
gently at first, later driving down in blinding sheets
throughout the night. Consuming gallons of coffee
to help them endure the long vigil, the crew of the
Adventurer remained alert for any emergency.

In the hour before dawn Brian came into the galley. "Are you all right?" he asked Sydne as he took a
mug of steaming coffee from her hands. With half of
the crew at the ready and the other half sleeping or
resting, she had taken over the watch from Gus.

"I'm fine," she replied with a weak smile. The
howling wind could still be heard outside. "Any
news?"

"We just heard from Miami," Brian replied. "The
hurricane is passing through as originally forecast.
We're on its fringe, but we're okay. The danger is
virtually over."

"Oh, that's good news!" she exclaimed warmly,
devouring him with her eyes. She couldn't prevent
the rush of love she felt at the sight of his weary face.
It was almost morning, and he had been on constant
alert for the past forty-eight hours. "Is Chuck on the
bridge now?" she asked. At his nod she added,
"Why don't you get some sleep, Brian? You look
dead on your feet. Chuck will call you if he needs
you, I'm sure."

"You could do with some rest, too," he said, taking her hand. "Let someone relieve you here and come with me."

A crewman was found to take over in the galley. Sydne hadn't wanted to shut herself up in her cabin while Brian was on the bridge monitoring the storm, but now she followed him docilely. A few minutes later she watched him stretch out fully clothed on the bunk.

"Come here," he said, extending a hand to her. She took it without hesitation.

The space was too narrow to share unless they curled up together. Brian put his arms around her, drawing her body closely against his. In seconds he was asleep, his even breathing stirring the strands of hair lying across her cheek.

Sydne felt safe and content. In the circle of his arms nothing would ever harm her. And it was so very comfortable. . . .

"Wow!" RANDY CRIED. "I thought I was in Vegas! It was like playing the slot machines and hitting a jackpot! Look, Sydne. Take a look at these!"

The ordinary rubber bucket being passed around came to her, but its contents were not at all ordinary. It was filled with golden *escudos* like the one she had found during her first dive to the shipwreck.

"We're rich! We're rich!" Randy and Kenny were chanting and doing a jig. "We hit the jackpot!"

Brian swept Sydne off her feet. "We hit pay dirt, babe! We made it through!" he cried, giving her a hearty hug and a smacking kiss. When he put her down, he propelled her to the forward section, where the divers and other members of the crew were whooping and hollering, dancing with joy and stamping their bare feet.

"Whooee! Whooee!" Randy yelled, swinging the lengths of gold chain he had draped around his neck. Kenny, Bernardo and the others were following suit in a kind of crazy square dance into which Brian and Sydne were immediately drawn.

"This is just the tip of the iceberg," Brian said to her, indicating the blazing jewels collected on deck. "I'm going to cover you with diamonds, babe."

Sydne would have traded all those jewels for a simple band of gold around her finger. All she wanted was Brian, but it was wonderful to see him so happy. At long last, after weeks of arduous excavation, they had gained access to the shipwreck. He had worked hard, had taken great risks to reach this goal, and the fact that he had succeeded was a more precious reward to her than all the gold and silver in the world.

One after another the men emerged with precious relics wrenched from the deep. Both sacred and profane had journeyed together. Chalices and other religious objects once destined to grace the altars of churches had shared their watery grave with idols whose jeweled eyes had looked down upon pagan worshipers. There were heavy candlesticks of blackened silver, and the spilled contents of a pouch revealed a field of iridescent ivory and black pearls. Then the hoist began hauling aboard sealogged coffers that, when pried open, disclosed glittering discs of gold.

"Did you ever dream of anything like this?" Brian

grinned, lifting a handful of gold coins and letting them trickle slowly through his fingers. "Feel it, Sydne," he encouraged. "It's fantastic!"

Mesmerized by the golden glitter, Sydne ran her hand over the coins. She and the crew were the first people to see them in over three hundred years! At Brian's insistence, she dipped both hands into the pile as he had, and the coins clinked musically as they fell into a shimmering heap.

Another coffer contained blackened silver ingots. Selecting one, Sydne wiped away the coating of sulfide to disclose initials and Roman numerals.

"Brian, I think we might be able to identify the ship from these," she said thoughtfully. "Do you still have the cargo manifest for the *Conde*?"

"Sure, Syd. I'll get it." He climbed the ladder to the bridge and reappeared moments later with a thick manila folder.

Sydne leafed through the photostats of documents until she came across what she was looking for, an entry for a shipment of ingots, the weight of which was given in marks and ounces. "Here it is," she said triumphantly. She made some quick calculations on a piece of paper and checked the tally numbers on the ingots. "Have we a scale aboard?" she inquired.

"You bet!" Brian said, and sent a man to fetch it.

The crewman returned after a few minutes and set the scale down. It wasn't the best type for the test, Sydne realized, but it would have to do. Several men had gathered to watch, and even Dr. Marín had abandoned his work to join them.

"Excellent, my dear," he approved when Sydne

explained her theory. And to Brian he said with a wink, "You've got a smart girl there."

Sydne blushed at Brian's grin, and to hide her confusion used her most businesslike tone when she said, "If the bars weigh approximately sixty-eight-and-a-half pounds, I think you've found the *Conde*."

There was complete silence as Sydne began to set the silver bars on the scale. When the last one was in place, the needle wavered from side to side before it finally settled. It indicated precisely sixty-eight pounds and seven ounces.

Around them the men were pumping hands, thumping backs, laughing and congratulating each other. Confirmation that they had found the *Conde de Santander* was icing on the cake. But Sydne was oblivious to the noise and merriment around her. All she could see was Brian's eyes, and the pride that shone in them.

Like the thieves' cave in the *Arabian Nights*, the steel deck of the *Adventurer* was strewn with marvelous treasures. Religious objects continued to pile up, and gleaming jewelry that had adorned the distinguished passengers of the ill-fated *Conde de Santander* now joined the gold and silver coffers once destined for the imperial armies of centuries past. Exultantly, everyone made plans for the riches that would soon be theirs—riches that exceeded their wildest dreams.

The flow of treasure from the sunken ship seemed inexhaustible. Even after the hold was emptied, more and more items were discovered under the floorboards—contraband some wily Spaniard had secreted in hopes of lining his own pockets. There were more gold and silver bars, brooches and bracelets and rings set with diamonds, rubies and emeralds, a pouch filled with unpolished gems. Also unearthed from the bowels of the ship was a complete set of delicate china that had survived the sinking, miraculously intact. Even fragile crystal stemware was recovered, needing only a good washing to sparkle like new.

And other more mundane articles the passengers had carried with them on the voyage were found. The steel blades of a pair of scissors had rusted away, but their brass handles remained. Crockery, some chamber pots, pewter and even a pair of ivory dice were unearthed.

With so much booty to process, Brian delegated a few of the crewmen to lend Sydne and Dr. Marín a hand. There was little time to waste. Each item had to be prepared for shipment to the bank vaults of the capital without delay.

Sitting in the middle of a reef with all that treasure aboard was unnerving, and even though she was tired, Sydne strongly objected when Brian made her take a break in the early afternoon.

"But there's so much to do!" she protested. "It's not fair to Dr. Marín!"

"He's the first one to agree that you've been driving yourself too hard," Brian answered, taking her by the arm and propelling her below decks to her cabin. "Now take a nap, read—do anything you like. But I don't want you back on duty for at least a couple of hours. And that's an order."

"Well, there's at least one thing that hasn't changed," she sighed as he was leaving.

Brian paused at the door. "What's that?"

"You still enjoy ordering me around."

"Ah, but that's not all I enjoy doing with you," he grinned meaningfully. Closing the door, he came back and stood next to her.

"No, Brian, don't," she breathed, reading his intentions.

"You little liar," he said gently, knowing her resistance was halfhearted. "Your lips might be saying 'no,' but all the time your eyes are sending me an open invitation to do this." He drew her into his arms and covered her mouth with his.

Still Sydne tried to resist, but his tongue, coaxing her lips apart, probed and explored...touching, caressing, enticing her, until her arms curled around his neck and she twisted her fingers in his hair. When he slipped his hand upward to cup her breast she still protested breathlessly, "No, Brian, no!"

"I'm going to enjoy teaching that delicious mouth of yours to forget that word and start saying what it really means."

"Please!" she whispered, unable to bear the sensations he was arousing in her.

"Please what?" he murmured, nibbling her earlobe. At the same time he was unbuttoning her shirt.

"Please stop." But her tone carried no conviction.

"That's not what you want!" He had unfastened her bra and now pulled it away. Her jutting breasts tumbled free into his hands, which circled slowly in a hypnotic teasing caress. "Tell me what you really want, Sydne."

She wouldn't admit defeat. But at the same time she offered no real resistance as he slipped her jeans to the floor, leaving her with only a pair of flimsy bikini panties to cover her nudity.

"Tell me, babe. Don't hold back," Brian coaxed in his husky voice.

The hair on his chest teased her taut nipples, and as his fingers languorously stroked the curve of her back, Sydne was deliciously aware of the intensity of desire his body, locked against hers, betrayed. Meanwhile his hungry lips continued to trace a burning path on her skin.

"Say, yes, Sydne," he whispered passionately. "I want to hear you say it."

Suddenly she was unable to deny any longer what her heart and her flesh were clamoring for. Dropping her defenses, Sydne opened herself to him, bare and vulnerable at last. "Oh, yes, Brian, yes!" she breathed. "I love you! I love you so much!" her body shivering with the intensity of her need, she went on pleadingly, "Love me, Brian. I want you to love me, please!"

She was aware only of his touch, of the taste of his mouth and his skin, of the weight of his body pressing her onto the bunk and the exquisite feel of rippling muscles under her fingertips as she stroked his shoulders and back. She didn't care anymore where they were, or that only a few feet overhead the crew was returning to work. She was oblivious to everything except Brian and their love.

But Brian tensed suddenly and lifted his head. Vaguely Sydne heard an unfamiliar roar, as if an engine came near and then faded away.

"What's wrong?" Sydne murmured, pressing her

burning cheek against the warm moist skin of his shoulder.

Brian seemed to be listening—for what she couldn't fathom. "It's nothing, babe," he replied, giving her a quick smile. But instead of kissing her again, he got to his feet.

"Brian?"

"I'm sorry, Sydne," he said, lifting her head to plant a single passion-filled kiss on her lips. "I'll be right back." Before she could react, he was gone.

What had happened, Sydne asked herself, bewildered. Her eyes filled with tears, which soon traced hot tracks down her cheeks. Her body was still throbbing from his touch and demanding release. Why had Brian brought her to such heights, only to let her fall flat on her face? There had to be some explanation for his actions.

He came back less than a quarter of an hour later, and by this time Sydne was almost frantic. "What happened?" she asked as soon as he walked in.

"Something I forgot," he said casually, apparently unconcerned. To her surprise, he undid the tie of the wrap she had put on and slipped the silky garment off her shoulders. Taking a thick gold chain from his pocket, he settled it around her neck. The heavy cross hanging from the chain was encrusted with emeralds and glistened between her naked breasts.

"What—"

"I told you I'd cover you with diamonds," he murmured. "This is the down payment. I want you to wear it while I make love to you."

Her eyes widened with horror. Before she knew it

her hand had reached up to smack him across the face, the loud crack seeming to echo in the confined space.

"Get out!" she all but screamed. "Get out!"

Brian's face was impassive even as the imprint of her hand began to appear on his cheek, an angry welt. "No!" he returned coldly, "you get out. I want you off this ship immediately. You have five minutes to pack."

He turned on his heel and strode out of the cabin, leaving Sydne, broken and dismayed, staring in disbelief at the closed door.

CHAPTER EIGHT

"YOU LOOK GORGEOUS, SYD," Andrew greeted her. "That stint on the ship certainly put roses in your cheeks."

Sydne blinked back the tears that were threatening to flow and fondly kissed the withered cheek. "Hello, Andrew," she said, desperately trying to keep her voice from breaking. She resisted the temptation to hug him tight, to seek the comfort of his fatherly affection. "I've missed you!"

"And when did you have the time to miss me, with all those young men dancing attendance?" he teased.

Her laughter was forced and brittle. "They're a nice bunch, but they lack your finesse."

Andrew gave her a probing look. "Even Brian?"

"Please," she said, the catch in her voice betraying her, "I'd rather not discuss him."

Andrew's craggy face creased abruptly in a worried frown. "What's wrong, Syd? Don't tell me you and Brian are still at war."

Avoiding his probing gaze, she took a deep breath to steady herself. "The war is over, Andrew. I'm going away." But with the words her composure finally cracked, and she could no longer stem the flow of tears.

"Sydne!" Andrew exclaimed, taken aback. "What's the matter?"

"Oh, Andrew," she mumbled, "I've been such a fool!"

"Now, now, my dear," he consoled, offering his handkerchief, "It can't be as bad as all that." She snatched the square of linen from his hand and pressed it to her face as if to hide behind it. Andrew let her cry for a moment, then he poured a tall glass of lemonade from a pitcher that had been left on the side table. "Here, my dear, drink this," he said finally, offering it to her. When she shook her head, he insisted, "Do as I say. Take it."

Sydne wiped her eyes resolutely and blew her nose before accepting the glass.

"Drink it," he commanded, and waited while she took a few sips of the icy lemonade. "Now tell me what happened," he went on gently.

Embarrassed by her loss of control, Sydne said with effort, "I have to go home."

"Home?" Andrew repeated, knowing what Sydne had left unsaid—that home was an empty apartment in a strange city. She had moved to Minneapolis when she'd taken the job at his private museum. She had no family and didn't know many people because she had shunned social activities during the six months she had lived there. Most of her friends were married and had their own families. Her few single acquaintances were involved in absorbing careers that didn't allow much time for socializing. She really had no one close to her. "Suppose you tell me what happened," he suggested.

Sydne forced herself to take another drink of the lemonade. The simple action seemed to help restore her equilibrium. "I'm sorry," was the first thing she said, inviting a wry smile from Andrew.

"Why do you want to go home?" he prompted when she seemed unable to go on.

"There's nothing left for me to do here," she said dismally. "Brian ordered me off the ship." When he didn't seem surprised, she said, "You probably knew that. He must have contacted you by radio."

Andrew's silence was answer enough. "I thought—Oh, it doesn't matter." She took a deep breath to steady her voice. "I love him, Andrew. Like a stupid fool, I love him."

"And you're running away," Andrew stated quietly. "Like a fugitive—not a stupid fool. Why?"

"Because love isn't what he's offering me."

"Are you sure?"

"Of course I'm sure. That's why I have to get away."

Andrew gave her a probing look. "You don't have to rush away like this, you know. Brian must have had a reason to do what he did."

Yes, he had, she mused ruefully. He had accomplished her surrender. She felt another wave of desolation wash over her. "There's nothing to think about, Andrew. I want to leave as soon as possible—today."

"All right, Sydne. I'll charter a plane or a helicopter to fly you to Santo Domingo tomorrow," he said without further argument. "It's too late in the day now." When the anguished expression didn't leave her face, he went on, "You're overwrought, my dear. Things may not be as bad as you think. Now why don't you get some rest and compose yourself, because you're going to a party with me tonight."

"A party!" Sydne exclaimed. Nothing was further

from her mind or her mood. "Oh, Andrew, I couldn't!"

"I know you'd prefer to be alone, but I don't think that's wise. Do it for me," he said persuasively. "I couldn't leave you behind, knowing how you feel, and canceling at the last moment would be a slight. We need the goodwill of the people of Samaná, and Francisco Lozano is a very important man. Besides," he added casually, "you might meet someone interesting. Who knows?"

"Lozano!" Sydne gasped.

"Yes. They live nearby—at the top of the hill, as a matter of fact." Misinterpreting her dismay he added, "We don't have to stay late, Syd. A handicapped person always has a good excuse to leave."

WITH ITS ENORMOUS BAY, which had once been coveted by the United States for the establishment of a naval base, the small town of Samaná offered one of the best sportfishing spots in the world. Beautiful beaches made the area a popular summer resort, as well. The cottages Sydne and Andrew occupied were part of the choice accommodations the large local hotel offered to its clients—those who came from as far as the capital for a weekend, or even a day, to enjoy the surf and sun.

There were other people on the beach when Sydne went down to the cove in the late afternoon. After using up her excess energy in a vigorous swim, she lay down on the sand in the shade of a coconut grove and watched a young couple play with their children. The little boy couldn't have been more than four or five; the girl was a toddler who took unsteady steps on the sand before landing on her rump.

Sydne could picture a similar scene in her mind, but the players were Brian, herself and their children. The little boy had Brian's bright blue eyes, his light brown hair streaked by the sun, his—

Why did she continue to torture herself like this, she asked herself despairingly. Such a future was impossible for them. In another day she would be leaving the island, and Brian would disappear from her life forever.

Why did she always have to fall in love with the wrong men. First Paul, now Brian. But it wasn't the same at all, she realized. Her feelings for Paul had been more like those of a star-struck teenager, disappointed when she discovered that the idol she worshiped had feet of clay. With Brian.... For the first time in her life she truly loved a man—a man of flesh and blood, of passion and tenderness who made her feel totally alive in a way she had never felt before. A man with whom she had yearned to share her life and her love, only to have it flung back in her face. What a fool she had been—an easy mark, a willing victim of her own design.

Because there was no one to blame but herself. All along she had suspected his motives, and still she had disregarded all her survival instincts. Why? Because she loved him, and she had wanted so desperately to believe in him. Even now....

The trip ashore had been a nightmare. She had thrown a few things into a bag, which Chuck had taken up on deck for her. Conscious of a dozen eyes fixed on her when she came up on deck, Sydne had felt as if the entire crew knew about her humiliating encounter with Brian. She hadn't let herself even look at Chuck, and she hadn't heard his words because her ears had been buzzing and her heart thumping so wildly. Holding her head high and looking straight ahead, she had crossed the deck and boarded the motor launch. And all the while she had felt dead inside.

There had been no sign of Brian. She'd been grateful for that, because if she had seen him she didn't know what she would have done. Stiff and erect, she'd seated herself on the same bench she had occupied on two previous occasions, not looking back when the launch pulled away from the *Adventurer*. She didn't even know who had been steering the craft. It didn't matter; it was over.

WEARING A DRESS AGAIN FELT GOOD, Sydne discovered while getting ready for the party. After a steady diet of jeans and work clothes for weeks on end the gauzy white dress with its print of fern leaves made her feel soft and feminine, as did the strappy, high-heeled white sandals she slipped on her feet.

Her auburn hair still retained the style created by Oskar's excellent cut, even though her hair had grown. Her white dress had never looked so good, now that she had acquired the golden tan she had always longed for. Gold loop earrings, a set of gold chains and a spray of light floral perfume put the finishing touches to her preparations and made her feel much better. Perhaps going to a party wasn't such a bad idea after all, Sydne mused. If only Julia Lozano weren't going to be there!

A sudden thought occurred to her. Was Julia's presence the reason she had taken special care with her appearance? Did she want to make sure she could compete with the Dominican woman?

Sydne shrugged the idea away. What would be the point in that? "She's not my enemy," she told her reflection in the mirror, silencing the nagging voice inside her head. The poor girl was probably as much in love with Brian as she herself was. Why else would she be risking scandal? It was Brian who was to blame, Brian who had no scruples about using them both.

THEY COULD HEAR the lively music before they reached the house, which, seen through the trees, was ablaze with lights. The many late-model cars parked on the driveway and along the street announced a large attendance.

If the house was impressive from the outside, the interior was even more so, with white marble floors and gilded Louis Quinze furniture. Elegant crystal chandeliers reflected their myriad lights in the wide windows, which afforded a sweeping view of the bay.

The familiarity with which the Lozanos greeted Andrew McCallum made Sydne aware that he must have become a friend and frequent visitor of the family's. Don Francisco's bantering remarks about a recent chess game confirmed this. Their host, a distinguished portly man, was well into his fifties, although his dark hair showed few traces of silver. His wife, Matilde, personified the affluent Dominican woman—exquisitely gowned and coiffed, and beautiful in a sedate matronly way.

Their daughter was everything Sydne had heard. Petite and delicate, Julia was so beautiful that she reminded Sydne of a porcelain doll that children are allowed to admire but not to touch. Her hair was glossy black and tumbled around her soft shoulders like a curtain of silk. Her complexion had the texture of a child's, and her dark expressive eyes were fringed with thick sooty lashes. She was perhaps two inches shorter than Sydne's five foot four, and her figure was slender yet well formed. There was no artifice in the young woman, whose eyes reflected the warmth of her charming smile.

If any doubts had remained in Sydne's mind about a possible involvement between Brian and the girl, they vanished at once. A virile man like him would never pass up such a beauty, Sydne realized with a sinking heart. Perhaps he even loved her. But what had she expected? What difference did it make if Julia was beautiful or not? Perhaps she would feel better if she could actually hate her, Sydne supposed, but somehow she couldn't.

The Lozanos proved to be as charmingly hospitable as most of the Dominicans Sydne had met, and to her surprise the evening passed by quickly in their pleasant company. The women present seemed fascinated by the fact that she had spent five weeks aboard the *Adventurer*, but their admiration increased when they learned she had actually dived to the shipwreck. Since most of the older ones had little knowledge of English, they were agreeably surprised when they discovered that Sydne could speak their language quite fluently. They began to pepper her with questions.

No, she had not been afraid to be the only woman aboard the salvage ship, Sydne answered. She was urged to explain the work she had performed with Dr. Marín, but the ladies seemed even more interested in her personal life. Was she engaged to that handsome man who ran the salvage operation? Sydne was surprised that they knew Brian. Perhaps he was a frequent visitor to the Lozano household, especially if he was having an affair with Julia.

Their own lives revolved around their homes, their husbands and their children, Sydne learned, with charity work to occupy the extraordinary amount of free time afforded them by the many servants at their disposal.

Julia's older brother, Rafael, finally rescued Sydne by volunteering to teach her the steps of the merengue, the national dance. Sydne accepted the offer at once—anything to escape questions about Brian! For the next hour or so she was claimed in turn by most of the young male guests, who boldly and flirtatiously praised her beauty. It should have boosted her ego, but it didn't.

Out of courtesy, Sydne tasted the tempting delicacies available from the ample buffet. She had no appetite and now wished the evening would end, but seeing Andrew in animated conversation with their host, she decided to wait patiently. She had been introduced to so many people in such a short period of time that she couldn't remember very many names or faces, except for Julia's fiancé, Lorenzo. He was a reasonably attractive man, but he couldn't hold a candle to Brian. But then, what man could? There was such vitality in him, such power, that any woman he set his cap for was bound for trouble. She should know....

"Sydne?" a voice said at her side, and Sydne turned to find Julia smiling at her. "May I have a word with you?"

Linking arms with her, Julia led her away to a corner of the room where they wouldn't be overheard. Meanwhile Sydne was trying to fathom what Julia could possibly have to say to her that was confidential. There was only one subject, of course: Brian.

"I wonder if I could take advantage of such a short acquaintance to ask a favor of you," Julia began uncertainly.

Sydne tried to hide her apprehension. "What is it?"

"Could I...could I ask you to take a letter to the *Adventurer* when you go back?"

Good Lord, Sydne thought, *she's asking me to take a letter to Brian!* "I'm sorry," she said dryly. "I'm afraid that won't be possible. I'm not going back."

"You're not?" Julia was visibly disappointed.

"I'm flying to Santo Domingo in the morning, and on home from there."

"Oh, I'm sorry to hear that."

Sydne was puzzled by her apparent sincerity. "Why?"

"Oh, no reason," Julia said quickly, then changed her mind. "Please forgive me for saying this, but I was hoping things would work out between you and Brian. Your leaving now—"

"What?" Sydne blurted out, almost dropping her glass.

"Please forgive me," Julia repeated contritely. "I didn't mean to pry. It's just that Brian has been a good friend, and I. . . ."

"I don't understand," Sydne admitted, frankly puzzled.

Julia gave her a questioning look. "He never told you about Chuck and me?" When Sydne shook her head dumbly she added, "Of course. I should have known he wouldn't betray a confidence."

"Are you telling me that you and Chuck are involved?"

"I love him more than I can say, Sydne," Julia said with a wistful sigh.

"But I thought—I mean. . . ."

Julia gave her a puzzled look, and then threw back her head and laughed. "You thought Brian and I were lovers, didn't you?"

Sydne's blush spoke for her. "I saw him meet a woman the night we arrived in Samaná," she said rather sheepishly. "I didn't know it was you then, of course, but it wasn't difficult to find out."

"And you were jealous?"

Yes, even then she had been jealous of Brian looking at another woman, Sydne realized. "I've always had a very active imagination," she confessed guiltily. "I could have sworn I saw the two of you embracing."

Julia laughed again infectiously. "It wasn't your imagination, Sydne. I did hug him—as a friend, of course," she added. "And if you're wondering about why I met him secretly, I'll tell you that also. You see, Brian had brought me a letter from Chuck when he was on his way to Santo Domingo. I asked him to stop by when he returned so that I could send my reply with him. It was that simple."

"He told me there was nothing between you two," Sydne admitted ruefully, "but I didn't believe him." It was too late now, anyway, she reminded herself, and besides, it hadn't made any difference in the end. He had also told her that he loved her, but she couldn't believe that was true. She'd been told that before by a man who merely wanted her physically, and she still hadn't recovered from that blow to her self-esteem.

"Perhaps now that you know the truth you'll change your mind about leaving," Julia suggested hopefully, interrupting her train of thought.

Sydne wondered if the other woman was concerned about her relationship with Brian, or about the letter Julia wanted to send to Chuck. Lovers were selfish, she knew. "I'm still going away, Julia," she said. "Things didn't work out between Brian and me. It had nothing to do with you."

"I'm sorry." Julia squeezed her hand in sympathy. "Love is such a complicated thing, isn't it?" she asked with a sigh. "I love Chuck and he loves me, yet there can be no future for us, either."

"But does it have to be that way?" Sydne said. "He's a good man, Julia. I'm sure he could make you very happy."

"Don't you think I know that?" Julia's eyes were bright with unshed tears. "He asked me to marry him, Sydne, but I couldn't accept. I love him, but I was engaged to Lorenzo before I even met Chuck. Lorenzo and I pretty well grew up together, and our families have always been very close. Our parents

have always hoped that we would marry someday—
you know how those things are. To end the engagement would not only create a scandal, it would break
their hearts. I couldn't do that to them. And besides,
Chuck is a foreigner. My parents would never accept
him, and I'm not strong enough to defy them. That's
why we have to content ourselves with stealing a few
moments whenever we can."

None of these reasons she'd mentioned took
Chuck's feelings into consideration, Sydne realized.
She thought of the fondness in his voice when he had
spoken of his little nieces, the same ones whose pictures he had finally showed her. He was a quiet, solid
gentle man—not the type to fall easily in or out of
love. Julia was throwing away what Sydne would
have given anything in the world to have with Brian,
even now. "And what of Chuck?" she asked Julia.
"What of his feelings?"

"Men are different," Julia said bleakly. "He loves
me now, but he'll go away and forget me—find
someone else. And after Lorenzo and I are married,
all I will have will be the memory of Chuck's love."

"I can't understand you, Julia," Sydne admitted
frankly. "Why settle for just a sweet memory when
you could have the real thing? If Chuck asked you to
marry him, it must be because he loves you. You're
throwing away not only your future, but his as well.
Think about it, Julia, before it's too late."

"Oh, Sydne, I wish I could be as strong as you!"
Julia sighed.

"Me, strong?" Sydne laughed. "You don't know
what you're saying!"

"Yes, you must be," Julia repeated emphatically.

"Otherwise Brian would not have fallen in love with you. Chuck told me how the two of you locked horns at the beginning. Brian is a very forceful man, and he needs a strong woman to match him."

Julia actually believed that Brian loved her, Sydne realized. If only it were true! But no, she couldn't afford to hope against hope. Brian himself had made his intentions perfectly clear. He wanted her, and in return he offered pleasure and luxury. And when he tired of her or found someone else, he would send her on her way without a backward glance.

No, she wanted his love, she wanted a commitment, and she wouldn't settle for anything less.

"So you're still determined to go away?" Andrew asked when Sydne appeared at his cottage the next morning, inquiring about the arrangements he had promised to make on her behalf.

"Did you really expect me to change my mind?" It was obvious now that Andrew had dragged her to the party for a reason. He had either been stalling for time, or he had hope that she would stay in the Dominican Republic after finding out about Julia and Chuck. That meant he was probably aware of a lot of what was going on, both between Brian and her and between Julia and Chuck. "Have you arranged for my transportation to Santo Domingo?" she prodded.

"There's nothing available today," Andrew said evasively. "I'm afraid you'll have to wait a little longer."

"How much longer?" she inquired with growing apprehension.

Andrew looked away from her probing gaze when he replied, "Probably tomorrow."

"Why are you doing this, Andrew?"

"Doing what?"

"Trying to keep me here. You're hiding something from me. I can feel it."

"Sydne, please wait a little longer," he said persuasively. "By tomorrow everything will be all right."

Sydne couldn't understand what he was talking about. Yet he seemed on edge, and he wasn't a man to get upset over trifles. Something was very wrong. "Either you tell me what's going on or I'll leave right now, Andrew," she said firmly. "I'll walk to Santo Domingo if I have to. Did Brian ask you to keep me here?"

"Yes," he finally admitted with a sigh of exasperation.

"Did he tell you why?"

"Yes, Sydne, he did, but I'm afraid I can't tell you that right now."

She felt betrayed, and her hurt and her surprise were reflected in her face. "Oh, no, Andrew, not you!"

"Please have a little faith, my dear," he told her. "Believe me, Sydne, I only want what's best for you—and so does Brian."

"Brian!" she cried jumping to her feet. "How can you say that when you don't know what happened between us?" She added warily, "Or do you?"

"The details, no," Andrew admitted, "but I have a pretty good idea about your basic misunderstanding."

Her cheeks were flushed with anger and embarrassment when she sputtered, "And you still expect me to wait here for him?"

"You love him, don't you?"

That deflated her. "Yes," she admitted ruefully.

"Then trust him, Sydne."

She opened her mouth to reply, but at that moment an urgent crackling message from the radio across the room broke the silence.

"Mayday! Mayday! Mayday! This is the *Adventurer* calling the coast guard. Come in, coast guard, come in. Mayday! Mayday! Mayday!"

Sydne recognized Chuck's voice immediately over the airwaves. She could hear what sounded like gunfire in the background.

"It's started," Andrew said in a tight voice, wheeling himself toward the radio apparatus. At that moment Tim Robbins walked into the room, but Sydne didn't even notice.

CHAPTER NINE

"MAYDAY! MAYDAY! MAYDAY! This is the *Adventurer* calling the coast guard. Come in, coast guard, come in. Over."

"What's going on?" Sydne cried, her voice fraught with anxiety. Her hands were balled so tightly into fists that her knuckles were turning white.

Neither of the men answered. Andrew's brows were knitted in a frown, and Tim, too, looked very worried.

"Mayday! Mayday! Mayday! This is the *Adventurer* calling the coast guard. Come in, coast guard, come in. Over."

"Where is the coast guard?" Sydne demanded, biting her lip. "They're supposed to be protecting them!"

"A distress call came over the radio more than an hour ago," Andrew replied. "I was sure it was just a trick to lure the coast guard away from the *Adventurer*. They probably suspected as much, too, but they couldn't let the call go unanswered. We've been expecting something like this since yesterday."

"Yesterday!" Sydne cried, aghast. "And you didn't tell me?"

Andrew shook his head. "I couldn't, Sydne. Brian asked me not to." He fell silent when another transmission calling for help came across. The sounds of fighting in the background seemed heavier now—short bursts of gunfire and the report of what must have been rifle shots.

"Couldn't we answer them?" Sydne asked almost hysterically. She couldn't bear to stand by while the *Adventurer* was under attack. Perhaps someone had been hurt. She couldn't even bear to think about Brian.

"I don't want to be jamming the waves when the coast guard responds," Andrew replied shortly.

The seconds of silence became minutes and seemed to stretch into forever before a second voice was heard. "Coast guard to *Adventurer*. What's your situation? Over."

Chuck's voice came on again. "*Adventurer* to coast guard. We have a pirate on our tail. What's your ETA? Over."

"Coast guard to *Adventurer*. Our ETA is twenty minutes. Repeat. Twenty minutes. Can you hold off the pirates for that long? Over."

"Twenty minutes!" Sydne cried. A lot could happen in that time. Andrew silenced her with an impatient gesture of his hand. The *Adventurer* was replying.

"We'll hold them off. But step on the gas, friend. They have machine guns. Over."

"Coast guard to *Adventurer*. We're on our way. Over and out."

"Machine guns!" Sydne blurted out. Of course! That was the rattling sound they had heard. Were there any firearms aboard the *Adventurer*, she wondered frantically. She'd never seen any. But there must be; otherwise the crew couldn't have held off the pirates for even this long. "Could we call them now?" she asked Andrew.

"Let's stay out of it, Sydne, in case they have to contact the coast guard again. There's nothing we can do for them."

Sydne had to admit that he was right, yet she desperately wanted to establish at least voice contact with the *Adventurer*. She wanted to let them know that... that what? What could she and Tim and Andrew do but sit tight and pray?

There were more crackling noises. Then Chuck's voice was heard again. "*Adventurer* to coast guard. We—" Following a burst of gunfire, the radio went dead.

"What happened?" Sydne cried.

"The radio is out," Andrew answered. "Probably hit."

Sydne could feel the blood draining from her face. An icy shiver of fear trickled down her spine. "What are we going to do? We can't just sit here and wait for news! Couldn't we at least get in touch with the coast guard?"

"I don't want to use the radio," Andrew stated with a shake of his head, "and the nearest phone is at the hotel. I don't think they'll let us tie up their lines."

But Sydne had to know what was going on. "How far is the nearest coast guard station?"

"There's one about fifteen kilometers from here," Tim offered.

"Could we go there?" Sydne asked hopefully, looking from one man to the other.

Without a word Tim started wheeling his employer toward the door. Minutes later they were driving off in the blue Dodge van.

"Brian called me on the radio after you left the ship," Andrew explained while Tim concentrated on the road. "He asked me to keep you here if I had to tie you down. For a while there I thought I would have to resort to such extremes," he added in a half-hearted attempt at levity.

"He must have been expecting the attack," Sydne said, aware of a tightness in the pit of her stomach.

"He said there had been an aircraft circling overhead, spying on the ship. He knew what was coming and he didn't want you there."

"So that's why he ordered me off the ship so suddenly!" Sydne said pensively. "But why didn't he tell me, Andrew?"

"Apparently you decided to remain aboard after he told you he was expecting a hurricane, didn't you?"

"Yes, but—"

"There you are." Andrew nodded. "He let you stay then because they would have had time to get out if the hurricane turned," Andrew explained. "But he didn't know how soon the pirates would attack. You're a very stubborn young woman, Sydne, and since he didn't have time to argue with you, he opted for the quickest course of action."

"It was quick, all right." And painful, Sydne added to herself. But that wasn't important now. What counted was that he had been thinking of her safety. Did that mean he really cared for her? If she hadn't been so worried, Sydne would have been jumping for joy. *Oh, God, please let him be safe,* she prayed silently, over and over.

The Dominican flag, a white cross on a field of red and blue, fluttered over the coast guard station, a small building of whitewashed concrete slabs. With the flag was a banner bearing the insignia of the coast guard. The only vehicle parked in front was a Jeep, and Tim parked the van next to it.

Consumed with impatience, Sydne suppressed the impulse to run inside alone. She waited while Tim settled Andrew into his wheelchair, and then the three of them went in together.

A young lieutenant seemed to be in charge. The man spoke English, and Sydne and Tim stood by while Andrew introduced himself and his companions and explained the reason for their visit.

"The last transmission from our cutter indicated they had the *Adventurer* in sight," the lieutenant replied.

"How long ago was that?"

The officer glanced at the clock on the wall before he said, "Ten minutes ago."

Sydne also glanced at the clock. It seemed impossible that only eighteen minutes had elapsed since the final transmission from the salvage ship. "They must have reached the *Adventurer* by now," she suggested.

"That is correct, *señorita*."

"Please, is there any way we can find out what's happening?"

Sydne's anxiety must have impressed the lieutenant, a man obviously accustomed to dealing with the barriers of military red tape, especially where civilians were concerned. "I'll check with our radio operator," he agreed. "Please excuse me for a moment."

"Thank you," Sydne breathed gratefully.

Too tense to sit still, she paced the floor while the lieutenant disappeared into another room. Andrew began drumming his fingers on the arms of his wheelchair, while Tim Robbins, hands jammed into his pockets, leaned against the wall and observed his companions.

"What's taking him so long?" Sydne exclaimed when minutes had slipped away and the lieutenant failed to appear.

"Patience, lass," Andrew advised.

"Patience!" she cried. "How can I be patient when Brian might be hurt!" Catching sight of Andrew's worried frown, she immediately regretted her outburst. "I'm sorry," she said contritely. "I know how fond you are of him, too. Oh, I'm so selfish! I'm thinking only of Brian when the others could be hurt, too. They're good men, Andrew, all of them. They're my friends."

"Love is selfish, Sydne," the older man said gently, reaching for her hand. "Don't feel too bad. It's only natural."

"If anything happens to Brian, I—"

"Don't think of that now."

"I should have had more faith in him," she admitted ruefully. "I thought he was only amusing himself with me—that he ordered me off the ship because I wouldn't meet him on his terms. And all the time he was only trying to protect me."

"Don't torture yourself, my dear," Andrew said fondly. "I'm sure Brian understands."

"I hope he forgives me."

"You only reacted the way he expected you to. That's why he provoked you the way he did."

"Oh, Andrew, if he gives me another chance I'll spend the rest of my life trying to make it up to him."

"You'll get your chance, don't worry."

"If he lives—"

"Of course he'll live!" Andrew protested. "Brian served in the navy, remember? He's perfectly capable of defending his ship." In a gentler tone he added, "You said you should have had more faith in him. Well, you can start believing right now that you're getting another chance. Grab that chance with both hands, girl. Brian will come back to you."

Seeing Tim snap to attention, both Sydne and Andrew looked up abruptly. The lieutenant was back.

"We just contacted the cutter," he said before they could ask. "The pirate vessel has been destroyed. Apparently it fired on the cutter, but its gas tank was hit when fire was returned. It blew up."

None of them gave the pirate vessel a second thought. "And the *Adventurer*?" Sydne asked anxiously. "Is it all right?"

"No damage to the ship as far as they could see," the lieutenant answered. "Our cutter is coming in with the casualties."

"Casualties?" Sydne's voice was a whisper. She had never known such fear.

"I'm afraid there were some casualties among your friends," the lieutenant said. "I'm sorry."

Sydne stared at him, the room blurring before her eyes.

It became strangely dark; then began to spin.... "No one was killed," the lieutenant quickly assured her. "Please forgive me. My English is not so good. Not dead, only hurt by bullets."

"Wounded," Andrew asserted. "How bad?"

"Two men," the lieutenant replied. "One only slightly, the other more seriously. I didn't get the name, only that he is an officer."

That meant Brian or Chuck, Sydne realized with dismay. "How bad?" she asked. Her own voice sounded as if it belonged to someone else.

"The officer was hurt in the chest," the lieutenant said, but he touched his shoulder. "It was said that he is losing much blood. The cutter is bringing him in."

"How soon will they arrive?"

Again the lieutenant consulted the clock on the wall. "They were starting back when we contacted them. No more than one hour."

"Will there be an ambulance waiting?" Andrew inquired.

"Ambulance?" the lieutenant repeated with a blank look on his face. "There is no ambulance in Samaná."

"Then we'll meet the cutter," Andrew said resolutely. "We have a van outside. I'm sure we can make it ready to transport the wounded man, couldn't we, Tim?"

"Yes, sir. I'll take care of it."

"Good." Andrew turned back to the officer. "Where is the nearest hospital?"

"In Samaná, just outside of town. I'll send someone with you to show you the way."

"Thank you, lieutenant," Andrew said. As an afterthought he added, "Perhaps we could request a helicopter to transport the wounded man to Santo Domingo."

"As you wish, Mr. McCallum," the officer said courteously. "But if I were you, I would not waste any time getting the man to a hospital. From what our radio operator tells me, he's losing a lot of blood."

Sydne died a thousand deaths waiting for the cutter to arrive; and all that time anxious thoughts churned in her brain. Each word, each precious moment she had spent with Brian came back to haunt her. He had exclaimed once about how much time they wasted sparring with words when they could have been loving each other. Now she regretted every wasted moment. For that she had only herself to blame.

But if Brian came back to her, if God granted her another chance, she wouldn't make a single demand. *Only let me love him,* Sydne prayed to herself over and over during an hour that stretched into eternity. She would be grateful for whatever time they had together. If only he lived!

"It's coming, Sydne." Andrew's voice brought her back to the present. She sprang to her feet, immediately alert. The boat was still a good distance away from the pier, and the van had been prepared. A pallet lay on the floor of the cargo space in back, and blankets provided by the coast guard were neatly folded on the seat.

Frozen, unable even to think any more, Sydne watched sailors from the cutter jump onto the pier and secure the lines. Others lifted the wounded man on an improvised stretcher. He was a big man—like Brian, she realized numbly, mechanically putting one foot in front of another like an automaton as she moved toward them. Then she caught a glimpse of the man's face.

"Chuck!" she breathed, and moved into action.

Tim Robbins had already taken charge. He helped the men put Chuck into the van, while another sailor assisted Andrew. And the male nurse didn't object when Sydne got in with the wounded man.

"How is he, Tim?" she asked anxiously.

He had made a brief examination of the wound and was applying pressure to stop the bleeding. "He's gonna make it, Syd," he said with an encouraging wink. "He's lost a lot of blood, but he's gonna make it."

Chuck opened his eyes as the van set into motion. "Julia?" he whispered. "Julia?"

"Is he delirious?" she asked.

Tim shook his head. "He's in shock. But go ahead and talk to him. He won't know the difference," he added as Chuck called out again.

Sydne took Chuck's hand in hers. "I'm here, darling," she said softly, her eyes filling with tears. "I'm right here."

"Don't leave me, Julia. Don't leave me," Chuck pleaded in a weak voice. Yet his grip was so tight that it made Sydne wince.

"I won't, darling. I'm here with you. Be still; don't talk."

Soothed by her warm crooning voice, Chuck relaxed his hold and seemed to fall into a kind of stupor. Sydne cast an anguished glance at Tim. "Do you think he hears me?"

"He knows you're here. That's the main thing."

A few minutes later the van pulled into the hospital driveway. Chuck moaned and held fast to Sydne's hand while he was being moved, and Sydne had no choice but to follow him into the emergency room.

"I'm sorry, miss," a nurse said. "You can't stay here."

"Julia!" Chuck became agitated when Sydne tried to release her hand.

The nurse watched in sympathy for a moment, then she gave the doctor an inquiring look.

"We'll give him a sedative," the doctor said to her. "He won't know you're gone."

The injection worked in seconds, and Sydne was able to free her hand. She stepped into the waiting room, which was furnished with a scarred wooden bench set against the wall of the hospital corridor. Andrew had been waiting in the room for quite some time. "How is he?" he asked immediately.

"The doctor gave him a sedative," she replied, shaking her head.

Tim came out then. In response to their expectant look, he said, "He's going into surgery."

"Julia should be here," Sydne announced firmly.

Andrew regarded her quizzically. "Will she come?"

"If she loves him as much as she says she does, she will," Sydne replied. After a pause she added, "I'm going to fetch her. May I take the van?"

"You're in no condition to drive," Tim pointed out.

"Yes," Andrew agreed. "Let Tim drive you, Syd."

It was true. Her hands were still shaking. She gave them both a grateful smile before she turned toward the door.

Would Julia give up her plan of secrecy and come to Chuck, Sydne wondered as she followed Tim to the van. If it were Brian in that operating room, she would cross half the world to go to him. Of course Julia would come! At least she deserved the chance to make her choice.

Before she knew it, Tim was parking the van in the Lozanos' driveway. "I'll wait here," he said as Sydne started to get out.

Strangely reluctant, she approached the front door and rang the bell with a trembling hand. What if Julia refused to come?

The servant who answered couldn't mask her surprise, and it was then that Sydne realized the front of her dress was stained with blood. The girl showed Sydne into the living room, where she had been the night before under more pleasant circumstances, then went in search of Julia.

"Sydne!" the young woman exclaimed as she appeared in the doorway minutes later. "Rosita said that. . . ." Her words trailed off at the sight of Sydne's appearance, and her face went pale. "What happened? Is it Chuck?"

There was no gentle way of breaking the news. "He's hurt, Julia," Sydne said, affecting a calm she was far from feeling. "He's going to be all right, but he needs you."

"Oh, no!" Julia gasped.

"He's been wounded and he's calling for you. I thought you should know."

"Wounded? But how?"

"The *Adventurer* was attacked early this morning. Chuck was brought to the hospital by the coast guard cutter. He's in surgery now."

"Is he—"

"He's doing okay," Sydne cut her off. "Tim Robbins, Andrew's nurse, says he'll be all right. But he's lost a lot of blood. He was in shock when he was brought in."

Julia was twisting her hands with indecision as Sydne added, "He needs you, Julia. He was calling for you, over and over."

"Oh, Sydne, I want so very much to go to him!" Julia declared, her face twisted with worry. "But if I do...my parents...."

"If you love him, Julia, come with me." Sydne's voice was deadly serious. "But if you don't come, I don't think you should ever say again that you love him."

Julia stared at her, her dark eyes wide and questioning.

"I don't have time to waste," Sydne went on, resolutely turning toward the door. "Please forgive the intrusion."

"No, wait!" Julia begged.

When Sydne paused on the threshold she added, "Would you take me to him?" Wordlessly they walked out to the van, and Tim started the engine.

Julia cried softly as they drove down to the hospital, but Sydne couldn't offer any comfort. Her own concern over Brian's safety still weighed heavily on her mind. She'd been told that the injuries were minor and that Moose was able to handle them, but she knew she'd have no peace of mind until she saw Brian with her own eyes.

It was only a short drive, and Andrew was still waiting outside the operating room when they returned. Sydne realized that she had been gone for less than half an hour. Time seemed to be dragging; it was only ten-thirty. It seemed as if a week had gone by since she'd walked into Andrew's cottage that morning.

"Any news?" she inquired.

"He's still in surgery." Andrew shook his head.

Tim bought coffee in small paper cups, which Andrew and Sydne accepted gratefully. Julia, however, sat on the bench, hardly moving. Sydne took a cup of coffee over to her.

"Julia," she said quietly, sitting down next to her, "have some of this."

Julia shook her head. "I couldn't."

"Drink it," Sydne insisted. "It'll do you good."

At last Julia accepted the cup. "I really love him," she whispered, after taking sip of the steaming liquid. "It's just that— Oh, Sydne, I'm so frightened!" she sobbed.

"He's going to be all right, Julia," Sydne protested, trying to comfort her.

"You don't understand! I'm afraid of what's going to happen, Sydne. My parents. . . ."

"Have you ever tried to tell them how you really feel?" Sydne asked gently. "You're their only daughter. They love you. I'm sure your happiness is more important to them than the threat of scandal. Give them a chance, Julia. They might surprise you."

"But that's just it." Julia wept. "I'm afraid that they will!" She paused. "I've just realized that I've been hiding behind my parents—using them as an excuse. The fact is, I'm afraid to marry Chuck. It will mean leaving my family, my country—everything that is familiar to me. That frightens me. Perhaps Chuck knows this," Julia continued. "I think he does, and that's why he hasn't spoken to my parents. He wanted to, only I wouldn't let him."

It made sense, Sydne thought. She didn't know Chuck too well, she had to admit, but he didn't strike her as a man who would stand by and let the woman he loved be railroaded into marrying someone else.

"I do love him," Julia repeated, "but is it enough?"

"Don't you think it is?"

"We're so different, Chuck and I," Julia sighed. "We come from two different worlds. What will happen when he stops loving me? I'll be all alone."

"What makes you think he'll stop loving you?"

"Because sooner or later it usually happens," Julia said dejectedly. "Maybe not in a year or two, but it will. Oh, he may not leave me, but he'll find someone else, someone younger and prettier who will make life exciting for him again. I know I can take that with Lorenzo; I will still have my family around me. But what will I do in a land that is not my own, one with such different customs? I'll be far from my family and will have no one to turn to."

Sydne realized what Julia meant. In many societies, men kept mistresses as a symbol of their affluence and manhood. In certain social circles it was almost expected, and many wives ignored the situation.

"I've known Lorenzo all my life," Julia went on. "His family is like my own. I know what to expect if I marry him, but with Chuck.... Oh, Sydne, you couldn't possibly understand. You are independent. You have your career. You can stand on your own two feet. My situation is different. I've never been away from my parents. My life has been geared toward the home, the man who will be my husband, the children I will have by him. If I defy my parents to marry Chuck, and then he turns away from me, I'll have no one!"

She had a point, Sydne had to admit. Yet Sydne herself had paid dearly for her independence. She had had lots of experience in being shifted from place to place. Her father had worked for a large corporation that had moved its executives from one city to another as a chessplayer moves pieces around on a board. She had never stayed in one place long enough to establish lasting relationships.

A kind of modern-day Gypsy, Sydne had always been the new girl in class. And each time she had had to say goodbye to her friends they had exchanged promises to keep in touch. But she had quickly discovered that well-meant promises were hard to keep long distance. Only once a friendship had survived the transition, but when the two finally met again, after years of sporadic correspondence, the reunion had been disappointing. She and Jean realized they had grown apart.

Sydne had found losing her parents quite a sobering experience—in more ways than one. Grief-stricken, she had turned to her current companions for comfort, but they had turned away from her. Suddenly she no longer belonged to their carefree world. Some of them had been cruel in their snubs when she'd been forced to work as a waitress to support herself.

Strangely enough, those bitter experiences had made her even more determined to make her own way and not to abandon her studies. But it had been a long arduous road, until her grades had earned her a partial scholarship at another college. There she had met Paul, who had inspired and encouraged her to go on. After all she had gone through alone, he had become her guiding light, and his betrayal had been so painful that she now found it hard to believe in anyone.

And Brian had paid the price. She had been so afraid to lay herself open to hurt that she had fought her love for him from the start. But that didn't matter anymore. She loved him, and she would take the consequences. Julia had to do the same.

"It's not an easy choice, I know," Sydne said gently, "but you will have to make it sooner or later. And you'll have to live with your decision for the rest of your life."

Julia bowed her head, tears gliding down her pale cheeks. "I love him so," she confessed.

Not knowing what to say, Sydne squeezed her hand warmly.

A few minutes later the doors of the operating room swung open, and Chuck was wheeled out to the corridor by two attendants. A plastic bottle containing a clear liquid hung from a steel frame above him, attached to his arm by a plastic tube. Julia sprang to her feet, then faltered as she took in the pallor of Chuck's normally tanned face. Sydne slipped a supportive arm around her. A man in a pastel green operating gown approached them.

"We've removed the bullet," he said, addressing himself to Andrew. "The patient's young and in excellent health, which is in his favor, but he's lost a lot of blood. We're giving him plasma at the moment until we can find a donor for a transfusion. Unfortunately his blood type is rather rare. Are any of you AB negative?"

They all looked at each other before shaking their heads.

"Well, I'm going to call the capital to see if they can find a donor," the doctor sighed.

"Please let me know right away if they don't," Andrew said. "We can call San Juan or Miami to have it flown in. Don't spare any expense, doctor."

The man nodded before he walked away, and the others followed Chuck and the attendants down the hallway. The room they took him to was small, and there was only one chair next to the bed. Julia sank into it naturally, as if it were her right, and Sydne, Andrew and Tim waited outside.

"I wonder if there's been any further contact with the *Adventurer*," Sydne said after a while.

"I called the coast guard station a few minutes ago," Tim replied. "Their radio is still out, but a cutter is on its way back."

"Brian must be terribly worried about Chuck,"

Sydne said pensively. "He must be very busy or else he wouldn't stay away."

"There must be a lot to clear up after what happened," Tim said. "But the station is contacting the cutter, and they'll inform Brian of Chuck's condition."

"How long do you think it will be before we get some blood?"

"If it's coming from Santo Domingo, maybe less than two hours," Andrew replied. "If we have to contact San Juan, probably about the same. Miami will take longer."

Thirty minutes later the doctor returned. They all looked anxiously at his face, which gave no clue to his news. "Both Santo Domingo and San Juan are looking for donors," he told them. "Miami is our best bet, since they have a donor on file. They're trying to locate him."

"How soon will we know?" Andrew asked.

The doctor shrugged eloquently. Then Tim inquired, "How long can Chuck wait for the transfusion, doctor?"

"His chances will be much better if we can get some whole blood into him within the next six hours."

"Tim, get on the phone to Miami," Andrew said immediately. "Get a plane ready to fly in the blood as soon as they find the donor."

"Yes, sir."

"You may use the telephone in my office," the doctor said, leading the way.

Once again, they waited. There was nothing else to do as minutes became hours. When the doors at the end of the corridor finally swung open once again, Sydne turned expectantly. What she saw did not raise her spirits. "Oh, no!" she exclaimed under her breath. The Lozanos were coming toward them, and the frown on Don Francisco's brow was definitely ominous. Señora Lozano followed her husband with quick nervous steps.

CHAPTER TEN

"WHERE'S MY DAUGHTER?" Don Francisco demanded without preamble.

Before anyone could answer, Julia stepped out of the room. "Papa," she said in a low voice, "please do not be angry."

Don Francisco soberly regarded his daughter's pale face. "What is this man to you?" he said abruptly. "This man Rosita tells us of?"

Julia took two more steps toward her father. "I love him, papa," she replied quietly.

A muscle twitched in Francisco Lozano's jaw. "You're coming home," he ordered curtly.

"No, papa." Julia's voice was firm. "I'm staying here with Chuck. He needs me."

Don Francisco was clearly taken aback by Julia's refusal, as if his orders had never before been disregarded. Matilde Lozano put a restraining hand on her husband's arm, as if she knew he might be tempted to strike his daughter's face. Sydne was full of admiration for Julia, who stood up to him firmly, yet without hostility.

"Father, please, listen to me," she pleaded. "I love Chuck, but I will keep my word to marry Lorenzo, since it is your wish. Only please, let me stay with Chuck until he's out of danger. He may die, papa," she said, her voice breaking.

Her grief seemed to take the edge off of Don Francisco's anger. "Is that true?" he asked Andrew.

The man in the wheelchair nodded soberly. "I'm afraid so. He needs a transfusion, and the doctor has been unable to match his blood type, which is somewhat rare."

"Rare?" Don Francisco repeated. "What is the type?"

"AB negative," Tim answered.

Francisco Lozano fell silent. He seemed to be debating with himself. "Call the doctor," he said at last. "I can help."

"Papa," Julia cried, "is that true?"

"My blood type is the same as his," Francisco Lozano told his daughter. "I will give him my blood."

"Oh, papa—" Julia rushed to embrace her father "—thank you!"

"But that won't change anything," he told her sternly. "Do you understand?"

"Oh, yes, papa." Julia smiled through her tears. "It's all right as long as Chuck gets well again."

Tim went in search of the doctor, who couldn't hide his relief at having found a donor. When he saw who it was he became more deferential, and chattered effusively as he led Don Francisco away to be prepared for the transfusion.

Matilde Lozano, who had stood by quietly until now, put a protective arm around her daughter's shoulders. "Your young man will be all right, darling."

"Oh, mother, I'm so glad you came!" Julia sighed. "By the way, how did you find me?"

"Rosita told me that Miss Matheson had come

looking for you, and that her dress was stained with blood," Matilde explained. "She overheard you mention a hospital, and when you disappeared so suddenly I supposed something must have happened to Chuck."

"You know about Chuck?" Julia exclaimed in surprise.

"There is very little I don't know about my children, Julia," her mother said with a wry smile. "But that is something you will find out for yourself when you have your own."

"Oh, mother, I wanted so much to tell you! Only I—"

"It's all right, darling," the older woman said gently. "The important thing is that Chuck will be well again. We'll worry about the rest later."

In less than half an hour a nurse exchanged the bottle of plasma for one containing blood donated by Don Francisco. Tim got busy canceling the emergency arrangements he had made to transport blood from Miami, and the doctor announced that the patient was now probably on his way to recovery. Barring any complications, Chuck could be released in a couple of days, though he would still have to be watched closely for some time.

Don Francisco was given a hero's welcome when he rejoined the group waiting outside the patient's room. He graciously accepted the appreciation of Chuck's friends, while his wife insisted that a comfortable chair be brought to him so that he could rest.

"Stop fussing, Matilde," he protested, trying to appear stern. Everyone could see he was enjoying the attention nonetheless.

After her husband was comfortably installed in a chair, Matilde said pensively, "The facilities of this hospital are rather limited—for a comfortable recovery, I mean. Mr. McCallum agrees that perhaps it would be best to move Chuck to a hospital in Santo Domingo."

Andrew, who hadn't said a word on the subject, kept his mouth shut, but gave Sydne a quick glance. Both of them were wondering what the woman had in mind.

"Of course," Matilde went on, "that will be very inconvenient for Julia."

"For Julia?" Don Francisco frowned, regarding his wife warily.

"I suppose I'd have to go to Santo Domingo with her," Matilde continued, as if unaware of her husband's frown of displeasure. "Or she could always stay with friends. I'm sure the Robles or the Tejedas will be delighted to have her."

Before her husband could say anything she went on, "Still, I hate the idea of Julia being alone with strangers at a time like this, especially when it's so unnecessary. We have so much room in our house—"

"If you're thinking of bringing that fellow into our house," Don Francisco interrupted, "it's completely out of the question."

Doña Matilde looked properly chastised. "Of course you're right, my dear," she admitted. "I was just thinking of Julia. I'll call Susana or Adela tonight to make the arrangements. They might be a little suspicious," she added as an afterthought, "that Julia has so much interest in this young man, but I suppose I could convince them that he's a very good friend of the family.''

It was plain that Don Francisco didn't relish the idea of bringing others into the situation, that he was reluctant to let his wife stay away for any prolonged period of time. Sydne was amused—and impressed— by Doña Matilde's tactics. The woman was obviously an expert at handling her husband, surmounting his objections while appearing to be in perfect agreement with him. She wondered how long it would be before he agreed to have Chuck stay with them.

By now Andrew was showing the effects of strain, but he brushed aside Tim's suggestion that he return to the cottage, determined to wait for Chuck to come out of the anesthesia.

At four o'clock, when Chuck woke up, Brian still hadn't come ashore, Sydne's concern over his absence was increasing.

"Father," Julia called from the door, "Chuck would like to speak to you."

Francisco Lozano rose from his chair, but before he entered the room Julia whispered, "Papa, he's very weak. Please don't upset him now, I beg of you."

The older man nodded curtly at his daughter and went in. Chuck was propped up in the bed, his left shoulder wrapped in bandages and his arm in a sling. On his other arm an i.v. dripped glucose into his vein.

"Don Francisco," he said weakly, extending his hand to the older man, "Julia told me what you did. I want to thank you."

"Anyone would have done the same." Francisco Lozano shrugged, cautiously taking the proffered hand. "How are you feeling, young man?"

"Much better—" Chuck smiled "—thanks to you."

There seemed to be much more to say, but now wasn't the time. "Yes, well, I'd better not keep you up," Julia's father said awkwardly. "There are other people waiting to see you anyway. May God grant you a swift recovery."

He left quickly, and Sydne and Andrew came into the room.

"Chuck!" Sydne exclaimed softly, kissing his cheek with affection, then standing aside to let Andrew approach the bed.

"You're looking much better, my boy," Andrew said with a grin. "I must admit you gave us quite a scare."

"I had a scare myself!" the patient said with a wry smile. "Any news from the *Adventurer*?"

Andrew shook his head. "Their radio is still out," he said. "We're expecting Brian at any moment, though. Can you tell us what happened?"

"Perhaps we should let him rest," Sydne interrupted, even though she was eager to hear what Chuck had to say.

"I'm all right," Chuck claimed a little groggily. Although his color had improved, he was still suffering the aftereffects of the anesthesia and the drugs he had been given to control the pain. "I'll start from the beginning," he went on slowly, "since Sydne probably doesn't know what happened after she left the ship." In spite of his assurances, he had to pause to take a breath. "After we spotted the aircraft circling overhead, we contacted the coast guard. But we didn't know if the pirates would appear before the cutter did—if indeed the pirates were coming. We got ready to defend ourselves just in case, but since nothing had happened by the time the cutter arrived, and because the probability of attack after dark was highly unlikely, we were beginning to think it was a false alarm. But when a distress call came in early this morning, we suspected it was a trick to lure the coast guard away from us."

"I thought so!" Andrew put in.

"And so did the coast guard, but they had to answer the call just the same," Chuck replied. Andrew nodded at this confirmation of the conclusions he had reached earlier in the day.

"Did you have any arms aboard?" Sydne queried.

"A few," Chuck replied, "and the coast guard transferred several armed men to the *Adventurer* before they left us."

Again he paused, and his friends could see that he was tiring.

"We should let you rest," Sydne insisted again.

"I'm all right," Chuck assured her. "Just thirsty."

Immediately Julia picked up a glass of water and held it to his lips. Chuck gave her an adoring smile before he took a sip. Then he continued, "About thirty minutes after the cutter left, we spotted a cabin cruiser approaching our position. There were only two men aboard that we could see and they looked okay, but we still warned them away. They told us that they had engine trouble and asked if we could send someone to help them but we didn't like the idea of providing them with hostages if attack was in their minds, so instead we told them to come aboard, warning them that we had guns trained on them."

Chuck paused to take another sip of water. "When they pulled alongside," he went on, "the two men started to climb aboard. Suddenly three others came out of hiding and opened fire on us. At that point some very anxious fellow made a mistake that worked in our favor. One of their men was caught in the cross fire and fell into the sea. I stayed at the radio and called the coast guard back."

"We heard you," Andrew told him.

"And the machine guns," Sydne added with a shudder.

Chuck nodded soberly. "I was calling for help when a burst of gunfire hit the radio. I guess that's when I was hit, too, because it's the last thing I remember."

Andrew filled in the details of the destruction of the pirate vessel and answered Chuck's questions about other casualties. Sydne remained silent, wondering how long it would be before Brian came ashore. As if reading her thoughts, Chuck said, "I'm sure Brian will get here as soon as he can, Syd. Don't worry about him."

"Is someone asking for me?" came a voice from the doorway.

Sydne spun around. Large as life, Brian was standing there, leaning lazily against the door frame. Even though there was a bandage on his cheek, a flood of relief invaded her body.

"How are you, old buddy?" Brian addressed Chuck as he came into the room.

"Looks like I'll be around for a while longer." Chuck smiled feebly. "How are things on the *Adventurer*?"

"It was quite a mess—" Brian shrugged "—but we're shaping up." He looked at Sydne, who still couldn't find her voice. "Are we back on speaking terms, Ms. Matheson?" He grinned at her.

What Sydne really wanted was to fly into his arms. But her legs wouldn't move, so she simply nodded briefly, her heart in her eyes.

"I'm glad," Brian said, giving her a look that made her cheeks grow hot. He turned his attention to Andrew, offering his hand. "Thank you, my friend."

"Anytime. Well," he said, rubbing his hands together, "I think I've earned my nap today. Tim!"

"Yes, sir!" Tim said cheerfully, his own face split in a wide smile.

"Goodbye, Andrew," Chuck said as he and Tim left the room. "Thanks for everything."

Uncertain about what to do next, Sydne started to follow Andrew. Now that everything was over and that she was sure Brian was unharmed, she felt terribly shy about facing him again. She dreaded discussing that last awkward scene between them, yet it would have to be faced—preferably later. Before she reached the door, however, Brian caught up with her. "You're not going anywhere," he declared, slipping a possessive arm around her waist. For a few more minutes he continued talking with Chuck. Then the doctor came back and ordered everyone out of the room so that he could examine the patient.

"Remarkable," he said, shaking his head when he came out. "The young man's excellent health should make for a speedy recovery. But he will need good care after he's released."

"You can leave that to us," Matilde Lozano said

to the doctor. "My husband and I have agreed that
he can stay with us until he's fully recovered."

"Mother," Julia cried, "is that true?"

"Of course, darling." Matilde smiled at her
daughter. "Where else can we keep an eye on the two
of you?"

Julia hugged her mother ecstatically, and then
Matilde said, "Well, we might as well go home and
let Chuck get some rest. You look about to pass out,
Sydne," she said kindly. "If I'm not mistaken, you
haven't had anything to eat all day."

The woman was right, Sydne realized. She had
been so anxious to get away from Samaná that she
had gone to Andrew's cottage before breakfast.
After that the events of the day had put all thought of
food out of her mind.

"Come along," Matilde said, starting for the
door. "We'll all feel better after a good meal."

No one argued with such splendid logic.

SYDNE WAS GRATEFUL for the Lozanos' invitation to
supper. She still didn't feel ready to be alone with
Brian, who dropped her off at her cottage so that she
could shower and change her bloodstained dress
while he drove Julia and her mother home. Don
Francisco had left the hospital after his conversation
with Chuck.

Sydne was waiting when Brian came back. She had
changed into a wrinkle-free polyester knit dress, one
of her favorites, which she had hastily rescued from
her packed suitcases. The material was silky and soft
to the touch, and yellow suited her. The dress was
buttoned down at the front and belted with a sash

that accentuated her narrow waist, while the V neck showed the long column of her slender throat to advantage.

Fearful of asking Brian into her cottage, Sydne stepped outside as soon as she heard the car return. He got out to open the car door for her, apparently amused by her anxiety to be under way.

After he took his place behind the wheel again, he gave her a long look that brought color to her cheeks. "You're beautiful," was all he said before starting the car.

"I'm sorry I couldn't get here earlier," he went on after a pause. "Things were pretty hectic on the *Adventurer*."

"Was anyone else hurt?"

"Nothing more serious than a few cuts and bruises," he replied. "Nikko hit the deck so fast when bullets started flying that he bumped his head on a crate. He'll have a lump for a couple of days," he added wryly. "Chuck was the one I was worried about. It was good of you to bring Julia to him."

She wasn't ready to talk about Julia yet. "What happened to your face?" she asked instead.

"Wounded by a flying fragment from a pottery jar. It's just a scratch, but Moose insisted on my wearing this—" he touched the bandage "—my badge of courage."

They pulled into the Lozanos' driveway, and Sydne waited while he got out and went around the car to open the door for her. The contact of his hand as he helped her out was warm and firm, and as if she had to be reminded, made her aware once more of her feelings for him. They walked up to the house.

Uncertainly, she looked at him. He seemed about to speak, but the door opened almost immediately, and they were ushered into the Lozanos' parlor, where the family was waiting.

"You'll be glad to hear that we're serving dinner right away," Matilde told Sydne. "I hope you like *arroz con pollo*."

"I've heard it's delicious—" Sydne smiled gratefully at her hostess "—but I've never tasted it."

"No one makes it like our cook," Matilde assured her. "It's one of her specialties."

Brian was introduced to the family members he hadn't met, and then they all gathered around the long table, beautifully set with fine linen, delicate bone china, crystal and silver.

Despite her forced fast, Sydne was not terribly hungry. The tomato stuffed with crab meat that was served as an appetizer would have satisfied her appetite, but it was followed by a tempting array of other dishes. An exotic avocado and pineapple salad was sprinkled with olive oil and tangy lemon juice. The sweetness of fried ripe bananas made a delicious accompaniment to the entrée, which, Sydne discovered, consisted of pieces of chicken carefully simmered in saffron rice and delicately spiced with wine. Garnished with peas and colorful pimientos, the dish was as pleasing to the eye as it was to the taste buds. It certainly merited its claim to fame. A caramel flan flavored with brandy completed the delicious meal— followed, of course, by aromatic Dominican coffee.

After supper Julia's brothers asked Brian many questions about the events of the day while Don Francisco enjoyed an aromatic cigar.

Sydne was relieved that the social gathering didn't allow her any time alone with Brian. She still felt uneasy in his presence, a feeling, she realized, that stemmed from her own guilt. Why hadn't she believed him when he denied any involvement with Julia?

At nine o'clock, after a telephone call to the hospital that reassured them about Chuck's condition, Sydne and Brian said good-night to their hosts.

Sitting next to him in the car, Sydne felt tongue-tied and unsure of herself. She went over and over in her mind what she wanted to say to him, trying to find the words to express how much she loved him and how sorry she was for having doubted him. The awkward silence during the downhill drive ended when Brian parked the car in front of her cottage.

"Tired?" he said gently, caressing her with his eyes. "It's been a rough day for you."

"Oh, Brian!" she blurted out unhappily.

He reached for her instantly and held her close, evoking within Sydne a surge of emotions that made speech difficult. It was so wonderful to be held this way, to find comfort in his strength.

"Why didn't you tell me?" she asked when she found her voice.

Brian drew back so he could see her face. "Don't you know?" he asked fondly. For the first time Sydne wasn't afraid to offer her heart. "I love you," she whispered.

Tenderly, Brian lifted her chin to look into her eyes, eyes that were softened by tears of love. "Do you still want to run away?"

"Not anymore," she breathed.

His lips touched hers, tentatively at first. Then

they moved seductively to the corners of her mouth, as if to prolong the moment before her surrender. Her lips parted finally beneath his in a kiss that deepened, compelling yet entreating. She responded fully, offering all her love, all her trust, all her dreams and hopes. There was no holding back.

No words were needed when Brian raised his head. The unspoken message was in their eyes as he gently rubbed her chin with his thumb. Then, touching her lips lightly with his own, he opened the door on his side and got out.

Trembling, Sydne remained in the car as he went around it, but when he opened her door and extended his hand to her, she didn't hesitate to take it. A full moon cast its silver glow over the sultry night. The breeze, heavy with the tang of the sea, carried with it the cadence of gentle waves breaking on the nearby shore as Brian and Sydne walked up to the cottage, their arms around each other.

The gloom inside was broken by the moonlight spilling through the open windows. Every detail was clear in the ghostly light, even after Brian closed the door behind them and held her close to claim her lips.

"Oh, babe," he said huskily, gently stroking her cheek with his knuckles, "how I've waited for this moment!"

Somehow the gentleness of his touch seemed to reassure her that she would not disappoint him in spite of her inexperience. Above all else she wanted to please him in the giving of her love, and unable to find words to express her feelings, she took the hand he put to her cheek, and pressed her lips to the open palm before lovingly kissing each finger.

Tenderly lifting her in his powerful arms, Brian carried her into the bedroom, where he put her down. His love-filled eyes didn't leave hers as he untied the sash at her waist. Then his fingers deftly loosened the buttons at the front of her dress, and he let it swirl to the floor around her feet. Freed of their lacy confines, her full breasts jutted forward tantalizingly, longing for his touch. With each garment that he removed the longing became more of an ache, and Sydne was in a kind of agony when Brian finally bent his head and moved his lips over the smooth column of her throat.

She in turn unbuttoned his shirt to caress his warm muscular chest, and she heard his own murmurs of pleasure when her lips found his heated skin.

She had seen him in scanty clothing before, but naked Brian was even more beautiful. His shoulders seemed more powerful, his chest broader, perhaps because of the uninterrupted line to his long, well-muscled legs. The cloud of dark hair covering his chest extended across his flat taut stomach to his groin.

"You're so beautiful," he whispered, lowering her onto the bed.

She felt no embarrassment when his gaze traveled over her body—only delight that he found her as beautiful, as desirable as he made her feel.

Gently he stroked her neck and shoulders, setting her skin on fire as he rained teasing kisses over her face. When he reached her lips, he traced their contours with the tip of his tongue before claiming their sweetness. Then he sensitively probed and explored the recesses of her yielding mouth, savoring the feverish responses she was powerless to hold back.

With a shudder of pleasure Sydne ran her hands over his lean hard body. He continued to explore and fondle, to stroke the smooth warmth of her flesh. He moved without urgency, taking his time and evoking a surge of maddening sensations. He touched the soft mounds of her breasts, teasing their crests with his tongue until her rosy nipples tautened and became alive with feeling, as did every pore of her body when his knowing hands caressed her thighs and touched, at last, secret uncharted places.

Breathing raggedly, Sydne thought she would die from bittersweet agonizing pleasure as his lips glided silkily over her fevered skin. And when the pulsating yearning inside her could no longer be denied, he came to her, a jet of molten fire. Wrapped together in ecstasy, they found at last the hidden treasure of fulfillment, the blissful shores of love. And when at last their passion ebbed, they sank together into a precious world of peace.

CHAPTER ELEVEN

WITH THE MORNING LIGHT, Sydne lay nestled in Brian's arms, drowsy with sleep and sated with love.

"I love to touch you," he murmured, running the tips of his fingers over her warm silken skin.

"And I love it when you do," she purred contentedly.

In the union of their flesh, Brian had shown her a dimension of fulfillment that she had never dreamed of even in her wildest imaginings. There were no words to describe the rapture that in a few hours had changed her world.

He brushed her lips, warmed by kisses, with his own before asking, "Where would you like to get married?"

Her eyes widened. "Oh, Brian," she breathed, "do you really mean it?"

"Don't tell me you still don't trust me!" He smiled lazily.

"Brian Stevens, quit teasing me!" she protested, touching the tips of her fingers to his lips.

"Well, then? Would you like to make it a local affair, or would you prefer to fly to San Juan or Miami?"

"Anywhere is all right with me."

"Then let's do it here—" he kissed the tip of her nose playfully "—and soon. I'm not giving you any time to change your mind."

"Not a chance!" she breathed, slipping her arms around his neck and snuggling closer to him provocatively.

THE QUIET COUNTRY CHURCH where they exchanged their vows was so small that it seemed crowded even with their few guests. Andrew, smiling widely as if the whole thing were his idea, gave the bride away. Chuck, well on his way to recovery, was the best man and Julia the only bridesmaid.

Under the loving care of Julia and her mother, Chuck's recovery had been just short of miraculous. Don Francisco was still adamant in his stand, however—refusing to accept the foreigner as his son-in-law. But even this cloud couldn't mar the joyful occasion.

Sydne's dress was simple, and instead of a veil she wore a floppy, wide-brimmed hat. Yet despite the understated quality of the affair, there never was a more radiant bride. All her dreams were coming true. Her love for Brian was obvious to everyone, her joy reflected in her eyes each time she looked at the man in whose arms she had known heaven. And it was only the beginning, she knew. There would be so much more for them as they created memories from their life together.

It had been a hectic week, what with wedding preparations and completion of the salvage work. Sydne had been grateful for their connection with both Andrew and Francisco Lozano. The two influential men had helped them cut through a fair amount of red tape.

Sydne was delighted with the arrangements Brian had made for their brief honeymoon—a cottage in the lovely village of Sosúa. They would move on from there to Santo Domingo, where Brian had to complete all the arrangements for the salvaged treasure.

"We'll have a proper honeymoon later," he had promised, adding mischievously, "You married a very selfish man, and we have a lot of catching up to do. For the next few days I'm not letting you out of my sight. No work, no distractions. Just you and me, babe."

If that was being selfish, then Sydne was selfish, too!

The Lozanos had graciously offered their rambling mansion for the reception which, like the wedding, was an intimate affair. Later the bride changed in Julia's room for the trip to Sosúa. Julia seemed a little downcast as she helped pack away the wedding gown, and Sydne realized that she was probably thinking ahead to her own wedding. Would it be the man she loved or not? Sydne gave Julia a sympathetic hug before she hurried back down the stairs to where Brian was waiting. Today she refused to let anything spoil her happiness. And the thought of having Brian all to herself for the next few days filled her with heady anticipation.

Only now did Sydne really understand what Doña Cristina had revealed in her diary about her love for Felipe. There was so much more than physical pleasure in becoming one with the man you loved!

They drove out to Samaná to the west, along a well-paved road. Brian was at the wheel, Sydne curled up on the seat beside him. Whether they chatted casually or remained silent didn't matter; they were communicating with every gesture.

"I hope you like the cottage," Brian said. "I was there only once when my friend Jim and his wife were in Sosúa, but I think it's the ideal place for us."

"Any place is fine as long as I'm with you." Sydne pressed her cheek against his shoulder.

Brian brushed her hair with his lips. "By the way, my darling, I have a present for you."

"A present?" Sydne sat up expectantly.

He held the steering wheel with one hand for a moment while he groped in his pocket. Then he handed her a small package. Sydne opened the box eagerly. Inside, wrapped in tissue paper, was a bracelet.

"Read the inscription," he told her.

The inside of the bracelet bore two names: Sydne and Tina. "It's Doña Cristina's!" Sydne exclaimed, looking at Brian in delight. "But how did you get it?"

"Out of the sea, naturally. I've been saving it for you as a surprise."

Sydne felt her eyes mist over as she held the plain circle of gold in her hand. The faint inscription was proof enough that, long ago, that had been a gift from Felipe to his lady. That Brian had chosen it as his wedding present to her was an indication of his sensitivity. He must have somehow understood how close she felt to the woman who had written so frankly and sincerely of her love. The night he had found her crying over the salvaged diary had been the turning point in their relationship. It was the first time he had put aside his anger to comfort her, and he had held her with such surprising tenderness.

Almost reverently Sydne slipped the bracelet on her wrist. "Oh, Brian, it's the most wonderful gift," she breathed, kissing his warm cheek shyly. "Thank you, my love."

"I hope you show more appreciation than that when we get to the cottage," he growled, pulling her close and nipping gently at her neck with his teeth.

Sydne laughed with him, then sighed deeply when his fingers moved down from her shoulder to stroke the incipient mounds of her breasts left exposed by the low-cut neckline of her silk dress. She was dying to be in his arms again, and suddenly she couldn't wait any longer to touch him. His sharp intake of breath when she unbuttoned his shirt didn't stop her. Slipping her hand inside, she caressed his broad muscular chest, letting her fingers tangle sensually in the cloud of curly dark hair.

"Don't do that, babe," he told her.

"But I want to touch you!"

"Not while I'm driving," he said tersely. "We'll be at the cottage in less than an hour."

With a disappointed sigh, Sydne drew back.

Brian cast a quick glance in her direction, and at the sight of her quivering lips, explained wryly, "If you keep that up I'll be in no shape to drive." He took her hand and pressed his lips to her open palm. "God, I'm so hungry for you I don't even dare kiss you," he added hoarsely.

"Oh, Brian, I love you so much!"

Again he drew her close, kissing her hair when she laid her head in the hollow of his shoulder.

The colors of the sunset sky were reflected on the water when Brian pulled out of the main highway onto a gravel road that ran toward the sea. Behind tall fences along the way were houses covered with a profusion of bougainvillea, hibiscus, oleander and clinging vines.

What Brian had called a "cottage" turned out to be a bungalow-style house with a generous-sized patio in the back, located at the end of a narrow unpaved street. The fruit-laden branches of a huge mango tree provided shade not only to the entire patio, but also to part of the house and the garage, where Brian parked their car. The bungalow's facade featured a wide veranda facing the ocean, red hibiscus and purple bougainvillea strung in profusion along the railing. There was also an enchanting rock garden, and among the flowering shrubs were flagstone steps that ran from the veranda to the beach below.

Brian deposited their luggage on the porch and fished inside a flowerpot for the key. He grinned as he opened the front door. "We're going to do this right," he declared, lifting Sydne in his arms and crossing the threshold. "Welcome home, Mrs. Stevens."

He didn't put her down until they reached the bedroom.

IT WAS THAT HOUR just before sundown when daylight gently pales and the blue of the sea turns softer. Wearing the scanty bikini she had bought especially for their honeymoon, Sydne lounged lazily in a long rattan chair, letting the cool breeze play over her body and savoring the memory of Brian's lovemaking.

In the four days they had been married they had rarely left this lovely setting. They had been too busy swimming in the ocean and making love, exploring the beach and each other, dancing to the music of old phonograph records; relishing their solitude and treasuring each magic moment.

From inside came the tinkling of ice on glass, and moments later she heard Brian start up the phonograph before he came out to her, two frosty glasses in his hands.

"Hi, gorgeous," he said, offering her one as he sat down on the edge of her chair.

Sydne lifted her face to receive his kiss. Her lips parted eagerly under his, returning the languorous caress.

"Mmm," he said, finally drawing away, "a woman after my own heart."

If someone had told Sydne a few weeks before that she was a very sensuous woman, she would have laughed. That side of her nature had remained dormant until Brian had unleashed it. Now that they were so intimately involved she was coming to terms with her own sexuality—not only accepting it, but reveling in it. She loved to arouse him, knowing instinctively that a man with Brian's strong physical needs could never be satisfied with a prim wife.

Brian went to sit on the rail that bordered the veranda. Sipping his drink, he gazed out across the water, reddened by the last rays of the setting sun. But his distracted frown indicated his thoughts were elsewhere.

"Brian?"

"Mmm?"

"Is anything wrong?"

He turned and gave her a questioning glance.

"You seem worried," she asserted. "Are you expecting problems next week?"

"Not really," he replied. "The Dominicans aren't giving anything away, but they're trustworthy. Besides," he added, "we have a battery of lawyers to handle any legal complications that might come up. We should be okay."

His attitude puzzled her. He had had such a long and arduous struggle to find and salvage the *Conde*, but now that the rewards were at hand he appeared almost indifferent to the project. Why?

The weeks Sydne had spent aboard the *Adventurer* had been exhausting both physically and emotionally, and this wonderful interlude with Brian had seemed like a dream come true. Making love had occupied a large portion of their long lazy days. Each time they came together a new dimension was added to their intimacy, another link in the chain of love that bound her to him. On their walks along the beach, and even during their silences, Sydne felt in perfect tune with him. But moments like this made her realize how little she really knew her husband.

"What made you take such a risk, Brian?" she asked suddenly. "Putting so much into the search for the *Conde*?"

His eyes were fixed on his drink, and she couldn't see their expression when he replied lightly, "It seemed like a good idea at the time."

There had to have been more to it than that, she knew. He must have started the project somewhere around the time of his divorce. Had that been one of the reasons he had committed himself totally to the search—to forget? "Did you begin the salvage operation before or after your divorce?" she asked timidly.

Immediately his eyes turned dark, as if her words had made him angry. "That had nothing to do with it," Brian stated abruptly.

Sydne berated herself for bringing up the subject. It hurt even to think that he had loved another woman before her, perhaps to the point that he had been willing to risk everything he owned to win her back.

"It will take a while to collect our profits," he said, seeming to read her thoughts, "but I can assure you that you have nothing to worry about in the meantime. I can provide adequately for you."

What a curious thing to say, Sydne mused. Aloud she murmured, "I know we'll be very happy, darling."

As he sat on the veranda railing in the gathering dusk his eyes were unreadable, but Sydne could see that his expression was still remote. Something really was wrong, and she was at a loss to know what to do about it.

Brian put an end to her indecision. "Come here," he told her.

Sydne got up from the lounger and moved toward him. She felt a thrill course through her as his gaze skimmed over her, lingering on her soft breasts, which were at his eye level. With one deliberate gesture he loosened the ties that secured her skimpy swimsuit, but made no effort to touch her after it dropped to the deck.

Sydne rested her arms on his shoulders and whispered, "I love you, Brian Stevens."

"Then show me," he answered huskily.

His skin still tasted salty from their late afternoon swim as she trailed her lips across his bare chest, lingering at the pulse in his throat before following the strong line of his jaw. Slowly brushing her bare breasts against his heated skin, she became deliciously aware of the pulsating need of his body. "Let me love you," she breathed against his mouth, teasing his lips with her own and kneading the nape of his neck with her fingers. He moaned with pleasure when she playfully nibbled at his earlobe, and a shiver went through his frame. There was a wild frantic hunger in his response then. His arms closed tightly around her naked body as she feverishly gave him her love.

"HEY, AMBER EYES, look at this one," Brian said, turning around at the jewelry-shop counter. He was holding up a beautiful beaded necklace that ended in a teardrop-shaped pendant. Trapped for eternity in the pendant was the blossom of a prehistoric flower. "How do you like it?"

When Columbus landed on the island he'd made a gift of amber beads to the local chieftain. Ironic, Sydne thought, since the area itself was now so well known as the Amber Coast, the Dominican Republic was one of the prime sources of the organic gem.

She knew that the flower and bits of twigs and leaves embedded in the beads Brian was holding would make the price of the necklace prohibitive. "It's beautiful," she agreed, "but it must cost a fortune."

"Ah, but it goes so well with your eyes," Brian said. With a meaningful look he added, "And with your...personality."

Sydne blushed. She was perfectly aware of what he meant—that far from being a cold mineral, amber is warm to the touch and could burn up in a flame, just as she did in his arms.

Waving her objections aside, Brian bought the necklace, and to her relief the price was not as high as she had feared. From the shop they drove along the palm-lined seaside boulevard to the Fortress of San Felipe, which had recently been restored to its former glory. It had once defended the small town of Puerto Plata, which was now covered in gingerbread and curlicued wrought iron, from attack by pirates and the fierce Carib Indians.

Upon landing on the spot on December 5, 1492, Christopher Columbus had written that the beauty of the sierras, the mountains, the valleys and fields was so inspiring that after seeing it one would never want to leave. And this was exactly the way Sydne felt as she and Brian took the cable car up to the Mirador, a lookout on top of a nearby mountain. The vista from the summit, of forest-covered mountains outlined against an azure sky, of lush green hills and the glimmering sea, lifted her spirits with its magnificence.

During lunch at the mountain-top restaurant Sydne proposed that they visit the ruins of Fuerte Navidad, the fort built in 1493 from the lumber of the *Santa Maria*, which had run aground. When Columbus returned from Spain a year later, Sydne recalled, he found that the entire garrison he'd left behind on Hispaniola—then called Española—had been massacred by the Caribs.

Brian readily agreed to the excursion and added, "If we get back early perhaps we could go horseback riding on the beach before returning to Sosúa."

"That sounds wonderful!" Sydne exclaimed. "Oh, Brian, it's been ages since I've been on a horse. I'd love to!"

"Are you a good rider?"

"Fair," she admitted modestly. "I even entered a few jumping competitions during my 'horsie' phase. Perhaps the hardest thing of all after my parents died was losing Buttercup. I really loved that horse."

"You could get another one." Brian covered her hands with his.

"Oh, that was a long time ago," she said, smiling a little sheepishly because her eyes were filling with tears. "I certainly don't need a horse!"

But it was wonderful cantering along the sandy crescent beach with Brian; wonderful with no one but the sea gulls to witness their passionate kisses when they rested the horses before turning back.

Two days later they took the Duarte Highway toward Santo Domingo, pausing in Santiago de los Caballeros to have a look around. The second largest city on the island, it had immaculate wide streets and beautiful homes. This was the hometown of Julia's fiancé, Lorenzo, the town they would live after their marriage.

"Do you think Julia will ever marry Chuck?" Sydne asked pensively at one point.

"Who knows?"

"I hope she does," she said, mostly to herself.

"She's a fool if she doesn't follow the dictates of her heart."

"Well, I don't know about that," Brian chuckled, casting an amused glance in her direction. "If I remember correctly, not too long ago I was having one hell of a time convincing a certain someone I know to do the same."

"It's not the same at all," Sydne argued with a laugh. "I thought you were having an affair with Julia and only amusing yourself with me. Chuck has actually asked her to marry him. I can understand her obedience to her father, but to marry a man out of duty is going a little too far." Brian refrained from comment, so she went on. "I'm almost positive Matilde is on Julia's side—that she arranged for Chuck to stay with them just so Don Francisco could get to know him. Still," she admitted, "he hasn't shown any signs of changing his mind. Oh, why does he have to be so stubborn! Julia is old enough to know what she wants. Why should she let her father decide who she should marry anyway?"

"Things are different here, babe."

"They sure are—like the double standard that prevails. A man may keep a mistress—discreetly, I suppose—but if a woman strays, God forgive her!"

"That's the way things stand." Brian shrugged dismissively.

"Well, it's unfair! Take it from a woman's point of view. What if *I* were to find a lover? I suppose you would be completely accepting," Sydne scoffed.

Suddenly the humor disappeared from his blue eyes, and he spoke in an oddly strangled tone. "Well, you're dead wrong. I wouldn't stand for it at all!"

SYDNE WAS STILL SHAKEN by Brian's abrupt change of mood by the time they drove through La Vega, not bothering to stop. The passion and romance of the past weeks had made her forget that angry side of Brian she had first encountered, that cold judgmental mask.

What a fool she had been, she chastised herself, joking about such a sensitive subject with a man who had perhaps been on the losing side of adultery. Maybe Helene had had an affair during their marriage. After all, she had left Brian to marry someone else.... Oh, if only he would tell her what had really happened! But after the way he'd reacted earlier at the mention of his divorce, Sydne hesitated to bring up the subject again, especially after his latest outburst.

His face was no longer set in grim lines, but the uneasiness persisted between them and was becoming too much for Sydne to bear. He must have read her mind, for he suggested tentatively, "Would you like to stop up ahead for a cup of coffee?"

"I'd love to," she readily agreed.

Alta Gracia was the next town. They stopped at a roadside food stand, where Brian encouraged Sydne to try the crackling *chicharrones*. She found them delicious, as was the fresh fruit they enjoyed before coffee. Sydne was sorry to turn down piles of the marvelous-looking fruit the cheerful vendor tried to press on her, but what would they do with it in a hotel in Santo Domingo?

The hotel Brian took her to was on the Calle Las Damas, in the heart of the colonial section of the city. Built on the foundations of the very house erect-ed by the first governor of Hispaniola, it followed very closely the original building's floor plan, and combined all the charm of the old with modern conveniences such as central air conditioning. Massive carved mahogany doors, beamed ceilings and beautiful tile floors and exquisite antiques completed the illusion of an old Spanish palace. Their room, on the third floor, overlooked the Ozama River as well as the lovely courtyard of the hotel, where tables had been set around a swimming pool.

"Would you like to go for a swim?" Brian suggested after the bellboy had left them in their spacious room. Still feeling a bit uncomfortable about their earlier argument, Sydne immediately accepted.

Brian must have felt her uneasiness, because he didn't try to make love to her when they returned from the pool. Instead he proposed that they go out to dinner, and selected a beautiful restaurant-nightclub actually built underground.

A mouthwatering paella, the specialty of the house, was brought to their table in a shallow clay dish. The saffron rice was generously layered with succulent shrimp, tender chunks of crab, lobster, chicken and chorizo, a spicy Spanish sausage. It was topped with mussels and clams in their shells. The meal was excellent, but Sydne had little taste for food. Instead, in an effort to relax, she sipped the light German wine Brian had ordered. Even so, she was tense when he drew her out onto the dance floor. But as his hands on her back molded her body to his, Sydne let her head rest on his chest with a heartfelt sigh.

What was happening to them? Their brief flare of

temper was turning into a nightmare of unspoken doubts. She loved Brian too much to let something like a silly argument come between them, erasing all the magic they had known. She was just being a fool. Yet, wanting to delay their return to the hotel, Sydne suggested they walk along the Malecon, the busy street that bordered the sea, where they paused to listen to the music of a lonely guitar.

"Tired?" Brian asked when they finally reached their luxurious room.

"A little," Sydne admitted. The stroll back to the hotel had been longer than she had anticipated. But even though the walk had relaxed them both, she was still a little unsure of what to say to him.

Brian framed her face with his hands and lifted her chin. His mouth touched hers, tentatively at first. But when his kiss deepened her lips parted and she clung to him in desperation. Sydne couldn't bear another minute of the estrangement that had developed between them. She needed the comfort of his arms holding her, needed to become a part of him. "Oh, Brian, I love you so much!" she murmured passionately. "Love me back, my darling. Oh, please, love me!"

Abruptly she was crushed against him as he possessed her mouth, and she gasped with a mixture of pleasure and surprise at the fever of his passion. His frenzied caresses ignited her blood.

"You're my woman," he whispered as he carried her to bed. "And you'll never leave me."

They had to talk, Sydne knew, but that could wait....

IN A VERY SHORT TIME after it was founded by Bartolomé Columbus, the famous explorer's brother, Santo Domingo became the most prosperous city of the New World. It enjoyed a period of flourishing growth during the first half of the sixteenth century, and many Spanish ships that discovered and conquered previously uncharted territory first put in at its shores. Hernando Cortés, conqueror of Mexico; Francisco Pizarro, en route to Panama and the conquest of Peru; Vasco Nuñez de Balboa, who discovered the Pacific; and Ponce de Leon on his way to colonize Puerto Rico—these were only a few renowned explorers who were entertained in the great reception halls of the splendid governor's palace, the Alcazar, during this dazzling age.

But as the gold of the Aztecs and the Incas drew the attention of the world, Santo Domingo declined dramatically in importance and affluence—to the point where when it was attacked and plundered by Sir Francis Drake in 1586, the city was put to the torch street by street, because its citizens were too poor to pay the ransom demanded.

The next four turbulent centuries—centuries that took the city through periods of prosperity as well as pirate sieges and wars—wrought countless changes in Santo Domingo. But, miraculously perhaps, the Alcazar survived, and was even restored to its former glory. The forty-inch-thick coral limestone walls of its majestic facade no longer bore the scars of the bullets they had deflected during the last civil strife. Austere but beautiful, the palace once again reflected the life-style of its original illustrious occupants.

In the morning Sydne and Brian strolled arm in

arm through the Alcazar's historic halls, then went across the plaza to explore the museum, which housed countless Spanish relics. They even stopped to visit the cathedral of Santa Maria Le Menor, which guarded the mortal remains of Christopher Columbus.

After lunch, taking advantage of the fact that Brian had business with some government officials, Sydne spent some time in a beauty shop, then decided to pick up a few gifts for their friends in Samaná. The numerous stalls of the Mercado Modelo offered everything from mouthwatering fruits and vegetables to mahogany ware, baskets and hats. Sydne was delighted by an exquisite set of brushes with tortoise-shell backing, and was about to pay the price the vendor had asked when a masculine voice interrupted her. "Excuse me, ma'am, but he's asking too much. You're expected to barter a little."

Surprised at hearing an American accent, Sydne turned around to find a nice-looking young man smiling rather shyly at her. He was tall and slim but well built, with light brown hair and brown eyes. He couldn't have been more than seventeen or eighteen. Sydne had noticed him the day before at the hotel, accompanied by an older couple she had presumed were his parents.

"Oh, hi." She smiled at him. "I'm afraid I've never been very good at bartering. It always makes me feel a little guilty," she admitted wryly.

"No reason to feel that way," the young man responded in a friendly tone. "It's a time-honored custom, and we shouldn't disappoint them, should we? May I?"

"By all means," Sydne agreed readily. She listened with interest as he bargained with the vendor in accented but correct Spanish. Finally the price of the brushes was lowered to everyone's satisfaction, and the bargain was struck.

"Thank you," Sydne said, smiling gratefully at her young savior. "You were great! By the way, I'm Sydne Ma—Stevens," she corrected, offering him her hand.

"Eric Masters," he replied with a firm handshake.

"Well, thank you, Eric. I really appreciate your help. Are your parents with you?"

"They're back at the hotel having a siesta."

"My husband is busy this afternoon, too. If you have no other plans, what would you say to our shopping together?"

Eric agreed, so they spent the rest of the afternoon at the various shops on Conde Street, pausing only to enjoy delicious fruit milk shakes.

Eric was a high-school senior from southern California, he told her, and he and his parents were planning to leave for Puerto Plata the following day. Since snorkeling was one of his hobbies, he was very interested in the kind of work Brian did and in Sydne's description of her own underwater adventures. By the time they arrived back at the hotel she realized she had learned more about her new friend in one afternoon than she knew about her husband.

Brian had just returned, too, as Sydne and Eric walked into the lobby. When he had collected the key at the reception desk, she introduced the two men. They chatted together for a few minutes about skin diving before they parted.

"I'm going to have to keep an eye on you," Brian said to Sydne on the way up to their room.

Sydne's mouth opened in protest, but she saw with relief that he was only teasing. "He's a nice boy," she said simply.

"And one with excellent taste," Brian said, unlocking the door to their room. Once inside, he drew her into his arms. "Can't say I blame him for looking at you the way he did," he added before he kissed her. "I missed you this afternoon."

Sydne rubbed her nose against his chin. "And I missed you."

"How about a swim before dinner?"

"Sounds great."

But as they changed into their bathing suits, Sydne found herself mulling over her reaction to Brian's comment. She was being silly about the whole thing, she chided herself. Brian wasn't really jealous of her and Eric.

CHAPTER TWELVE

THE DARK HAIRS on Brian's chest were damp under Sydne's cheek after their passionate lovemaking, despite the cool breeze floating through the open window of their bedroom. The breeze brought with it the fragrance of lush tropical gardens, and their two-story, red-tile-roofed *casita* was so close to the sea that they could hear the murmur of waves breaking on the shore.

They had left the capital during a lull in negotiations with the Dominican authorities, and were spending the brief respite at Casa de Campo, a luxurious hotel near the well-known resort town of La Romana. There were many celebrities among the guests, especially since a polo tournament was about to take place.

Arriving early at the hotel, Sydne and Brian had gone horseback riding, taken a lazy siesta and spent the afternoon on the beach.

"Brian, when can we go home?" Sydne asked now, propping herself up in bed on one elbow.

He lifted a hand to stroke her hair. "Anxious?"

"In a good way," she agreed. She had never been to Fort Lauderdale, where Brian had his business headquarters and maintained a penthouse apartment, but to her it was already home. Home! What a marvelous word it was, and for the first time in many years it had meaning for her.

"It won't be long now," Brian said. "The artifacts will be displayed at the museum in Santo Domingo for a couple of months, but we can head for home as soon as all the papers are signed."

"What are you going to do with your share of the goods?"

"Our share," he corrected. "They'll go on auction in London. After paying off the expenses, some of the proceeds will go into the business."

"Are you planning to look for another galleon?" she asked, unable to hide her apprehension.

"Not right away," he chuckled. "There are other kinds of marine salvage, babe. Commercial, for instance. You know, repairing underwater construction, oil rigs, laying cables and the like. Not very romantic, is it?" he said wryly. "I'm not a professional treasure hunter or a man of leisure." He regarded her soberly before adding, "Disappointed?"

"No—" she smiled "—I'm glad."

"Why?"

"Because I don't want you taking so many risks."

"What makes you think I do?"

Sydne touched the scar on his thigh. "This."

His expression softened. "That was a fluke. I wish I could impress you with a dramatic story, like wrestling with a moray eel or something of that nature, but I just cut myself on some rocks years ago. Like most animals, eels don't attack unless they're threatened."

"And sharks?"

"They seldom bother anyone." Brian smiled, kissing her shoulder before he rolled over onto his back. "Don't take everything you see in the movies so literally, Syd. You saw what happened when we met the blue."

When she remained pensive he added, "I'm not going to sit behind a desk from nine to five, so you'd better get used to the idea. I won't deny there can be danger in the sea, but if you know what you're doing and don't take unnecessary risks there's no reason to be afraid. You saw how much beauty that world holds. I could have talked myself hoarse and still you wouldn't have really understood how fantastic it is until you had seen it for yourself. That's why I took you there, babe. Were you afraid?"

"Only when we met the shark," she admitted. "But otherwise it was so beautiful that danger didn't even occur to me."

"That's my girl!" Brian laughed, pulling her against his chest in a hearty squeeze. "When we get back to Fort Lauderdale you can take scuba lessons and become a certified diver. Then we'll be able to go diving together."

The idea appealed to her. "I still have to move out of my apartment in Minneapolis," she said after a pause.

"How long will you need?"

"No more than a couple of days. I don't have a lot of knickknacks, or books."

"Good. I like a woman who travels light." Brian grinned. Running a proprietary hand over her body, he said possessively, "And I'm glad I've got you."

Sydne loved horseback riding, and the stables of the Casa de Campo were full of splendid animals. By the second morning she seemed to have adopted a roan mare that would have presented a challenge to a lesser rider. She and Brian spent relaxing, sun-warmed days alternately horseback riding and snorkeling in the clear waters.

The dining room, situated on a large outdoor terrace overlooking the pool and gardens, was filled each evening with slim tanned women in glittering jewels and men in blazers and ascots. Here and there Sydne caught sight of faces that appeared frequently in newspapers, magazines, television—a famous clothes designer, a TV actor, a socialite, a politician. Conversation was always subdued, and there was a cultivated air to the gathering. But Brian didn't seem pleased with the setting.

"Brian, darling!" someone called out one evening as they made their way to the secluded corner table he had requested. Both Sydne and Brian turned in the direction of the voice.

Sydne couldn't begin to guess the age of the woman who had spoken. Her beautifully styled hair owed its rich chestnut color to chemistry, she was fairly sure, and her tanned complexion was smooth. But her hands, where diamonds glittered in profusion, betrayed that she was not as young as she appeared at first glance. The man with her was middle-aged and overweight, his complexion florid. He rose as Sydne and Brian approached their table.

"Hello, Maude," Brian said politely, taking the bejeweled hand the woman offered and accepting the kiss she planted on his lips.

"What a delightful surprise, darling," the woman said in a low husky voice. Indicating her companion, she added, "This is my new husband, Harry Webster. Harry, say hello to Brian Stevens, a dear friend."

Brian shook hands with the man, and to Sydne he said, "Darling, meet Maude and Harry Webster. My wife, Sydne."

"Your wife!" the woman gushed. "How do you do!" She squinted her eyes slightly as if to see her better.

Sydne was taken by surprise. She had had no idea that Brian moved in such exclusive circles, but there was no doubt Maude Webster knew him well. With a sinking heart she realized that the woman must have known Helene, and that she was now probably comparing her to Brian's first wife. Sydne was wearing a new dress, one she had purchased in Santo Domingo to wear with the amber necklace Brian had given her. It was pretty enough, but in comparison to Maude's designer creation and to the fashions worn by the other women present, she suddenly felt underdressed.

Harry Webster, at least, seemed like a genuinely jovial sort. "Won't you join us?" he invited cordially.

"Thank you," Brian replied, to Sydne's relief adding, "but we'll take a rain check if you don't mind."

"Are you here for the polo tournament?" Maude inquired, pointedly ignoring Sydne.

"As the matter of fact, we're here on our honeymoon," Brian replied, slipping an arm around Sydne's waist.

"So you want to be alone with your little bride." Maude's smile carried a subtle note of sarcasm. "How quaint and charming."

"Well, it was nice seeing you again, Maude," Brian said insincerely. "If you will excuse us, our table is ready." He nodded to Harry Webster before steering Sydne away.

"I'm sorry about that, babe," he said once they were seated at their table.

"Who is she anyway?" Sydne inquired after the waiter had taken their order.

"One of the 'beautiful people,' who have nothing better to do with their lives than move from one place to another in an endless pursuit of pleasure. The south of France, Acapulco, Palm Beach—you name it, they're there."

"Harry Webster seems like a nice man," Sydne commented for lack of anything else to say.

"Poor man," Brian agreed. "I wonder if he knows what he's got himself into. Maude changes husbands as often as she changes the color of her hair. He must be her fourth or fifth."

"Were you...a part of that crowd?" Sydne inquired after a thoughtful pause.

"Not really."

His vague answer spoke volumes. It must have been Helene who had moved with the jet set—and now Sydne was definitely being compared to her!

Brian must have sensed her uneasiness. "Would you like to go back to Santo Domingo tomorrow?" he suggested.

Was he ashamed of being seen with her, Sydne wondered for a wild moment. She could still hear the note of malice in Maude Webster's voice when she had called her Brian's "little bride." No, returning to the capital would only prove to Maude and her crowd that Brian felt he had to hide her away. Sydne was too proud to allow that.

But was there another reason why Brian wanted to leave the Casa de Campo? Was he afraid to run into his ex-wife? "Do *you* want to go back?" she asked in turn.

Something in her tone must have communicated a challenge. "It doesn't matter." He shrugged.

"Then I'd like to stay," Sydne replied as casually as she could. "I've never seen a polo tournament."

A HIGHLY REFINED and sophisticated game that combined elements of horse racing, hockey and soccer, polo was perhaps the oldest organized sport being played today, Sydne knew. Most historians believe it originated in Persia and was played there in the first century A.D. as a training game for elite cavalry troops, before becoming the sport of the nobility. From there it made its way to Turkey, India, Tibet, China and Japan. In the nineteenth century it was revived in India, where it was discovered by British soldiers and taken to Europe.

Once played only by aristocratics, the game retained, even today, that special glamour reserved for the wealthy, and the crowd attending the tournament at the Polo Club La Romana reflected the fact. The occasion was even more prestigious than usual—a charity benefit for some international organization—and the very best players had arrived with their entourages and their ponies.

Drawn almost inevitably into the ensuing social whirl, the Stevenses were attending a party the next night when a waiter delivered a message to Brian and he excused himself. At that point Sydne was engrossed in conversation with Jorge Zamora, a handsome Argentine playboy whose exploits in international boudoirs had received as much publicity as his feats on the polo field.

It was amazing how much confidence a woman could gain simply by changing her dress, Sydne had decided earlier. The previous evening she had felt totally out of place. But now, wearing a new creation she had acquired at the resort boutique, she was totally at ease. She had always been clothes conscious, perhaps because her mother had been a well-dressed woman and had passed on her good taste. During the lean years Sydne had become an expert at getting the best for the least, taking advantage of marked-down items and combing secondhand shops that sold clothes discarded by wealthy women after one or two wearings. Still hanging in her closet in Minneapolis was a Cardin suit she had bought for a song at one of those thrift shops.

The prices in the hotel boutique had made Sydne wince, but grimly reminding herself that she had married a man accustomed to elegant women, she had bought a particularly flattering black dress. With its handkerchief skirt and flounced round neckline, the gown was simple but elegant, and the way she felt in it made it well worth the investment.

Sydne's attention wandered from Jorge Zamora's conversation when Brian returned to the party. He came over to her right away, and she turned to smile at him.

"Excuse us," he said taking his wife by the arm.

"I had a call from Samaná," he told her when they were out of earshot.

"Is Chuck all right?"

"Couldn't be better." Brian grinned. "He and Julia are getting married."

"Married!" Sydne cried, and realized her voice had risen in her excitement. Embarrassed, she looked around to see if anyone had heard. No one appeared to have noticed. "When?"

"In two weeks."

"So soon?"

"It seems Doña Matilde's plan worked," Brian conceded. "Don Francisco has finally relented."

"Oh, I'm so happy for them!" Sydne exclaimed.

"You women always manage to get what you want, don't you?"

Something in the way he said it gave her pause. "What is that supposed to mean?" she asked on a sharp note.

"Nothing." Looking around at the elegant gathering he asked, "Have you had enough of this for one night?"

Sydne smiled and took his hand. "Uh-huh. Let's go to bed, shall we?"

Next day the tournament began in earnest. The two teams of four players each were lined up in the center of the huge playing field. The ponies, their manes clipped and their tails braided so they wouldn't get in the way, had their legs bandaged from ankle to knee for protection.

Wearing colored shirts bearing their numbers, whips and mallets at the ready, the players waited for the mounted umpire to bowl the ball between their lines. Sydne noticed that Jorge Zamora was playing pivot man, the number three position that Brian said was usually reserved for the best player on the team.

The moment the little ball was released the field became a confusion of horses, riders and mallets. Jorge fielded a ball to number two, while helping numbers one and four maintain a solid defense. There was little doubt that the Argentinean was a superb player. Number two hit the ball through the goalposts and scored.

The heavy stress placed on the horses made it necessary to change mounts at the end of each chukker, as the periods of play lasting seven and a half minutes were called. By the end of the first period Zamora's team was in the lead, and it maintained the advantage to the end of the game.

Sydne enjoyed the spectacle more than she anticipated. It was fast-paced and exciting, and each horse was a joy to watch.

Brian, sitting next to her, looked into her eyes, which were bright with excitement. "I'm going to Santo Domingo this afternoon," he announced.

"Are the negotiations being resumed?"

"Looks that way."

"Should I come with you?"

"I'll be in meetings all afternoon. It's up to you."

With Andrew back in the States and her own work on the artifacts completed, there was nothing for Sydne to do in the capital. Brian didn't seem to expect her to go. It was less than an hour's drive to the city, after all. "I suppose I could stay here and spend the time on the beach," she said at last.

"Suit yourself," he answered casually, finally releasing her from his intent appraisal.

Brian left after lunch, and about an hour later
Sydne decided that reading at the beach would be
more pleasant than staying in the *casita*. She took the
resort's horse-drawn buckboard down to the immaculate little beach, where an attentive waiter set up a
lounger for her in the shade of a thatch-roof cabana,
disappearing after she declined a drink. Liberally applying coconut oil for protection, she then began to
read her novel, until the warm breeze playing across
her body made her drowsy. Giving in to the languorous feeling, she put her book aside, pulled her straw
hat over her face to shield it from the glare and fell
asleep.

Eventually the sound of feminine voices from the
other side of the cabana filtered through her stupor,
but since she had little inclination for conversation,
Sydne decided to remain as she was. Her two neigh-
bors, she deduced, had come to Casa de Campo from
the polo tournament, and they entertained themselves by discussing their mutual acquaintances. A
few minutes later a third woman joined them, apparently a new arrival at the resort, who was greeted
effusively by her friends.

"It was a total disaster," she was saying after the
initial greetings. "The flight from Sardinia was late,
and I missed my connection in Rome. Otherwise I
would have been here yesterday. How was the
match?"

"Who cares!" The second woman laughed, and
the others joined in.

"True," the newcomer agreed. "Maybe I should

have asked instead, 'who is here?' And by the way,'' she continued before her friends could answer, "you'll never guess who I just met as I drove in. Brian Stevens!''

Sydne, who had just made up her mind to take a swim in order to get away from their gossip, froze in her chair.

"And he looks divine!" the woman was saying.

"What else is new?"

"I was so surprised to see him," she continued. "He seemed to disappear after Palm Beach, and he was the last man I expected to meet here."

"You might as well stop drooling, Jackie," her friend warned. "He's here on his honeymoon."

"He's remarried?" Jackie was obviously surprised. "What a pity—but no matter. Who's the lucky girl?"

"A little nobody, from what I hear."

"Well, well, well, what do you know?" she chuckled. "So he's got over Helene."

"Don't be too sure," the first voice said smoothly.

"What do you mean?"

"Well, I haven't met his new wife, but from what Maude tells me she could pass for Helene."

"Oh, no! The poor girl," the second woman commiserated.

"Nonsense!" Jackie argued. "She's caught herself a man who is gorgeous, sexy and rich to boot. How often do you find that combination?"

"I never understood how Helene could leave him," the second woman commented. "He was crazy about her."

"Well, he was a little...unconventional," Jackie offered in her dry cultured voice.

"Unconventional? In what way?"

"You know, he had this crazy idea that he had to work for a living."

The women burst out laughing. "Well, sometimes a book isn't as good as its cover leads you to believe," one of them pointed out.

"In this particular case, it is." Jackie's throaty laugh was charged with meaning. "Take my word for it, girls."

Despite the tropical sun, Sydne felt herself grow cold.

"And I thought Helene was your best friend!"

"She is," Jackie replied easily. "Actually, some of my favorite lovers have been married to my best friends. It sort of keeps everything in the family. Now, take Brian for instance...." She lowered her voice.

Too stunned to move, Sydne listened as the woman discussed his sexual prowess, boldly describing shockingly intimate details of what had clearly been a very physical affair. The pain in Sydne's heart was so sharp that her breathing became labored. They were talking about the man she loved! She wanted to scream at Jackie to stop, yet another part of her listened with morbid fascination as the woman went on and on.

"Now that he's back, I wouldn't mind at all renewing that friendship," Jackie confessed silkily. "Actually I'm looking forward to it."

Finally Sydne couldn't bear to hear any more. Without looking at the nearby women, she got up from the lounger and began to collect her belongings. But she couldn't walk away without taking at least one long look at the woman who had known her husband so intimately.

She must have been in her thirties, sophisticated and beautiful, Sydne decided. Her light blond hair contrasted with the golden tan of her skin, and the brief white bikini she wore hid little of her slim body—the small high breasts, narrow waist and softly rounded hips that tapered down to long slender legs. Jackie's icy blue green eyes were examining Sydne's figure rather absently at the same time, until their gazes met. Perhaps the woman saw the pain in Sydne's eyes, for her expression changed to one of recognition, and then a contemptuous smile curved her sensuous mouth.

Sydne held her head erect as she walked away, but the derisive laughter that rang in her ears convinced her the woman must have guessed who she was.

Once safely inside the *casita*, Sydne stood uncertainly in the middle of the small parlor and looked around, as if seeing the room for the first time. She had no recollection of how she'd got there. The pain inside her was still so sharp that she couldn't even cry. An icy coldness was taking over, and she found she was actually shaking. She sat down cross-legged on the floor, her teeth chattering. Hugging herself and rocking back and forth, she sought relief in tears that refused to come.

Brian didn't love her; he never had. He had married her because he couldn't have Helene! Each time he held her, it was Helene he was loving, not her. For him the real Sydne didn't exist. And God only knew where Jackie came into the picture.

She couldn't seem to stop torturing herself with

bitter thoughts, and dusk was turning into darkness before Sydne finally returned dully to reality. Brian would be returning at any moment, she realized. How could she face him, knowing what she did? The answer was clear: she couldn't.

In a fog she ran to the bedroom, threw the closet doors open and pulled out her suitcase. She began piling her clothes into it, and the suitcase was half-full before she stopped to think. No, she couldn't run away again like a fugitive. Brian was her husband, the man she loved more than life itself. He deserved a chance to tell his side of the story.

But to what end? If he denied what Jackie had revealed, Sydne knew deep in her heart that she wouldn't believe him, no matter how much she wanted to. The doubt would never leave her. And if he admitted that she was only a substitute for Helene, her pride wouldn't allow her to stay with him another minute.

Pride, she mused. What was pride compared to love? Never to be held in his arms again, never to know his kisses and his warmth, or bear his child. . . .

A few hours ago Sydne had been the happiest woman in the world. True, she'd known so little about Brian—so little when she wanted to know so much—but they had only been married two weeks. She had been confident that time would bring them closer together, that Brian was reluctant to talk about his past because the subject of his divorce was still painful. She had hoped he would open his heart to her when he learned to believe in her love. But this was the end of her hopes. . . . Or was it?

Sydne thought of the times she had awakened in

the night just to touch him, almost to reassure herself that he was real. He had become the center of her world. The thought of life without him terrified her.

Suddenly Sydne had a feeling of déjà vu, as if she had lived this same situation before. It was then that she remembered Doña Cristina's diary, the woman who through space and time had seemed to reach out to bring her and Brian together. Cristina, too, hadn't been able to bear the thought of life without her husband, and in the end Felipe had come back to her.

Sydne touched the gold bracelet on her wrist, as if it were a magic talisman that would give her the strength she needed to win her husband's love.

She was more composed by the time Brian returned for dinner. "Hi, babe," he said, catching her in his arms and giving her a hungry kiss.

She was dressed and waiting for him, having used the time to think things over, but she still couldn't bring herself to put much enthusiasm into her response. "How did things go?" she asked, disengaging herself from his embrace.

Brian gave her a curious glance. "Great," he replied, emptying his pockets and beginning to take off his clothes. "I think everything will be settled by the end of this week. Whew, it was hot in Santo Domingo today," he added. "You were right to stay here. Did you enjoy the beach?"

"It was nice," Sydne replied, collecting the clothes he had discarded on the floor. Naked, Brian came up behind her and captured her in the circle of his arms. "Mmm, you smell sweet," he said, burying his face in the hollow of her shoulder. "What would you say to a moonlight swim later?"

Her skin tingled where his lips had touched it, but when he slipped his hand inside her dress to cup her breast Sydne tensed. "Don't!" she gasped, stepping away from him.

For a moment there was silence between them as Sydne averted her eyes. "All right, Sydne," Brian said at last. "What's going on?"

She was sorely tempted to confront him with what she had learned that afternoon, but she faltered at the last minute, terrified that he would tell her it was all true. No, she couldn't. She needed more time. "Nothing really," she said quietly.

His expression softened. "Something is bothering you, babe. I know you." He sat down on the bed and drew her onto his lap. "What is it?"

His gentleness unhinged her. "Oh, Brian!" she blurted out, flinging her arms around his neck and burying her face in his shoulder.

"Honey, what's the matter?" he asked, alarmed by her sudden tears. "Won't you tell me what's wrong?"

Oh, if only she could tell him the truth! Wildly Sydne groped for something to say. Anything would do. Then she thought of the dress she had purchased. Wiping away her tears, she managed to say, "It's just that I have nothing to wear. All my dresses are so... so ugly!"

Brian was taken aback. "What?" he exclaimed.

Sydne swallowed hard. Lying didn't come easily to her. "You saw the way Maude Webster was dressed," she said, forcing herself to go on. "All the women here are so elegant and beautiful. Oh, Brian, I feel terribly shabby next to them.''

She felt his body tense. "If you need clothes there are shops right here, Sydne," he said, unable to hide his impatience. "Buy anything you want.''

"Anything?" she repeated, regarding him through the haze of her tears. She could tell he was angry. "The prices are so high," she reminded him. "Can you afford them?"

"You didn't marry a pauper," he said tersely, then added, "I'd better take a shower."

Sydne rose from his lap, and without even looking at her again he went into the bathroom. Moments later she heard the shower running.

What a mess, she sighed inwardly. Now Brian was angry. Perhaps he thought she was a fool for making such an issue over some silly gowns. Well, better that than a confrontation that could end everything.

The first person they spotted when they went into the dining room a while later was Jackie, who was sharing a table with Jorge Zamora and the Websters. In full regalia she appeared as beautiful as Sydne had dreaded. When she waved them toward the table they had no choice but to stop and say hello.

"Brian, darling!" Jackie rose gracefully from her seat and flung her arms around his neck. The kiss she planted on his lips was more than friendly.

Brian threw an uneasy glance at his wife, but Sydne had carefully schooled her features to betray no emotion.

"Darling," he said, gently removing Jackie's arms from around his neck, "this is Jackie Newton." And to Jackie, almost as a warning, "Sydne, my wife."

"Hello, Sydne." Jackie's smile was charged with innuendo. "I hope you don't mind my kissing your husband. We're very old friends."

Her meaning was perfectly clear, and Sydne suppressed the wave of anger that threatened to engulf her. "Me—mind old friends?" she said instead. "Of course not, Jackie, darling. Only young ones."

The other woman's face blanched, and Sydne saw the quirk of amusement curling the corners of Brian's mouth. Ignoring them both, she greeted the other people at the table, aware of the sullen look Jackie was throwing in her direction.

But Jackie was not about to let them go. "Please join us, darling." Her invitation was accompanied by a seductive smile directed at Brian. "It's been such a long time."

Perhaps it would have been better to make excuses and find another table, but Sydne was on the warpath. "We'd be delighted," she accepted, without giving her husband a glance. "I'm sure you two have a lot to talk about." She took the seat Jorge rushed to offer her, since Jackie was still clinging to Brian's arm.

"You were wonderful today, Jorge." Sydne smiled at the Argentinean.

But before he could reply Jackie broke in. "I didn't know you were a polo aficionado, Sydne."

Obviously still smarting from the younger woman's remark, she added, "I thought it was still the domain of more exclusive circles."

"As a matter of fact, today was the first time I've seen the game played," Sydne admitted, disregarding the dig. "And I didn't know it could be so exciting.

The horses are magnificently trained," she said, moving on to more familiar ground. "You must be very proud of them, Jorge—especially of that chestnut mare you rode in the last chukker."

"That's Mariposa," Jorge Zamora replied.

"She's a grade thoroughbred, isn't she?"

"You know your horses." He seemed genuinely pleased that she'd noticed. "Yes, she is one-fourth quarter horse."

"Tell me about Mariposa. How old is she?"

"Nine years old. She's in her prime now."

"Did you train her yourself?"

"For the most part—at least since she was five. I keep her out on the pampas of my *estancia*, which is near Rosario, Argentina."

"Estancia?" Sydne repeated.

"My ranch. That's where I raise ponies, and where I trained Mariposa."

"She really does you proud." For a moment Sydne was pensive, then she went on, "Mariposa is such a lovely name. And she really did look like a butterfly out there in the field. She seemed to have wings."

"Ah, so you do know the meaning of the word!" Highly gratified, Jorge added, "You speak Spanish, then, no?"

"Un poquito, señor," Sydne replied with an impish grin. "But I'm afraid it's a little rusty with disuse."

"Then you must allow me to help you remember," Jorge Zamora offered gallantly, a wealth of meaning in his tone.

Once set on this dangerous course Sydne couldn't turn back, and she smiled briefly into his eyes before

turning her attention to the rest of the group. To her
chagrin she discovered her entire performance had
gone for naught, since Brian's attention hadn't wavered from Jackie.

"I've really missed you, darling," Jackie was telling Brian in her low husky voice, giving him a low-
lidded glance that oozed seduction. "Tell me, what
have you been doing with yourself besides getting
married again?"

"Salvaging a galleon," Brian replied, and it was
obvious to Sydne how much he was enjoying Jackie's
attentiveness. "As the matter of fact, that's how
Sydne and I met."

"Sydne?" Jackie arched a delicate brow. "Don't
tell me she's a diver!"

"No, not yet." Laughing, Brian qualified, "But
she will be in due time, I hope. No, Sydne is an
archaeologist."

"An archaeologist!" Jackie exclaimed. "My dear,
what a plebian way to make a living! Isn't it terribly...boring?"

"On the contrary," Sydne replied sweetly. "It's
really fascinating. And one of the things you learn
right away is how to recognize a relic when you see
one."

Jorge Zamora choked on his mouthful of champagne, and if looks could kill, the one Jackie sent in
Sydne's direction would have crystallized her on the
spot.

Silence fell over the table while the waiters served
the sumptuous meal, and afterward it was the Argentine playboy who suggested a visit to the nightclub on
the grounds.

Dancing a bit later with Jorge to the rhythm of a Latin band, Sydne felt a stab of jealousy when she glanced across the crowded floor at her husband. He was dancing with Jackie, their bodies so close that they seemed to be glued to each other.

Sydne's own partner was a marvelous dancer, but although she tried to derive pleasure from his skill and from the compliments he whispered in her ear, she was totally unmoved by them. All she felt was relief when the music ended and a comedian took the stage.

Jackie monopolized Brian's attention with her whispered conversation as soon as they returned to the table. Sydne pretended interest in the performance until Jorge, who was sitting on the other side of her, leaned forward to murmur in her ear, "What are your plans for tomorrow?"

"I don't really know," Sydne replied, also in a whisper. "Brian hasn't mentioned anything in particular. Why?"

"I thought you might like to play some tennis after the polo match."

"Doubles or singles?" Sydne smiled sweetly.

Jorge gave her a meaningful look. "That will be up to you."

Her inclination was to refuse, but when she glanced again at her husband and saw that he was still absorbed by Jackie, she turned to Jorge again. "I'll let you know tomorrow," she whispered.

Sydne couldn't recall ever having been as miserable as she was that evening. She made all the right moves, laughing at the comedian's jokes when the others did, but if anyone had asked her to repeat one, she would have been at a loss. She was so glad when it was time to say good-night that she had to stop herself from jumping to her feet and hurrying out of the nightclub.

But her misery didn't end there. Brian was so quiet during the short drive back to their *casita* that Sydne felt a wild urge to scream—anything to break the silence in the car.

She was becoming hysterical, she admonished herself. Everything would be all right once she and Brian were alone together. He would take her in his arms, and their love would make everything all right. This horrible day was only a nightmare; it wasn't real. Brian loved her. He didn't love Jackie Newton!

Her sigh of relief was audible when he pulled up in front of their *casita*.

Brian turned to look at her. "Tired?" he asked as he switched off the ignition.

"A little," she admitted.

"You'll be able to sleep as late as you want tomorrow," he said before he got out and went around the car to open her door. "I'm driving into Santo Domingo early in the morning."

She accepted his hand and stood up. "Again?"

They walked together to the front door, and Brian waited until they were inside before saying, "More meetings. I'd expected as much."

He hadn't even asked if she wanted to go with him, Sydne thought as she walked into their bedroom and flipped on the light switch. "Perhaps we should just go back to Santo Domingo, Brian," she suggested as she began to undress, hoping with all her heart he would agree. "There's really no need for you to be doing all this driving."

She didn't know if Brian's shrug meant something or if he was simply removing his shirt. "It doesn't bother me," he replied. "It's not that far to drive. Besides, I thought you wanted to stay the week."

Afraid to sound too insistent, she let the matter drop. Instead she asked, "How long will you be gone?"

"Probably all day. Why?"

"Oh, nothing. I just wanted to know if I should wait for you or do something on my own."

Sydne's frustration increased with every minute of conversation. Why couldn't she go to him right this minute, throw her arms around his neck, tell him exactly how she felt and clear the air between them? She wanted to, but when she looked at Brian's reflection in the mirror, she lost her nerve. He was staring at her with a grim expression on his face. Their eyes met for just an instant, and then he looked away and got into bed.

That glance, Brian's whole attitude, left Sydne almost paralyzed as she sat at the dressing table. Was it possible that since Jackie had come back into his life, he was realizing his mistake and regretting their marriage?

Unable to lie down next to Brian as if nothing had happened, Sydne switched off the bedroom lights and stepped restlessly out onto the small balcony overlooking the sea. The fine crescent of a new moon made for a dark night, and although she could hear the sound of the waves, all she could see were elusive white caps running toward the shore, mysterious white spirits that soon vanished in the gloom.

When she opened her eyes in the morning the first thing Sydne noticed was the empty space beside her.

Turning to the bedside table, she discovered that it was nearly ten o'clock.

She would have to hurry if she wanted to catch the polo match at eleven, she told herself, starting to get up. But then she stopped, realizing that she really didn't care whether she missed it or not. What was the point anyway, she asked herself, staring at the ceiling. All she cared about in the world was Brian, and he seemed to be slipping away from her even before their honeymoon was over.

Last night had been the first night since their marriage that they hadn't made love. How different things had been between them during those marvelous days spent in the cottage in Sosúa. In that relatively simple little house, without many of the luxuries surrounding them now, they had shut themselves away from the world and just lived for each other. She wanted desperately to go back there, to recapture the magic before they lost it forever. But they couldn't hide from the world for the rest of their lives, she realized with a heavy heart.

The telephone on the bedside table shrilled twice before she reached for it. "Hello?"

"Good morning, Sydne." It was Jorge Zamora.

She tried not to sound depressed when she answered, "Good morning, Jorge. All set for the match?"

"Of course. Since your husband is away, I wondered if you would like to drive with me to the *rancho*." She knew he was referring to Rancho Cajuiles, where the polo match was to be held. Occasionally mini-rodeos featuring local talent were staged there for the amusement of the resort guests.

"You seem very well informed about my husband's activities, Jorge," she stated rather primly. But despite his reputation in the romance department, Sydne had found Jorge very good company, and when she heard his chuckle she was glad he hadn't been offended by the sharpness of her tone.

"Ah, Sydne, *querida*," he exclaimed, slipping the endearment in smoothly, "I just can't bear the thought of your being alone when you and I could be together. Besides, it's too beautiful a day to be wasted. We could have lunch after the match, then either play a little tennis or laze on the beach. Your wish is my command."

"I don't know if I can be ready in time, Jorge. I just woke up."

"I've been told that I'd make a fair ladies' maid," he murmured softly, his tone insinuating. "I could be over in a minute to help you dress."

Sydne couldn't help laughing. "No thank you, Jorge. I believe you'd be much more experienced at undressing than at dressing a lady. But all right, I'll meet you by the pool for lunch."

"Then I'll see you later, Sydne, *querida*."

"Good luck at the match, Jorge."

"*Gracias,*" he replied. "But I believe we make our own luck."

Sydne was pensive when she hung up the phone. Perhaps Jorge was right—at least she *wanted* to believe she controlled her own destiny. If that were true she could win Brian's love in the end.

Feeling considerably more optimistic than she had before the phone call, Sydne got up and stepped out onto the small balcony, where she had felt so lonely only hours earlier. Today she was greeted by the cheerful sight of clear skies and turquoise water shimmering in the sun. She went back inside to call the restaurant, ordering coffee and orange juice to be brought to her *casita*. Lunch with Jorge Zamora was a good two hours away.

CHAPTER THIRTEEN

"I CAN'T BELIEVE this is truly happening!" Julia exclaimed as the powder-blue Mercedes 450SL turned the corner on Bay View Drive and headed west. "Sometimes I'm afraid I'm going to wake up and find that I'm still living in Samaná, and that all this was just a beautiful dream."

Sydne, who was driving, couldn't bring herself to answer. She was glad her friend had found happiness with Chuck, but she couldn't help feeling a little envious of them.

Their afternoon visit to the doctor's office had confirmed Julia's suspicion that she was pregnant. Had only two months gone by since the day she and Brian had attended their friends' wedding, Sydne wondered. For her the time had taken on an unreal quality, had evolved into an emotional limbo through which she and Brian moved as if nothing had happened—both of them staunchly pretending that all was well, perhaps afraid to delve too deeply and uncover the harsh truth.

The pretense had started so soon after their wedding that at times Sydne wondered if those ecstatic moments she and Brian had shared were only a figment of her overactive imagination. Had there really been days and nights of total intimacy, in Sosuá, or had she only dreamed about them? More vivid in her mind were the days at Casa de Campo—days when Brian had made no attempt to keep Jackie Newton in her place, but had instead encouraged the horrible woman's efforts to drive them further and further apart.

During that excruciating week Sydne had taught herself to hide from both of them the pain his callousness caused her, to ignore the glint of malice that flashed in Jackie's blue green eyes each time she held Brian's attention. And more and more Sydne had found herself accepting the company of Jorge Zamora, who hadn't bothered to hide his admiration for the lonely newlywed. Jorge was as charming as he was handsome, but for Sydne the attentions of the notorious playboy had been meaningless. Only one man possessed the key to her heart, and that man was her husband.

Over and over Sydne asked herself if she hadn't unconsciously encouraged Jorge in the secret hopes of awakening Brian's jealousy. But if that were the case, her efforts had met with dismal failure. Brian had been too involved with Jackie to notice, too confident of his wife's devotion, or else indifferent— Sydne couldn't decide which. Yet he had taken her completely by surprise one day. She had come back from an afternoon of horseback riding with Jorge to find that Brian had suddenly—and without explanation—decided they should return to the capital. They had spent a few days there before going back to Samaná to attend the wedding of their friends, a splendid occasion that had seemed like the culmination of a fairy tale.

Julia and Chuck had certainly been blessed with a fairy godmother. Just as Matilde Lozano had intended when she'd taken Chuck into her home, the time the patient had spent there had been sufficient to impress Don Francisco in his favor. Lorenzo and his family, the only stumbling blocks remaining, had been easily won over when Julia's former fiancé had admitted, much to everyone's relief, that he, too, had accepted the betrothal more out of duty than choice, since *he* was in love with someone else.

"Chuck is going to be so happy when I tell him!" Julia chatted on, dragging Sydne's attention back to the present. "Oh, and I must call mother right away. She and papa will surely want to come. Imagine, Sydne, this is going to be their first grandchild!"

"Don't start setting up the guest room yet," Sydne warned. "Babies don't appear overnight."

"Oh, Syd," Julia said cheerfully, "I'm making a fool of myself, I know, but it's just that— Oh, just wait until you're in my shoes!"

Sydne couldn't help feeling relieved when they arrived at their destination. Until Julia learned to drive and obtained her license, Sydne had volunteered to serve as chauffeur during their frequent outings together. But sometimes, as now, listening to her friend's happy chatter only served to make her more painfully aware of all that she was missing with Brian. Still, she doggedly clung to the glimmer of hope that their relationship would improve.

Sydne pulled the blue Mercedes over to the curb and stopped in front of the house Julia and Chuck had purchased when they arrived in Fort Lauderdale. Located in one of the best residential districts of the city, it was a home meant for a large family, as were most of the other houses on the wide, tree-lined street. Abandoned toys were scattered on the sidewalks and in the front yards. Julia maintained that what had sold her on the house was the large backyard, a perfect place for children to play.

Sydne liked the house. When she had gotten married and had given up, for the moment at least, her work in archaeology, she had dreamed of a place just like it. It was what she would have wanted if she and Brian— *Stop it,* she admonished herself sternly.

"Would you like to come in?" Julia invited before opening the car door. "Lucia made a cheesecake this morning, and her baking's out of this world."

"I must get going," Sydne said, shaking her head. "Brian said he'd be home early."

Julia hugged her irrepressibly. "Thank you, Sydne, for driving me to the doctor's and for being with me. You're the best friend I've ever had."

Sydne was so moved that all she could say was, "And so are you." Feeling her eyes mist over, she added, "You better get out before I make a fool of myself."

Julia drew back, smiling warmly, and got out of the car. Shutting the door, she leaned forward to look at her friend through the window. "Bye, Syd. Give my love to Brian."

Sydne waved and started the car. After she pulled away from the curb she drove instinctively. Almost oblivious to her surroundings, she crossed several of the graceful arched bridges over canals and waterways that have earned Fort Lauderdale the title Venice of America. On Atlantic Boulevard she stepped on the gas, and the blue Mercedes took off at a speed well above the legal limit.

Sydne didn't know how far she had driven when the sound of a siren brought her back to reality. She looked in the rearview mirror to see the flashing lights of a police car behind her. Heaving a sigh, she pulled over to the curb, and her hands were shaking while she waited for the officer to get out of his patrol car and approach her window.

"May I see your license, miss?" he requested courteously.

"Yes, yes, of course," she blurted out, knowing her face had flushed with color.

The middle-aged and rather heavyset patrolman waited while Sydne fumbled through her purse. "Please take it out of your wallet," he told her, when in her confusion she tried to hand him the whole thing. When he finally took her ID he added, "You were speeding, miss."

"I know, officer. I'm sorry," Sydne admitted guiltily. She was silent while he wrote out the ticket for her traffic violation.

"I've been following you for the past two miles, you know. Didn't you see my signal?"

Her flush deepened. "I really am sorry, officer. I—I guess my mind was elsewhere."

She accepted the notebook and pen the man handed her, and after she had signed the citation he peeled off the ticket. With a frown of reproach, he handed it to her together with her license. But before walking away, he said, "Look, ma'am, it says there that you're married. Next time you have a fight with your husband, don't take it out on the road. I'd hate to be the one to have to tell him his pretty wife became another traffic fatality.'' He must have known he had guessed the reason for her distraction, and went on, ''Why don't you go home and make up with him? A woman with your looks shouldn't have too much trouble convincing him.''

Sydne gave him a tremulous smile. ''Thank you, officer. I might do that.''

The patrolman grinned and gave her a friendly wink before finally walking away.

Through her rearview mirror Sydne watched him get into his car. It was only then that she realized she had been so distracted by her own troubled thoughts that she had driven a considerable distance in the wrong direction.

She started the car again, but instead of turning around she drove on a short distance and parked near the ocean. She inserted a cassette in the tape deck, and almost immediately the notes of a Chopin étude blended with the sound of the waves.

She was still reluctant to go back to the penthouse. It had never really felt like the home she had hoped for. But then, she thought wryly, brick, mortar and a luxurious decor do not a real home make. There was nothing wrong with the dwelling itself; far from it. It was beautifully and expensively furnished to satisfy the most fastidious taste, and it commanded a sweeping view of the oceanfront as well as of the marina where Brian kept his weekend pleasure boat. But the place lacked the warmth that would make it feel like home. Sydne knew it was up to her and Brian to provide that main ingredient.

As she sat there Sydne pondered the friendly

patrolman's advice. Could it really be that simple to put an end to the difficult situation between her and Brian? Since their return from the Dominican Republic he had played the part of the devoted husband, she had to admit. If she hadn't overheard Jackie's shocking revelations, she would never have questioned his love. But even after learning the bitter truth she had chosen to remain his wife, to try to make their marriage work. Then wasn't she defeating her own purpose with her reluctance to confront him? It wasn't enough to pretend that Brian loved her, she was finding out. She had to *believe* it.

Why couldn't she accept his love at face value— put all her doubts aside? Once before he had asked for her trust, Sydne reminded herself. She had refused to believe him, only to discover later that he had been telling the truth all along. How many times did he have to prove himself to her?

And wasn't trust an important ingredient of love? How could she say that she loved him, and in the same breath refuse to believe in him? She had to stop wondering each time he held her if he was picturing himself with someone else....

During the long minutes she sat there, her mind racing on its familiar unprofitable track, Sydne realized that she alone held the key to the future of their marriage. On one side of the scale was love, happiness, a home, a family; on the other suspicion and doubt, loneliness and despair. There could be no in-between, and unless she recognized her mistake and changed her ways, all she could hope for was to drive Brian away. Well, she would do something about it immediately. She would start once again to believe in him, to put their marriage back on the right track!

Once she had decided to turn over a new leaf, Sydne's heart felt lighter than it had for ages. The traffic ticket had been the best thing that could have happened to her, she decided as she started the car, turned it around and headed for home.

Along with the apartment, Brian had acquired the services of Hiroshi, a very efficient Japanese manservant. In addition to taking care of all the household chores, he was an excellent cook, specializing in the many varieties of sushi, those tempting minute works of art that delight the senses with their color, texture and flavor. For Sydne Japanese cuisine was a new experience, but Brian couldn't have been happier, since he had developed a taste for Oriental food during his tour of naval duty in the Far East.

Since cooking was not one of Sydne's fortes, she and Brian usually dined out on Hiroshi's days off. But for that night she hurriedly formulated other plans. A romantic dinner by candlelight, soft music and a chilled bottle of wine would set the right mood to start the evening—an evening that she was determined would lead to a complete reconciliation. Given her limited culinary skills, Sydne realized she would have to keep the meal simple, yet elegant. On her way home she stopped at a meat market where, after great deliberation over their display, she bought half a dozen lamb chops.

As soon as she arrived at the apartment Sydne searched through the collection of cookbooks Hiroshi kept in the kitchen. Finding what seemed to be a simple recipe, she followed the instructions on how to prepare the chops for the oven. When she had finished, she set them aside while she shampooed her hair and luxuriated in a long bubble bath.

After blowing her hair dry she experimented with different hairstyles, but then remembered that Brian had once commented on the sensuous appeal of her long silky hair worn loose around her shoulders. That settled it. Tonight she was bent on seducing her husband, on making him forget that any other woman even existed.

A few strokes of fawn eye shadow accented her almond-shaped eyes, and her lips glistened moist and inviting with a thin layer of lip gloss. She debated for a while before dispensing with her bra. The silk pajamas, in sizzling magenta and pink with a matching belted kimono top and bell-like sleeves, didn't need one.

After selecting a pair of strappy flirtatious sandals, she touched perfume to her throat and wrists, and as an afterthought, to the hollow between her breasts, before she took one last appraising look at her reflection in the mirror. Only after a few strokes of blusher added a glow to her cheeks was Sydne satisfied with the result of her efforts. She knew she wasn't unattractive, but in spite of having been called beautiful by many men, she had never really thought of herself as such. Only Brian had the power to make her feel truly beautiful and desirable.

At five-thirty Sydne put the lamb chops in the oven, set the table complete with candles and fresh flowers and selected soft romantic music to play on the stereo. She experimented with the lighting until she had achieved the exact effect of light and shadow that she wanted. Logs were ready in the fireplace, awaiting the touch of a match, and she hoped the evening would be chilly enough to warrant a cozy fire.

The living room had never appeared more inviting, Sydne thought as she examined her surroundings with a critical eye. It was a beautiful room—one that until this moment she had never truly appreciated. Two large twin sofas near the fireplace faced each other across a table of gleaming glass and chrome. A number of pillows added bright and earthy tones to the muted color of the couches, and to the comfortable chairs upholstered in complimentary colors. Occasional tables, plants and other accessories blended with tastefully selected paintings on the walls to complete a well-balanced, pleasant effect.

A wide sliding-glass door opened onto a large balcony, where a profusion of flowering plants and shrubs created the illusion of a garden in the sky. Wicker and rattan furniture was combined here for an exotic touch. Gazing out at night, they could see the lights winking from the boats in the marina below.

A glance at the clock told Sydne that only fifteen minutes had elapsed since she'd put the meat in the oven. Brian would be home any minute. Not wanting to appear impatient, Sydne poured herself a glass of white wine and settled down on one of the sofas to wait.

A moment later she sprang to her feet again. Here she had prepared the setting and herself, but hadn't given a thought to Brian's comfort. This would be a perfect occasion for him to wear the beautiful velvet smoking jacket hanging in his closet. She ran into the bedroom and layed the jacket on the bed. Then she thought of his slippers, which she couldn't find on the floor or under the bed.

Brian's closet could easily have passed military inspection, she thought for the hundredth time as she searched the boxes lining its shelves. She'd never dared until now to rummage through his belongings. Instead of the slippers she found a photograph album in a large square box. Curiously she flipped the cover open.

The picture on the first page made her look twice. There was a striking resemblance between the younger Brian and the man in uniform who was standing beside him. Even though the photograph was in black and white, it was easy to guess that his eyes were as blue as Brian's and they shared the same strong features, except that Brian's chin was firmer than the older man's. She was looking at Brian's father, Sydne realized, and to make certain she slipped the photo from its plastic shield. "Greg Stevens, 1960" was written on the reverse side, confirming her suspicions.

There were other photographs, too, mostly of Brian's father with a beautiful woman on his arm, taken in what appeared to be a tropical setting. From the way they looked at each other in the photographs, there was no mistaking the magic that had existed between them.

Quickly Sydne flipped through the pages, looking for photos of Brian as a little boy. But there were none, and she put the album aside, planning to look at it again more carefully some other time. Then the shrill peal of the telephone broke the silence, and she rushed to answer it.

"Hi, babe."

When Brian's voice came over the line Sydne felt a surge of dismay. The call could only mean that he would be late coming home. "Brian, where are you?" she asked.

"Tampa. I'm sorry, honey. I tried to reach you this afternoon, but I guess you were out."

Oh, no, Sydne groaned inwardly. "What happened?"

"We had an emergency. One of the men working on a job here was rushed to the hospital with a case of the bends, so I flew over. He's all right now."

"Who was it?"

"Jerry Trent, a new man. You haven't met him."

"Will you be home tonight?" There was a note of expectancy in her voice.

"I'm at the airport now and should be home in a couple of hours at the most. Don't worry about dinner. I'll grab something on the way."

"Oh, no!" she exclaimed before she could contain herself. To cover her blunder she quickly added, "I mean, I'll fix you something when you get home. Hurry home."

There was a pause at the other end. "Sydne, did you have plans for tonight?"

She was tempted to tell him, but that would only spoil the surprise. "Nothing special. Just hurry home, darling."

"Miss me?"

"You know I do."

"Syd, I— They're calling my flight. I'll see you in a little while, hon."

Before she could say anything else the phone clicked in her ear.

Well, her plans weren't entirely ruined, Sydne consoled herself. There was still time for a quiet dinner— Dinner! Sydne rushed to the kitchen and took the meat out of the oven so it wouldn't dry out. She would finish cooking it later.

Leaving the roasting pan on the kitchen counter, Sydne collected her glass of wine and went into the living room. Kicking off her high-heeled sandals, she curled up on one of the sofas to look at the photograph album in more detail. At seven o'clock she put the lamb chops back in the oven and lit the log in the fireplace, since the evening was turning chilly. . . .

The logs were glowing embers by the time Brian let himself into the apartment. The first thing he noticed was the acrid smell of something burning. Rushing to the smoke-filled kitchen, he turned off the oven, which he opened to retrieve the roasting pan. The crispy lumps inside resembled smoldering briquettes, he decided, opening the kitchen windows to let the smoke out. As he slid open the glass doors leading to the terrace, he spotted Sydne lying on the sofa, sound asleep, with a photo album in her lap. A glance at the table set for two told him the rest of the romantic story.

Cursing himself for spoiling her surprise, Brian knelt down on the floor next to his wife. Even in her sleep Sydne responded to his kiss, and curled her arms around his neck.

"Hello, babe," he said softly, stroking her cheek. "I'm sorry I'm so late."

"What time is it?" she murmured drowsily.

"Past ten."

She sat up with a start. "The lamb chops."

Brian held her back when she tried to get up. "It's all right, hon. I took them out of the oven."

It was then that Sydne became aware of the acrid smell pervading the apartment. "They burned?" She was crestfallen.

"I'm afraid so," he said gently. "But it's all right, honey, really."

"Oh, Brian!" she cried on dismay. "I wanted to surprise you! I wanted it to be so perfect, and I forgot to set the timer!"

"What a nice idea, though." He held her as gently as he would a child. "It was my fault for being so late. I'm sorry."

"What happened?" she sniffled.

"The flight was delayed because of engine trouble," he explained, handing her his handkerchief. "Unfortunately I couldn't get to a phone to warn you."

Sydne dried her tears and blew her nose. "Are you hungry?"

"Ravenous!" He grinned.

"I could fix you something—" But Brian didn't let her finish.

"It's not food I'm hungry for," he said pointedly before his lips covered hers.

For a fleeting moment the doubts that had plagued her threatened to return, but Sydne shoved them aside. Parting her lips to his caress, she responded without reservation to his kiss, which deepened urgently until it absorbed her completely. Nothing seemed to exist but this moment as she gave herself to him fully for the first time in a long, long while.

Oh, yes, the magic was still there, stronger than ever, Sydne thought as she lay peacefully in Brian's arms much later. Was it her imagination or had he been aware of the change in her? With her head resting on his warm chest she listened to his heartbeats, which had once again become regular.

By now Sydne had convinced herself that the estrangement between them had been her own fault. Brian loved her; she must cling to that belief and never let go of it. There were no ghosts except in her own imagination. She had nothing to envy Julia or anyone else. She and Brian could be happy together; all she had to do was put aside her fears.

"I took Julia to the doctor this afternoon," she said, stirring at last.

"Is she ill?"

Sydne smiled up at him. "She's going to have a baby."

Brian chuckled, and his chest rose and fell beneath her cheek. "Does Chuck know?"

"I imagine he does by now. Julia was so excited I don't think she could keep it a secret if she wanted to." Sydne lifted her head to look into Brian's eyes. "Would you like a baby of our own?"

"Of course I would!" Brian regarded her quizzically. "Are you—"

"Not yet." Sydne smiled wistfully and shook her head.

Brian heaved a sigh of relief. "I'm glad."

"But you said—"

"I said I wanted a child of our own," he interrupted. "But not now, not yet." At the wary glance Sydne couldn't disguise he framed her face with his hands. "I warned you you'd married a very selfish man, remember? I don't want to share you with anyone, babe—not yet."

He held her questioning glance until he saw her doubts fade away.

"I'd love to have your baby," Sydne sighed, tracing the contours of his lips with her fingertip. "A little boy who looks just like you." After a moment she asked, "What were you like as a child, darling?"

"A handful," he chortled.

"I found a photo album when I was looking for your slippers this evening. I always wondered why you didn't keep any old photographs around. Why didn't you show it to me before?"

"You—the subject never came up." He shrugged, but his slip hadn't escaped her. Of course, she realized guiltily, she had never asked. She'd been too wrapped up in her own insecurities.

"You resemble your father very strongly," she said. "He was a very handsome man. And your mother was beautiful. They made a striking couple. Even in the photographs you can see how much they loved each other." At his silence she went on, "But I couldn't find any photographs of you as a very young child, Brian. Where are they?"

"I suppose Bea has them all."

"Who is Bea?"

"My mother."

"Your mother!" Sydne cried, startled. "Your mother is alive?"

"And living in Philadelphia," he added wryly.

"But I thought your parents were dead."

"Only my father. He was killed when I was fourteen, but Bea was married to someone else by that time anyway."

Divorced! That accounted for Brian's silence at her earlier comments.

"I never knew my parents were even separated until Bea remarried," Brian said. At her puzzled frown he explained, "Dad was a navy pilot and spent most of his time overseas. Bea hated living abroad. For her the world began and ended in Philadelphia, so she stayed at home. I never spent much time with dad," Brian continued after a pause, "but when he was around life was exciting. I always wanted to grow up to be like him. The only problem was that he was never around for long." He fell silent for a moment, then added, "For many years I blamed Bea for the divorce, but it wasn't really her fault. She and dad were worlds apart, Sydne. Each wanted different things out of life. Perhaps under normal circumstances they would never have married in the first place, but there was a war going on when they met. Everybody was afraid time was running out, I suppose.

"After the war Bea wanted dad to settle down in Philadelphia—go into the family business. I think he tried it her way for a while, but I guess he missed the excitement and went back to the navy. That must have been a blow for Bea. To give her her due, she tried to follow him, but it was another disaster. I think the only reason they stayed married at all was because she came back pregnant. I don't know how many times they got back together, only to separate again. I was too young to understand, and dad's career kept him away most of the time. I was about ten when Bea married a man who had been in love with her for years, even before she met dad. To make a long story short," he sighed, "if Bea hadn't sent me away to boarding school, I might have wrecked her second marriage. I didn't appreciate it at the time, but now I'm glad she did. Harold is a good man who has given her the home, the family and the kind of life she always wanted. You can't ask for a steadier man than a judge," he finished with an attempt at levity.

Many things began to fall into place. "Do you ever see her?" Sydne prodded.

"Occasionally."

"Are there any other children?"

"I have two half sisters."

"Is that why you joined the navy, Brian—because you wanted to be like your father?"

"That's one of the reasons," he admitted with a crooked grin.

Sydne gazed lovingly at him. "Oh, Brian, I do want to have a child who takes after you!"

FOR SYDNE, discovering the part of him that Brian had kept hidden only served to make her love him more. She could picture Brian as a boy, torn by the divorce of his parents and shipped off to boarding school. She could understand his hating the man who in his eyes had taken the place of the father he

adored. And she understood now his desire to postpone parenthood, to keep her undivided attention for
just a little longer, as if he needed to make up for
some of the love he had lost as a child. In her eyes the
man she had believed to be so strong, so self-
possessed and so invulnerable became more human,
more sensitive, more in need of her love. How mistaken she had been in deciding that he was capable
only of hurting, not of being hurt.

Now Sydne was able to laugh again, to love again
without regrets or reservations. The ghosts of Helene
and Jackie Newton had been exorcised at last.

"How would you like to take a trip to London?"
Brian asked her a week after their unspoken reconciliation.

"When?"

"Next month. The *Conde* artifacts will go on auction then."

"Oh, Brian, that's wonderful! You'll be a millionaire."

Not that they lacked for anything now, she admitted to herself. Sydne had never inquired about the ex-
tent of her husband's fortune, but considering the
experiences she had suffered after the death of her
parents, she was worried that Brian couldn't really
afford their luxurious life-style—without touching
his profits from the salvaged galleon, that is. His
business seemed prosperous enough, and he was
generous to a fault, but still, Brian seemed extremely
touchy about the subject of his finances, and Sydne
was reluctant to press the point. Yet in addition to
the elegant penthouse apartment and the expensive

pleasure boat he maintained, they were members of
an exclusive country and sporting club, where she
had expanded her circle of friends. His first surprise
to her had been the Mercedes; the latest a beautiful
chestnut quarter horse she rode every chance she
got—not to mention her collection of jewels. Practically nonexistent before their marriage, it was now
large enough to satisfy a very demanding woman,
which she wasn't.

"You'll be glad to hear that Andrew will be there
for the auction," he announced dismissing her remark.

"Dear Andrew," she said pensively. "I'd love to
see him again. I owe him a great deal, Brian. He was
very good to me during a very difficult period of my
life—much more so than an ordinary employer
would have been. And most of all I owe him for introducing me to you."

This was the first reference Sydne had ever made to
her past, but even though she really had nothing to
hide she was glad when Brian didn't inquire further.
The episode with Paul seemed totally unimportant
now. Perhaps if, similarly, she had disregarded
Helene and Jackie, she would have saved a lot of
unhappiness for both her and Brian.

A FEW DAYS LATER Sydne dialed the number of
Brian's office. His secretary answered at the second
ring, and after a pleasant greeting put her call
through immediately.

"Hi, babe, what's up?" he asked.

"I was wondering if you're free for lunch."

Sydne could almost feel his hesitation. "Honey, I'd love to," he said at last, "but—"

"It's all right, darling," she said hurriedly, trying not to let her disappointment show in her voice. "I just took a chance you'd be free. I won't keep you if you're busy."

"I'm never too busy for you."

"Will you be home early?"

"Of course."

"I'll see you then. Love you."

When the phone went dead in her hand, Sydne was vaguely disappointed. Brian hadn't said that he loved her back. Oh, well, she was being foolish again. He probably had someone in his office.

With a shrug she dialed Julia's number. It was busy, as it was for several more tries. Julia was probably talking to her mother in the Dominican Republic. Chuck was always teasing his wife that bringing Matilde Lozano for a visit would be much cheaper than Julia's phone bills. With a sigh of resignation Sydne decided that she would do her shopping alone.

She left the car in a parking lot and walked down the street, reveling in the beauty of the day until it made her feel almost drunk with happiness. The boutiques, art galleries and fine shops of the tree-lined Las Olas Boulevard occupied most of her afternoon. Finally, with one more item on her list to find, Sydne drove to the shopping center in Pompano Beach, where she knew she could get just what she was looking for.

What made her glance at the man and woman driv-

ing out of the hotel on Atlantic Boulevard, Sydne
never knew. The long black Cadillac was not a familiar car, but the faces were. Brian, intent on the road,
didn't see her, and Jackie Newton was too busy looking at him to notice anyone else.

CHAPTER FOURTEEN

"I THOUGHT we were staying home tonight," Brian said when, upon his arrival home, Sydne informed him that they had a dinner date.

"I'm sorry. I forgot to remind you."

"I'd rather stay home with you," he said, capturing her by the waist. "Couldn't we get out of it?"

"I'm afraid not," she replied, stepping away to avoid his kiss.

It had taken her a few calls to find another couple available on such short notice, and she didn't want to spend the evening with Julia and Chuck. Even less did she want to be alone with Brian after what she had seen that afternoon. Her husband had been too busy to have lunch with her—too busy with Jackie Newton.

It was obvious they had renewed their affair. What else would they be doing, leaving a hotel together? The very thought of his duplicity made Sydne feel ill. She had fallen in love with a man who simply couldn't be faithful to one woman. He had loved Helene—perhaps loved her still—but that hadn't prevented him from having extramarital affairs. What hope was there for Sydne herself? She just wasn't the type of woman who could share the man she loved.

Jody Quinn, who had agreed to have dinner that

night, was a frequent tennis partner at the club where Sydne played. Her husband, Ralph, was rather dull, but the entertainment provided during the supper cruise Sydne had hastily arranged for would allow little time for conversation.

The evening was a total flop. The vaudeville comedian's jokes were appreciated by the Quinns, but Sydne had to force brittle laughter that sounded false even to her own ears. Brian sat mostly in silence, speaking only when directly addressed. It hadn't taken him long to discover that she had arranged the evening at the last minute.

"Would you mind telling me what that was all about?" he asked impatiently when they finally got into their car.

"I don't know what you mean," Sydne replied, refusing to meet his probing gaze.

He gave her another long questioning look before starting the car, and the ride back to their apartment was brief and silent. The basement garage was deserted when they parked the car and took the elevator to the penthouse.

As soon as they were inside the apartment Brian wouldn't be put off any longer. "All right, Sydne, what's bothering you now? That dinner date with the Quinns was not planned ahead."

Sydne fought the temptation to confront him with the truth. Only pride held her back. "I was bored," she said instead. "We've been spending too much time at home."

"I thought you enjoyed our evenings together." She couldn't have missed the note of regret in his voice.

Those evenings had been precious, Sydne admitted in her heart. Aloud, however, she said, "There's such a thing as too much togetherness, Brian. We should lead a more active social life."

She couldn't read the expression on his face because he had turned away and was ambling toward the bar. He poured himself a drink before saying, "Don't tell me you enjoyed tonight."

"No," she admitted, "I guess I didn't."

"So what's really bothering you?"

How could she tell him that she knew about Jackie, that she couldn't trust him any longer and that she still couldn't stop loving him? No, she wouldn't act the part of the jealous wife, but she couldn't live with the knowledge that there would always be someone else standing between them. The past few days had been pure heaven, had been everything she had ever hoped for, but they had only been an illusion. She had to put an end to her misery before it was too late—before she began to despise herself.

"Our marriage was a mistake, Brian." Sydne forced herself to keep her voice even, but she couldn't look him in the eye as she added, "I think we should end it now, before it's too late."

Brian was speechless for a moment. "Damn you!" he growled suddenly, slamming the glass in his hand down on the counter. He crossed the distance between them in two long strides, and when he grabbed her to make her face him his fingers closed around her upper arms like a steel vise. "Damn you!" he repeated. "If you think I'm going to let you walk out on me just like that, you're very much mistaken.

We're married, Sydne, and that's the way it's going to stay."

Sydne tried to get away, but her struggles only served to make him hold her tighter. "You're hurting me." She winced when she could no longer bear the pressure of his grip.

Brian jerked his hands away as if he had been burned. He turned and walked slowly toward the bar, keeping his back to her after he poured himself another drink. Numbly Sydne collected her evening bag and her fur coat from the chair where she had dropped them earlier, and made her way to the bedroom.

Her reflection in the dressing-table mirror was that of a white-faced stranger. Mechanically she began to remove her jewelry, concentrating on the task of replacing each item in its case as if to block any other thoughts from her mind. Desperately she tried to keep a tight rein on her emotions. No, she couldn't break down.

When she had finished she went into the dressing room, where she took off her two-piece silk dress and hung it up in her closet, donning a white satin nightgown trimmed with lace. Going back to the dressing table, she cleansed her face of makeup with shaking hands and directed her attention to brushing her hair. When Brian walked in she refused to meet his eyes in the mirror as he stood behind her. Her body tensed when he touched the faint imprints his fingers had left on her arms.

"I'm sorry, babe," he said huskily. "I didn't mean to hurt you."

Sydne bit her lower lip when he sat next to her on

the velvet-padded bench. Her skin prickled when his lips traced the hollow of her shoulder and began to explore her throat. He had only to touch her to make her forget all her resolve! Fighting down the weakness that threatened to invade her, she drew away and got to her feet. "I think I'll use the spare bedroom tonight," she said as steadily as she could manage.

A muscle twitched in Brian's cheek, and his jaw was clenched angrily as he rose from the bench. "Don't bother," he rasped, stalking out of the room.

Sydne rushed to lock the door behind him, and only then did she allow herself the luxury of tears.

SYDNE WAS AT A LOSS; she didn't know what to do next. There was no question in her mind that the marriage was over, but she couldn't bring herself to simply walk out without reaching some sort of agreement with Brian. She couldn't help but wonder about her reluctance. Was it possible that she was stupid enough to still hope for a miracle to happen—to wish that Brian would come back and hold her, tell her that he couldn't live without her and beg her to stay?

The idea of him begging was as incongruous as a beggar wearing diamonds. Why should he beg when he knew he could have any woman he wanted simply by snapping his fingers? There could only be one explanation for the violence of his reaction. He had already gone through one divorce; the prospect of another couldn't be pleasant for him. Perhaps given the chance to cool off, he would realize that going their separate ways was best for both of them. She wouldn't ask for anything, of course—only to be released from the bonds of marriage. If only her heart could be released as easily, she reflected ruefully.

To all intents and purposes it was a day like any other. The fact that her own world had collapsed didn't stop the rest of it from following its normal course, and Sydne went through the motions of everyday living as if nothing had happened.

Whether or not it was a good idea, when Julia called and asked her to lunch Sydne accepted. The conversation, naturally enough, centered around Chuck and the preparations for the arrival of their baby. Looking more beautiful than ever in the maternity dress she was wearing, even though it was much too early, Julia showed her friend the room the proud parents had converted into a nursery.

Swallowing the lump in her throat, Sydne voiced her admiration for the results of hours of loving work, the delicate pastel hues, the cheerful wallpaper print, the crib, the dressing table. Even without its new occupant, the room smelled like a baby. But that was only her imagination, Sydne chided herself.

How often had she dreamed of having Brian's baby? Like all her other dreams, this one would never come true. She would never have a child, because in her heart of hearts she knew that there would never be another man for her. The love she had for Brian would live for as long as she did.

And yet when he came home that evening, Sydne seemed cool and collected, elegant in her fashionable striped purple dress with a strand of pearls at her throat. Her hair was swept into a French coil at the back of her head, making her high cheekbones stand

out more prominently. She hid her pallor behind
carefully applied makeup.

Brian examined her appearance. "Don't tell me
we're going out again tonight."

"Dinner and theater," she replied.

"Cancel it."

"It's too late, Brian. We're supposed to meet the
Bradleys at the restaurant in an hour."

"I said cancel it," he clipped tersely. "We're staying home."

"But the evening was planned a week ago," she
tried to argue. It was obvious that Brian was still
angry, and she wanted to avoid another scene at all
costs. "If you want to stay home, I'll meet the Bradleys and make your excuses."

"You would go by yourself, wouldn't you?"

"Brian, please, let's not argue," she said, trying to
placate him. "You don't have to go if you don't want
to, but I need to get out."

"Out of our marriage, Sydne?" he said scathingly.
"You might as well forget it."

"Why don't we wait until we've both had a chance
to calm down and discuss it rationally," she said,
summoning her courage. "You're angry now, and
I. . . ." She faltered.

He gave her a curious look. "Give me fifteen minutes," he said at last.

With Brian behaving as if nothing had happened,
the evening went better than Sydne had hoped for.
She even had to remind herself that it was just an act.
He was a man who looked at ease in anything he
wore, be it diving gear, work clothes or the elegant

dark suit he had donned that evening. The number of admiring glances women of all ages sent in his direction only served to remind Sydne how easy it would be for him to replace her.

He was not handsome in the exact sense of the word. The features of his hard-boned face were too strong, too angular. Rugged was a word that described him best. Only his eyes were truly beautiful. Of the deepest blue and fringed with thick dark lashes, they eloquently reflected his emotions when he allowed them to. They could cut through a person like cold steel. And yet how much tenderness she had seen in those deep pools of blue, how much they could convey in a single glance and how many feelings they could stir within her. The times she had seen those eyes darken with passion. . . .

But how many other women could say the same thing? No, it had to be all or nothing, and to believe that she could hold him was folly—as she had discovered.

And so, when they returned to the apartment Sydne said a hasty good-night and locked herself in the bedroom, while Brian headed straight for the bar and poured himself a nightcap. An hour later, still unable to sleep, Sydne heard him pause outside her door before he continued on to the guest room.

Lying awake in the great bed where she had spent so many hours of love, Sydne wondered how much longer the present situation could last. Even if Brian could bear it, she knew she wouldn't be able to stand the pressure much longer. Yet the days were passing without a marked change in their relationship. At times Sydne caught a glance from Brian that she couldn't fathom, because immediately a mask would fall in place to hide his thoughts. The mask was as impenetrable as it had been in the very beginning, only the tension between them was even worse now than they were man and wife.

THE NEXT WEEK there was a dinner dance at the country club, an event that had been planned months in advance. Julia was very excited about it, since it was the first gala occasion she and Chuck were to attend after their marriage. Helping Julia adapt to her new environment had occupied Sydne's attention after their return from the Dominican Republic. But in spite of the fears she had voiced after the attack on the *Adventurer*, Julia had made the transition with an ease that had surprised her friends.

"I don't expect you to understand," Julia had answered when Sydne had brought up the subject. "All my life decisions have been made for me. I don't deny it bothered me at times, but on the whole it made life easier. When I fell in love with Chuck I was terrified. I suppose I used every excuse in the world to avoid facing the fact that there was one decision no one could make for me, the most important of my life. Chuck is a very perceptive man. He knew what I was going through, and he did the best thing he could do—let me work it out by myself."

Of course she understood, Sydne had mused wryly. Especially now that the tables had been turned. Her own parents had always encouraged her independence, and although they had offered their guidance, they had allowed their only daughter to make her own decisions. It was something Sydne had appreciated when, overnight, she had found herself alone in the world.

What she couldn't understand now was her own inability to act. Had love destroyed her courage? No, Brian was a forceful and obstinate man—those qualities were part of his attraction—but she wouldn't let him browbeat her into staying with him against her will. But she couldn't just walk away. Something held her back.

Sharing a table with them at the dinner dance were the Bradleys, a young couple with whom Sydne and Brian had established the beginnings of a promising friendship. Harry Bradley, president of an electronics firm, was an energetic but pleasant man, while Karen, his wife, was an excellent tennis player who invariably beat Sydne at the game.

Motherhood seemed to lend an added glow to Julia, who had discarded her maternity clothes for the black-tie affair and looked radiant in a long evening gown of plum taffeta. Her long black hair was done up in a Gibson Girl style that didn't hide the sparkle of her dangling diamond earrings.

Sydne's own black satin gown was strapless, and the slit of the long narrow skirt exposed a slender leg encased in the sheerest of black stockings. She wore long black gloves to above her elbows, and her hair, smoothed away from her face and swept into a chignon at the back, accentuated her delicate bone structure. The glitter of diamonds completed the picture of sexy elegance. In his tuxedo, Brian seemed at ease and enjoying himself.

"Nice turnout, isn't it?" Karen commented with approval.

· The orchestra, popular because of its forties big-
band sound, had attracted a large crowd, offering as
it did a bit of nostalgia to the older generation as well
as novelty to the younger one.

It opened with a good imitation of Glen Miller's
"Moonlight Serenade," and Brian turned to Sydne.
"Shall we?"

"You're beautiful," he murmured, taking her in
his arms as they reached the dance floor.

Sydne closed her eyes and thought how easy it
would be to yield to the temptation of romance at
this moment. Everything seemed to conspire against
her—the mellow music, the soft lights, his nearness.
The combination was too heady, too strong to resist,
and refusing to succumb to her weakness, she opened
her eyes to look at the other dancers. There were
older couples dancing close together as she and Brian
were, their eyes shut as if they were transported back
to the past by the magic of the music. The gray hairs,
the wrinkles, the extra pounds had disappeared. In
their own minds, tonight they were what they had
once been.

They were the survivors, Sydne mused. There must
have been so many other casualties along the way—
casualties of the war, of time, of love. Brian's parents had been casualties, and now they themselves
were, too.

Sydne endured the dance until the song ended.
Then she and Brian returned to the table. Many of
the younger couples who had remained on the dance
floor moved aside to watch some older couples provide impromptu choreography to the lively rhythm of
"In the Mood."

"They're great!" Karen cried, joining in the applause that followed. "Gosh, Harry, why can't you dance like that!"

Her husband heaved a comic sigh of resignation. He was a gifted storyteller who kept everybody entertained with his jokes, although there were a few that went over Julia's head. Although her English was excellent, she missed out on some of the puns.

It was turning out to be a bearable evening—bearable until a familiar voice called, "Brian, darling!" The men rose from their seats as Jackie Newton approached their table, her latest escort at her heels.

As Sydne had expected, Jackie had no compunction about throwing her arms around Brian's neck as she kissed him fully on the lips.

With more years and experience, Karen was better able to hide her surprise than Julia, whose mouth fell open in dismay. Her innocent face reflected her outrage before she took her cue from Sydne, who seemed impervious to the liberties the stranger was taking with her husband.

"Hello, Sydne, darling," Jackie said in her low husky voice. "Nice to see you again." She introduced her escort, a middle-aged man shorter than she, and Brian presented the two of them to the group.

"You don't mind if we join you for a bit, do you, darling?" Jackie's blue green eyes seemed to laugh at Sydne as she seated herself next to Brian without waiting for an invitation. Extra chairs were immediately produced by alert waiters, and the Bradleys reestablished the conversation, smoothing over the awkwardness of the moment.

When Jackie leaned toward Brian, everyone at the table was aware that the deep V of her white silk gown was intentionally displaying her cleavage to his gaze.

"Will you show me the way to the powder room, Sydne?" Julia asked after a moment.

"Yes, of course." Sydne stood up, secretly relieved to have a reason to escape.

Once there, Julia couldn't contain herself any longer. "I can't believe it!" she cried. "How can you sit there and let that—that—" She was speechless with rage.

"Simmer down, Julia." Sydne was amazed at her own calm. "What do you expect me to do?"

"If she were making those passes at Chuck, I'd scratch her eyes out!" Julia said hotly. "How can you sit there as cool as a cucumber?" She gave Sydne a probing look. "Sydne, are you and Brian having problems?"

Sydne would have liked to unburden herself; she had no one at all to talk to. But Julia wouldn't keep any secrets from Chuck, who was Brian's best friend. No, it would get too involved. "Nonsense! What ever gave you that idea?" she replied with a straight face.

Julia didn't appear convinced. "Who is that hussy anyway?"

"Someone Brian. . . used to know."

Conflicting emotions played over Julia's face, and she bit her lower lip as if to restrain herself from voicing her suspicion that there had been much more than friendship between Brian and Jackie.

Instead Sydne took the initiative. "It wasn't important, Julia. I know all about it." Her tone implied that she didn't want to discuss the subject any further.

Julia took Sydne's hand and gave it a warm squeeze. "If you ever need me," she said at last, "remember, I'm your friend."

Sydne swallowed the lump in her throat and smiled. "I know, Julia."

With that support in mind, somehow she managed to survive the rest of the evening.

FEELING LIKE SHE WAS WAITING for a time bomb to go off, Sydne filled her days with activity, and her and Brian's evenings with social engagements. She knew she was only torturing them both with her evasive tactics, yet she faltered each time she decided to face Brian and put an end to the intolerable situation that existed between them.

On Hiroshi's night off a week later, Brian failed to appear by seven o'clock for their dinner engagement with the Bradleys and the Morrises. Tired of waiting, Sydne dialed his office, but the phone went unanswered even though she let it ring for a long time. If Brian wasn't at the office, he was either on the way home...or with Jackie Newton.

The idea made her bristle. Well, if he thought she was going to sit around the apartment waiting until he tore himself away from Jackie—or whoever else he was with—he was mistaken.

She decided to give him another five minutes. If he wasn't home by then, she would go meet their friends and make his excuses.

Four minutes later she was gathering up her purse and her fur coat. Even though winter days were warm in Fort Lauderdale, nights could get chilly.

She left a note telling him where she'd gone, and was at the door when the phone rang. She ran inside again, but as she reached for the phone something made her hesitate. It could only be Brian, telling her that he would be late and to cancel the engagement.

The phone continued to ring. No, she wouldn't answer it. Without further hesitation she walked out.

The other two couples readily accepted her explanation that Brian had been detained and would join them later if he could. As wives of businessmen, the two women had gone through the same experience often enough. But Sydne was unable to enjoy the evening. The elegant atmosphere of the restaurant was a blur. She was only vaguely aware of the conversation going on around her, and if someone had asked her later what she had had to eat, she would have been at a loss to answer.

Her distraction didn't go unnoticed by her friends. "I felt the same way the first time I went out without Harry," Karen sympathized. She wasn't much older than Sydne.

"It happens to all of us, dear," Susan Morris agreed. Her husband was a marketing executive for a large corporation, and he traveled extensively. "I used to go on business trips with Norman when we were first married, but the twins put an end to that," she recalled.

But there was a difference, Sydne knew. The Morrises had been married for eight years to the Bradleys' five. Both couples seemed happy and well adjusted. She and Brian had been married for little more than two months, and everything was over between them. Her nerves stretched as taut as violin strings, Sydne expected an angry Brian to appear at any moment. But he never came.

When she arrived home the sight of his car in the underground parking lot made her shudder. He was back, and most likely angry.

As she rode the elevator up to the penthouse Sydne braced herself for the scene that was sure to follow. But perhaps it was for the best. They had evaded the issue long enough. Brian would have to accept the fact of divorce, and in the morning she would go away. Where, it didn't matter.

The look on Brian's face was ominous. "Where were you, Sydne?" he demanded.

"We had a dinner engagement, Brian," she replied as calmly as she could. "You were late. Since I couldn't reach you I left you a note. Didn't you see it?"

He made a gesture of dismissal with his hand. "Why did you do it? You know perfectly well I don't want you going out alone."

Sydne took a deep shuddering breath to summon her courage. "Brian, this situation has gone on long enough. I meant what I said. We— What are you doing?" she cried when he swept her up in his arms. "Put me down!" She pounded his chest with her fists and kicked ineffectually as he carried her into the bedroom, where he dumped her unceremoniously on the bed.

"What are you doing?" she demanded again indignantly.

Brian began to undress. "What I should have done weeks ago. Take off that dress."

"What?"

"You're right about one thing, babe," he said, continuing to shed the rest of his clothes, "this situation has gone far enough. From now on there'll be no locked doors between us. Now take off that dress!"

"I will not!"

He advanced toward her. "Take it off, Sydne, or I'll rip it off your back."

"You wouldn't!" she cried, but even as she spoke the expression on his face left no doubt in her mind that he meant exactly what he said.

Scrambling to her feet, she made an attempt to escape, but Brian caught her before she could reach the door and collapsed back onto the bed with her. He held her flailing arms above her head with one hand, while with the other he made short work of removing her dress. Her breasts heaving, Sydne ceased her struggles as he removed her underthings, as well.

"You're my wife," he said hoarsely. "I want you—right now!"

"It'll be rape!" she panted.

"Rape?" He laughed without humor. "No, I don't think so."

As his lips moved along her neck and found the pulse at her throat, Sydne willed herself to fight the response she felt. "No," she moaned, her resolve weakening at the unrelenting sensuality of his mouth on her breasts, which already ached to be caressed and fondled.

He knew her well, and he played on that knowledge, invading those secret places of velvet pleasure and silken delight to which only he held the key. Her love for him and the passion he was able to arouse were his powerful allies in this battle where there could be no winner, no loser.

He wound his fingers on his left hand into her hair to hold her still when she thrashed her head from side to side, trying to escape. "Oh, God, Sydne, please," he groaned in anguish, and she couldn't help but see the pain in his eyes. Then his compelling lips coaxed hers to part and yield their sweetness, breaking down the last of her defenses.

Sensing her surrender, he released her arms, which immediately coiled around his neck as she returned his fevered kisses with a hunger of her own. Finally, writhing in the height of passion, her cries joined with his, and when she became a part of him, like an exploding star the all-consuming fire within her reached out for freedom—overwhelming, satisfying. She was his, as he was hers, and their hearts pounded as one.

Then came the stark realization of her weakness, and she had to make a supreme effort to hold back the tenderness she felt for this man who could arouse her so completely. Failing miserably, she wept.

After a moment Brian rolled away from her. Then he was gone.

SYDNE SLEPT IN the next morning, until a light rap on the door awakened her. Hastily throwing on a robe, she rushed to answer it. Instead of Hiroshi, however, she found Brian standing there. The fact that he was still home although it was late morning didn't really surprise her.

"May we talk?" he asked seriously. When she hesitated he added, "Please?"

Without replying she stood aside to let him in.

"Sydne, about last night—"

"Don't," she cut him off. The memory was still too fresh in her mind, too painful.

"It won't ever happen again, Sydne." His face held no emotion. "I've asked Hiroshi to move my things to another bedroom."

"And you think that will make everything all right?" she said bitterly.

Brian looked away. "Is it really a divorce you want?"

Of course she didn't want a divorce, Sydne wanted to scream at him. She wanted to love him, to be loved in return. "I . . . think so," she said instead.

The strong planes of his face were made more prominent by his grim expression. "Look," he said finally, "we have both been under tremendous strain. Perhaps we should wait a little longer before reaching such a final decision."

Sydne looked at him warily. "Are you proposing a marriage in name only?"

"For the moment. I don't want to end this marriage, Sydne." Before she could voice any objections he went on, "The London auction is scheduled for next week. I want you to fly over with me. Andrew will be there. He'll be glad to see you."

Sydne considered his proposals. "Do you think it's wise?" she said at last. "I'd prefer to have him believe all is well between us. He's very perceptive, as you well know."

"We could try, for his sake."

Sydne sighed. "I suppose we could at that."

Brian seemed to have something else on his mind.

"I realize that perhaps this isn't the best moment to ask you, Sydne, but I want you to consider this carefully. Would you like to visit the Continent after the auction? I promised you a proper honeymoon. Maybe...."

Sydne turned away, unable to hide the despair his words caused her. Did he really expect her to accept such an outrageous proposition? She swallowed hard to clear her throat and said as evenly as she could, "Let's not make any plans, Brian. One day at the time is all I'm able to handle right now."

CHAPTER FIFTEEN

ARMFULS OF FRESH FLOWERS WERE MASSED atop the console table in the ornate glittering entry hall of the hotel, just as they had been years ago when Sydne had stayed there with her parents. For a fleeting moment it seemed as if time stood still. But no, her parents were gone, and it was her husband who was at her side. She glanced briefly at Brian's somber face. It was not the face of a man on his way to collect the fortune he had earned.

They had exchanged only a few words during the long flight from New York—or for that matter during the entire week. Sydne had seen little of him during that time.

Andrew had left a message for them at the reception desk. It was an invitation to meet him in his suite at seven o'clock for drinks before dinner.

Sydne and Brian followed the bellboys who led them into a two-bedroom suite. With its sprigged wallpaper, Regency curtains and graceful antiques, the room re-created the pleasant atmosphere of an old English country house.

Sydne had never been able to sleep on planes, so after unpacking her suitcases and taking a hot shower she slipped between the fresh-scented sheets of the antique bed, where she would sleep alone.

How little time it had taken her to become accustomed to sharing a bed with Brian, she mused sadly as she started to relax. Days could be filled with activity that allowed no time for reflection. Only in the stillness of the night did brooding thoughts and memories resurface. She had come to dread the nighttime, because it was then that Brian's absence was hardest to bear. And after hours of pursuing the elusive release of dreams, she would awaken in the morning on his side of the bed, where she had moved in her sleep as if seeking the comfort of his body. . . .

"SYDNE, HONEY, WAKE UP."

Her eyes fluttered open. All she could see in the gloom was the outline of a tall figure standing near the bed. For a fleeting moment she had the crazy notion that he had kissed her. Then Sydne realized it had just been a dream. "What time is it?" she asked.

"Six-thirty."

Exhausted, she had slept the afternoon away. She sat up and reached out to turn on the bedside lamp, but when Brian remained in the room she decided against it.

"You don't have to meet Andrew tonight if you're still tired," he said, misinterpreting her hesitation. "I'm sure he'll understand."

"No, I'm all right. I'll be ready."

He seemed reluctant to leave, and she wished she could read his face.

"Sydne," he said after a moment, "have you given any thought to visiting the Continent after the auction?"

Yes, she had, many times, and she still couldn't

reach a decision. As if aware of her inner struggle Brian added, "I'm not asking to return to your bed, Sydne—only that you give our marriage another chance."

And what would that accomplish, Sydne wondered, except to prolong the agony? Twice before she had seen her illusions trampled. She couldn't bear another disappointment.

But if she refused, how could she ever live with the knowledge that it had been she who had refused to make one last effort to save their marriage? Wasn't a future with Brian well worth this last try? "In that case," she said, still unable to lay down her arms, "I accept. Now, please, I have to dress."

Andrew was as cheerful as ever when he met them in his suite. "My dear Sydne," he cried, giving her a warm affectionate squeeze when she bent over to kiss him, "let me look at you." Sydne was wearing perhaps the most expensive designer creation she had ever owned, a gown of raspberry silk that derived its beauty and elegance from the richness of its color and the exquisite simplicity of its lines. The fitted bodice was low-cut and strapless, and a flowing jacket open at the front offered a tantalizing view of the swell of her breasts. The slit at the side of her narrow skirt afforded seductive glances of long slender legs. Her hair, gathered at the back of her head in a coil, enhanced the slenderness of her throat, and she was devoid of jewelry except for the tiny clusters of diamonds and rubies dangling from her earlobes. "You look fabulous," Andrew said when he finished his examination. "Marriage certainly agrees with you."

"You always were a flatterer," she said. "I've missed you, you old fox."

"And you, my boy," Andrew said as he shook Brian's hand. "Good to see you again." Jerking his head toward the well-stocked liquor cart, he added, "Why don't you pour us something to drink. Bob will join us momentarily."

"How is his leg?" Sydne inquired.

"His leg?" Andrew echoed absently. "Oh, fine. No complaints."

"I'm so glad."

"Yes, of course." Andrew nodded, and changing the subject he said to Brian, "Well, by the end of this week the *Conde de Santander* affair will be over, and you'll be richer by quite a sizable sum—not to mention me. How does it feel?"

"Fine." Brian shrugged.

"Is that all you have to say?" Andrew raised a quizzical brow. "After the risks you took, I must say I expected a little more enthusiasm. Oh, well, the first million is always the most thrilling," he went on philosophically. "After that they just pile up, don't they? Money has a tendency to make more money— unless it's wasted, of course."

Sydne was puzzled by his remarks. Was Andrew saying that Brian was already a rich man, even without the profits from the *Conde*? And all this time she had been worried! What an idiot she had been! At that moment she was glad that a knock on the door gave her an excuse to hide her confusion, and she went to answer it.

"Dear Sydne," Bob Hamilton greeted her when she opened the door. Younger than Andrew by a couple of years, the curator was also shorter and more slightly built. "How nice it is to see you again. You look more beautiful than ever."

Sydne hugged him affectionately. "I'm so glad to see you're all right, again, Bob." She linked her arm through his as they walked into the parlor.

"Why shouldn't I be?" Bob inquired with a puzzled frown.

"I meant that your leg healed so well," Sydne clarified.

Bob's face flushed slightly. "Oh, yes, my leg," he repeated. "Well, as you can see it's as good as new."

Brian stood up to greet Bob, shook hands and inquired about his recovery. When everybody had drinks they all toasted their reunion.

"And your marriage," Bob offered. "May the years bring you much happiness," he added, raising his glass.

His words brought a lump to Sydne's throat. She couldn't look at Brian; all she could do was smile.

"I suppose you'll be taking Sydne on that delayed honeymoon," Andrew said conversationally. "Got any plans?"

"We're flying to Italy after the auction," Brian replied without looking at her. Apparently he had been so confident of her acquiescence that he had already made the arrangements.

The conversation turned to the auction, with Bob and Andrew going over the list of those items that held their interest. Brian related an anecdote involving the actual discovery of a piece in question.

Sydne herself said little, but smiled on cue as she sat next to Brian on the sofa, their bodies not touching. She tensed involuntarily when Brian casually threw an arm around her shoulders and drew her closer. Although she forced herself to smile at her husband she felt ill at ease, and was greatly relieved when she heard Andrew suggest they go downstairs to the restaurant for dinner. She knew her old employer well enough to realize that very little escaped him, and in the intimate surroundings of his suite she was afraid he would be able to see through the facade of married bliss she and Brian were trying to present for his benefit.

In his usual expansive style Andrew had ordered a special dinner for his friends, and the excellent food and wines plus the convivial conversation and elegant ambience made for an enjoyable evening. Many acquaintances paused at their table to say hello, some of them joining the party.

"And they say Scots are tightfisted," Sydne teased her host after the lavish dinner.

"Ah, well—" Andrew shrugged philosophically, selecting a tart from the gleaming dessert trolley presented by a deferential waiter "—they also say you can't take it with you. So you might as well enjoy it!" he finished with a roguish wink.

The old man glanced at his wristwatch when Tim Robbins appeared at the entrance of the glowing oak-paneled dining room. "Bedtime already!" he groaned comically. Taking Sydne's hand, he added, "It's been wonderful seeing you again, my dear. If you can tear yourself away from that lucky husband of yours, perhaps we could take in some of the sights."

"I'd love to," Sydne replied fondly, kissing his

cheek. "Good night, Andrew. I'll see you tomorrow."

"I think I'll say good-night, too," Bob Hamilton said as Tim Robbins was about to wheel Andrew away from the table. Together the three men left the dining room. Andrew was pensive while waiting for the elevator, so much so that Bob inquired, "Is anything wrong? I'm sorry about that slip. I almost gave myself away when Sydne asked about my leg," he added.

"So did I," Andrew admitted absently, "but that's not it. They're trying very hard to look like a perfectly happy couple, but something is wrong between those two." The elevator came, and when they were all inside he added thoughtfully, "I hope I didn't make a mistake bringing them together."

LONDON HAD ALWAYS BEEN Sydne's favorite city. With her parents she had explored the town endlessly, but the streets now appeared narrower and grayer than she remembered. Was it because of the dismal weather or her own state of mind?

Once again she wondered if she had made a mistake in accepting Brian's offer of a delayed honeymoon. But then perhaps her first error had been to remain with him at all after finding out his reasons for marrying her. Would he one day look at her and really see that it was Sydne—not Helene or Jackie—whom he held in his arms, who returned his kisses, who responded to his passion? And would he love her then or cast her aside?

The shops of Bond and Oxford streets failed to tempt her with their displays, and she returned to the hotel empty-handed, having no heart for material acquisitions. She was married to a wealthy man, she could buy anything she desired, but there was no joy in her heart as long as the most precious gift of all, Brian's love, was missing.

As she had expected, Brian was still out when she arrived. "Room 510, please," she told the desk clerk who handed her the key. "Any messages?"

"For Mr. Stevens, madam."

"I'll take them."

"Thank you, madam."

Sydne accepted the slips of paper without glancing at them and took the elevator to the fifth floor. She let herself into the suite, and discarding her coat and purse on a chair, glanced briefly at the messages as she set them on the antique table with the key. A name leaped out from one of them—Countess Beaumont. It could be no one but Helene, Sydne realized with a shudder of apprehension. She had left a number so that Brian could return her call.

Sydne's hand trembled. "Helene in London!" she whispered in dismay. She felt an urge to destroy the message, until she realized that Helene's physical presence in London might resolve once and for all the situation between her and Brian. If they wanted to be together, fine, she wouldn't stop them. She had just turned away from the table when Brian walked in.

"Any messages?" he inquired, taking off his coat and loosening his tie.

"Three," Sydne replied, not looking at him. "On the table."

Brian glanced at the messages, and his brow creased in a frown when he read the last one—Helene's.

"I just got back myself," Sydne said, feeling compelled to say something. Standing in front of a gilded mirror, she removed her hat, oblivious to the framed shepherdess who smiled down at her from the wall.

"Did you do any shopping?"

"Window shopping." Sydne smoothed and patted her hair, then turned to face her husband. "Would you like a drink?"

"I'll have a Scotch, thank you."

Obliquely Sydne watched him take off his tie and loosen his shirt collar as she poured them each a drink. Brian wasn't fond of wearing a coat and tie. He found them confining and preferred casual sports clothes. He seemed to be trying to act naturally, but the set of his jaw gave away his tension. It was obvious he had no intention of returning Helene's call while Sydne was in the room.

"What time is the auction?" she asked as she handed Brian his drink.

"Nine o'clock. We're having dinner with Andrew first."

"I'm going to bathe and rest for a while, then." Taking her glass, she went into the bedroom. She was about to close the door, then thought better of it and left it ajar. She went into the bathroom, poured a capful of bubble bath into the tub, and turned on the taps. When she went back to the door, Brian was giving the hotel operator the number Helene had left. She must have been at a hotel, because after a moment he requested a room number.

"Helene," he said in a low voice.

All along Sydne had known it was she, but hearing the name on his lips was surprisingly painful. With the sound of the water running she could barely hear the one-sided conversation. She couldn't even see Brian's face, but it didn't matter; he had said it all when he had pronounced her name.

Sydne was scarcely aware of her actions as she undressed and went into the bathroom. Numbly she climbed into the old-fashioned tub and settled down among the scented bubbles. She took a sip from her drink, and finding it bitter, set it down on the small glass table next to the tub. Fighting the temptation to pick up the extension, she lay back and tried to relax. But she couldn't.

NOTHING IN THE DISCREET FACADE of the building on Oxford Street advertised the nature of the business, only a small placard with the name Romwell's in gold letters. The interior spoke of wealth, however, with plush red carpets and elegant furniture. In a wood-paneled parlor a number of well-dressed people spoke in whispered tones, cradling champagne glasses in their hands. The collection of artifacts to be auctioned was displayed in a separate room, locked in shatterproof glass cases that were jealously protected by uniformed private guards.

Attendance was by invitation only, and there was a hush over the room in spite of the number of people inspecting the items to be sold. In one of the glass cases Sydne recognized the emerald necklace Brian had hung around her neck the day he had ordered her off the *Adventurer*. After discovering his motive, she had taken that action as proof of his love. But that was in the past, and she felt nothing now as she looked at the glittering ornament that by the end of the evening would belong to someone else.

To Sydne's secret relief Andrew wasn't there, for
he had come down with a slight case of flu, and Tim
was making sure he stayed in bed for at least a day.
So far she and Brian had managed to maintain their
"happy couple" pretense, but how long that would
last she didn't know. Andrew was too inquisitive, too
shrewd to be fooled for long, and Sydne couldn't yet
bear having any of her friends know the truth about
her marriage—not even Andrew. Especially not Andrew. She had wished a thousand times that she herself had never discovered Brian's duplicity. For a
while she had been so happy in her illusions, and she
didn't want Andrew's to be destroyed.

One item after another fell to the auctioneer's
gavel, and by the end of the long evening a fortune
had been added to Brian's credit column. But he
seemed unimpressed. Sydne could understand how
he felt, because she herself felt the same. Riches
meant nothing to her without Brian's love; riches
meant nothing to him without Helene.

The next morning dawned gray and gloomy, a typ-
ical London day with rain falling in a steady drizzle
that never changes, never stops. Earlier, from the
window of her hotel room overlooking Hyde Park,
Sydne had watched the Queen's Household Cavalry
making their way to Buckingham Palace from their
barracks in Knightsbridge.

Brian had gone to meet Helene, and when he came
back he would probably ask Sydne for a divorce. Although she herself had originally brought up the subject, she had never really wanted it. Perhaps it had
been a subconscious ploy to seek his reassurance. Perhaps she had expected Brian to take her in his arms
and tell her she was the only woman he loved. Instead

he had angrily rejected her request and presented her with the outrageous proposition of farcical marriage.

But now everything had changed. He would want his freedom to go back to Helene, and that Sydne couldn't bear. Her decision had been made during the long sleepless night, but she had been too much of a coward to tell him in the morning. It had been easier to remain in her room, pretending to be asleep when she had heard him in the parlor of their suite. He'd gone out very early.

Sitting at the antique Harrow writing table, Sydne tried to pen the farewell that she knew she would never have the courage to deliver in person: "Dearest Brian; I'm going home."

No, she couldn't say that, because without him there was no home for her. She crumpled up the sheet of paper and began again. She started many notes, but eventually discarded each one. She didn't want to burden him with the knowledge of her grief, and in the end her message was brief and cold.

Dear Brian,
Now that you have another chance with the woman you love, I won't stand in your way. By the time you read this I'll be out of your life forever. I will agree to any terms you set for our divorce.
    Be happy.

                                          Sydne

She wrote his name on the envelope, enclosing the letter as well as the receipt for the jewels she had deposited in the hotel safe. Then she sealed it and left

it on the mantel, where he couldn't fail to see it when
he came in.

THERE WERE LONG LINEUPS at the TWA counter at
Heathrow Airport, but Sydne had taken the precaution of calling from the hotel, and her name was already on the standby list.

"What are my chances of getting on the next
flight?" she asked the airline clerk after giving her
name.

"You're third on the list, madam."

"How long before I know for sure?"

"The names will be called fifteen minutes before
boarding."

"Thank you."

The flight was scheduled to depart in another thirty minutes. Determined to wait, Sydne turned away
from the counter. The lounge area was crowded, but
she spotted a vacant seat next to a fat man in a heavy
tweed overcoat.

As she started to pick up her bag Sydne saw Brian
advancing toward her. The expression on his face
was ominous.

"Oh, no!" she heard herself say. How had he
managed to discover her disappearance so soon?

Brian was already beside her, and taking her arm,
he propelled her away from the line of waiting passengers. "Where the hell do you think you're going?" he demanded in a low voice.

Sydne's knees weakened. "Please let go of my
arm." She winced. "You're hurting me."

Immediately he relaxed his grip. "Well?"

"Pardon me, miss. Is this man bothering you?"

They turned in unison toward the voice, and came face to face with an elderly man in a pinstriped suit, the image of an English gentleman. Before Sydne could reply, Brian said, "Stay out of it, mister. The lady is my wife."

"Oh, I beg your pardon," the man said, tipping his bowler hat before he ambled away.

"Brian, please, let me go," Sydne pleaded in earnest. "There's no need for any of this. I left you a note at the hotel."

"You mean this?" Brian pulled a crumpled envelope from his pocket. She recognized it immediately. "Would you mind explaining all this nonsense?" he added.

"Why do you insist on tormenting me?" she said in a strangled voice, fighting back her tears. "Haven't I suffered enough?" No, she wouldn't cry, she told herself sternly. Brian was scowling, but she found the courage to go on. "You know as well as I do that our marriage was a mistake, Brian. I'm not Helene, and you don't have to pretend anymore that I am. I know that it's her you've always wanted, and I won't stand in your way if you have a chance to be with her now."

Brian gave her a puzzled look. "Where on earth did you get such a stupid notion?"

Sydne looked up swiftly at him. The grim lines of his face had softened.

"Mrs. Stevens, Mrs. Sydne Stevens," the airline clerk called over the PA.

Obviously she had procured a seat on the overseas flight. Sydne stood there, torn with indecision. If she didn't act quickly she would miss the flight, but Brian's words had left her baffled .

"Mrs. Stevens, Mrs. Sydne Stevens," the man called again. "Report to the TWA counter."

"Babe, we have to talk," Brian said in a tone of voice she hadn't heard in a long time. "If afterward you still want to leave, I'll put you on the next plane myself.' And without waiting for her answer he went over to the harried clerk at the desk. "Mrs. Stevens has changed her mind and doesn't want a seat on this plane." He held her gaze, expecting her acquiescence, and she did not disappoint him. "Let's see if we can find a quiet spot in this madhouse," Brian said, taking her bag in one hand and leading her away.

There were quite a few people crowding the counter in the cocktail lounge, but they found a vacant table in a quiet corner.

"Would you like a brandy?" he inquired after seating her.

"Please."

Sydne tried to compose herself while Brian made his way to the bar. A few minutes later he was back with two brandy snifters in his hands.

For a moment there was silence between them. Sydne played nervously with her drink, but Brian took a long swallow from his before he spoke, keeping his eyes fixed on his glass.

"I know I haven't made you happy, Sydne," he began, "but please believe me when I say that I love you." He looked up, straight into her eyes, when he added, "More than anything else in the world, I love you, babe."

Sydne drew her breath in sharply, unable to believe what she had just heard.

"I know I've made many mistakes along the way," he went on. "My only excuse, if that's what you want to call it, is that I've been scared—scared to death of losing you."

Her eyes were brimming with tears when she reached for his hand. "Oh, darling! But why? Don't you know that I love you?"

"You don't know how much I've wanted to believe that, babe, but I just couldn't be sure." At her puzzled expression he said bitterly, "I never gave you much of a choice, did I? First I kept you almost a prisoner aboard the salvage ship—because I knew you'd never come back if I let you go."

Sydne gazed at him mutely, unable to deny this.

"Afterward," he continued, "I rushed you into marriage before you had a chance to change your mind. I could see that you were beginning to have doubts while we were still on our honeymoon, but when you told me our marriage was a mistake and that you wanted to end it, I felt as if I'd been kicked in the gut." He paused, and the pressure of his hand on hers increased slightly when he added, "I've never been very good at begging, honey, so instead I took by force what you denied me. But in forcing you, I pushed you even further away from me, and that frightened me more than ever."

"You never forced me, Brian."

He looked away. "Didn't I?" There was no mistaking the bitter edge in his voice. "Don't make excuses for me, Sydne. We both know the truth."

Her hand on his cheek, Sydne made him look at her. "Darling, the truth is that I love you, that I need you as much or more than you need me. You never forced me, Brian. I couldn't stop loving you even when I thought you were still in love with Helene."

His expression was puzzled. "But what made you believe that?"

"A conversation I overheard at Casa de Campo. Actually I was confused about who you were involved with—Jackie, Helene, or both. I tried to put it out of my mind, but you were always so reluctant to tell me anything about your ex-wife that I thought you still loved her, that you had married me because I reminded you of her."

He shook his head wryly. "You don't remind me of her at all. In fact, no two women could be more different from each other than you and Helene." He hesitated again before confessing, "It was mostly pride, I guess. A man doesn't relish the thought of telling his wife what an idiot he made of himself over another woman. It took me a long time to realize that I never really loved Helene; I only loved the illusion she created."

He fell silent and thoughtfully picked up his glass again. Sydne waited until he had finished his drink, knowing that Brian was at last ready to tell her about his first marriage.

"I became a minor celebrity after the salvaging of the first galleon," he said finally. "Even though I didn't want the publicity, I was interviewed or at least photographed by every existing newspaper and magazine, it seemed. And I don't know how many invitations I turned down to appear on those television talk shows that are so popular.

"After things began to quiet down a bit, a cub reporter from a Palm Beach newspaper came to see me. The only reason I agreed to an interview was that she was the most beautiful woman I had ever seen. One thing led to another, and we started dating, but she only went so far with me because she said she was a virgin and was saving herself for the man she would marry one day. That turned out to be me, after all," he added wryly, shaking his head.

"At first I was too blind, too emotionally involved to see the truth about Helene. She was the only child of wealthy parents, so I wasn't surprised that she was a little spoiled; it was to be expected. But it went much further than that. To make her happy we moved in the circles she wanted to move in—constantly. But she was never satisfied, and when she began putting on pressure for me to claim my inheritance, I realized that, even before she came to see me, she must have done some research into my background and found out about my family. After that it didn't take me long to discover that the reason she'd married me was because her family was ruined financially. She had planned the whole thing, and I had fallen for it like a fool."

"I'm afraid I don't understand," Sydne interrupted.

"I know, honey." Brian nodded. "I only mentioned to you that mother wanted dad to go into the family business in Philadelphia after the war." He paused briefly before asking, "You've heard of H.T. Winthrop & Sons, haven't you?"

"Who hasn't?" Sydne replied automatically. It was a retail chain, as much a household word as F.W. Woolworth. It was then that the implication hit her. "Oh, no!" she gasped, looking at Brian through wide bewildered eyes.

"My mother's maiden name was Winthrop. My grandfather was the founder of the business, and he left me a considerable trust."

Sydne's mouth had fallen open. "But—Andrew said you had gone to him for financial backing for your first salvage, as well as for this last one," she argued.

"And I did," Brian admitted. "For many years I wasn't on the best of terms with Bea, so I wouldn't go to her to ask for money to finance anything, not even my business," he explained. "I had many offers of help—all because of my family connections—but that wasn't what I wanted. Andrew was the only one who accepted my terms. I didn't tell you because—"

"You were afraid I'd be influenced by your fortune," she finished for him.

He reached for her hand, and his tone was apologetic. "I'm sorry, honey. It's just that, after Helene, I wanted to be sure about you. There were times when I thought you loved me for myself, but others—"

"Oh, you're impossible, Brian Stevens!" she snapped, snatching her hand away. "Have you any idea at all what you put me through? All this time I thought you were still in love with Helene. Why didn't you tell me?"

"Helene used sex as a weapon to get what she wanted from me, Sydne," he tried to explain. "When you started being so cold and distant I was afraid you were using the same tactics."

Remembering the way she had behaved when Brian returned from Santo Domingo, the day she had overheard Jackie's conversation, Sydne couldn't really blame him. That silly excuse for her tears—about clothes and other nonsense—was one of the worst mistakes she'd ever made.

She turned her attention back to Brian, who was saying, "Helene's plans backfired, because I had no love or desire left for her after discovering her little games. But with you, babe. . .that was another story. You have no idea how hard it's been for me to stay away from you."

"So you consoled yourself with Jackie Newton," Sydne put in tartly.

"Honey, I was only using Jackie to make you jealous." He grinned sheepishly. "I know it was a foolish thing to do, but you were so wrapped up with that Argentine playboy that I hoped my being with Jackie would shake you up a bit. When you didn't seem to care—"

"That was in the Dominican Republic," Sydne pointed out. "What about Fort Lauderdale?"

Brian looked at her and frowned. "The only time I saw Jackie after that was at the country-club dinner dance."

She looked at him quizzically. "So what were you doing leaving a hotel on Atlantic Boulevard with her? And don't deny it. I saw you with my own eyes."

"Oh, yes, that day!" He had such a guilty look about him that Sydne could have laughed if she hadn't been so angry. "That was the day you called me at the office, wasn't it?" She didn't reply, so he went on, "I had taken a client to lunch, and when I drove him back to his hotel I ran into Jackie quite by accident," he explained. "I gave her a ride because she said her car was being serviced."

Sydne wasn't convinced. "And whose car was the black Cadillac?"

"It belongs to the salvage outfit, babe. We use it when we entertain clients."

It was precisely the simplicity of the explanation that reassured Sydne that her husband was telling the truth. She didn't draw away when he reached for her hand. "Honey, I truly believe marriage is something to be taken seriously. Even my affair with Jackie happened after Helene and I had split up. It was very brief, and it was over a long time ago." Cupping the nape of her neck with his hand and rubbing his thumb over her chin—something he hadn't done for ages—he added, "And besides, what would I want with Jackie or anyone else when I have you, babe? You're the only woman I want, the only one I'll ever want."

"Oh, Brian, I'm so sorry. I hate sounding like a jealous wife."

"Honey—" he grinned, kissing her softly on the lips "—it's your indifference I can't take. I love you, Sydne. From the first moment I saw you I knew I wanted you. That was why I was so rude to you. I was pretty bitter at the time, and figured you'd keep away from me if I couldn't keep away from you. But do you know when I really fell in love with you? The day I found you crying over that diary, with your eyes all puffy and your nose red."

"Oh, Brian!" she cried, overcome with tenderness.

"That was the first time I saw you looking rumpled and vulnerable, honey," he explained, regarding her lovingly. "Mind you, I still thought you hated me. But then I saw your face after the earthquake, when you thought I was in danger. It was then that I realized there was no hope of escape for me. I had been caught in those amber eyes forever, and you know what? I didn't mind it one bit."

Brian moved to the bench next to her and slipped his arm around her. Their lips met in the sweetest kiss Sydne had ever known. With a sigh of contentment she leaned her head against his shoulder.

After a moment Brian spoke again. "You know, one good thing that came out of my first marriage was that, for the first time, I understood my mother. Helene and I were as different from each other as Bea and dad were. She wanted the glamour of the international jet set, a kind of excitement that to me wears thin very quickly."

He paused briefly, then confessed, "I can't deny that curiosity was part of the reason I went to see her today. I mean, why would she so conveniently show up in dreary old London when I happened to be here? I figured she was up to something if she would desert the haunts of the rich."

Sydne nodded. "What did she have to say?"

"She put on a very convincing act—that she's divorcing her count because she wants to come back to me," Brian replied. "Only I knew the real reason—money didn't go with the title. And apparently the settlement she got from me was used for the restoration of the count's estates. But that's only a small setback for her," he said dryly. "She'll make out all right." Taking Sydne's hand, he looked into her eyes as he said, "I'm just an ordinary guy, Syd. All I want is to do the kind of work I enjoy, have you to come home to, maybe raise a couple of kids. Does that sound terribly mundane to you?"

"Perhaps," she replied, squeezing his hand warmly, "but it's all I want myself."

"Then we could have it, babe," he said, a smile illuminating his blue eyes. "Unless, of course, you still want to catch that flight. Do you?"

Laughing, Sydne threw her arms around his neck. "Not on your life!"

ANNE MATHER
Stormspell

A major new bestseller by Anne Mather— the author whose Harlequin Romances and Harlequin Presents have sold more than 90 MILLION COPIES!

When a tropical storm unleashes its fury on the tiny Caribbean island of Indigo, Ruth Jason's sheltered life is dramatically changed... as she loses her heart to the shipwrecked Dominic Howard.

Later in London, Ruth struggles to build a new life for herself, always haunted by her lover's image. But she knows their love is impossible. For although Dominic's spell holds her still, he is bound to another woman...

Stormspell

Almost 400 pages of spectacular romance reading for only $2.95!

Watch for it in November wherever paperback books are sold or order your copy from Harlequin Reader Service:

In the U.S.
1440 South Priest Dr.
Tempe,
AZ 85281

In Canada
649 Ontario Street
Stratford, Ontario
N5A 6W2

Begin a long love affair with
SUPERROMANCE.
Accept LOVE BEYOND DESIRE, **FREE.**

Complete and mail the coupon below, today!

- -

FREE! Mail to: SUPERROMANCE

In the U.S.
1440 South Priest Drive
Tempe, AZ 85281

In Canada
649 Ontario St.
Stratford, Ontario N5A 6W2

YES, please send me FREE and without any obligation, my
SUPERROMANCE novel, LOVE BEYOND DESIRE. If you do not hear
from me after I have examined my FREE book, please send me the
4 new **SUPERROMANCE** books every month as soon as they come
off the press. I understand that I will be billed only $2.50 for each book
(total $10.00). There are no shipping and handling or any other hidden
charges. There is no minimum number of books that I have to
purchase. In fact, I may cancel this arrangement at any time.
LOVE BEYOND DESIRE is mine to keep as a FREE gift, even if
I do not buy any additional books.

NAME _____ (Please Print) _____

ADDRESS _____ APT. NO. _____

CITY _____

STATE/PROV. _____ ZIP/POSTAL CODE _____

SIGNATURE (If under 18, parent or guardian must sign.)   PR210

This offer is limited to one order per household and not valid to present
subscribers. Prices subject to change without notice. ●ffer expires April, 1983

Now's your chance to discover the earlier books in this exciting series.

Choose from this list of great
SUPERROMANCES!

SUPERROMANCE

Complete and mail this coupon today!

- -

Worldwide Reader Service

In the U.S.A.
1440 South Priest Drive
Tempe, AZ 85281

In Canada
649 Ontario Street
Stratford, Ontario N5A 6W2

Please send me the following SUPERROMANCES. I am enclosing my
check or money order for $2.50 for each copy ordered, plus 75¢ to
cover postage and handling.

☐ # 8	☐ # 14	☐ # 20
☐ # 9	☐ # 15	☐ # 21
☐ # 10	☐ # 16	☐ # 22
☐ # 11	☐ # 17	☐ # 23
☐ # 1?	☐ # 18	☐ # 24
	☐ # 19	☐ # 25

Carson
xander

...es checked @ $2.50 each = $_____
...ents add appropriate sales tax $_____
...ing $_____.75
                            TOTAL $_____

...e _____.

...ease send check or money order. We cannot be responsible for cash
sent through the mail.)
Prices subject to change without notice.   Offer expires April, 1983

NAME_____
          (Please Print)
ADDRESS_____ APT. NO._____
CITY_____
STATE/PROV._____
ZIP/POSTAL CODE_____
                                              2015600000C